Justin was in a [...]
ated him. He reached for Penny's arm and pulled her roughly
to her feet. "You'd better come with me."

"No!" cried Penny.

Jonny saw the fear in Penny's eyes and jumped to his
feet. He placed a hand protectively on her shoulder.

"Sorry, but Penny's staying with me."

"Take your hand off her," ordered Justin.

Jonny felt Penny shrinking against him.

"Come on, man," he hissed to Justin. "Pull yourself together. You're behaving like an idiot."

What happened next was like a slow moving picture.
Penny never forgot it: Every gesture, every motion was etched
in her memory forever. With eyes cold and calculating, Justin
took out his gun and smashed the barrel over Jonny's head.
Jonny keeled over. With a scream, Penny rushed to his side.
Justin seemed to kick out at Jonny, but at the same time he
aimed his gun at Violet and fired. There wasn't a sound. Violet crumpled in silence.

Penny threw herself over Jonny's body, certain that Justin was going to kill him next. She may have screamed again,
but all she remembered afterward was the nightmarish silence.

Justin landed a well-aimed kick right into the side of her
face. She felt the bones crack, then she fell into a black, very
empty space. . . .

The BRIGHT FACE of DANGER

WINSLOW ELIOT

SMP

ST. MARTIN'S PAPERBACKS

THE BRIGHT FACE OF DANGER

Copyright © 1993 by Winslow Eliot.
Teaser for *The Last Innocent Hour* copyright © 1991 by Margot Abbott.

Cover illustration by Edwin Herder.

ISBN: 0-312-95124-8

Printed in the United States of America

St. Martin's Paperbacks edition/October 1993

10 9 8 7 6 5 4 3 2 1

To My Mother Who Helped Me and My
Daughter Who Let Me

Acknowledgments

Thanks to Cynthia Cannell, Charlotte Carter, Jefferson Eliot, Jane Winslow Eliot, Alexander Eliot, Ron Gustavson, Mark Hardy, Beverly Hendricks, Jennifer Kellen, Sam Knapp, Eva Lewin, Randye Lordon, May Paddock, Adriana Reyneri, Peter Scibetta, Jill Sprecher, Thomas Stier, and Dr. Barry Zide for their help and advice, their support, faith, encouragement, and inspiration. I would also like to give special thanks to my agent Loretta Fidel and my editor Jennifer Weis.

CHAPTER ONE

"SHUT up, you ass!" Penny laughed as Graham dropped two beer cans on the stone-flagged kitchen floor. "Do you want my father to hear?"

Graham caught the cans before they rolled under the sink and stuffed them in his denim jacket pocket.

"God, is he here?" asked Billy, nervously. "If my mom finds out I'm not in school she'll kill me."

"I don't know where he is," said Penny. "Probably in the barn. C'mon, let's go."

Jumping down the porch steps, she waved to the two boys to follow. They climbed over the low white picket fence instead of using the gate, and hurried across the cornfield to the shelter of a grove of birch trees. By the time they reached their favorite hiding place in a comfortable ditch near the Taconic Parkway, they were sweating from the warm spring sunshine. Penny tossed her jean jacket on the ground then opened a can of beer and drank. The boys followed suit.

Penny turned her freckled face to the sun, running her long fingers through the tangled mass of dark curls. She wore loose-fitting jeans belted around her slim waist and a yellow tank top.

"One more year till we graduate," she sighed, leaning against an oak tree, "and then I'm outta here. Good-bye Dogwood Farm, good-bye Northkill, good-bye upstate New York! I can hardly wait."

"Why not go now?" said Graham. He was a tall, soft-spoken youth with quiet gray eyes.

"I need a high school diploma."

"What for?"

Penny lit a cigarette. "College."

"Oh," said Graham, indifferently. He planned to work in his father's copy shop in Northkill when he graduated. There would be no money for college.

"Want one?" Penny offered her cigarettes to the boys. They shook their heads.

"I'd like to go to college," mused Billy. "I hear it's like a four-year party. But we couldn't afford it."

"Oh, *money.*" Penny shrugged. "Dad couldn't afford it either. But there are lots of ways to get around not having money!"

"Like what?"

"Loans . . . scholarships . . ."

"I'm not smart enough," said Billy.

"Stealing . . . borrowing . . . joining the army . . ." Penny's earnest blue eyes closed tightly. "I can't wait. I'm so bored here I can hardly stand it. Sometimes when I'm cleaning the henhouse and collecting eggs for Dad I think I'm going to go crazy. I just want to march into the house and tell him that I'm quitting."

"What would he do?"

"He'd horsewhip me."

"What's it like to be horsewhipped?" teased Graham. "Does he use a horse?"

"Does he really whip you?" asked Billy.

"All the time," lied Penny.

Billy eyed her admiringly.

"C'mon," she exclaimed, jumping to her feet and tossing the empty beer can into a bush. "Let's do something exciting."

"Like what?"

"I dare you to run across the highway," said Penny.

"Forget it," said Graham.

"Poultry! Poultry!" taunted Penny.

"*What?*" asked Billy.

"Poultry," she repeated.

"She means chicken," Graham explained to Billy.

Penny climbed out of the ditch, swayed a little from the effect of the beer, then suddenly dashed into the road.

The blast from a car horn made her leap hastily back into the ditch. A black Spider swerved to miss her, still honking furiously. Peering over the edge of the ditch, Penny saw the sports car pull over to the side of the road. A man got out and headed purposefully toward them.

"We'd better split," said Penny excitedly, grabbing her jacket. "He might tell Mr. Jackson." Mr. Jackson was their principal.

"What about the beer?" said Graham, eyeing half a dozen unopened cans piled neatly in the ditch.

"Leave it! It'll be here tomorrow."

She was already jumping over some shrubbery, her dark curls flying in the wind. She knew they were in sight of the highway the whole way back to the farmhouse, but she figured it was unlikely that the driver would bother to chase them all that way.

When they reached the marsh grass bordering the driveway, Graham said that he was leaving. "School will be over in an hour, and I said I'd help Dad out at the shop this afternoon. Billy, you want a ride?"

"That man's not going to follow us," Penny objected.

"We'd better go anyway."

Disappointed, Penny watched them leave, then she turned back to the house. It was a hundred years old, not ancient by local standards where houses often went back two hundred and fifty years, but it showed its age. The white paint was peeling badly. The porch steps needed fixing, and the screens were torn in several places. She noticed the windows on the two main floors needed cleaning. The cellar and attic ones were opaque with dust.

Flinging her denim jacket over her shoulder, she went up the rickety stairs and slammed open the screen door into the front parlor. As usual, it was filled with junk. All the rooms were. Her father never threw anything away. Not even an out-of-date offer for a cruise he'd never go on. Newspapers, bills, old letters, old birding lists were piled on every surface, in every drawer, and over much of the floor. Broken furniture lay tipped against the wall. There was no way for Penny to keep the old place tidy, much less clean.

But it had been so beautiful when her mother was alive.

Penny wandered into the kitchen. It was her favorite room, with its big open wood shelves, the large potbellied wood stove, and the deep gray soapstone sink. Pewter plates and jugs glowed among the wooden boxes and bowls. A sweet-smelling stack of firewood stood near the stove. The kitchen table was made of thick raw maple, smoothed and polished over many decades.

She debated opening another can of beer, but she didn't really like beer. She took a Coke from the refrigerator instead, then went out onto the back porch, wondering where her father was. Lately he had been spending more and more time indoors, sitting at his cluttered desk or staring sightlessly at the blaring television. But now the house was empty, silent. Through the torn screens she could see their large red barn, and beyond it down the hill to the highway. Mountains ringed the distance. The majestic maple trees rustled with squirrels and crows who shared the large, leafy branches with busy blue jays and elegant redwings. Their busy play stitched the nearby forest to the farm.

She heard a car coming up the long drive. Curious, she returned to the front porch. A moment later the black Spider that had almost run her over roared up to the front of the house and skidded to a stop.

The driver got out and she eyed him nervously through the screen.

"Hey!" he called when he saw her. "What the hell were you doing back there?"

Uh oh, thought Penny. *If Mr. Jackson finds out I cut school again he'll definitely tell my father.* She wasn't afraid her father would punish her, but she dreaded the heavy disappointment in his eyes. It seemed she had been a disappointment to him for as long as she could remember.

"What the hell are *you* doing here?" she called back impudently.

The man started toward her. He was tall and lean, with dark brown hair jutting up from his high forehead. When he came closer, she realized from the flash in his eyes that he was furious.

Galvanized into action, she turned and sped inside the house, locking the door behind her. She stood uncertainly in the middle of the living room, wondering what he would do. Suddenly she heard the back door flung open.

"Hey!" the man shouted from the kitchen.

Penny backed into the unused dining room, thinking fast. Could she lure the stranger upstairs and lock him in one of the rooms? Then she would find her father and make up some sordid story about the stranger, before he told about her skipping school and running out into the highway.

She heard his footsteps coming closer. Nimbly, she crossed the living room and dashed up the stairs, not sure if she felt more nervous or excited.

The stairs creaked loudly; he heard. She barely had time to slip into the bathroom, hop in the shower, and pull the curtain.

Who was he, anyway?

She heard him searching the other rooms and stifled a laugh. She was tempted to strip out of her tank top and jeans and turn on the shower, just to embarrass the heck out of him, but just then he opened the bathroom door and ripped aside the shower curtain.

He glared.

"Now it's your turn to hide," she said mischievously.

"Are you crazy? What the hell made you run in front of my car like that?"

"What car?" She hopped out of the shower and edged toward the door.

"What are you doing here anyway?" asked the man. "Who are you?"

"I live here." Penny slipped into the narrow hall. The stranger guessed what she was going to do, and crammed his foot in the door just before she slammed it shut. He winced, but effortlessly pushed open the door. They stood staring at each other in the hall. The varnished planks tilted and dipped, matching the low ceiling which missed the man's cropped hair by less than an inch.

"You must be Penny," he said abruptly.

"Good guess." She was surprised that he knew her name. "Who are you?"

"Dom Whitfield. I didn't realize you were still here. I was staying in Connecticut for the weekend and thought I'd drive up to take a look around."

"What for?"

"Don't you know who I am?" He looked puzzled.

"No."

"I thought your father would have told you," he said.

Anxiously, Penny glanced out the window from the dim hallway in which they stood. In the distance, she saw her father, stooped and slow, emerging from the barn. Chickens clamored about his feet. Glancing at the house, he saw the black Spider and stiffened. Then he turned and went back inside the barn, closing the door. The sky was a clean, pale blue in the warm spring afternoon; the pastures were already psychedelic green with new growth. But Penny felt cold. She turned back to the odd stranger, with the tawny, intelligent eyes that had changed so dramatically from blazing anger to puzzlement.

"Told me what?" she asked sharply.

"He's sold the farm," said Dom slowly. "The sale was arranged last fall although we made special arrangements so you wouldn't have to leave till May. My mother is moving in this weekend. I assumed you and your father were gone by now."

CHAPTER TWO

THE sun must have gone on shining, but it was as though someone had drawn the dusty curtains. Now the long winter months when her father had been so silent and withdrawn were explained. He had known all along that the farm no longer belonged to them.

And he hadn't told her! She felt shocked by the betrayal.

"Did you say you're moving here this weekend?" asked Penny, sounding more astonished than upset.

"Yes." Dom added, gently, "That is, my mother is. She's moving here from New York City. She's retired and she always wanted to live on a farm."

"It won't pay!" said Penny earnestly. "Dairy farms around here are having a real bad time."

"She's not going to run it as a dairy farm. She just wants to live here."

"She must be crazy. Why would anyone want to live here?"

"It's peaceful . . ."

"You mean boring."

"Quiet."

"You mean dull."

"Beautiful."

"You mean stupid."

Dom hid a smile. "Anyway, my brother and I will visit. We're not too far from New York City. She can go there if she gets lonely."

It had never occurred to Penny that they weren't far from

New York City. The two-hour trip might have been two hundred hours. She had never been there.

"I wonder what we'll do?" she said, half to herself.

Sympathetically, Dom touched her bare arm. "I'm sure your father will have made plans."

His touch sparked something in her. Staring at Dom, she rubbed the skin he had so fleetingly touched. A ray of hope gleamed in her narrow blue eyes. "Plans?" she repeated. Might they leave Northkill? Start life somewhere entirely new?

Just then they heard an explosive report from the barn. Penny turned white.

"Oh, God," she whispered.

"What was that?" asked Dom.

But Penny had already disappeared down the narrow stairs and rushed outside.

"Daddy!" she cried, leaping over the white picket fence. Dom was at her heels. Georgia, her retriever, barked wildly outside the red barn. Penny wrenched open the door and rushed inside.

Jan Houten lay facedown on the floor, a pool of blood by his head.

He had been cleaning his revolver. The grease wax and chamois cloths were on top of the wood table. Another revolver lay in its case.

The hens clucked frantically as Penny threw herself on her father's body.

Dom knelt beside her and felt for the man's pulse, but he knew it was pointless. Penny's father was dead.

"Oh, God!" she screamed. *"Oh, Dad!"*

Dom gripped her shoulders and forced her to her feet. He was afraid she might turn him over and see his face.

Penny tried to struggle out of Dom's hold, but she had to give in to his strength. Finally she allowed him to lead her out of the barn.

"Penny . . . I'm here," Dom tried to reach her. "Penny . . ."

She clung to him. Georgia trotted beside them, whimpering. Dom led Penny to the back porch and pushed open the kitchen door. Once inside, Penny broke away from him. She wasn't crying, but the absence of tears worried Dom more than her sobs would have done.

"It'll be all right . . . you'll be okay . . ."

He went over to her and put his arms around her again. He had never felt a body so rigid. Rubbing her back, he murmured helplessly, "Penny . . . talk to me . . . Penny dear . . . it'll be all right."

He couldn't tell if she heard, but after a while he realized she was clinging to him as though he were a life raft. He pulled out a chair and said gruffly, "Here, sit down. Do you have tea or coffee or something I could make for you?"

She didn't answer, but she did sit down. Dom put water on to boil and found a box of tea bags in one of the cupboards.

"Milk? Sugar?" He placed the steaming mug in front of her and brought out a pitcher of milk from the refrigerator. Automatically, Penny added milk and sugar to the tea and took a sip. The warmth brought some of the color back to her face.

Dom went to the wall telephone and dialed the police.

"There's been an accident at Dogwood Farm," he spoke into the receiver, slightly dazed by the sound of his own voice. "Mr. Houten . . . No, I'm afraid he's dead. Dominic Whitfield. I'm the new owner of the farm. Yes, I'll be here."

He replaced the receiver and turned back to the dry-eyed Penny.

She was staring, unseeing, at the blue tablecloth. Georgia crouched beside her. Every now and again she licked her hand. Penny didn't appear to notice.

Dom drew up a chair. "Do you want to lie down? I can handle the police when they get here."

She shook her head.

He wished he knew what to say. He had been an infant when his own father died.

"It's a terrible accident," he began.

Penny finally spoke. "It wasn't an accident," she stated flatly, still staring at the tablecloth. "Daddy killed himself. He'd never leave the farm, I know he wouldn't. He'd rather die."

Dom went over to her and massaged her rigid shoulders. "We can't be sure of that, dear," he said.

"Yes, we can. The farm meant everything to him."

Dom stared down at the mass of glossy dark curls on top of her head and felt such a poignant tenderness for the girl he wanted to kiss the top of her head. Instead he asked gently, "Is there anyone you want to telephone? Any grandparents or other relatives?"

"There was only Daddy and me."

"We'll think of something to do. Don't worry, Penny."

After some time, a siren screamed up the drive. From the window Dom saw a white ambulance following the police car. He went to the door and opened it. A sheriff was getting out of his car.

"Morning," said the sheriff, approaching the house. "Are you Mr. Whitfield?"

"Yes, I am."

"Name's O'Mara," he said, stepping inside the kitchen. He was large, straight backed, with a soft stomach hanging over the top of his belt. He glanced at the silent girl sitting at the table. "Hello, Penny." His voice gentled.

Penny did not look at him.

The sheriff cleared his throat and addressed Dom. "Where's the old man?"

"In the barn," said Dom.

He followed the sheriff outside.

The sheriff shouted to the ambulance driver, "He's in the barn. Better bring the stretcher."

"Do you have a sedative for Penny?" Dom asked. "She's in a state of shock."

The sheriff went to speak to the ambulance driver. He returned with a plastic bottle which he handed Dom. "Valium. It'll help."

"What will happen to her?" asked Dom, as they crossed the gravel driveway and headed toward the barn.

"She must have relatives who'll look after her."

"She says not."

The sheriff shrugged. "Then a social worker will look into

the situation and decide what's best for her. She's only six-teen."

He pushed open the barn door. Hesitating, Dom glanced at the small bottle in his hand. He would be of more use to Penny than to the sheriff. He returned to the house.

She wasn't in the kitchen.

"Penny!" he called out.

There was no answer.

Dom grew alarmed. The narrow stairs creaked under his weight as he went upstairs. Dom took them two at a time.

He looked in the open door on his right. Penny's room, he guessed, from the pink flannel pajamas flung carelessly on the unmade bed. All the drawers in the chest of drawers were open. On some narrow shelves by the open window were a dozen books: some childhood favorites and a dozen mystery novels.

A quick search of the rest of the upstairs yielded no sign of her. He glanced into a messy master bedroom, then into an-other room that looked as though it had never been used for anything but storage, and the bathroom. Anxiously, he looked out the small window toward the front of the house.

In the distance, he saw her walking purposefully across the cornfield toward the highway.

Dom tore out of the room. If she was planning to throw herself in front of a truck it would require a miracle to reach her in time. Taking the entire flight of stairs in one leap, he was out the door in a flash.

Penny stood in the same place from where she'd darted onto the highway earlier. She watched the cars and trucks that passed as though in a trance. Panting, Dom grabbed her arm and pulled her into the safety of the ditch. It took him a moment to get his wind back.

"I know what you're thinking," he finally gasped. "It's im-possible for you to believe me, but you'll get over this, Penny. You'll never forget it, but you'll get over it. I know you will."

"How do you know what I'm thinking?" she asked, still gazing at the highway.

"I know my mother will do what she can to help you too,"

he went on. "Don't give up, Penny. You have a whole life ahead of you."

She looked confused, and then she broke into a comprehending smile. "Oh, don't worry. I wouldn't ever do what Daddy did."

"Then what are you doing here?"

"I guess I wanted to run away. I was watching the cars going by and I felt so free, as though I could do anything—go anywhere in the world."

"Oh." Dom was still trying to catch his breath.

She turned to him. "But I don't have any money or anyplace to go."

They stood looking at each other.

"I've often thought about running away," she said. "But now there's nothing to run from really."

Dom thought she finally might break down and cry, but she didn't. After a moment, he tucked her arm through his and they headed back to the farm. "I think everyone gets that feeling at some time or other," he said understandingly. "To go somewhere where no one knows you."

Penny's eyes were again fixed dazedly on the horizon. Dom guided her back toward the house. Once inside, he led her up the stairs to her bedroom, pausing in the bathroom for a glass of water. Penny obediently swallowed the pill.

"Now, lie down. I'll be here when you wake up."

Penny lay down and closed her eyes. Dom waited until her breathing became even, then he quietly left the room.

CHAPTER THREE

THE sheriff stood by the large wood stove in the kitchen. "Tragedy," he said when Dom entered.

"What's going to happen to her? Apparently her father didn't tell her about the farm being sold."

"Just like him."

"Where will she go?" asked Dom.

"She's not of age. Unless she has some relatives that we don't know about, she'll become a ward of the state. She'll either be put in foster care or a place in Albany will take her."

"She'll have to leave Northkill?"

"We'll see." The sheriff hesitated. "I don't suppose there's any question that it was an accident? I mean, Houten not wanting to tell his daughter about the farm being sold makes it look . . ."

"I don't know anything about that."

"Doesn't matter. If his life was insured, the insurance company will investigate."

The siren screamed again as the ambulance sped down the drive, carrying Jan Houten's body to the morgue. Dom winced at the thoughtlessness of the driver. He hoped the noise hadn't woken Penny.

"When are you moving in?" asked the sheriff.

"My mother's the one who will be living here. She's coming this weekend."

"I'll speak to the social worker then. She'll have to make arrangements for Penny right away."

Dom opened his mouth to tell the sheriff that his mother would take care of Penny, at least temporarily. But then he closed it again. His mother was recovering from a heart attack and was coming to Dogwood Farm for a much-needed rest. The last thing she needed was to be saddled with an unruly teenager.

"Meantime my wife'll look out for her," the sheriff continued. More confidentially, he added, "Penny doesn't like her, but that doesn't matter. Penny's a bright girl, but she's wild. Talks back to you—my wife doesn't like that."

"What happened to Penny's mother?"

"She died ten years ago. Jan never knew how to control Penny. She's in with a bad crowd at school. They skip classes —get into trouble. Penny's been caught shoplifting a few times. We don't let our daughter come to the farm anymore. I suppose Penny holds that against us. We'll start the paperwork right away and try to get her into a home."

"I'm going to let my mother know what happened," said Dom as he walked the sheriff to his car. "Maybe she'll have some ideas."

The sheriff brightened at his words. "Then I'll wait till I hear from you before I send the wife over. Nice to have met you, Mr. Whitfield. I hope your mother likes living here."

"I think she will. She fell in love with the farm the moment she saw it."

"It's nice enough."

When the sheriff had gone, Dom went back inside and dialed his mother's number from the rotary wall telephone in the kitchen.

"Hello?" Susan Whitfield answered.

"It's Dom."

"Hello, dear. Back from Connecticut?"

"Not yet. I decided to drive up to Northkill and make sure the house was ready for your arrival."

"How nice! How does it look?"

"I'm here now."

"What's the matter?" she asked, sensing something was wrong.

As succinctly as possible, Dom described what had happened.

"That poor girl!" his mother exclaimed, appalled. "How awful! Is she there now?"

"Yes, she's asleep. I couldn't possibly leave her. Someone should stay with her. The sheriff said his wife would look after her but—"

Susan Whitfield interrupted. "You stay right where you are. I'll be there as soon as I can."

"Wait a minute," protested Dom. "There's nothing you can do." He knew it was futile to argue with his mother. Besides, hadn't he been vaguely hoping she'd come up with some sort of solution?

"Of course there is," insisted Susan. "When the sheriff's wife comes, tell her to leave Penny where she is. I'll look after her."

"Mom . . ."

"You sit tight. I'll be there before you know it."

"But you can't look after her," said Dom, helplessly. "Anyway, how will you get here?"

"I'll get Toni to drive me. She'll jump at any excuse to see you."

She hung up before Dom had the chance to argue any further.

CHAPTER FOUR

"**W**HAT are you going to do?"

They were floating along the Taconic Parkway in Toni Sumner's sporty red Mazda. The speedometer read seventy-five, but inside the car it didn't feel as though they were going that fast. Soft classical music floated from the Jensen speakers.

Susan Whitfield settled back in the soft beige leather seat. She loved this drive along the Taconic toward the Berkshire mountains. She'd seen the parkway being built years before. It was beautifully engineered. Now the trees had grown tall and the forsythia was bursting gold along its edges. She smiled at the highway ahead as she replied to Toni's question.

"I'm going to look after the girl, of course. I'll adopt her if I have to."

Toni laughed. She had a charming laugh. In fact, practically everything about Toni was charming. Her slender hands, with their perfectly manicured nails, her platinum blond hair that framed her oval face in a stylish pageboy, her sparkling green eyes with the catlike yellow centers, her willingness to work hard, and her delightful ability to play hard too, were all part of her charm.

But the nicest thing about Toni was her sensitivity to what went on around her. Susan was continually surprised by her assistant's ability to assess peoples' moods and her subtle tact in dealing with them. She had been Susan's assistant at Whitfield Communications for three years. Looking back, Susan was impressed at how the company had changed under Toni's increasing authority. It was a less competitive publicity firm, and yet far more popular. Clients hired them because they knew they could count on Toni's personal involvement in their needs. And Toni loved the work—spending late nights and most of her weekends at the office. Now that Susan was planning to retire, Toni was taking over. Susan would remain president and be available for consultation, but she knew the company would be more than safe in Toni's capable hands.

"Adopt her!" exclaimed Toni. "You haven't even met her! What if she's horrible?"

"No one is 'horrible,' certainly not a sixteen-year-old." Susan was irritated.

Toni glanced at the woman whom she hoped one day would be her mother-in-law. Susan was still striking at sixty. Her cheekbones were high, her dark hazel eyes large and intense. She wore little makeup apart from pale peach lipstick. Her chestnut hair was cropped short and tightly curled. Toni couldn't imagine Susan on a farm, far from her sophisticated city friends and her beauty parlor. It seemed a drastic move to make simply because she'd had a mild heart attack.

"Why are you smiling?" asked Susan.

"Just the thought of you in the country, looking after a teenage girl. You've always seemed so corporate. You belong in the city."

"I'm not sure about that. My work was a question of survival. With regard to the girl . . ." Her eyes clouded. "I had a daughter who died. She was just a baby. It was a long time ago, before Dom was born."

Toni was sympathetically silent.

"I don't suppose women of your generation can understand how totally we devoted ourselves to our children back in the fifties. I was devastated when my husband died and I was forced to leave Jonny and Dom to the care of baby-sitters and schools and go out and make a living. But you young things seem to think nothing of it."

"I'm not sure about that," mused Toni. "If I had children I'd want to stay home with them, at least for the first few years."

"Really? Now *you've* surprised *me.* I thought nothing could tear you away from your career."

"I love working, it's true. But I'm almost thirty. Almost every career woman has to feel a bit conflicted. I love babies. I've always wanted lots of children." She saw Susan laughing and laughed too. "Incredible, huh? But it's true. I even like the idea of a knight in shining armor sweeping me off my feet and us riding off into the sunset together."

"It's not so incredible. That's what happened to me."

"There you go."

They drove in silence for a while. Susan leaned over and patted Toni's hand.

"Thank you so much for taking the time off to drive me to the farm this afternoon. I hope I didn't mess up your schedule too much?"

"It was a light day," Toni lied with a smile. "No problem at all." She hadn't minded Susan's call because she appreciated any opportunity to see Dom. She did have to delay their departure, for she couldn't cancel an appointment with her most important client: Congressman Justin Groome. Even Susan had seen that, although she had offered to call the congressman, who was an old friend, and make excuses for Toni. But Toni had refused. Instead they had left at four, and now they were almost there.

"Did you tell Dom your plan?" asked Toni.

"About looking after the girl? No, but it'll make sense to him, I'm sure. Here's our exit."

Toni skillfully eased the car onto the exit ramp, then followed Susan's directions to the long gravel driveway.

Dom was sitting on the front porch. Looking relieved, he skipped down the rickety steps to greet them.

"Where's Penny?" asked Susan, getting out of the car.

"Still asleep." Dom gave her a hug. "I gave her a Valium earlier. Hi, Toni. Come on inside." He kissed her cheek, then led them into the kitchen.

"Is there anything to drink?" asked Toni, opening one of the kitchen cupboards.

"Beer? Tea? Or coffee?"

"I'll make coffee. Susan?"

"Please." Susan took off her houndstooth tweed jacket and sat at the large wooden table. She looked inquiringly at Dom. "Now tell me exactly what happened."

Dom went over the events of the morning again. He'd had several hours to mull over Penny's predicament and reluctantly had come to the conclusion that, deeply as he found himself caring for the girl, his mother was simply too frail to take care of her. "As far as I know Penny has no other relatives," he finished. "According to the sheriff she'll be put in foster care or placed in a home in Albany."

"Did you tell her she can stay here with me as long as she wants?"

"No . . ."

"Then I'll tell her when she wakes up."

"I know you want to help out somehow. But she can't stay on here. You don't even know her. Besides, you're here to get better."

"Looking after a sixteen-year-old will probably make me feel a whole lot better. She can show me around Northkill and she'll keep me young."

Remembering the wicked glint in Penny's eyes when he'd pulled aside the shower curtain, Dom was still hesitant.

"She's a little hellion, Mom. When I first saw her she was drinking beer and playing 'chicken' with some friends—daring each other to run across the highway. I almost ran her over."

"Sheer high spirits, my love."

"No, it's more than that. Her mother died ten years ago, and she's had no sort of discipline since then. She just may be too much for you to handle."

"Give me some credit for being your mother. You weren't a piece of cake when you were a teenager."

"Don't bring me into this," Dom argued, annoyed by the teasing smile on Toni's face. "Penny's been caught shoplifting. She skips school all the time. The sheriff won't even let his daughter come to the farm anymore."

"The sheriff probably has a nightstick up his ass."

Amused by their argument, Toni poured the coffee into three solid white mugs. The kitchen faced east, so now that the sun had set the room was almost dark. She switched on the table lamp. She liked the old farmhouse, but she knew she liked it especially since it meant Susan would be turning over the reins of the business to her. For herself, she couldn't imagine living so far from the city. It was like moving into a cemetery.

She thought she heard a noise in the hall, but the others didn't notice. Dom paced the room, running his fingers through his short hair in frustration. "You're crazy. You'd be embarrassed by her when your friends came to visit."

"The girl just lost her father," said Susan sharply, "and she learned her house had been sold. And you're concerned that I might be embarrassed? I'm more embarrassed by your heartlessness."

"I'm not heartless. I'm worried about you. At least wait till you meet her before you decide anything."

"I won't change my mind no matter what she's like."

"You're recovering from a heart attack," Dom raised his voice. "You need a complete rest. Taking on a teenager like Penny won't be restful even if she should be any help at all. And that's unlikely. She's practically a delinquent. You should have seen how she behaved earlier. She had me chasing her all over the house."

Toni saw a shadow in the doorway. "Dom," she said warningly. But he went on, unheeding, "You're moving here to recuperate. Running after a sixteen-year-old isn't my idea of rest, and I don't think it's Dr. Goodman's either."

"Dom," Toni said again, more loudly, "I think someone has joined us." She nodded toward the door.

Penny stood there with her arms folded, smiling defiantly at them.

CHAPTER FIVE

THERE was an uncomfortable silence, then Susan rose and went toward her.

"You must be Penny," she said, softly. "Come on in."

Penny didn't move. Toni thought Dom was right about Penny. She did look like a juvenile delinquent with her wild, dark hair, dirty T-shirt, tight blue jeans, and insolent expression. And how could anyone be so thin? Toni dieted constantly, but she never dreamed of being so scrawny.

"I'm sorry," Dom apologized at once. "I didn't mean for you to hear what I said. My mother—"

"Never mind me," interrupted Susan. "I want to talk to Penny by herself. You two go for a walk, will you?"

Dom looked as though he might argue, but a warning glance from his mother changed his mind. Abruptly, he turned and went out the door. Toni followed.

Left alone, Susan put out her hand to Penny. Penny kept her arms folded.

"It's been a day of shocks for you," said Susan. "Dom didn't mean what he said. It's just that I've had a heart attack and he thinks it would be too much work to take care of you."

Penny raised an eyebrow. "Who said anything about taking care of me?"

"It was my idea. I hoped you'd like it. We could take care of each other. Would you like some coffee?"

"No." Instead Penny opened the refrigerator and took out a beer. Her expression dared Susan to stop her.

Susan didn't say anything.

"Why would you want to take care of me?" asked Penny, opening the can.

"The plan has merit. I'd have a companion here and you wouldn't have to leave your home."

Penny took a sip of beer. "I can look after myself."

"Of course you can. I was hoping you'd be generous enough to look after me a little too."

"He"—Penny jerked her thumb at the door—"wouldn't like it."

"Eventually he would."

Penny put down the beer and went over to her jean jacket, now hanging on the back of a rocking chair. She fished for her cigarettes. When she struck a match, her hand was shaking. Quickly, she blew it out.

"Forget what Dom said when you weren't in the room," Susan said sharply, watching her. "He wasn't talking about you, he was talking about me."

Penny smiled her disbelief.

"He was worried about me," Susan explained. "He said things he didn't mean because he was trying to change my mind. It had nothing to do with you."

"I don't care anyway."

Susan wanted to put her arms around her. As if sensing this, Penny folded her arms again and moved away.

"We could try out the arrangement for the summer," Susan suggested. "If it works out we'll stick to it for the school year. If it doesn't, at least you'll have time to make other plans."

Susan sat back down and poured herself another cup of coffee. She had felt an immediate affection for the child. She longed to cradle her in her arms and comfort her. Was Penny desperately holding back tears, Susan wondered, or was she still too stunned by her father's death to cry? As she watched Penny wandering around the kitchen, occasionally glancing sidelong at her, Susan kept her expression devoid of any pity. She had a feeling if Penny were to glimpse that, she would refuse help under any circumstances.

"Okay," Penny said at last, abruptly.

CHAPTER SIX

"**W**HAT do you do with the old woman?" asked Mary, the sheriff's daughter, between classes.

"We see lots of movies," said Penny. "She has a VCR and she sends off for movies from movie rental places all over the country. She's crazy about them."

"That doesn't sound too bad," said Graham.

"You know her son is Jonny Whitfield, the director."

Mary and Billy had never heard of him, but Graham had. "He made some pictures back in the seventies. Pretty good stuff."

Mary regarded Penny critically: "You look different."

"She's into that beauty parlor stuff," Penny said carelessly. "I said I'd check it out with her. She wanted them to cut my hair. They did my nails too. She doesn't think I should bite them." Penny held out her long-fingered, square-tipped hands for inspection. The nails had been painted with translucent rose.

"Nice," said Mary.

"Here." Penny fished in her pocket and tossed her two small bottles of nail polish. "I picked these up when they were doing my toes."

"You stole them?"

"Nah—just borrowing them. Help yourself. Anyone got a cigarette?"

The boys didn't smoke and Mary didn't have any.

"She won't let me smoke in the house," said Penny. "It'll

be a bitch in winter when I have to go outside every time I want a cigarette."

"Are you going to stay with her for the winter?" asked Graham.

She shrugged. "I guess."

"Dad says she's going to be your foster mother," said Mary.

Penny didn't answer. When Susan first told her she was going to apply for the license needed to provide foster care, Penny hadn't believed her. But then Susan went to an orientation meeting, and she submitted to a physical exam, and now she was in the midst of six weeks of training.

All for a girl she hadn't met before a month ago.

"She must be real nice," said Mary.

Susan was nice, Penny had to admit. She was also the busiest person Penny had ever met, and she kept Penny busy too. First of all she needed Penny's help in clearing out the clutter inside the house. They went through old letters together, and threw out brochures, newspaper and magazine clippings, and boxes of mildewed old paperbacks. Then she wanted to redecorate the rooms, and they spent hours discussing color schemes and types of furniture before taking a day trip to Albany to look at what the department stores offered. While they waited for the wall-paperers to come, Susan ordered custom-built shelves for the dining room.

"It's going to be our library from now on," she decided. "We'll eat in the kitchen. That's my favorite room anyway, and we're not going to change a thing in it."

Penny said nothing, but she felt relieved for she loved the large, cozy kitchen. She was thrilled when she discovered that Susan had hundreds of books—many of them mysteries—in the boxes she'd stored in the barn. The new "library" became a source of constant delight to her.

Susan took Penny to the country antique stores that Penny had always despised and persuaded her to select some special objects to place around the now shiny, airy home: a colorful French papier-mâché box, a bronze Victorian scale in the shape of a horse, two Italian cupids made of cherry wood.

Then Susan wanted to sell the hens, the cows, and the milking machines. She was thrilled by the rapidly growing corn and the pumpkins in the field and Penny had to tell her everything she knew about growing and harvesting the vegetables. Six tall sunflowers grew close to the house; on a couple of occasions Penny heard Susan talking to them. Penny laughed to herself when it happened, but she didn't tell her friends about the incident. She didn't want anyone else laughing at Susan. Strangely enough, she felt almost as protective of Susan as she knew Susan felt about her.

Susan also loved to cook—strange, exotic dishes from every kind of recipe book. When she had guests they spent most of their time in the kitchen helping her: chopping, cleaning, measuring. Penny figured if Susan's sophisticated city friends helped, she could too.

The kitchen had not been changed, but it felt different to Penny now that it was used as the main room of the house. Susan hired a woman from the village to clean it thoroughly once a week, and there seemed always some sort of activity going on there.

Dom, Susan's son, was their most frequent visitor. In the first few summer weeks he came almost every weekend. He was always unfailingly kind to Penny, but she couldn't forgive him for calling her a delinquent and trying to talk his mother out of taking care of her.

Early one hot Sunday morning, Dom came downstairs and found Penny gazing moodily out the back screen door at the highway in the distance.

"I'm going into town to pick up the *New York Times*," he told her. "Want to come?"

She was on the point of refusing, but the temptation to ride in his black Spider was too much to resist. She slipped her bare feet into her running shoes that had been left under the table. Dom held the door open for her.

The car roared down the driveway. Penny's curls were whipped around by the wind. Her eyes shone. *When I finally leave Northkill,* she said to herself, *I want it to be in a car like this.*

"You okay?" Dom smiled at her.

She nodded shortly.

"I meant in general—with my mother and everything. It's working out all right for you?"

She nodded again, surprised. She thought he hadn't given a damn about her since the afternoon her father died.

"She's awfully fond of you," Dom went on. "Says you've been an enormous help in getting her adjusted to the place and fixing up the house. You've been working very hard."

Penny didn't reply. She felt embarrassed, because the truth was that right from the beginning she'd been especially nice and helpful to Susan simply in order to prove Dom wrong.

Dom didn't appear to mind her silence. They pulled up in front of the grocer and Dom hopped out of the side of the car without opening the door. "Be right back."

Penny wished some of her school friends would see her sitting in the sporty Spider, but it was still too early for any of them to be up.

Dom returned. "Anything you want to pick up now we're in town?"

"No."

"Mom'll probably have a great breakfast ready for us when we get back or else I'd take you out somewhere." They drove off again. "Why do I get the feeling you like sports cars?"

"It's a nice car."

He smiled at her reserve. "I never told you I'm sorry for what I said that first night my mother arrived."

Penny's face grew scarlet.

"I really didn't mean any of it. I was just worried about my mother. She's been very sick."

"I know."

They soared along the Taconic.

"You must miss your father terribly," Dom said at last.

"I don't want to talk about it." She stared straight ahead.

"Okay. But I want you to know I'm here for you. If you ever need something or just want to talk, let me know."

They reached the farmhouse at last. Still embarrassed, Penny flung herself out of the car and went upstairs to her room. Dom followed more leisurely.

But Penny couldn't forget Dom's words. "I'm here for

you." No one had ever said anything like that to her before. She felt touched. After he had left that weekend, she tried even harder to be as helpful as possible to Susan.

Another frequent visitor to the farm was Congressman Justin Groome. He was big, broad-shouldered, with a tremendous laugh. He had been a congressman for many years, and had twice lost the race for senator. His father, grandfather, and two uncles had all been in politics, and Groome was carrying on the family tradition.

In addition to his own staff, Congressman Groome hired Whitfield Communications as consultants when he staged a major event such as running for office. He was one of the company's most illustrious clients. Often Toni drove to Dogwood Farm with Justin Groome in order to talk over a campaign strategy with Susan.

Justin Groome fascinated Penny, with his booming voice, contagious laugh, his charming manner. He treated her like a lady. When he brought flowers for Susan, he always remembered to bring a bouquet for Penny as well. When he invited Susan to lunch at a famous little tavern overlooking the Hudson, he included Penny in the invitation. His eyes were hard, light blue, but they were interested when they turned to her. Penny was flattered that a famous politician would bother with her, much less actually seek out her company.

"What's he like?" asked Mary curiously.

"Weird," replied Penny. "Weird and rich. He's always buying me presents."

"Why?"

"He says he's trying to make up for my losing my father. I guess he sees himself as a sort of father figure."

"Is he going to marry Susan?"

"I don't know. They've known each other for years. They would have done it by now, wouldn't they?" Penny couldn't figure out their relationship. She knew Susan had managed Groome's political career almost from its inception thirty-five years earlier. But she seemed reserved toward him in spite of their long friendship. "He's actually nicer to me than he is to her."

"I'd watch out for him," warned Graham. "Politicians never do anything without a reason."

"Maybe the reason is that he likes me."

"Maybe."

"But it's weird that he buys me so many presents, isn't it?"

It wasn't just the presents that bewildered Penny; it was how frequently Justin Groome touched her. Since her mother died, Penny had rarely been caressed, and she found she disliked the congressman's hands on her, even when he merely patted her shoulder. She also didn't like him kissing her on his arrival, and again on his departure: His large lips were wet and repulsive to her.

She couldn't bring herself to tell Susan how uncomfortable Justin Groome made her, since it appeared he was one of Susan's oldest, dearest friends. But one weekend she hesitantly remarked to Dom that Justin Groome "grossed her out."

"Why?" asked Dom.

"He's always pawing me."

Dom laughed. "He just can't wait till you're eighteen."

"What'll happen when I'm eighteen?"

"You'll vote for him, of course. Justin cares for very little other than being reelected."

Penny felt young and very unsophisticated. Maybe people in the city did hug and kiss more often than she was used to.

Maybe she was being silly.

Driving back to New York after that visit, Dom told Toni that he had the feeling Penny still had not forgiven him for what he'd said to his mother their first night at the farm.

"Relax." Toni laughed. "The reason she hasn't forgiven you is that she's madly in love with you. She knows it's hopeless, she has to keep some sort of emotion going, so she opts for anger. It's obvious."

"In love with me! She's just seventeen!"

"Do you know how many thirty-year-old men I fell in love with when I was seventeen?"

"She hardly looks at me."

"Not when you're looking at her. But get a glimpse of

those brazen blue eyes when you're not looking at her. I've never seen a girl more in love."

For some reason, indefinable even to himself, Dom could not bear to listen to his girlfriend making light of Penny's crush on him. From then on, he was silent on the subject of Penny.

CHAPTER SEVEN

ONE afternoon Penny met her friends at the ditch near the highway looking excited. "Look what I found!" She waved a MasterCard over her head.

"Whose is it?"

She tossed it to Graham.

"Justin Dwight Groome," he read out loud. "Jesus, Penny, you'd better give it back to him."

"Why?"

"You're not going to use it!"

"Sure I am. Remember the Minimum Rage concert we wanted to go to in Albany? I've already phoned in for four tickets. It's all set."

"I can't go," Mary wailed. "Mom'll never let me."

"Don't tell her where you're going, you yellow banana."

The concert was on Friday night. Penny told Susan she was going out with some friends and she'd be home late.

"Be home by midnight," Susan said mildly. "Who's driving?"

"Graham."

Susan trusted Graham. "Have a nice time."

Penny, Billy, and Mary drank beer and smoked a joint while Graham drove. When they arrived at the concert hall, they were all high, except for Graham. "Forget it: I gotta drive," he objected when Penny kept urging him to take a hit.

"We have to pick up the tickets at the ticket booth," said Penny, going ahead of the others. "Let's go."

She lit another joint while they waited in line.

Just as she was handed the four tickets in an envelope, Justin Groome appeared. Penny jumped in fright when she saw him.

"I thought it might be you," he said, yanking the envelope from her hand and grabbing her elbow. "Did you really think you could get away with a stunt like this?"

"Ow. You're hurting me." She saw Billy and Mary duck behind a group standing in line. Graham stood by manfully until Groome turned on him with a cold glare.

"These tickets were obtained by fraud. Better go home right away if you don't want to get into serious trouble. I'll take care of Penny."

Graham struggled with himself. "I'll be okay," Penny encouraged him. "Go ahead."

Dragging her by the elbow, Justin strode to the parking lot. "Get in," he said, opening his car door and shoving her inside.

Penny sat in the front seat, wishing she hadn't smoked that last joint. "How did you find out?"

"My dear girl, as soon as I discovered my credit card had been stolen I had my bank trace back how it had last been used. When it turned out it was for a rock concert I suspected you and your juvenile delinquent friends immediately."

He eased the Lincoln out of the parking lot.

"Are you going to tell Susan?" asked Penny in a small voice.

"We'll see," he replied harshly.

They drove in silence. Penny stole a glance at him, wondering if she could persuade him not to tell Susan what had happened.

"I'm sorry. I won't do it again."

"Damn right you won't."

He took an unfamiliar exit. Penny wondered, but didn't say anything until he turned onto a deserted dirt road and pulled over.

"Get out," he ordered.

"What?"

He got out of the car. Nervously, Penny did too.

"What are we doing here?"

He stood just inches in front of her.

"Penny, I know you better than you realize. You're a liar, a pickpocket, a thief. I've watched you and I've heard talk about you. I haven't said anything, knowing you've had a big shock this summer, losing your father like that. But you're too much for Susan to handle. You need someone with authority to keep you in line. So I'm going to punish you."

Her eyes grew round. "What are you going to do?"

"You're going to get the worst spanking of your life," replied Groome. "Pull down your pants."

"You're kidding!"

"Do what I say."

She only stared.

"Okay, then I'll help you."

Hardly seeming to use any force, he tore open the fly of her jeans and yanked them to her knees. He turned her around so her stomach was pressed against the car. One hand squeezed her neck.

She screamed as his hand struck her.

"That's for lying to Susan. That's for smoking pot. That's for stealing my credit card. That's for simply being a bad girl." He paused, surveying her, and as she craned her neck around to see him she saw he was smiling. "And here are a few extra ones because you need to be punished."

He released her at last. Gasping with pain, Penny reached for her pants.

"I can't believe you did this," she whispered. "Susan would kill you if she knew!"

He eyed her blandly. "Would she?"

Penny was confused. Would Susan think she ought to be punished like that? She knew there was something terrible about what Groome had done, and yet she wasn't sure whether she had deserved it.

All her life she had been told she was a bad girl. Her teachers had said it, and her father had said it, over and over, hopelessly, as though she would never change. Clear as a bell she remembered him exhorting her not to spill the pail of milk she had picked up from under one of the cows. The cow had moved her leg, the bucket was kicked out of Penny's hand. "Bad girl—bad, bad girl!" her father had shouted. "No, you can't help me anymore, *you bad girl!*"

She had been five years old.

"Get back in the car," ordered Groome.

They drove back to the farm in silence. Susan had already gone to bed. Penny fled to her room, grateful that she didn't have to face her.

Oh, Dad, she thought miserably, lying fully clothed on top of the bed. *Why did you do it?*

Her anger at her father for abandoning her by killing himself kept her awake half the night. All the rage that might have been directed at Justin Groome, she directed instead at her dead father. If her father had been alive, Groome would never have dared do what he had done.

In the morning she heard Susan and Justin talking on the front porch. Evidently they didn't realize her window was just overhead and she could hear every word.

"Dom spoke to his lawyer about Penny's father's life insurance," said Susan. "He says it's impossible to try to claim it since he committed suicide."

"Susan—Susan. You rely too much on Dom's advice. Trust me."

"I do trust you, Justin, but in this case I think he's right. He's also taking Penny into consideration. Trying to justify the claim would be very stressful for her."

"On the other hand, getting a nice sum of money from the insurance company might take away some of the stress."

"I don't think so. Although it is a shame that her father was so deep in debt there's no money left for her from the sale of the farm. Most of it went to back taxes."

"Why don't we ask Penny if she'd be interested in trying to claim her father's insurance?"

"I'd rather not," Susan said firmly.

Groome laughed. "You know she'd jump at the chance."

"That's not fair, Justin. She's still in a state of shock from her father's death. Refuses to talk about it, never cries. Dom said she didn't even cry when it happened."

"But, Susan, I'm trying to get reelected. The story would be gold for me. A young girl screwed by an insurance company, championed by the sensitive congressman. The polls would reflect the whole thing."

"It's too risky. You might lose the case."

"We'd still come out smelling like a rose. I need to get known in this neck of the woods if I'm going to run for senator. They're all goddamn rednecks up here—won't even look at a Democrat. I plan to change that."

"We'll come up with another plan. Maybe you can offer to build a new town hall or something like that."

Groome snorted.

"I thought Penny was going out with Graham last night," Susan said after a moment. "How come you drove her home?"

Penny held her breath.

"They dropped her off at the end of the drive," said Justin. "I happened to pick her up. God, what a gorgeous day it is."

"Why wouldn't they drive her all the way home?"

"She said something about an argument. I wouldn't mind some more of this delicious coffee."

They went inside.

Penny clasped her knees, thinking. She did not want to try to prove that her father's death had been an accident. She knew it wasn't and she didn't want to have to lie. But she was appalled that there was no money left over from the sale of the farm. She had not thought about it before, since Susan had seemed to take for granted that she would pay for whatever Penny wanted. But now Penny decided she would offer to get a job. Perhaps she could work at the beauty parlor on weekends.

That way, she wouldn't see so much of Justin Groome. He had been very wrong to spank her like that. She understood that now, because otherwise why wouldn't he tell Susan what he had done? He must be counting on Penny not to say anything about it, so long as he didn't mention the stolen credit card. He was setting her up.

Penny debated with herself, absentmindedly rubbing her buttocks. She still felt a little sore.

For the time being, though, she would keep the spanking a secret. The congressman was definitely weird. You never knew when knowledge like that might come in useful.

Chapter Eight

PENNY turned seventeen that summer.

"How would you like to celebrate your birthday?" asked Susan.

"I don't know."

"What do you usually do?"

"Nothing."

"Well, we'll do something this year," said Susan. "Seventeen is a marvelous age. Let's have a barbecue. Dom and Toni would come for it, I'm sure. And we can invite any of your friends that you'd like."

To Susan's delight, her older son, Jonny, and his wife, Emmy, were in New York for a couple of weeks and planned to be at the farm for several days. They arranged their visit to coincide with Penny's birthday.

Penny was excited about meeting Jonny. "What's he like?" she asked Susan.

"Charming. Everyone loves Jonny. Even Emmy, his wife, loves him, which is amazing considering the fact that he treats her like a doormat."

Susan had refused to let Penny work at the beauty parlor. Now that she was officially her mother, she said, it was perfectly okay for her to support her daughter. She wanted Penny to spend more time on her homework, and helping around the house, and watching movies together.

Jonny and Emmy arrived late one night, after Penny had

gone to bed. In the morning only Emmy and Susan were at breakfast; Jonny was sleeping late.

"Hi," said Penny.

"Hello," said Emmy. Her voice was clear and low-pitched. "It's nice to meet you." She was definitely striking, Penny thought, with bright turquoise eyes and rich auburn hair, cut short. Taller than Penny, Emmy wore a sheath of purple voile. On her tanned feet were slim Italian sandals. She was a reporter, and told Susan and Penny about the story she was researching: "The contrast between being homeless on the West Coast versus the East Coast. *Monday Week* assigned it. I have to go to Boston and Washington as well as spend more time in New York."

"You look exhausted," said Susan. "Are you sure you're not overdoing it?"

Emmy shook her head. "It's not the job."

"Things aren't going well." Susan stated the question.

Interestedly, Penny looked from one to the other.

"Not too well."

"He couldn't hope for a better wife . . ." Susan said indignantly.

"It's not just me. He needs to get funding for *Flaming Forest*. You know how obsessed he gets. Everything's taken a backseat to that."

"I wish I knew what to say."

"There's nothing to say."

Jonny was dark haired, like Dom, but his eyes sparkled and flashed in a way that Dom's never did. Dom's gaze could pierce into someone else, but he rarely let any of himself show through his eyes. Jonny showed everything. He laughed boisterously, he kissed exuberantly, he joked, he wept, and—he drank.

Penny had never seen anyone drink as much as Jonny did. He seemed always to have a glass in his hand, except at breakfast, when he was heavy lidded, ominously quiet, and drank strong, black coffee by the potful.

"What's this movie you want to make?" she asked him on the morning of her birthday. It was a hot, muggy day and they were-sitting on the front porch. In the distance they heard thunder.

"Flaming Forest? It's an action adventure set in the Amazon rain forests. Everyone agrees the movie should be made. It'll raise the public's consciousness about what's happening there. It'll bring to light the truth about so-called environmental groups who're actually encouraging the despoilation by setting ridiculously high quotas for the exportation of hardwood. It's a fabulous project—everyone agrees about that. But no one wants me to direct it."

"Why not?"

"I'm too expensive."

Penny was drinking coffee for the first time since Susan had arrived. Susan always made herb teas. Jonny wouldn't touch them.

"It sounds boring," she said.

Jonny's eyes flashed. "It'll be the most exciting thing ever made. The story's the tragedy of the decade! There's action, tension, murder, rape, suspense . . ."

"How can you have any suspense?" she goaded him. "You know they're going to go on cutting down the forest until there's nothing left."

"You're a fatalist. I'm an optimist. I'm hoping my movie will change peoples' attitudes."

"Good luck." He was so enthusiastic she couldn't help teasing him. "But personally I don't think movies change peoples' attitudes. They're for entertainment."

Jonny cocked a dark eyebrow. "I could argue with you all day. Too bad I have to get more coffee."

Susan was right: Jonny was charming. Only Dom seemed immune to his charm. The tension between the brothers surfaced almost as soon as Dom arrived. Standing around the barbecue while Dom skillfully cooked the hamburgers and hot dogs, Jonny angrily described his most recent, unproductive meeting with a producer.

Dom interrupted coldly. "You haven't even got a script together, or any stars, apart from Jeannette. Why should anyone risk backing you?"

"I've got a tremendous treatment, and a lot of stars are

interested. Besides, someone should back me because the movie's so damned important! The whole face of the earth is changing because of those rapists!"

"Don't tell me you care more about what's happening to our planet than to yourself," said Dom sarcastically.

"I've yet to see your TV station trying to educate the public about anything," said Jonny, munching on fresh-picked corn.

"Sure—I'm just in it for the money, not for the good of the world," agreed Dom.

Toni flared up in Dom's defense. "You know he backs environmental groups," she told Jonny. "And he also makes sure his station carries even more public service announcements than are required by law!"

Emmy put a hand soothingly on Jonny's arm. "Everyone's doing what they can, in their own way. You can't fight about whose way is better."

The argument ended without any resolution. Penny was fascinated. This was the best birthday she'd ever had. She and her father had hardly spoken to each other, much less argued.

She loved seeing Dom looking so annoyed. But she saw that Susan looked distressed. She went over and put a hand on her shoulder.

"Thank you for everything," she said softly. "I'm having a wonderful time."

Susan took her hand and squeezed it. Penny bent over to kiss the top of Susan's head. She was starting to let the brown turn gray instead of dyeing it as she used to. Penny liked it better now—it reminded her of a fall morning when the frost lay on the fallen brown leaves. As she lifted her face, she found Dom gazing at her with an expression so tender she flinched. But she could not look away.

Involuntarily, her fingers stole up to the gold chain he had given to her as a birthday gift. He gave a half smile and turned back to the barbecue.

Penny stayed beside Susan, feeling a little sick. She didn't want to fall in love with Dom. Loving anyone was a terrible thing, because the person you loved always left you in the end.

CHAPTER NINE

THUNDER shuddered ominously on the horizon, then retreated. It didn't rain but the city air was thick and damp.

"Jonny, don't you think you should try to get a job?" asked Emmy.

"No. Why?"

"I know you want to get the money to make *Flaming Forest* but so far no one's biting. My income's not enough to support us in the life-style you're accustomed to. I don't even make enough to pay taxes on your house."

They were in New York City; Emmy was still researching her article on the homeless and Jonny was still trying to get investors interested in *Flaming Forest*.

The air-conditioning had broken down in their hotel room. Ignoring her, Jonny went to stand in the open window looking at the rushing commuters on the street below. They poured like lumpy syrup out of the office buildings and into the subway entrance. How had they ended up where they were? Why hadn't they tried to escape from their jobs before they became automatons? Did they harbor a festering ambition beneath the hardened crust they presented to the world? Did they sigh angrily at the end of each day because they knew they were no closer to a dream they might have had? Did they squirm in disbelief as the days wound them pitilessly toward death and oblivion? Did they think about it?

Emmy wanted him to get a *job!*

He watched a group of homeless men standing on the street corner, drinking something in a paper bag. It made him feel thirsty.

"How's your article coming?" he asked.

"Okay."

It occurred to him that Emmy rarely talked about her work. Or was it that he rarely listened?

He went on watching the bums on the street. He would rather be a bum than get a job. When you were a bum the rigid beginning and end to each day—and night—become fluid and blurred. Your life wasn't merely a fishing reel pulling you inexorably to your doom.

Emmy was lying on her stomach on the wide bed, writing. She was naked. Her long back glowed faintly with freckles. Jonny went to lie beside her. But it was too hot to touch each other, even to hold hands.

"I can't get a job right now," he said. "This might come through any day now."

"Couldn't you get a job until you hear of something?"

"No."

He could tell she was annoyed, and yet she wasn't sure whether or not he was right and funding for the movie would come through any day now.

Jonny put his arms around her.

"I love you."

"It's too hot," she said, putting down her pen.

He kissed the back of her neck. "I love it when you sweat."

Emmy resisted, then stroked a damp curl from his forehead. Wherever their flesh met sweat broke out.

"Darling." Then she said, "We'll wait a bit longer. Something's bound to come through eventually."

"Okay," said Jonny.

Then the heat again drove their bodies apart and they lay with the damp air solidly settled between them.

CHAPTER TEN

SWIFT, cool autumn winds swept down the valley and frolicked around the farmhouse. The pumpkins ripened. Crisp apples fell from the half dozen trees in the tiny orchard. For the first time in her life, Penny enjoyed school. Susan was always willing to help her with her homework, and she was impressed by the compositions Penny wrote. "You have quite a talent," she said. "Have you ever thought about trying to get something published?"

"No." But Penny's eyes lit up. "Do you really think I'm any good?"

"Oh, more than just good."

As the days grew shorter and colder, they kept the potbellied wood stove burning all day long and the kitchen was the warmest room in the house. Penny spent more and more of her time there, and less time alone in her room.

Susan encouraged her to invite her friends to the farm. She persuaded Sheriff O'Mara to rescind the ban against Mary visiting. One evening Penny gave a slumber party, just for girls. When Susan had initially suggested it, Penny had sneered.

"It'll be so boring."

Susan laughed. "Because there won't be any boys? But think what fun it will be to talk about them."

The boys teased the girls about the party, but Penny knew it was because they were jealous and she liked their teasing.

Susan was usually tolerant of Penny's mischief-making.

When Penny got into trouble, she tended to take her side. It was obvious she didn't like Penny smoking but she didn't say much about it. Penny grew conscious of the stale smell of the smoke in her clothes and hair, and the yellow stain at the tips of her fingers, and began to wonder why she smoked at all.

The only thing Susan was adamant about was that Penny didn't take drugs.

At first Penny was sullen when Susan broached the subject. "Drugs are deadly," Susan said firmly. "They're also evil. I don't mean to sound melodramatic, but the people bringing drugs into this country are thugs and murderers. They think nothing of torturing and killing anyone who stands in the way of their business. In effect, you're handing money and encouragement to a torturer and murderer. That's what's really bad about taking drugs."

Penny thought about their talk. The next time a joint was passed to her during a movie, she refused it.

"You feel okay?" asked Graham when the movie was over.

"I don't feel like getting high anymore, that's all."

In early December Susan took Penny on her first trip to New York City. They planned to stay overnight at the Plaza Hotel. Susan wanted to show Penny the Empire State Building and a couple of museums, then they had been invited to a cocktail party at Justin Groome's apartment. Afterward they would go to Lincoln Center to see the "Nutcracker" ballet.

Penny was thrilled by the skyscrapers, the shops, and the crowds.

"So many people!" She laughed breathlessly, as they pushed their way down Fifth Avenue, stopping to gaze at the magical store windows which had their Christmas panoramas set up inside. The tree in Rockefeller Center, over thirty feet high and strung with thousands of colored lights, dazzled Penny too.

Her excitement was contagious, and Susan had almost as good a time as Penny. But eventually she was worn out by the shoving crowds and noise of the heavy traffic. She slipped her arm through Penny's and leaned against her as they gazed at the Christmas tree.

"You're tired," Penny realized. "Let's go somewhere we can rest."

"We're due at Justin's cocktail party at five," Susan reminded her. "It's almost that now. Maybe we could find a cab to take us there. I don't think I can walk another step."

"I should have noticed before that you were tired. How do we find a cab?"

Fifth Avenue had a stream of yellow cabs crawling along, but they were all occupied. Penny suggested they hire one of the horse drawn carriages standing near Rockefeller Center.

"It'll take longer but it will be fun," Susan agreed.

She gave the driver Justin Groome's address on the Upper East Side and they settled back to enjoy the ride. A few large snowflakes drifted by, adding to the magic.

Groome used his Park Avenue penthouse for large, official receptions, personal luncheons, and delicate negotiations. A private elevator, decorated in brass, red silk, and mirrors, lifted them slowly to the top floor. The brass doors opened onto a small reception room where they were greeted by a butler ready to take their coats. As they fixed their hair in the silver mirror by the entrance, they listened to the festive sounds of talk and laughter from guests already arrived. Penny tingled with anticipation.

She took Susan's arm and propelled her into the crowded living room. But she stopped on the threshold to look around. It was almost as bare as the entrance. One wall was all glass, overlooking the East River and beyond to the lights of Queens and Brooklyn. The two side walls were white and bare. The back wall held a large painting of swirls and squiggles.

"That's a Jackson Pollock," Susan told her, catching her look. "It cost Justin two million dollars. Probably worth ten times that now."

They walked toward the wonderful window. Along the far side wall stretched the crowded bar. A plain white door was centered directly across.

Six chrome and leather chairs were spaced like sentinels around the edges of the room. "Those are Charles Eames's Barcelona chairs," Susan said.

"Why doesn't anyone sit on them?"

"They cost two thousand dollars apiece. No one dares."
Susan laughed. "Justin did a favor for a company that distributes them, so he got them cheap."

A black marble table stood in front of the glass window.
On top, a black vase held tall yellow asters. Behind them the
twinkling lights of the river bridges, and the buildings to the
east and south, spread out like a fairyland in the December
dusk. Boats plied the waterway. Penny looked back into the
room. The sparseness only served to emphasize the glamorous
people who moved elegantly about the vast space. Penny wondered what was behind the white door, centered so dramatically, and yet so discreetly shut tight.

A head taller than anyone else, Congressman Groome stood
near the bar, surrounded by women. His eyes constantly
roamed through his guests, even while he talked and laughed.
As soon as he saw Susan and Penny he excused himself and
came over.

"Ah, my favorite guests have arrived," he said, kissing
them both. He held on to Penny's hand. "Drinks?"

"Susan's tired," said Penny, trying unsuccessfully to free
her hand. She added mischievously, "Let's find her a chair."

Unperturbed, Justin Groome steered them to one of
Eames's masterpieces. Gratefully, Susan sat down.

"I'd like a glass of ginger ale," she said. "Penny?"

"I'll have one too."

Groome spoke in an undertone to one of the waiters who
was passing around a silver tray of *saucissons en croute.*

Penny spotted Dom near a window. His eyes met hers and
he smiled. Pertly, she turned away.

Without bothering to wait for her drink, Penny wandered
around the room. She was drawn to the white door. Seeing
that Justin was occupied with his guests, she turned the brass
handle and poked her head inside. It was his private study. An
Aubusson carpet covered the floor, mostly in blues and ivories.
It picked up the colors in the large painting hanging on the
wall behind the couch. Penny went toward it: It was a portrait
that looked strikingly like Justin.

"That's not me." Justin closed the door behind him and

came to stand next to her. "An ancestor. Done by John Singer Sargent. Like it?"

"Uh-huh." Penny glanced at the closed door. Ever since "that night" of the concert, Justin scared her, yet fascinated her too. He was charming, but dangerous. He could probably convince anyone of anything, she thought now, meeting his eyes boldly.

He placed himself comfortably in the middle of the soft couch and patted the ivory-colored leather beside him.

"You look as if you could use a rest too."

"Are you kidding? I wouldn't sit next to you if you paid me."

"My dear," he drawled, "if I decide to spank you again, you can be damn sure I'll do it whether or not you sit next to me."

Still, she remained standing.

His hard blue eyes inspected her. "I like what you're wearing. It's a refreshing change from blue jeans."

Penny fingered the black silk dress that she and Susan had picked out at Saks earlier in the day. The sales attendant had wrapped up her old skirt and sweater and she had worn the new dress as they left the store. It clung to her slender body, showing every curve and most of her legs. It was the shortest dress she'd ever worn. Her black stockings were subtly patterned, and her high-heeled black sandals showed off her feet and ankles to perfection.

He patted the couch again. "Don't be gauche, Penny. Sit when I tell you to. You're not a child," he added sarcastically, his eyes wandering up and down her body. She felt naked under his scrutiny.

Abruptly she sat down beside him, holding herself stiffly. His after-shave smelled sweet.

"Where are you staying tonight?" he asked.

"The Plaza."

"With this snow it'll be hell trying to find a cab. Why not stay here with me instead?"

"I'd rather stay at the Plaza."

"Would you?" His fingertip tapped her thigh. "You should wear dresses like this one more often. You have pretty legs."

"I'll tell Susan you said so."

"I don't think you'll tell Susan I said anything," he said softly. "Will you, Penny?"

"Maybe. Maybe not."

"I have a feeling you're a dangerous ally," he murmured, patting her thigh again. "But I like that."

Penny didn't move. She didn't like where the conversation was going. She was glad when they were interrupted by a light tap on the door. Groome's butler stepped just inside the doorway.

"Mr. Sheehan is on the telephone, sir," he announced.

Groome jumped to his feet. "I'll take it in here." With a curt nod he dismissed both Penny and the butler.

Later that night, back at the Plaza, Penny soaked herself for a long time in a hot bath. She left the door open to the bedroom, talking to Susan about the party. Susan was already in bed. The bathroom was the best part of the hotel, Penny decided. It was mostly gray marble and thick white towels. Beside the large marble sink with its gold water taps were tiny bottles of sweet-smelling liquids, some for her hair, some to rub on her body, some to create more soap bubbles than she'd ever dreamed of.

The tub was long and deep, water covering her entirely, not like the stained shallow thing at home. She luxuriated in the bubbles, half-floating, letting her disgust with herself wash away. She remembered sitting beside Groome when he told her to. She should have walked out on him right then.

Jumping out of the tub, she toweled herself hard. The towel was almost as big as a blanket. She rubbed vigorously, watching her skin glow pink in the tall mirror on the back of the door. Then she massaged herself with the fragrant body lotion, starting with her arms. Finally, feeling relaxed and clean once again, she went back into the luxurious bedroom. There were two double beds with large gleaming white pillows and silk comforters. A low table was placed in front of the couch from where she could look out the window at the rumbling city. It was alive with lights and movement. Penny picked up her hairbrush.

Cautiously, she told Susan that Justin Groome made her uncomfortable.

"He thinks he owns me," she said.

"He thinks he owns everyone," Susan answered. "I wouldn't let it bother you."

"I don't think I like him."

But Susan only laughed. "As long as you can't vote one way or the other, Justin doesn't care whether you like him or not. He only likes people he can use."

"Why are you two friends?"

"He was a friend of my husband's," Susan explained. "They went to Harvard Law School together and they entered politics in Washington at the same time. It was the early fifties."

Penny sat on the edge of her bed. She wore a new peach flannel nightgown—another present from Susan.

"What happened to your husband?" she asked curiously. "You never talk about him."

"He died," Susan answered, her eyes distant. "I miss him very much."

"Of course."

"Not everyone misses their husbands," Susan said dryly. "But I really did miss mine. I didn't have enough money to support my boys. That's why I went into business. I would never have been as successful as I was without Justin's help. He stood by me emotionally and financially. I'll always be in his debt."

"I'm sure you would have been just as successful without his help," said Penny. "He probably just made you feel as though you owed him a lot."

"I was never much of a career woman. Justin encouraged me to believe in my ability to do something completely new and different. He can convince anyone of anything."

"Mm."

"He's very fond of you, Penny. He sees himself as a father figure."

Penny looked pained.

"What's the matter?" asked Susan.

"Nothing."

"Do you miss your father very much?"

"Sometimes."

"Do you want to talk about him?"

Penny didn't reply.

"Dom said you didn't cry when he died and I haven't seen you cry since. Why not, Penny? I feel as though you're still hurting terribly inside."

Penny shrugged. "I cried so long and hard when my mother died, I've never been able to cry since. Funny, isn't it?"

Susan's eyes were full. "You were only seven."

Penny got into bed.

"I've had a wonderful time today," she told Susan, before turning off the light. "Thanks for everything."

"I had a wonderful time too. And I love having you for my daughter."

Chapter Eleven

THE week before Christmas, Jonny and Emmy were on the East Coast again. Emmy went ahead to Dogwood Farm, leaving Jonny in New York. She was tired of Jonny's continued obsession with his movie.

They had another fight before she left. At Dom's suggestion Jonny had arranged to meet another producer. Emmy was impatient with him. "Perry doesn't even have a job! How on earth can he help you?"

"He might know someone, or hear of someone—"

"If he doesn't have a job himself, he's not going to get you one."

"I don't want a job. I want money."

"Some people work for their money."

"I don't mind working for my money. But I'll work on my terms, not anyone else's. I won't get a job."

"You're being unreasonable. We need money to live, not just to make a movie."

"Fuck that."

Emmy was relieved to arrive at the serenity of Dogwood Farm. Susan and Penny had draped the rooms with garlands of princess pine. They hung a ribboned wreath on the front door. Penny picked the bushiest tree from a local Christmas tree farm and Emmy helped her drag it home.

From an old trunk, Susan brought out colored Christmas balls and odd ornaments. "Some of these I've had since I was a girl," she said.

Penny didn't have any decorations to add, but she offered to make a star for the top of the tree. When Dom came, he brought a string of tiny white lights. He and Toni piled presents under the tree. Jonny, who'd gotten a ride with Dom and Toni, insisted that more greenery was needed around the house and he and Emmy returned from a shopping expedition laden with holly and mistletoe.

The mistletoe gave Jonny license to kiss indiscriminately. On Christmas Eve Jonny got drunk. Emmy went to bed early. She tried to read a mystery novel, but she fell asleep almost right away. She dreamed that she and Jonny were on a sinking ship in the middle of a storm. Huge waves threatened to sweep them into the ocean. Emmy started to scream. But Jonny kept saying, "Don't scream, Em. Think of it as an interesting experience."

The dream switched. Emmy was recounting the shipwreck adventure to the children they didn't have. Jonny was with them. His hair was white, and he was bent over with age. He went to his car—a gold Porsche—and drove away. Emmy put her old, wrinkled arms around her children.

"Even knowing," she said, "that shipwrecks have always happened, and will happen again, people go on building ships."

She was talking about love.

Her eyes opened. It was still night. Her light was on and she was alone in the cozy guest room. From downstairs came the rise and fall of voices, mostly Jonny's.

Sometimes she wondered how much longer she could go on living with him.

She had met him seven years ago. He had scraped the side of her old Hyundai with his Porsche as he was getting out of a parking place while she'd been doing some errands: When she returned there was a note on her windshield asking her to get in touch with him so that he could pay to have her car fixed.

They'd met on a windy, bone-dry day at Mort's in Pacific Palisades. He had been late. She'd waited, sharing a large wooden table with strangers, eating a pastrami on rye, wondering why she thought he'd show. But she'd waited anyway.

When Jonny finally dashed in, full of apologies, she saw an odd look of recognition in his eyes.

Afterward Jonny told her it had humbled him, that initial feeling he'd had. It wasn't only love at first sight, it was a miraculous sense of having found someone he'd been looking for for as long as he could remember.

Emmy had felt it too. They stayed at Mort's for hours, drinking coffee and talking, as though there were years and years to catch up on.

Jonny was a film director; she had seen all his movies. He had been divorced twice. She was a free-lance journalist.

Later that afternoon he took her home, and they made love, and for three whole days they hardly left his bedroom.

His house was on the edge of an iron-red cliff in Pacific Palisades, overlooking Los Angeles and the Pacific. A steep, flower-filled garden fell away from the back of the Spanish-style white mansion. Flowers bloomed everywhere: There were huge poinsettia plants, the flowers brilliant scarlet, long and pointed like fingernails. They were nothing like the little potted plants she was used to. These were as big as trees.

There was jasmine and sweet-smelling rose trees too, with fat blossoms—a perfumer's dream. Hibiscus, the color of fresh peaches, bloomed along the walkway to the front terrace. Their petals were scrupulously swept up by the gardener, almost as soon as they landed on the ground. A lemon tree grew outside her window, with lemons the size of papayas. Orange trees and lime trees added to the riot of color and fragrance. Monarch butterflies, large, golden-orange creatures with black velvet trim, on their long migration to Mexico, fluttered gracefully over the whole like blossoms blown free.

Hedgerows, twenty inches high, bordered the stone walkways. At each corner was a round blob of a short, trimmed bush as added ornamentation. Birds would perch on these, unmindful of Emmy as she took solitary walks through the garden. They perched so close she could see each soft, small feather on their plump bellies ruffled by the breeze.

When she wasn't working, she'd wander through this paradise for hours. There was nothing else to do. The Mexican maid kept the mansion immaculate, and the gardener took care of every stray leaf, every weed that she might have tugged up. She didn't speak Spanish, and they didn't speak English, so their conversations were confined to shy smiles and embarrassed back-turnings.

She used to go swimming in the heated pool at the bottom of the garden. It was a sparkle of aquamarine, a misplaced jewel amidst the gaudy flowers on the hill. The silver leaves of a giant eucalyptus tree leaned protectively overhead, whispering when there was a breeze, but usually motionless under the hot California sun. Sometimes she thought the solitary splashing of someone in a swimming pool was the loneliest sound imaginable.

There was a fountain in the garden too. She could hear the water falling onto the goldfish in the jade green pond all day long—and all night too. Next to swimming, the sound of a fountain could make her breast ache with loneliness.

Sometimes when she lay outside on the grass she heard voices from deep in the bowels of the cool mansion, reverberating like quiet, barely audible voices of people long dead. She would jump to her feet and run up the terra-cotta steps to see who it was. But the voices were always those of the maid or the gardener, and they talked only to each other.

She didn't mind being alone so much: She was by nature a solitary person. She'd lived alone for years before she married Jonny. Her work schedule didn't change: She went on getting assignments and researching and writing articles. She continued to visit her friends.

No, it wasn't being left alone that she couldn't stand. It was Jonny. She couldn't stand his extravagance, his dissipation, his egotism, his drinking. Most of all she couldn't stand his affairs.

After all this time it was still hard to realize she couldn't stand someone she loved so much.

CHAPTER TWELVE

TONI and Dom went upstairs soon after Emmy. Jonny stayed down with Susan and Penny and some last, lingering guests. Dom built a fire in their bedroom while Toni undressed. He kept one eye on her. It was always a treat to see what she wore under her clothes. Tonight it was a sheer red and black lace-trimmed bustiere, a red G-string, red garter belt, and sheer black stockings with seams going up the back.

"Brrr . . . cold . . ." She smiled at him.

"You'll be warm in just a minute." But he reluctantly gave her his burgundy dressing gown to keep her warm while they drank the champagne. The soft wool enveloped Toni, who was less than average height, and she curled cozily in the large armchair.

"Here—open this while I light the fire," he said, handing her the bottle.

She popped the cork expertly.

"I have some news," said Dom, bringing over the champagne glasses. "The job offer came through at APG that I told you about. I'll be moving to Los Angeles in January."

Toni waited, without pouring the champagne.

"I couldn't turn it down. It's a fabulous promotion."

"Why would you want to turn it down?" she said coolly.

He hesitated. "Because of us."

"What about us?"

"Long-distance relationships are hard," he admitted. "But I'm hoping we can manage it."

She was too disappointed to speak. She set down the bottle. "What's the matter?"

"Dom, I'm practically thirty!"

"Well?"

"I'm not interested in a long-distance relationship with you."

"But . . . I love you."

She took a deep breath. "You don't love me enough to want to marry me." She had finally said it.

Dom was silent. "There's so much happening just now. I don't feel ready."

"We've known each other for three years. If you're not ready by now, you never will be."

She blinked back tears, took off his dressing gown, and began to dress.

"What are you doing?"

"I'm leaving."

"Where are you going? It's Christmas Eve."

She pulled the short black velvet dress over her head. "So what? I've waited and waited—"

"Toni, let's talk this over reasonably . . ."

"Forget it. I've been hoping all this time that eventually you'd *want* to marry me. You don't think *I* wanted to be the one to bring up the subject, do you?"

She slipped into her high heels.

"For heaven's sake, don't be so damned impulsive."

"Explain to your mother for me, will you? I have a feeling she'll understand."

"At least tell me where you're going!"

"To my parents'. I *know* they'll understand."

She left.

Downstairs Jonny was talking earnestly to Penny who looked sleepy but amused. Everyone else had gone to bed. Toni took out her mink coat from the hall closet.

"Going to midnight Mass?" asked Jonny, looking up.

"It's way past midnight. Shouldn't you guys be in bed?"

"Is Christmas over already?"

"Yes, it's definitely over. 'Bye, Penny."

"Later," replied Penny.

They listened to her car roar down the snowy drive.

"Poor Toni," said Jonny, refilling his glass of Glenfiddich and splashing some water in it. "Did you know if you only drink scotch and water you can't get a hangover?"

"Sure," said Penny. "That's why you haven't been getting up till after noon since you've been here. Why do you say 'poor Toni' like that?"

"Because she's in love with an asshole like my brother."

"He's not an asshole!" Penny flared.

Jonny gave a mock groan. "Don't tell me you're in love with him too? Why is it that girls always go crazy over assholes?"

"Why do you call him that?"

"Because he's in a position where he could help me get backing for *Flaming Forest,* and he's done nothing."

"Maybe he doesn't think it's worth it."

"Why are you defending him? Mom said he was pretty rotten to you too."

"He wasn't! He was just worried about your mother, and I happened to overhear some things I shouldn't have."

"Thanks for understanding." Dom stood in the door, the open champagne bottle in his hand. He looked at Jonny. "Hey, don't hold it against me that Perry's out of work. I told you before you made the appointment."

Jonny waved a hand airily. "I know."

"Want to help me with this?" asked Dom, setting the full bottle on the table. "Toni and I didn't get very far with it."

"Sure," said Jonny.

"Sure," said Penny, who had never had champagne before. Dom sat down. Jonny got out fresh glasses and filled them.

"Where'd Toni go?" she asked, enjoying the champagne a lot. "She looked upset."

"Someone should teach you to be more tactful," remarked Jonny, before Dom could answer.

"But I want to know. You must have had a fight." She eyed Dom innocently.

"Leave him alone," said Jonny. "Tell us about your boyfriends instead. Who's this Graham fellow Mom's mentioned?"

"Nobody." Penny tossed Graham aside with a wave, embarrassed by the thought of her youthful friends.

Dom rested his chin in his hands, regarding her with an odd smile. "You're a character. Isn't she a character, Jonny?"

"She sure is. How'd you get so many freckles?"

Penny hated her freckles. "How come you two don't like each other?" she asked.

"We like each other," said Dom. "We just don't get along."

"Oh." She felt lightheaded.

Jonny refilled their glasses and the brothers looked at each other as though Penny weren't there.

"I'm sorry about Toni," said Jonny.

Dom only nodded.

"Maybe you should go ahead and do it," said Jonny.

"Do what?" asked Penny.

They ignored her.

"How is it you always seem to know what's going on, even when you're completely self-absorbed?" Dom smiled at his brother.

"It's not the end of the world."

"What isn't?" Penny insisted.

They still didn't seem to hear.

"I'm moving to L.A. in January," said Dom. "APG came through with the job offer."

"Congrats. Wouldn't she move?"

"Not without a signature on paper."

"What paper?" asked Penny. "What are you guys talking about?"

"It isn't the end of the world," Jonny repeated with a laugh. "I know it kinda seems like it, but you go on living, you know."

"Thus speaks a man who's twice divorced."

"I don't know what you guys are talking about," complained Penny.

"Marriage," said Jonny, still looking at Dom. "We're talking about marriage."

Penny refused any more champagne.

CHAPTER THIRTEEN

TWO days later, Dom went with Jonny to the sole jewelry store in Northkill. Jonny picked out a large, square emerald framed by tiny diamonds. "She'll never know it didn't come from Harry Winston's."

"Why would she care where it came from? It's what it means that matters to her."

"Welcome to the real world," Jonny encouraged him. "You'll probably like having her around. And kids too."

"I like her a lot," said Dom. "I probably love her. But marriage?" He stared gloomily at the ring. The salesman flashed it inspiringly in the cold sunshine that streamed through the window.

"Practically everyone's at least tried it," Jonny said cheerfully. "You might find you like it."

Dom drove to Toni's parents' Connecticut house that afternoon. The sky was a low, depressing gray. What was it about women that made them want to spoil a perfectly fine relationship with commitment? Still, he'd decided to go ahead and he would do it with good grace.

Toni opened the door for him, looking stunning in black spandex pants and an oversize white angora sweater.

"Come on in." She was still cool.

"No, you come out." Dom grinned at her. "Let's go for a walk."

"Don't you want to say hi to my parents?"

"When we come back I will. Come on. It'll be dark soon."

He waited outside.

"Which way?" he asked, when she emerged in snow boots and her fur coat.

She led him across the wide lawn and up a hill on the far side. From here they could see the village of Middleton in the distance. The streets were practically traffic-free because of the snow. The white clapboard houses created a ghostly effect against the snow: shades of white on white. A white church spire pierced the darker white sky.

Dom cleared his throat self-consciously. "Here's your Christmas present."

It was a plain beige velvet box. Toni's heart jumped wildly when she saw it.

"Oh, Dom," she breathed.

She opened the box and stared at the ring. She was acutely aware of the cold in her feet, the wind blowing on her face. The air was filled with the crisp scent of snow and pine. She knew she would remember these sensations forever. They hummed through her, overwhelming her.

Dom mistook her silence. "I'm not just asking you to marry me because of our fight the other night. I decided I really want to."

He took the ring from the box and slipped it on her third finger. Toni clung to him. He kissed her cheek, her closed eyes, her brow. Their lips met, then their tongues.

"I love you," Toni whispered.

Dom's hands found their way beneath the coat, beneath the sweater, beneath the satin bra.

"We can't do anything here," she whispered.

"Why not?"

They were alone, on top of the world. Twilight closed in. Toni clung to Dom, ripples of pleasure running from the tips of her breasts, down her belly, down to her thighs. She felt Dom pressing against her. His urgency excited her. They had been lovers for practically three years, and yet she had never felt such desperate desire for him before.

They half-fell into the soft, dry snow. Toni still wore her fur coat: It kept her warm while Dom tugged the tight pants down her hips. He straddled her within seconds, so that she barely felt the cold. Her breasts were exposed, but his hands warmed them. His mouth found hers again.

"You're mine," he murmured, "all mine."

"All yours."

He gave a shudder. "Toni—"

"I can't believe we're doing this—" But she was carried away too. She kept her eyes open, fixed on his, as they rocked more and more urgently, back and forth in the snow.

"Thank God for my coat," she groaned. "Dom . . ."

"I know . . ."

The moment came, burning cold, hot, wet, fierce, bright, dark. Dom lay on top of her, breathing hard.

"I'll never forget this," he said at last.

They straightened their clothing, laughing. Maybe marriage to Toni wouldn't be so bad.

CHAPTER FOURTEEN

O N Valentine's Day Susan and Penny went to New
York again. Susan wanted Penny to visit the Metropolitan Museum. Susan also had to talk to Toni about some
new clients.

They planned to go just for the day and return on the train
after an early dinner with Justin Groome. It was Friday:
Penny took the day off from school. She wore a white blouse
with a red lambswool cardigan over it, a black corduroy skirt
which flared down to her calves and low-heeled oxfords. She
was never entirely comfortable in the new clothes Susan
bought for her, but she wore them as a favor. For herself, she
still preferred jeans.

They spent the morning at the Metropolitan Museum of
Art, walking through Central Park to get there. Penny's eyes
were wide with wonder as they walked slowly through the
great rooms, each one filled with amazing and entrancing objects. When she couldn't take in any more, they took a taxi to
Enrico's on Lexington for an early lunch. The restaurant was
long, narrow, and noisy, the air marbled with delicious aro-
mas. They ordered Saltimbocca alla Romana and an Italian
salad and they ended up with tiny cups of the bitterest, black-
est coffee Penny had ever had.

"I'm going to leave you now," Susan said, putting on some
lipstick. "You can explore the shops and galleries by yourself.
You'll have about two hours, but you can't get lost. Let's meet
at the Prescott Gallery at four-thirty. It's on the corner of

Fifty-seventh Street and Madison. Have a good time till then."

Thrilled to be alone in the great city, Penny wandered over to Madison Avenue and up to Seventy-ninth Street. She went in and out of shops, trying on dresses, window-shopping antique stores. She rang the bells of the carefully locked doors into the small art galleries, impressed that she had the nerve. She liked best the light-inspired realism of her contemporaries. She must remember to tell Susan.

It was only four o'clock when Penny reached the Prescott Gallery. Susan had not yet arrived. Penny was tired, but, still eager, she wandered around the gallery. The show was of primitive African sculpture. "More Picasso than Picasso," the critics had called it. Rows of masks stared down at Penny from glossy white walls. The exhibit made her feel uneasy. It was too strange. The potbellied, baked figures inspired revulsion, even fear.

She found a seat and sat down. Four-twenty. She hoped Susan would not be late.

Four-thirty. Penny heard the imposing voice of Justin Groome fill the reception room. Expansive and genial, he sounded like a father trying to play Santa Claus. Her heart lifted, hoping Susan was with him. But when he found her, he was by himself.

"I'm thinking of buying one of these masks," he said, by way of greeting. "Any suggestions?"

"No . . . I don't really like them."

"But they're tremendous things. Look at this one."

He pointed to an ebony fantasy with eerily wide eyes and a mouth that might have been screaming.

"It's okay. How did you know I'd be here? Where's Susan?"

Groome smiled. "You like it? Then I'm going to buy it."

"I don't like it at all."

"We'll take it to my apartment and you can show me exactly where you think I should put it." He went to speak to the woman seated at a desk in the back of the room.

"We don't usually let pieces go until the end of the show, Congressman," she said. "However, if you insist . . ."

"Of course I insist," Justin Groome said grandly. He

caught sight of Penny's expression and scowled. "What's so funny?"

"Shouldn't you think it over? It's probably the most expensive thing here."

He shrugged indifferently. While the treasure was being wrapped, Penny asked again, "How did you know I'd be here?"

"Susan told me. I left her at the office trying to straighten out a few things with Marianne. Toni's not there—she's in L.A. for the weekend."

They went outside. The chauffeur opened the door of the waiting limousine. Justin put the wrapped mask on Penny's lap. "I want to show you something in my apartment that a friend sent me. I'm considering buying it for the museum in Northkill. I'd like to know what you think of it."

"I don't know anything about art."

"It'd be refreshing to have your point of view then."

The penthouse looked unfriendly without the crowds of guests who were there last time. Its emptiness made Penny uneasy.

"Is Susan going to meet us here?"

"Yes. Take off your coat, will you? I'll hang it in here. Want a drink?"

"No."

He made her one anyway, a strawberry concoction that he claimed was his own invention. Then he took a cigar out of an inlaid wooden box on the coffee table and lit it.

"What were you going to show me?" asked Penny.

"I'll get it in a moment. Sit down and relax. Tell me about your day so far. Where did you go?"

"To the Metropolitan Museum." She remained standing.

"What did you see?"

"Art."

Justin pushed a chair toward her. The chrome scraped on the stone floor. Penny winced.

"Anything in particular that you liked?"

"No."

She felt Justin's large, cold fingertip circle the back of her neck. "You're being a little rude," he murmured.

Penny stepped back, hastily. "What were you going to show me?"

He nodded complacently. "Of course." He left his cigar smoking in the ashtray.

His new sculpture was a cross, made of copper, bronze, and iron. A semiabstract naked woman was pinned to its center. Penny was disgusted.

"As I said, I don't know anything about art."

"Anyway, it's not a cross to kneel in front of." He refilled his glass and pointed to a tray with brie, crackers, and strawberries. "Help yourself."

"Thanks, I'm not hungry." She looked pointedly at her watch.

He smiled again, his eyes hard. "Don't play games with me."

"I'm not playing games."

"Good." Abruptly, he leaned down to kiss her.

Shocked, Penny pulled away.

"I said, don't play games." He pressed her against the wall.

She stared at him with loathing. His enormous, muscular arms snaked around her shoulders. He was so close it was as though she were seeing him through a magnifying glass. The pores on his nose seemed huge. She tried to squirm free, but his hands gripped her.

"You can't get away from me now. And you've been wanting this to happen for a long time, haven't you?"

"No." Fighting panic, Penny ducked away and hurried to the elevator. She pressed the button. Hurry up, she prayed. *Hurry up.*

Smiling, Groome followed. "Wrong way."

Grabbing her arm, he dragged her along the hall. Desperate, Penny kicked his leg.

He jerked her into his bedroom and heaved her onto the wide bed. She leapt off and made a dash for the door. Groome caught her easily and threw her back on the bed. Bending over her, he slapped her face hard.

Penny screamed.

"There's no one to hear." He looked relaxed. "We're surrounded by wind and sky. Why don't you admit that you've been leading me on? You want this as much as I do."

He took off his jacket. Under it he wore a holster with a gun.

She would not lie there helplessly. She rolled off the bed.

"Do you want me to tie you up?" Groome yanked her back by her hair. "I can be pretty rough. But maybe you like that sort of thing?"

With one hand, he pinned her arms above her head, and unbuttoned her cardigan with his other. Penny kept struggling.

"No," she begged. *"No, please!"*

He began to undo the bronze buckle of his belt. She watched his hand as if hypnotized. The belt was leather, wide and thick.

"You'll find it easier if you relax. With your experience, you should know that."

She tried to keep cool. "You're crazy. What about your career? What about the election?"

Squeezing her wrists with his right hand, he began lightly tapping her thighs with the tip of the belt.

She shuddered.

"I can be pretty convincing when I want to be. If it ever comes down to someone having to choose between your story and mine, I can assure you you don't have a prayer. But I don't think it will come to that. You've screwed around so much already no one's going to think you're anything but a lying nymphomaniac. And you wouldn't want them to think that, would you?"

The belt slapped her hips.

Penny screamed again and tried to writhe out of his grasp. Her struggles only amused him. He unbuttoned her blouse and ripped her bra apart. Then he pushed the skirt up around her waist and pulled off her cotton tights.

Holding her wrists again over her head with one hand, he turned her onto her stomach. The leather belt stung the backs of her thighs. It began to lacerate her buttocks.

Finally he let go of her wrists. Penny didn't move. Groome

turned her over. Eyes smarting from pain, she watched him take off his pants. He fell on top of her, the gun pressing painfully into her ribs. Groome had a mad, excited look in his eyes. Penny could hardly breathe.

He pushed inside. "Whore," he said.

The pain was extraordinary. Groome was breathing heavily.

"Does Susan know you're a little sex maniac, as well as a liar and a thief?" he panted. "Does Dom know?"

He moved up and down fast, grunting. Penny couldn't move.

Finally he stopped.

"There's a word for girls like you. It's slut." He rolled off her and stood up. "Ever heard it?" He tossed her the tights. "Put these on and try to be respectable. We're meeting Susan downtown."

Penny kept looking at the gun in his holster. Then she went into the bathroom and threw up. She showered and got dressed.

One thing was certain. She was not going to be able to sit through dinner with Justin Groome. She rinsed out her mouth again and went into the hall. Her coat was in the closet.

"Where do you think you're going?"

She pressed the elevator buzzer without answering.

"You can run away from me, but you can't run from yourself."

The elevator came and she got in. Groome made no attempt to stop her.

The door slid closed.

Shaking, Penny leaned against the wall. Outside, she hailed a taxi.

"Grand Central Station, please." Her voice came in a low gasp.

She leaned back against the seat. *Slut.* What would Dom think if he knew?

Justin can convince anyone of anything.

Could he convince Dom that she was a slut?

Groome had played his cards perfectly. She did have a reputation to live down. He had used that against her like the consummate politician that he was.

Penny buried her face in her hands, shuddering.

He knew she would never breathe a word to anyone about what happened.

Chapter Fifteen

DOM and Toni were also celebrating Valentine's Day. Toni had telephoned Dom at his office in the afternoon.

"I miss you," said Dom. In spite of their engagement, they were living three thousand miles apart.

"Do you wish we could get together this evening?" she asked.

"More than anything."

"Then come by the Beverly Hills Hotel when you're through with work. I'm here now."

He laughed out loud at his surprise.

She opened the door at his knock. She wore a pale rose teddy decorated with tiny hearts, a matching garter belt, ivory stockings, and rose high heels. Her blond hair fell over one eye. She smelled of jasmine.

"Hello." Dom's voice was husky. No other woman could arouse him as she could.

"Mmmm." She kissed him. "You taste good."

"You do too."

"I already ordered champagne. Want some?"

"I sure do."

He took off his jacket and tie and dropped them on an armchair while Toni poured the Moet & Chandon into glasses.

"Cheers." She stretched out on the wide bed, sipping the champagne.

"It's a wonderful surprise to see you," he said, surveying her.

She returned his gaze unselfconsciously. She was so glad to see him. Dom had no idea how terribly she missed him. He assumed that she cared about her job as much as she cared about him, but it simply wasn't true.

"How's business?" she asked.

"Great, although I'm exhausted. How about you?"

"Terrific."

"Have you seen my mother lately?"

"No. We were going to meet in New York today, but Justin gave me this ticket to L.A. and I couldn't refuse. A valentine's present. Nice, huh? He said Susan was going to be in town to take Penny to some museums. Justin says she's determined to turn your juvenile delinquent into a debutante."

"Penny's not a juvenile delinquent!"

"You called her that, not I. Anyway, let's not talk about her. She's Justin's favorite topic of conversation lately too."

"What do you mean?"

"He talks about her all the time."

"Why?"

Toni shrugged. "Maybe she represents his lost youth or something."

Dom kicked off his shoes. "I've missed you." He lay next to her, leaning on one elbow and looking down at her.

"Me too."

He kissed the tiny embroidered hearts on the edge of her teddy.

"I know we agreed to get married next fall, but why don't you quit your job and move out here now? We could live together."

"Why?"

Dom slipped his finger underneath the spaghetti strap and nudged it off her shoulder. He didn't want to say he thought they should see how they liked living together before committing themselves to anything as drastic as marriage.

"You'd have the chance to get settled in a new job," he said instead. He kissed the side of her throat.

"We haven't talked about my giving up Whitfield Communications," she replied slowly.

"But you'd have to, if you moved out here."

"Have you thought about your moving back to New York?"

"I can't do that."

"Why not?"

"It looks as though I'm going to be promoted to vice president soon," he said. "I'd never go so far, so fast in New York. This city was made for me. I love it out here."

Toni's long fingernails stroked the inside of his thighs. "I'm an old-fashioned girl, Dom. I don't want to live together if we're not married."

"I like old-fashioned girls."

Her lips were tantalizingly cool. Dom buried a hand in the nape of her neck. "I love you," he moaned. "I'll do whatever you want. We'll get married tomorrow."

"I love you too," whispered Toni.

But she really meant it.

Chapter Sixteen

SUSAN was furious at Penny.

"Don't ever, ever do that again. I was worried sick when Justin said he couldn't find you at the gallery."

Penny stood in the middle of the kitchen, her eyes downcast.

"If you wanted to come back for a date, all you had to do was ask."

"I didn't have a date."

"Then why did you come home without telling me? Don't you have any consideration? I was scared out of my mind."

All she had to say was: "I thought Mr. Groome would tell you I went home. I didn't realize he'd lie about having seen me."

But she couldn't say it. Susan would interrogate Groome about why he'd lied and he would say it was to protect Penny. He'd say, "I didn't want you to know she was a slut." Something like that. And then Susan would tell Dom.

"What did you do last night?" Susan persisted.

"I got on the train and came home."

"You didn't go out?"

"No."

"How can I believe you, Penny? If you'd wanted to go home early, I would have taken you."

In every sentence, Penny heard Justin Groome talking. *He can convince anyone of anything.* She turned away from Susan without answering and went upstairs to her room.

Susan didn't mention the incident again, but neither of them could forget it. Inwardly, Penny was upset with Susan. *She should have known about him,* she thought. *She's known him practically all her life. She shouldn't have left me alone with him. She should have protected me.*

Groome still visited the farm, but less often. Penny called him "Mr. Groome" and made sure she was never alone with him again. But she didn't tell anyone what had happened.

"I'm worried about Penny," Susan told Dom on the telephone. "She hasn't been in her usual high spirits this spring."

"Working too hard at school?"

"I don't think that's it. She's very bright."

"Maybe she's anxious about graduating. Doesn't know what the future will bring . . ."

"We've talked about that. We're planning to travel together next year, and then she'll go to college the following year. I want to give her a graduation party. I think she'd enjoy it. Would you be able to come?"

"Absolutely. It'll be the end of May, won't it?"

"Yes. I'll let you know the exact date."

"I'll bring Toni."

All Penny's classmates were invited. Several of Susan's friends from the city promised to come. Emmy couldn't make it, but Jonny and Dom both flew east just for the occasion. Dom brought Toni and Toni's younger sister, Violet. Jonny was feeling great because the company Dom now worked for —American Production Group—had finally agreed to produce *Flaming Forest,* his movie about Amazonia.

They strung up Japanese lanterns on the trees in the front yard and cleared the living room of furniture so there could be dancing. A delicatessen, the best in town, catered the affair. There was very little for Penny to do other than enjoy herself.

"Hello, Penny." Justin Groome approached her with a pleasant smile. "Congratulations."

Penny nodded coolly. She looked lovely. Susan had bought her a forget-me-not blue silk dress. Although the dress was high in front, creating a chaste appearance appropriate for an adolescent, the back plunged sharply in a low V, startling in its elegant seductiveness. Penny's brown hair, usually thickly tangled around her head, had been fashioned by a hairdresser in Northkill that afternoon, and was fastened on top of her head, leaving her freckled shoulders bare.

"Dance?"

"No." She turned away.

Groome caught hold of her hand. Penny wrenched it free. It was the first time he'd touched her since the rape. She swung away and bumped into Jonny.

"You okay?" He steadied her.

She broke into a sweat. Jonny glanced over at Justin who was looking sourly at him.

"Come on over here," said Jonny. He guided Penny to a window seat. A balmy fragrance of wisteria floated in through the open window. "How come our friend looks as though he'd swallowed a pickle?"

"Because I wouldn't dance with him."

"It's probably the first time he's been turned down." Jonny looked kindly at her. "What's up, Penny? I thought you two were friends."

But she didn't tell him. Jonny felt curious.

"I was just talking to Toni's sister," he said. "I guess she used to be Justin's girlfriend. I'm not sure if she's high or the elevator just doesn't reach the top floor. What do you think?"

Violet was a model, nine years younger than Toni, with the same platinum hair and high cheekbones. She had a peculiar habit of gesturing abruptly. Twice tonight she had knocked over someone's glass. She made Penny nervous.

"She's loose as ashes," she stated.

Jonny laughed. "She's that, all right."

"She looks scared, as though she just discovered that Mr. Groome carries a gun or something."

"Does he? I wondered why he never takes off his jacket." He eyed her. "You've seen a lot of Justin this year, haven't you?"

"He visits your mother a lot," Penny answered.

"Why do I get the feeling you don't like him?"

"Because I don't."

Penny watched Dom and Toni begin to dance. Dom's fingers slipped caressingly inside the waistband of her red mini-skirt. His eyes were closed and Penny felt intensely irritated.

"Can we go outside for some air?" she asked. "It's too hot in here."

Jonny jumped up. "Yes, let's. I'll find a bottle of champagne to take with us."

A moment later he was back with two glasses and a bottle. Tucking her hand through his arm, they went onto the back porch. As they passed the open library window they overheard part of an argument.

"You know I'd never tell, Justin." It was Violet's faintly whining voice.

"Oh, no?" Justin Groome sounded quietly menacing. "Then why did you bring it up just now?"

"I didn't realize you'd get so upset."

"About blackmail? Oh no, not I, girl!"

"But I need money. And it was a bad thing to do to me. I was only fifteen."

"You're old enough to know you'd better not bring it up now."

Jonny pressed Penny's arm and they hurried down the steps, out of earshot, hoping they hadn't been seen.

"That was ugly," said Jonny once they were out of earshot.

"Jonny . . ." she hesitated, "do you know what they were talking about?"

"No," he said shortly, "and I don't want to know. Let's sit here and open the bubbly."

Penny decided she would like to make friends with Violet.

Jonny chivalrously took off his jacket and spread it on the grass for Penny to sit on. He eased the cork off the bottle: It shot up into the starry night sky. They drank quickly; he refilled the glasses.

"Why didn't Emmy come with you?" asked Penny.

"She hates traveling with me on business. Says she never gets to see me. Well, that part's true enough, I suppose."

"Are you on business? I thought you were here for the party."

"I do business wherever I am. I'm trying to talk Justin into putting some money into *Flaming Forest*. APG has finally agreed to produce it for me, but their budget's too small. God knows Justin could afford to help out and the environmentalists would love him for it."

"Is he going to?"

"Of course not. He's an asshole." Jonny changed the subject. "What are your plans now that you're through with school? Mother says you want to go to college. Have you thought about where?"

"Not yet. I'm going to take a year off first and do some traveling. First your mother and I are going to see Europe."

"You've never been there, have you?"

"No and I can hardly wait. London . . . Paris . . . Can you imagine me in Paris?"

"Bien sur. You look very French tonight, by the way."

Penny blushed. *"Merci.* I've been studying French in school." She sipped the champagne. "We may even go to the Far East. It's funny, I've always wanted to travel but I never thought I'd actually get the chance. Even going to New York this past year with your mother was exciting."

"I'm afraid I've done so much traveling that I'm kind of jaded by it. Maybe I'll try to meet up somewhere with you and Mom. You're a bubbly creature. It could be fun."

They heard footsteps and a moment later Justin Groome emerged from the shrubbery. He seemed surprised and annoyed to see them there.

"Where's Violet?" he asked, looking around.

"We haven't seen her."

"What are you two doing here?"

"Enjoying the moonlight," Jonny replied smoothly. "Care to join us?"

Justin Groome was in a foul mood. Seeing Penny with Jonny infuriated him. "No, thanks."

Violet appeared, looking subdued. "Here I am."

Groome ignored her. He reached for Penny's arm and pulled her roughly to her feet. "You'd better come with me."

"No!" cried Penny.

Jonny watched the byplay curiously. He saw the fear in Penny's eyes and placed a hand protectively on her shoulder.

"Sorry, but Penny's staying with me."

"Take your hand off her," ordered Groome.

"Not until you take your hand off first."

"Why did you want me to come here?" asked Violet plaintively.

Everyone ignored her. Jonny felt Penny shrinking against him.

"Come on, man," he hissed to Groome. "Pull yourself together. You're behaving like an idiot."

"You—" Without any warning, Groome balled his hand into a fist and smashed it into Jonny's jaw.

Jonny staggered back, then he pulled himself up and lunged at Groome. Groome kicked him hard in the groin and Jonny doubled over with a moan.

What happened next was like a slow-moving picture. Penny never forgot it: Every gesture, every motion was etched in her memory forever. With eyes cold and calculating, Justin took out his gun and smashed the barrel over Jonny's head. There was no emotion in the movement. Jonny keeled over. With a scream, Penny rushed to his side. Groome seemed to kick out at Jonny, but at the same time he aimed his gun at Violet and fired. There wasn't a sound. Violet crumpled in silence.

Penny threw herself over Jonny's body, certain that Groome was going to try to kill him next. She may have screamed again, but all she remembered afterward was the nightmarish silence. She turned to face Groome to beg him to stop, but no words came. Then she saw Georgia charging at Groome from the bushes, and she must have been barking, but Penny didn't hear a sound. Groome aimed his gun at Georgia and fired again. Georgia fell back abruptly. Then Penny saw Groome say something to her, but she still couldn't hear anything.

Groome landed a well-aimed kick right into the side of her face. She felt the bones crack, then she fell into a black, very empty space.

CHAPTER SEVENTEEN

WHEN Penny awoke it was daylight. She was lying on a hard narrow bed. She opened her eyes. Susan's face was bent over her. Very blurred.

"Dear Penny. Penny, wake up. Can you hear me?"

Penny felt a stabbing pain in her head and closed her eyes again.

"Don't move," ordered Susan. "Just rest."

"Is she okay?" It sounded like Dom.

"As okay as she can be."

"Where am I?" It hurt to talk. She couldn't move her jaw.

"In the hospital."

She thought for a moment. "Jonny?"

"He's okay. He's back in California."

"How long?"

"You've been here a couple of weeks."

Slowly the memory drifted back to her. She opened her eyes and found Susan's close to hers. Behind their anxiety, Penny saw a funny expression of pity. She didn't understand it. Then she remembered Georgia.

"Georgia . . ." she moaned.

"Yes, dear. She had to be shot. She was going to attack you."

"No, no. Groome—"

"He'll be here to visit you soon. He's been asking for you almost every day."

"No!" cried Penny. Susan gripped her hand to calm her.

"Penny—"

"He killed Georgia. He was trying to kill me—"

"No, dear. Calm down. It was just an accident."

Penny struggled to sit up but couldn't manage it. "Just an *accident!*" she whimpered.

"All right, dear. It's all right." Susan tried to soothe her.

"He killed Violet."

Her face hurt so badly she had to stop talking. Her breast heaved.

"I know all about that," Susan said soothingly. "Don't worry. We'll see this whole thing through together."

Penny closed her eyes, bewildered and afraid. She had a strange feeling her face didn't exist anymore, but it felt so painful she knew she was wrong. At length she slipped back into unconsciousness.

When she opened her eyes she saw Dom instead of Susan.

"Mother needed a break," he said. "She's been here constantly."

"What did Groome say happened that night? I don't understand."

"Don't think about it yet. And don't try to talk. You've got wires in your jaw. We'll get you off. I know it was an accident."

"There wasn't any accident," Penny mumbled. "What are you talking about?"

"Violet . . ." Dom reminded her gently.

"He killed her."

"Who?"

"Groome. He killed her. I saw him."

Dom looked puzzled. He sat forward in the chair. "Are you sure?"

"Of course I'm sure! I saw him do it! Jonny saw him too! Ask Jonny."

"He's gone back to California." Dom was frowning.

"But he must have told you what happened."

"Yes." Dom held her gaze. "Let's talk about this later. I do want to hear your side of the story, and I know the police will want to also. But you're not strong enough yet."

"He did it," Penny repeated, but wearily. She felt extraor-

dinarily tired. Besides, the compassion in his eyes was as painful as her aching head.

After a moment, she asked, "I look pretty bad, don't I?"

Dom took her hand. "You could never look bad to me,
Penny."

Penny turned away but held onto his hand. He stayed until
she drifted off to sleep. The next thing she knew the room was
empty except for two nurses fussing with the machines by her
bed.

"You have a very important visitor," one of them said,
impressed by her young patient. "We're letting him visit even
though it is nighttime."

"Hello, Penny. How are you feeling?" It was Justin
Groome. The nurses left discreetly.

Penny shrank back against the pillows.

He sat on the edge of the bed and took her cold hand in his.
She tried to pull away, but he gripped it tightly.

"I don't think you've been told what happened the night of
the accident," he said gently. "Naturally you were too confused and upset to follow it all. What you told Dom this
afternoon is nonsense. I had nothing to do with it. You were
very jealous of my attentions to Violet, and so you shot her.
You've been in love with me for months. Jonny tried to stop
you from killing her, but he was too late. He knocked you
over, and you accidentally smashed your face on some rocks."

"Lies! Lies!" whispered Penny, realizing what Groome was
trying to do. "No one will believe that!"

"Shut up and listen to me."

Penny stopped. *He could strangle me right now with his bare
hands*, she thought. *He's capable of it.*

"Nothing stands in the way of my career," Justin continued
in an ominously soft voice. "Nothing. Violet found that out
and it cost her. I don't want you to make the same mistake she
did. Is that clear? Now, you're going to stand trial for the
murder of Violet. If things go well, you'll get off lightly.
Luckily you're still a juvenile. But one word about me and I
won't stop at smashing your face. Is that clear?"

Penny closed her eyes in terror, reliving the nightmare.

"What about Jonny?" she whispered at last. "He knows the truth."

"Jonny knows what's good for him, just like you do. Besides, Jonny was drunk, as usual. He didn't see Violet get shot. Even if he did, he doesn't want you to end up like her. He's no fool. You're the little fool," he added bitterly. "Jonny took my word for it that you were responsible. I had several minutes to prepare the scene to make it look like your doing. Your fingerprints were on my gun. No one will believe a drunken seventeen-year-old as opposed to a congressman."

"You killed my dog, Georgia." She had never felt such hatred. She reached for the nurse's bell by the side of her bed. Justin Groome stopped her hand in midair.

"Fuck the dog," he said mildly, squeezing her hand till it hurt. "I want you to tell me that you understand what I've said."

She swallowed. "I understand."

"Good." He let her go. "If you behave, I'll pay for the plastic surgery you'll be needing to put your face back together. And I'll buy you a new dog." He stood up. "I have a soft spot for you, you know. Good night. You need to rest."

Penny lay motionless after he left. Plastic surgery? Was her face that bad? She tried to feel her cheek, but couldn't through the bandages.

She had to think what to do. Her plans for next year were ruined. There would be no trip to Europe with Susan now, no visiting the Far East in the fall. There wouldn't even be college the following year, not if she was in prison.

There would be a long, drawn-out court case which, if she did not tell the truth about Groome, would end up with her in jail. If she did tell the truth, Groome would have her killed.

"Georgia," she moaned.

The faithful retriever had been her last link with childhood. A puppy when her mother died, Georgia had been Penny's companion all through adolescence. She'd been there when her father committed suicide. It was as though the last of her old life had vanished, leaving Penny floating in a sea of strangers and strange occurrences. Even Dom felt a stranger to her, with the new pity in his eyes. Susan more so, with her insatiable desire to be a mother rather than a friend.

At six o'clock in the morning the nurse came to check on her. Penny hadn't slept.

"What's your name?" Penny asked the woman as she bustled about her tasks.

"Alice, dear."

"I want a mirror, Alice."

The nurse looked worried. She was a young, very pretty woman, new on the job. "Not yet, dear. Wait until you're stronger."

"I want one now. I won't get upset, I promise." She added, scared, "My face is pretty bad, isn't it?"

"They do wonders with plastic surgery nowadays," Alice replied.

So Groome hadn't just been trying to frighten her. "Please give me a mirror."

The nurse brought her one later that morning. Penny waited until she was alone before looking at herself. The swelling around her eyes was still so bad they were almost closed. Tentatively she tried to push the bandages away from the rest of her face. Her jaw was wired; her lips were blue and split. She couldn't remove the bandages farther. But she could see one side of her face was different from the other.

She felt a scream rising inside her.

"There, dear, it's quite a shock, as I warned you it would be." Alice had been waiting just outside the door. She pried the mirror from Penny's fingers.

"What's under the bandages?"

"Take this, dear. It's a sedative. Here's some water."

"Tell me, first, please." Penny refused the proffered drink.

"I can only say your cheekbone and nose were broken. You'll have to talk to the doctor about it. Now be a good girl and take this. You must rest."

Penny sipped the thick liquid through a straw, then lay back on the pillows. Alice straightened the bandages, patted her hand, then hurried off to her duties.

Penny was overwhelmed with grief. Her face—her funny-looking, freckled face—was smashed. She hadn't realized be-

fore how fond she was of it. In a way, the Whitfield family
had gotten her into this. Susan should have known about
Groome. Jonny should have stayed to defend her. And where
was Dom? Why hadn't he come to visit again?

The minutes passed. Ever since her mother died she had
been on her own, she realized now. Even when her father was
alive. But then everyone in town knew where she belonged,
knew how to fit her in the scheme of things. She was the high-
spirited child of Jan Houten, who had the pumpkin field off
the Taconic. He'd failed as a dairy farmer, but he would have
protected her from Groome. He would not have believed
Groome before his own daughter. But who were the
Whitfields? They were Groome's friends.

She had three choices. One, she could stand trial and go to
prison for another man's crime. Two, she could defend herself
and risk getting killed by the same man.

Three, she could vanish.

She drifted into a deep sleep.

At visiting hours in the midafternoon, Susan entered with
tears in her eyes. She had just been told by the nurse that
Penny had seen herself in a mirror.

"Penny, dear!"

Penny couldn't speak. Susan took her in her arms and held
her close.

How can I leave her, thought Penny, clinging to her. *It isn't
her fault she doesn't know Groome raped me and that he murdered
Violet. All I have to do is tell her. But I can't tell her because then
he'd kill me.*

A knock on the door interrupted them. Susan sat up and
told Penny, "Sheriff O'Mara asked if he could stop by and ask
you a few questions. Do you feel strong enough?"

"No."

"He's not going to ask you anything that might incriminate you. He just wants to hear your version of what happened."

"I don't care." Penny was aware that the sheriff was standing inside the open door, listening. "I don't want to talk to
anyone."

"Maybe you're right," said Susan, glancing apologetically

at the sheriff. "She should have a lawyer present, shouldn't she?"

"If she likes. I guess we'll go ahead and file manslaughter charges. Does she want a court-appointed lawyer?"

"No," said Susan. "We'll take care of all that."

"Good." The sheriff coughed gently. "I'm sorry this happened, Penny. I really hoped you'd straightened out this year."

Penny looked at him with hostility.

"Your sons are in California?" the sheriff asked Susan.

"Yes, but they can be reached at any time if you want to talk to them some more."

"Dom left?" exclaimed Penny.

"He's returned twice. But he had to get back to his job."

"He went back to Los Angeles?" She was shocked. If it had been he accused of murder, with his face destroyed, she would never have abandoned him. Not in a million years.

Bitterly, she sank back against the pillows. She remembered the pity in his eyes when he'd looked at her. Horror and pity, both, in spite of what he'd said about her never looking bad to him.

She never wanted to see him again.

The sheriff agreed to postpone their talk; she and Susan were alone.

"Manslaughter," whispered Penny. "I can't believe it."

"Nor can I," said Susan, sadly.

"Does that mean I have a guard standing outside my door?"

"No, dear. Justin convinced the sheriff that you wouldn't try to run away. He also offered to put up any bail amount that's required so you can be at home with me."

I'll be damned if I take a dime from him, thought Penny.

Angrily, she muttered, "I don't understand why Mr. Groome is your friend. I just don't understand it."

"My dear—"

"I don't understand it," Penny repeated.

"Years ago, when my husband died, Justin put up the money for me to start my own business. It was a lot of money, but it wasn't only that. He brought me clients too. Whitfield Communications would never have been the success it was without his help. I knew nothing about business: He taught me everything."

"You already told me all this. Haven't you paid him back by now?"

"I paid him all the money he loaned me years ago. And I've done a lot to further his own career. But gratitude is a funny thing, Penny. Sometimes you just never get over feeling grateful, no matter how a relationship turns out. Maybe one day you'll understand what I mean."

"I don't think I will."

"He helped me in another way too," Susan said slowly. "He saved me from a disastrous marriage."

"What do you mean?"

"I was going to marry my husband's best friend after he died. But it turned out that he'd been responsible for my husband's death. Justin told me the night before the wedding."

They were silent. Penny agonized over the three choices she had before her. But she knew there was really only one.

Susan said, "Several of your friends want to come and see you. Graham especially. I said I'd ask you if it was okay."

Penny shook her head.

"Penny, dear, you're crying!" Susan was stunned.

"I . . . can't . . . help . . . it . . ."

"Why, dear? Tell me why you're crying."

"If anything happens to me," sobbed Penny, "I want you to know how grateful I am. You've been like a mother to me—"

Susan held her tightly. "Darling."

"I missed my mother so much when she died," Penny clung to Susan. "And then I met you and it was as though she'd come back to me—but I was almost grown up. I wanted you to be my friend as well as my mother. And you have been —oh, Susan—I love you so much. I can't bear the thought of being separated from you."

"You won't be," Susan assured her, anxiously. "We'll hire the best lawyers—"

"But if I don't see you again—if something happens, you'll remember?"

"You sound as though we'll never see each other again. But

in a few days you'll be back home. Just getting out of this place will make you feel better. Soon you'll be strong enough for surgery, then you'll look as good as new."

Still weeping, Penny held on to Susan as though she were drowning.

"I love you, Susan," sobbed Penny. "I never want to leave you."

Susan was crying too. "I won't let them take you from me! I won't, I *won't!*"

Vanishing would be the hardest thing Penny had ever done in her life.

CHAPTER EIGHTEEN

IT was another two weeks before Penny felt strong enough to put her plan into action. She was going to be released from the hospital on Monday but she told Susan it was Tuesday. That would give her a twenty-four-hour headstart.

On Sunday, Susan brought her an attractive outfit to wear home: a white sundress and matching sandals. "And here's some makeup too, so you'll look like a million when you leave here."

Susan handed Penny a box of eye shadow, eye liner, lipstick, and a compact. But neither of them was fooled. The right side of Penny's face was caved in, her nose broken. Two teeth were missing from one side of her mouth: She would need implants if she was ever going to look really pretty again. Her skin was marked by stitches. It would take a long time and a lot of money for Penny to "look like a million."

When Susan was getting ready to leave, Penny said, "Please don't come to the hospital tomorrow. It's my last day here, and there's no point in your driving all that way."

"I don't mind the drive."

"I'd rather you didn't. Just be here early on Tuesday to take me home."

Susan was reluctant, but she finally agreed not to come.

"All right. Good-bye, dear. It will be so nice to have you home again." Neither of them had spoken about the fact that she was to be indicted on manslaughter charges since Sheriff O'Mara's visit.

"Good-bye."

Susan left. Dusk closed in, but the nurse did not come in to turn on the light. Penny lay awake, thinking. How could she leave Northkill without anyone noticing? It was not just Susan that she was going to have to evade, it was the entire Northkill police force, and, when she crossed state lines, the FBI.

She would be a fugitive.

A *liar, a thief, a slut, a murderer, a fugitive.* Justin had played her to perfection.

"Excuse me. Penelope Houten?"

Penny turned her head. A doctor smiled at her in the dim light.

"How are you feeling?" he asked.

"Okay."

"You're leaving us tomorrow. Feel strong enough?"

"Uh-huh."

She had never seen him before. Perhaps he was an intern who had just taken over this shift.

"Have you thought about plastic surgery for your face?"

"Why?"

"I have the name of a surgeon who might be interested in helping you."

"I can't afford him."

"Because of the nature of your injury, he would be willing to help you at a fraction of his usual cost."

"Really?"

"He lives in London. I know it's a long way to go, but you might find it worth your while." The doctor reached in his pocket and took out a business card. "Here's his address."

Penny took the card. She noticed the doctor's hands were calloused and dirty. They did not look like a surgeon's hands. "Dr. Carl Bellamon," she murmured, curiously. The name seemed like destiny to her. "You really think he'll help me?"

"I'm sure he will."

Penny looked at the card again, and then at the doctor. Brown eyes twinkled back at her.

"Who are you?"

"Dr. Smith. I'm Dr. Bellamon's buddy. Tell him I sent you."

She looked at the card again, puzzled.

"Good-bye," said Dr. Smith.

Some time later Alice came in with her evening meal. Penny asked, "Who's Dr. Smith?"

"Who?"

"Dr. Smith. He was here an hour ago. I haven't seen him before."

"There is no Dr. Smith at this hospital."

"Maybe he's an intern or something?"

"I can check." Alice looked concerned. "What did he want?"

"He was just asking me how I felt."

Alice left. Ignoring her dinner, Penny began working out the next day's plans. She wished she could go back to Dogwood Farm just one more time for her jeans.

But she couldn't risk it. She couldn't take with her a single trace of the old Penny. It was the only way she would feel truly safe from Justin Groome.

At least now she had a destination. London. The little business card still in her hand seemed a ticket to a new life.

She refused to get discouraged at the difficulties ahead of her in getting to London.

She'd better get started with her plans.

She got up, put on her dressing gown, and walked down the corridor to the visitors' room. It was almost empty except for two patients who were smoking. Penny knew one of the men; he was in a room next to hers. He was in for a kidney transplant.

"Hi, Ben," she said, sitting on the arm of a chair. He was about her size.

"Hi, Penny. How're you doing?"

The men were playing cards. After a few minutes, Penny left them.

Ben's room was semiprivate, but luckily the patient in the far bed by the window was asleep. The room was dark.

She tiptoed over to the lockers against the wall where patients' personal property was kept. Reaching inside, she felt the coarse texture of a tweed jacket. Quickly and quietly, she extricated it. She reached in again and took out a pair of pants. Then a wallet; she left a set of keys.

"Who's that?"

The other patient had woken.

"Ben wants his cigarettes," Penny said quickly.

"Oh, yeah."

Her heart thumping, Penny waited till he closed his eyes, then carried the bundle to her room. She closed the door and turned on the light. The jacket was big but wearable. In the wallet she found a twenty-dollar bill, a driver's license, and a Visa credit card.

The credit card would be useful, if she could use it before it was reported missing.

At six in the morning, Penny was ready. She was dressed in the white sundress Susan had brought and white sandals on her bare feet. A floppy straw sun hat partially hid her face. She had spent a long time working on her face with the makeup. It wasn't too bad. In Susan's tote bag, she had her change of clothes.

Alice came in as she was getting dressed and smiled.

"Is your mother going to be here so early?"

"I hope so. I said I'd meet her downstairs."

"You'll have to check out at the reception desk there. Good luck, Penny. We'll miss you."

Downstairs in the lobby, doctors and nurses milled around. The morning shift had just begun. No one noticed Penny. She straightened her back and lifted her chin, trying to look more confident than she felt. Then she pushed the revolving door and stepped outside.

She hadn't realized before that it was raining.

Immediately the white leather sandals were soaked and her bare legs splattered with rain. The wide brimmed straw hat began to sag.

Damn, she thought. She looked conspicuous enough already. She walked briskly down the hospital drive to the bus stop. Self-consciously, she waited for what seemed like an eternity.

Dripping wet, she got on the bus at last, paid the fare, and sat down near the back. It was a bus to Albany. The windows were misted from rain; she couldn't see out. Good. That meant no one could see in, either.

In Albany she went first to a J.C. Penney, located near the bus station. There she bought a fedora; it cost almost nine dollars. She needed shoes, too, since the leather sandals had been ruined by the rain. She bought a pair of cheap, Korean-made running shoes.

She had very little money left.

The public rest rooms in the mall were open. She went inside, wondering how she was going to be able to dress up like a man and then leave the ladies' room without being noticed. An elderly woman was inside, powdering her nose.

"I'm soaking wet," Penny said, smiling. "And all I have to change into are my brother's clothes. I hope they fit."

The woman nodded, avoiding looking at her after one horrified glimpse of her face.

In one of the stalls, Penny slipped into the pants and the jacket. Then the running shoes.

The woman left. No one else came in. Penny stood in front of the full-length mirror, adjusting the jacket so that it covered her bra: She hadn't thought about a shirt and she didn't have time to unstitch the top of the dress from its skirt. She pulled up the pants around her waist so they wouldn't trail.

The fedora didn't cover as much of her face as the sun hat, but it was better than nothing. Her shoulder-length hair was too long, though. There were no scissors around. She tucked it inside the hat.

She stuffed her other clothes in the tote bag and opened the door. Directly across from her was a travel agency. "Hermes Travel," it was called. Penny debated a moment, then went to a pay phone and dialed information.

"I need the number for Hermes Travel in the Walt Whitman Mall, please."

She dialed the number she was given. "I need to get a flight from New York City to London leaving tonight or tomorrow," she said. "Would you be able to arrange it if I gave you my credit card number over the phone?"

"Certainly. Just one moment, please." She heard the click

of the computer keys. "There's a flight leaving at eight P.M. from JFK, arriving at Heathrow tomorrow at seven forty-five. Will you be traveling coach?"

"Yes."

"Credit card number, please."

She gave all the information the clerk requested.

"Thank you," he said. "You can pick up the ticket at any travel agency, or at the airport. Will that be all?"

She would pick it up at the airport. "Yes, thanks."

Penny was so nervous she felt a little faint. At any point she expected Groome to appear beside her and grab her elbow. Hurriedly, she left the mall and returned to the bus station.

"When is your next bus to New York City?"

She was discomfited by the ticket agent's shock at seeing her face, but he quickly regained his composure. "Half an hour. Gate twelve."

"I need a one-way ticket, please." She handed him the credit card.

As he punched the numbers into his machine, she surreptitiously kept her eyes on two policemen who were standing in the doorway. They looked as though they were on the alert for something.

Hurry up, she urged silently.

The man didn't even look at the signature on the slip. He gave back the Visa card and handed her a ticket. On the way to gate twelve, she dropped the credit card in a trash can.

In half an hour she was sailing down the highway on her way to New York City.

CHAPTER NINETEEN

THE telephone rang while Dom was in the bathtub. Toni sat on the edge of the tub, sipping a screwdriver. A month had passed since Penny's graduation; it was now the end of June and Toni was visiting again for the weekend.

"Can you get that?" asked Dom.

"Let the machine answer," Toni said lazily.

"Are you sure you won't join me then? There's plenty of room."

"My flight leaves at eight. There's no time. I'm going to refill our glasses."

Dom settled back in the tub. Toni had not turned on the light and twilight filled the room. The scent of hibiscus fluttered in the open window. Dom had lived in this wood and glass house in Topanga Canyon ever since he'd moved to Los Angeles six months earlier. He liked it up here in the rural hills; it helped him differentiate his hectic business life from his home life.

Toni thought the house too small and too remote for a man who was certain to be president of American Production Group one day. Jonny thought so too, but that was because Jonny was trying to sell his spectacular mansion atop the Pacific Palisades hills and he wanted Dom to buy it.

Toni returned with their drinks. She switched on the light. Dom smiled at her. Her jade eyes with the yellow centers smiled back at him.

Before long, she was in the bath too.

By the time Dom emerged and toweled himself dry, there were several messages for him on his answering machine. Toni went downstairs to the kitchen to fix a snack while he listened to them. The first message was from his mother.

"Dom, dear, please call me as soon as possible."

Frowning, Dom tied the towel around his waist. The next message was from Jonny.

"Has Mom told you about Penny? What should we do? We have to do something. I'll never forgive myself if anything happened to her—but he promised he wouldn't touch her—" Jonny sounded drunk and incoherent. The message ended on sobs.

Thoroughly alarmed, Dom listened to the third message. It was from his mother again.

"Dom, are you there? Please pick up the telephone if you're there—"

Dom cursed answering machines and dialed his mother's number. Toni came in the room, carrying a platter of crackers and cheese and two drinks on a tray. She stopped to listen.

"I just got your messages," Dom spoke into the phone. "What's wrong?"

"It's Penny," Susan said, her voice shrill with anxiety. "She's disappeared."

"What do you mean 'disappeared'?"

"She said she was going to be released from the hospital tomorrow but it was actually today. She was last seen getting on a bus headed for Albany. No one knows what happened to her after that."

"You mean she ran away?"

"But it's so unlike her, Dom! I never thought she'd run away from trouble."

"Oh, my God."

"She was saying things to me in the hospital that made us both cry, but it never occurred to me that she was planning to do this!"

"Are you by yourself?" he asked heavily.

"No, Justin's with me. That's how we found out she left today. He went to visit her and discovered that she'd gone. He came here, and—oh, Dom what should we do?"

"You've notified the police?"

"I had to."

"If they don't find her, they'll call in the FBI. Oh, God, I can't believe it."

"I can't believe it either."

"We could hire a private investigator. It's the only thing I can think of at the moment."

"I feel as though I'm to blame," cried Susan. "I should have reassured her more. We all would have stood behind her."

"You think she didn't know that?"

Susan blew her nose. "She seemed really upset when I told her you'd gone back to L.A."

"She must have understood that I had a job to get back to."

"I don't know. I just don't know."

"Look, I'll get on a flight as soon as I can. Maybe there's something we can think of if we're together. Some clue . . ." Dom spoke a few more words of comfort to his mother, and then hung up.

"What happened?" asked Toni from her perch on the arm of a chair.

Dom ran a hand distractedly through his wet hair. "Penny's run away."

"You're kidding."

Dom dialed Jonny's number. "Could you make me another drink, Toni? I have a few telephone calls I want to make." He did not really want another drink, but he wanted to talk to Jonny in private.

"Wait a minute! It's my sister's killer we're talking about here! I'm interested in finding her too."

Dom put down the telephone again. "I know that. But Penny's a part of our family. And you know I don't think she was really responsible for what happened. Justin said it was sort of an accident."

"I'd like a jury to make that decision, not Justin. Justin's always had a thing for young girls. He's prejudiced."

"I don't know anything about that."

They were close to fighting.

"Look, I need to talk to Jonny," said Dom.

Toni left the room, slamming the door behind her. Dom

vacillated between going after her and telephoning Jonny. He picked up the telephone.

"Hello, Jonny?"

"That you, Dom?" Jonny's words were slurred. "Didja hear what happened?"

"Yes, I just spoke to Mom. What did your message mean? Why do you feel you're to blame?"

"I shoulda spoken out and to hell with the consequences. I shoulda. I shoulda. I shoulda. If I'd known how scared she was, I woulda. But I was scared too."

Dom hated talking to his brother when he was drunk.

"Scared of what, for Chrissakes?"

He heard Jonny gulping from a glass. "Forget it—forget it. We're better off trying to forget it ever happened."

"Forget it?" exploded Dom. "What the hell are you talking about?"

"I cared about her too. But you were the one she was crazy about. She must've wanted to die when you saw her face."

Dom heard a car door slam and then Toni's rented Ford raced down the drive. "I don't know what you're talking about. I'm going to fly back to be with Mom for a few days. We have to do everything we can to find Penny. Maybe you should go with me."

"I'm scheduled to go to Brazil to begin shooting *Flaming Forest* next week."

Dom hung up without saying good-bye and dialed his travel agent.

"I need a reservation for this evening's flight from LAX to New York," he said. "First class."

When the reservation was confirmed, he went into his bedroom and saw that Toni's small suitcase was gone. She had even remembered her toothbrush.

He dressed hurriedly and threw some clothes in an overnight bag. Then he grabbed his car keys and went out to his car.

Why had Penny run away?

Toni was sitting self-assuredly in the TWA ambassador lounge, reading *Harper's*. He watched her from the door, seeing her as a stranger might. She was leaning forward slightly, exposing a discreet glimpse of lace-trimmed bra under the cap-sleeved silk blouse. Her blond hair fell across one side of her face. Her legs were crossed so that the pebbly muslin skirt draped almost to the floor. Her sandaled foot swung slightly. Apart from that movement she was completely still.

This is the woman I'm going to marry, thought Dom. She was by far the prettiest woman in the room, but she seemed opaque too.

She looked up as though she sensed him watching her. Dom went over and sat beside her.

"Hello."

She smiled warmly. One of the things he liked best about Toni was that she might lose her temper, but she never sulked.

"What are you doing here?" She put down the magazine.

"Going to New York too. I booked a seat on your flight—next to you."

"You're going to see if you can find Penny?"

"Yes."

"Violet was a silly girl in many ways, but she didn't deserve to die." Her voice was choked.

"I know that, Toni. It's been awful for you."

"It was my fault in so many ways. She was just a baby. A vain, silly baby."

"Don't go on blaming yourself. It had nothing to do with you." He put his arm around her, wondering why he had thought she seemed self-assured earlier. She was just a fragile, grief-stricken woman.

"Are we still getting married in September?" asked Toni.

Dom kissed the top of her hair. "If you want to."

"Now my parents think we should wait for a bit."

"I know how shattered they are. We can put it off if you want to."

"I don't want to."

Dom cradled both her cheeks with his hands, gazing at her. "Then we'll get married in September," he promised.

* * *

"I thought at least she would leave me a note," Susan said to Dom as soon as he arrived. "I can't believe she'd leave without a single word."

"Did the police get any kind of statement from her before she left?"

"No. She refused to say anything to them."

"Nothing about Justin?"

"Not a word."

"She insisted to me that he'd killed Violet. But then why wouldn't she say that to the police?"

"Maybe because it wasn't true," Susan said, upset. "She's lied before."

"She has?"

"I loved her very much, but I wasn't blind to her faults. As you said, she's had no discipline since her mother died."

"I said she was wild but I never called her a liar."

Susan told him about their trip to New York when Penny had returned to Northkill without telling her why.

"I still don't think she could have killed Violet," insisted Dom.

"If Justin hadn't seen it happen with his own eyes, I wouldn't have thought so either."

Dom persuaded Susan to lie down after lunch. He went into Penny's room and looked around. The room overflowed with clothes and objects. Each item was stamped with Penny's personality: a string of moonstones on the windowsill, her mystery novels, a teddy bear worn out by affection, a reproduction of a painting by Monet which he himself had given her.

He gazed around, as though searching out a secret.

He remembered chasing after her on the morning of her father's death, thinking she was going to commit suicide. When he'd caught up with her she'd said, "I wanted to run away. I felt as though I were free, as though I could do anything—go anywhere."

Her words came back to him as clearly as though she were in the room.

He was determined to find her. No matter what it took, eventually he would find her.

CHAPTER TWENTY

THE Greyhound bus arrived in New York City in the early afternoon. Penny followed the stream of people up an escalator onto a busy sidewalk. The noise of the traffic was intense and she had no idea where she was. Her head throbbed in intense pain.

She looked up at the bruise-colored clouds. Rain stung her eyes. What should she do now? A panhandler started toward her; she walked away quickly.

The street she was on was lined with X-rated video stores and pornographic movie theaters. Short-skirted, tired prostitutes stood on the street corner.

"Sens . . . hash . . ." a man muttered under his breath.

She walked faster.

If she didn't find a way of getting some money and escaping to England, might she too end up on this avenue, trying to survive in the netherworld of drug pushers, pimps, whores, and teen runaways?

Relentless hammers pounded inside her head. She felt faint.

She had to get out of here.

She touched a policeman on the arm and he spun around, his hand on his gun.

"Sorry," she said. "I just need directions."

He glared suspiciously, but then the sight of her face embarrassed him.

"Which way is Fifth Avenue?"

He pointed.

On crowded Fifth Avenue she turned north and kept walking. Central Park was up ahead. On a bench near the entrance sat an old woman, muttering unintelligibly. Her hair was flattened with dirt, her eyes half-closed. At her feet were two soggy paper bags, filled with newspapers and wool sweaters. The woman's hands, gnarled with arthritis, clasped and unclasped her wet skirt as she mumbled.

Penny stopped in front of her. Her initial revulsion turned to a queer empathy. It was as though she were seeing herself when she was old.

The Plaza Hotel loomed up against the heavy sky with lofty indifference. Portentously, the doormen held shiny, black umbrellas over each guest, escorting them to and from the lemony taxis which wound up to and away from the royal entrance. Penny remembered the wonderful evening she had spent there with Susan before her world had been smashed to pieces.

She turned toward the park. She longed to be back in the country, away from the craziness of the city. It was no wonder the old woman muttered to herself. In a moment Penny thought she might start muttering too.

The woman's gnarled hands reached out and grabbed Penny's tweed jacket. Her face was bright red, as red as a peasant's in a Brueghel painting. Her nose was thick with warts, her lips were wet and purple. Her eyes were black as jet as she stared at Penny.

Penny felt a profound, wordless kinship between them.

Then the woman spoke. Most of her teeth were missing.

"Fuckin' cunt! Fuckin' cunt! What're you staring at?"

Feeling faint, Penny tugged the jacket free and plunged into the park. The woman was crazy. But Penny wasn't. She absolutely wasn't. *She wasn't like that old woman.*

There was hardly anyone in the park. Rain poured thickly onto the gray sheets of road. She broke away to walk on the shiny clumps of grass under the black branches of the trees. She could have been in the heart of the country. A strange country, though, one filled with smoggy, dying trees and broken bottles, where if she walked too far in any direction she would end up where she had started.

CHAPTER TWENTY-ONE

P ENNY finally left the park and mingled with the crowd on Sixth Avenue. After a while, the colorful, shiny lights reflecting on the wet streets lifted her spirits a little. Somehow she would be on that flight to London that evening.

Somehow.

She paused in front of a coffee shop. The aroma of hamburgers and french fries made her mouth water. She had eaten nothing since the previous evening.

A young woman went inside, wearing a gray flannel business suit, white ankle socks, and white running shoes. Her umbrella had fishes all over it. A man went in a moment later, also in a business suit.

Penny followed them.

She sat at the counter and ordered a hamburger and a glass of water. As she ate hungrily, she looked around for the ladies' room.

She felt a surge of adrenaline. *She would be on that flight tonight.*

First, with her remaining change, she paid her bill at the front desk. Then, making sure no one was watching, she went to the ladies' room. She closed a lavatory door and took out the dress from her tote bag. Quickly she slipped it over her head. It was a little wrinkled, but it looked okay with the jacket over it. She left on the running shoes since every woman she'd seen wore them with their skirts and stockings.

The fedora would still have to do, but she let her hair out so that it bounced to her shoulders.

Someone went into the stall next to hers.

Penny stuffed the pants into the tote bag. Then she stood on the toilet and looked over the top of the partition to the occupied stall beside hers.

A woman was hanging the shoulder strap of her purse on the hook inside the door. Conscientiously, she placed toilet paper on the toilet seat and sat down.

Penny got down and unlocked her door.

She pulled out a stool that was under the sink and placed it in front of the woman's stall. Then she reached over the door and grabbed the purse by the strap.

A second later she was out the door, closing it against the woman's furious yells. She walked quickly past the counter. Once outside, she turned the corner and waved madly at a passing cab.

"Rockefeller Center, please." Her heart thumped like crazy.

The driver hardly looked at her as he drove off. Sliding low on the seat so that she couldn't be seen, she opened the purse hopefully.

It contained a hairbrush, a French novel, a French passport, a checkbook, and a wallet.

She took out the wallet.

Inside she found ten fifty-dollar bills, three ten-dollar ones, three credit cards, and a French driver's license.

She took out what looked like a checkbook. Inside was over two thousand dollars worth of American Express traveler's checks in one-hundred-dollar amounts.

Exhilarated, she put them away. She had to work quickly, before the loss was reported.

The traffic was heavy.

"I'm in a hurry," she urged the driver.

"It'd be quicker to walk," he replied brusquely. "You're only a block away now."

She paid him with one of the ten-dollar bills, and didn't wait for change.

At Rockefeller Center she walked into the first bank she saw.

"I wish to cash some traveler's checks," she said in her best French accent.

The teller held out his hand.

"These need to be signed," he said, annoyed, handing them back.

She wished she had known that. Imitating the signature at the top of the check as closely as possible, she signed them quickly.

"In feeftee dollar bills, *s'il vous plait.*"

The man hardly glanced at the signature. He counted the money and placed the bills before her in a fan shape.

Her next stop was Saks.

It gave her a pang not to be with Susan, but she was glad Susan had made the ways of the store familiar. She took the elevator to the third floor, where the designer dresses were displayed. She was kept waiting for a while, but eventually a saleswoman came over.

"Can I help you?"

Penny put on her best French accent.

"I need one outfit," she purred. "I need to go to ze funeral. You see my face—I am here to have ze plastic surgery, but first ze funeral. My mother die in ze accident."

The woman nodded sympathetically, but she didn't look convinced that Penny could afford the price that most of the dresses commanded.

"I do not wish to spend terribly much," Penny assured her, instinctively alert. "Possibly one zousand dollars? Not too much more, if you pleez."

The woman's eyes widened and she nodded again.

"What did you have in mind? A day dress? Or a suit?"

"A simple suit, *tres chic.* One that will not attract attention to ze dreadful face."

"You'll need a hat too," said the saleswoman, taking more of an interest. "With a veil."

"*Ah, oui. Parfait.*"

"Black, of course. We have a Chanel over here. I'll show you."

The jacket was cut long, the skirt narrow. Penny tried it on.

"Zis is perfect." The skirt reached her knees: She'd need black stockings, she pointed out. She did not want to appear to be in a hurry but she was jittery.

The saleswoman had had several hats brought up while Penny was trying on the suit. Penny picked a black skimmer with a delicately patterned veil that covered her face.

"Do you need shoes?"

"Just simple leettle pumps."

The simple little pumps that were selected for her cost two hundred dollars. High-heeled, exquisitely cut, they made her feel like a new being. She peered at herself in the mirror through the veil. No way to associate this dignified woman with a runaway teenager.

"How will you be paying for this?" asked the saleswoman, patting the padded shoulders as Penny slipped into the jacket.

Penny opened her purse. "MasterCard."

"Please come this way." She led her to a sales counter and left her in line.

"Zank you so much," said Penny, laughing inwardly. When the woman had left, Penny paid cash. She'd been right to go to an expensive store, but there was no point leaving a trail for Justin Groome to follow.

Nothing could stop her now. Nothing.

She pushed her way through the revolving doors. Outside three policemen were questioning a cab driver who leaned carelessly against the side of his car, second in line at the taxi stand. A small crowd had gathered.

"I think it was just a teenage punk purse snatcher," Penny overheard a cop say.

Then she recognized the driver as the one who had picked her up when she had fled from the coffee shop.

His eyes met hers. Penny stood rooted to the sidewalk. Terrified, she waited for him to point an accusing finger.

The moment passed. Nothing happened.

The driver went on talking to the three policemen. His gaze dropped away from her indifferently.

Penny turned and moved gracefully into the crowd, exuber-ant with relief. She was invisible.

She turned off Fifth Avenue toward Madison. Her feet, un-

used to high heels, were starting to hurt. It was already four
o'clock. Time to head out to the airport.

She waved down another taxi.

"I need to go to Kennedy Airport," she said.

As they neared the airport, the driver asked, "Which airline, miss?"

She hesitated. If Ben's credit card had been reported missing, her adventure would end right now. Police would be
waiting for her to claim her ticket. She would try a different
airline.

"British Airways," she said.

By checking the departure monitor, she saw there was a
nine P.M. departure for London that evening.

There was no one in line at the ticket counter. "I need one
ticket for your flight to London tonight," she said in her
French accent.

"Certainly, madam. How will you be paying?"

"Cash."

"That will be six hundred and ninety-six dollars."

She blanched. "I can only afford the economy class today."

"That is the economy fare. First class is one thousand nine
hundred and eighty-eight dollars."

"Very well."

He clicked some more keys. Penny gave him the money.
He made a few more noises on the machine. Eventually a
ticket was printed out and he handed it to her. "Any luggage
to check?"

"No."

"I can give you your boarding pass too. Would you like a
window? Smoking or nonsmoking?"

"Window, nonsmoking."

"You're all set then. You can proceed to gate seven. They
won't be boarding yet, but there's a waiting area."

"Thank you."

Penny turned away. Her high heels tapped loudly on the
linoleum as she walked. She stopped at a newsstand and
bought one of her favorite Raymond Chandler mysteries to
read on the plane.

Near the gate she paused to take all the money that was left in the purse and put it in her jacket pocket. Then she dropped the purse into a mailbox.

Her feet hurt like crazy. How could women wear shoes like these?

CHAPTER TWENTY-TWO

MARVELING, Penny couldn't sleep. She gazed out the small airplane window. Billions of stars glowed in the dark sky. The soothing drone of the engines lulled her into a state of tranquil anticipation. She knew she would never get tired of flying in airplanes.

After the evening meal had been cleared by the flight attendants, the cabin lights dimmed. Passengers settled themselves with blankets and pillows, and many went to sleep.

Snuggled under a blanket, Penny continued to look out the window. Below her a thick bank of clouds severed her from the earth. She felt invincible.

The airplane flew on into the unknown. A strange country lay ahead, where an unknown surgeon was going to make her invisible.

Even Dom would not recognize her.

She dozed. When she opened her eyes the sky was changing rapidly from light gray to shell pink. Other passengers began to open their eyes and stretch.

Penny took her makeup kit to the bathroom and worked on her face in the mirror. Once back in her seat the flight attendant brought her coffee. Penny enjoyed herself watching the groggy passengers.

The intercom crackled. "In a few minutes we will be landing at Heathrow Airport. Please fasten your seat belts."

Penny peered out the window again. Gray swirls of fog swam past the window. She caught fleeting glimpses of gray strings of roads tying green pastures together. Then they landed with a lurch and the engines roared into reverse.

Penny followed the passengers off the plane and along a corridor marked "Customs."

"Anything to declare?" asked an official in uniform.

Blankly, she shook her head, offering him her passport. He handed it back. "Carry on."

She "carried on," following the sign saying WAY OUT.

" 'Way out' is right," she giggled to herself.

Ahead of her was a currency exchange office. She took out all that was left in the wallet.

The teller handed her strange looking notes, a handful of change, and a little chart explaining the currency. She stuffed everything in her purse and went to the information booth.

"What's the best way of getting into London?"

"The bus is the least expensive and will take you to Victoria Station. You can queue at the stop just outside."

To Penny's delight, the bus was a red double-decker, just like those she'd seen in movies. She went upstairs and sat in the very front, amused by the fact they were driving on the left-hand side. The highway was busy, but once they were in the city proper Penny didn't care how slowly they went. She was too excited looking at everything. London! She'd made it against all odds.

The bus stopped at last; everyone politely filed out. Penny looked around.

"Excuse me, what time is it?" she asked a passerby.

"Half ten," he answered.

Now what did that mean? Ten-thirty, she guessed, although half ten was really five. A black, boxy taxi drove toward her and she stuck out her hand.

She gave the driver Dr. Bellamon's Harley Street address and settled back in the soft leather seat. After a moment, she pulled out the jump seat opposite and put her feet up on it.

Dr. Bellamon's reception room was decorated in muted rose wallpaper and a lot of mirrors. Flowering, exotic plants were displayed on the windowsills. The coffee table and four chairs were ebony hardwood with enamel inlay.

A receptionist looked up from a magazine with a bright, impersonal smile.

"I'm here to see Dr. Bellamon," Penny tried to sound confident.

"Do you have an appointment?" She glanced at the calendar on her desk.

"No."

"Dr. Bellamon doesn't see anyone without an appointment."

"Oh—well, may I make one?"

"Certainly. What time?"

"How about now?" Penny laughed anxiously.

The receptionist pursed her cameo pink lips. "Your name?"

Penny thought rapidly. "Uh . . . Lark." The receptionist waited so she added, "Lark Chandler."

"Who referred you?"

"Dr. Smith."

The receptionist rose. "I'll be right back."

While she was gone the telephone rang, but it was picked up somewhere else almost immediately. Penny went to stand in front of one of the long mirrors and lifted her veil. She couldn't imagine that she might ever look attractive again.

The receptionist returned.

"Dr. Bellamon has agreed to see you this morning. He won't be free for half an hour though. Would you like some tea or coffee while you wait?"

"I'll have tea."

Penny sat on a mauve velvet unholstered chair. The office seemed like a set for a movie. No one else came or left the office. Penny tried to decide what to tell the doctor about herself. She finished the tea just as the door to the inner offices opened. She stood up hastily, suddenly overwhelmed by anxiety.

A man stood in the doorway.

"Ms. Chandler?"

"Yes, hi." She shook his hand, scrutinizing him as she did so. They were the same height: She looked directly into battleship gray eyes circled with smile wrinkles. Deeply etched

crags shot up from his jaw and creased his tanned forehead.
"Thanks for seeing me without an appointment."

"Come this way," he held open the door. "Diana, hold my
calls, please." His voice had the trace of a foreign accent.

"Yes, Dr. Bellamon."

Penny walked down a wide hall to an office at the end. A
large oak desk stood diagonally in one corner with two Queen
Anne chairs in front of it. A bronze penholder gleamed under
the green desk lamp.

"I want you to take off your hat and lie down here." Dr.
Bellamon guided her to a white serge davenport by an open
window. She lay down, wondering. Outside, a tulip tree was
in full bloom. Its petals were large and of a pure, pearly pink
color. Fresh and pure and innocent . . . Penny gazed at
them.

Dr. Bellamon sat where she could not see him.

"I always do this on my first consultation," he explained in
a low, pleasant voice. "If I am going to work on a person's
face, I want to hear their voice, to really listen to them, without getting distracted by the visual reality. I want to hear who
you are and what you are like, what your favorite color is, your
favorite song. That way my first impression will be the truest
one."

She tried to place his accent. It was mostly British, but
there was a trace of something else too. Something almost
American.

"My name is Lark Chandler and I'm from a really poor
family in the Bronx in New York City. I was in a car accident
recently—"

She heard him laughing and stopped.

"No—no," he said. "You have to tell me the truth. I am
your doctor, remember."

Worried, she stopped. What had she done to give herself
away? How much could she trust this stranger?

"Trust me all the way," he said gently, as if reading her
thoughts.

She sighed. "I was brought up on a farm. My father got
into debt and was real depressed. A year ago he killed himself.

I've been on my own since then." She added, "My mother's dead."

She went on, even more hesitantly, "Something happened recently that put my life in danger. I saw something I shouldn't have seen. So I ran away. No one must ever find me or I might be killed. That's why I came to you. I hoped you'd give me a completely new face."

Dr. Bellamon came over and looked down at her. His gray eyes were kind.

"I will do what I can."

"The thing is, I don't have any money. I'll pay you back eventually but I can't do it right away. Dr. Smith said that would be okay."

"Dr. Smith was right. Your case interests me. Now come here to the desk and we will get down to business. First of all, where are you staying?"

"I just got off the plane and came straight here."

"You did exactly the right thing," he said.

Chapter Twenty-Three

DRIVING in his chocolate brown Mercedes was like sinking into a luxurious bubble bath, Penny thought. They were on their way to his house in Sussex.

"It will take forty-five minutes to get there, but it is only four miles from the hospital where we will be performing the surgery. So it is the most convenient place for you to stay."

"When do we start?"

"Not for at least four months. We must let the trauma to your face heal before we actually operate."

"Four months! What am I going to do till then?"

"You're going to stay with me. I have a nice, large house. I think you'll find there's plenty to do."

"I thought it'd all be over in a few weeks. What if someone finds me?"

"No one will find you." Dr. Bellamon changed the subject. "You may have heard of Sir McIndoe? After World War Two he specialized in reconstructing the faces of pilots who had been badly burned. He established Queen Victoria Hospital as one of the leading plastic surgeries in the country."

"Really?" But Penny wasn't paying attention. There was too much to look at. Everything seemed foreign to her, from the damp gray mist that could hardly call itself rain to driving on the left-hand side of the road. Once they had left the suburbs, she was struck most of all by how green everything was even though it was almost July.

"Sir McIndoe put a lot of work into making his patients

feel comfortable with how they looked, even prior to surgery. The inhabitants of East Grinstead—where the hospital is— got used to seeing the men in the pubs and after a while they were not shocked at their features. You must have found this out already—how peoples' reaction to your face can be quite disconcerting."

"Especially my reaction to myself! I get a shock every time I look in the mirror."

"You will probably experience that sensation for the rest of your life. But I hope the surprise will be a pleasant one."

Dr. Bellamon's Georgian house fronted a winding country road. It was white, with a pillared central porch leading to a glossy black front door. A square hall with a black and white marble floor opened into a large living room at the back of the house. Lead-paned windows overlooked a sumptuously green lawn. A black leather sofa and two brocaded wing chairs were arranged around the biggest fireplace Penny had ever seen. In the opposite corner stood an antique Florentine writing desk. A reproduction of a Madonna by Raphael graced the wall behind it.

Dr. Bellamon's housekeeper showed her upstairs to her room. Her name was Betts, a thin, polite woman who seemed anxious to please Penny.

Penny wanted to laugh at the unexpected turn her life had taken. Not only did she feel strangely safe with Dr. Bellamon, she had been pitched into a world of elegance entirely foreign to her.

Her room overlooked a small sunken garden with a gray stone birdbath in the middle. A poster bed and a cherry wood closet were the only furniture, but the thick violet broadloom carpeting the floor and the gold damask curtains framing two tall windows created an aura of splendor.

A fire burned brightly in the fireplace in the late afternoon light.

"A fire in July?" Penny scoffed laughingly.

"It gets quite damp in the evening, miss," Betts explained. "You'll be glad of it, you'll see."

After dinner, served by a young maid called Sara, Dr. Bellamon loaned Penny a too-large pair of Wellington boots and a raincoat that he called a macintosh. Then they went for a walk. Penny was glad of the knee-high black rubber boots as soon as they stepped onto the sodden lawn.

"I can't believe I'm really here," she said, sniffing the delicious twilight air.

He led her through a grove of silver birches, their leaves trembling in the misty drizzle.

"My property backs onto the forest," he told her. "You will find it pleasant for walking. In this direction lies Goodhall Farm. Mr. Goodhall has a nice little lake which he does not mind our swimming in. You may find it refreshing when it gets warmer."

"Does it ever get warm?" Penny laughed. "I thought it always rained in England."

"We see the sun occasionally."

Dr. Bellamon reached for her elbow to help her over a turnstile. She cringed at his touch and jumped over it by herself. They crossed the soaked pasture, avoiding the small piles of cow dung. She was unaware that he was regarding her curiously.

"I don't understand why you've invited me here," said Penny. "It seems incredible. I mean, you hardly know me."

"I suspect that you are younger than you told me. And it appears you have no one else to look after you."

"I can look after myself."

"Perhaps. You were certainly brave to come all this way by yourself. Were you afraid?"

"Oh, yes! But it was exciting too."

The pewter twilight faded so gradually Penny hardly noticed it was getting dark. It was ten at night and still she could see her way easily. In the distance, his mansion was a blurry white outline in the mist. Yellow lights glowed from the downstairs windows.

"Why is it that everything about England seems so charming?" said Penny, delighted. "It's like a storybook."

"I am glad you find it so."

"I guess that's why Hitchcock set so many of his movies here. It's so charming that anything even slightly sinister is magnified."

"You'll find nothing sinister about my house," Dr. Bellamon assured her.

"Oh, I don't know about that," she replied, relishingly. "Getting a whole new face is pretty sinister, don't you think?"

"Since that is my profession I can't say that I do."

They reached the front porch. Before opening the door, Dr. Bellamon said more seriously, "We will not talk about money yet. There may come a time when you can repay me, but there is no hurry. Let us take one step at a time."

Penny gazed back at him. She felt she was taking the final, irrevocable step across an abyss that would separate her forever from everything she had ever known before. A jolt went through her when she thought of Susan and she dropped her eyes.

"Penny?" asked Dr. Bellamon.

She looked up again. His eyes were still kind but there was another expression in them that seemed strangely familiar: a poignant tenderness that reminded her of Dom. Her heart jumped and then a feeling of enormous loss threatened to overwhelm her. She would never see him again.

"Penny?" prompted Dr. Bellamon again. "What are you thinking?"

"About someone . . ." She paused. "I wish I could have said something to him before I left. Just something to let him know how much he meant to me."

Dr. Bellamon reached for her shoulders and gripped them gently when she cringed. "A new face does not mean you are a new person. It is possible you will get a second chance to say this something to your friend."

"Never. When you're through with me I'm going to have a different name, a different country, and I'll be a different person." She took a breath and added, "But it's okay. I can't tell you how grateful I am to you for offering to help. And I still don't understand why you're doing it."

He smiled and released her. "One day you will understand. And in the meantime, understanding is not the same as trusting. You can trust me, Penny. I am your friend."

Penny nodded. "Okay, Doc. I'm in your hands."

CHAPTER TWENTY-FOUR

EMMY Whitfield looked around the room one last time. Her luggage was piled in the hall downstairs. For a moment she thought she would not be able to do it.

Then suddenly, like whirligigs sweeping at her in an amusement park, came the recollection of all the fights she and Jonny had had.

"Where were you?"

"Why didn't you call?"

"I hate you."

"I wish I'd never met you."

The fight over, there would be tears, apologies, lovemaking, promises—forgiveness. It made her sick to remember. Because you can forgive and forgive . . . and forgive. But you never forget. Jonny thought forgiveness was the same as forgetting, like a sand castle washed away by the tide. Each fight was like the first one to him. But Emmy would remember the time before, and the time before that, and unconsciously built a rising heap of sand in the place where Jonny thought nothing remained.

She heard him bounding up the stairs.

"Hello." He was deeply tanned from the weeks he'd been shooting in Brazil. His eyes were red with fatigue.

"I'm leaving, Jonny."

"We're both leaving. The house is sold."

"I'm going back to New York. I want a divorce."

His mouth hung open. He looked like a ten-year-old boy

who had been told his dog just died. She couldn't stand it. She pushed past him and went downstairs.

"Wait a minute!" He leapt past her and blocked her way at the bottom of the stairs. "What'd I do?"

"You knew it was coming."

"I did? Then how come it's such a surprise?"

"I tried to talk it over for months. You never wanted to listen."

"I'm listening now."

"If you'd gotten treatment for your alcoholism—"

"I'm not an alcoholic."

"Excuse me, you're a drunk."

"Right," Jonny said cheerfully. "Don't tell me you're leaving because I like a drink occasionally!"

"*Occasionally?* And what about Jeannette?"

"Jeannette who?"

"Oh, come on."

"Where's your sense of humor? Oh, I forgot. You don't have one." He cocked his head. "I didn't think you cared about my affairs. You don't seem to have minded up till now."

"Somehow Jeannette doesn't seem like just another affair." They looked at each other; Jonny didn't respond. Emmy dropped her eyes. "Anyway, we can't go on like this. We don't have any money. You must have made something from working on *Flaming Forest.* What did you do—throw it all back into the movie?"

"Most of it went to taxes."

"What about the money from selling the house?"

"Taxes too."

"I didn't know you owed them *millions.*"

"I didn't think you cared about money. You make enough to live on."

"On my own. But not enough to live like this—" A sweep of her arm described the fabulous mansion.

"I never liked the house anyway," said Jonny. "Who wants to live on a hill with a bunch of stuffy millionaires? Besides, we really didn't have a perfect view of L.A."

"So instead you're moving to a flea-bitten hotel in Hollywood."

"I didn't think you cared about that either."

"I wouldn't care if we were together."

"But we will be together."

"Maybe for a few hours."

He took a step toward her. "You look so pretty in blue."

"Jonny."

"At least if you're going to leave don't look so pretty."

"Stop it."

He turned and went into the kitchen to pour himself a drink. His hands shook. Damn Emmy.

"It's my fault too," she said, following him. "I wanted you to be different. I kept hoping you'd change."

He smiled at her. " 'I can change, I swear,' " he quoted.

"You've said that so many times this past year it's a joke."

"I'm glad you still think I'm funny. I love you, Em."

She turned away, and he thought she was crying. But her voice came out perfectly steady.

"It makes no difference if you love me or I love you. I can't live with you."

The telephone rang in the living room. Neither of them went to answer it. Eventually it rang itself out, then immediately started ringing again.

The answering machine had already been packed.

"You can't leave," he said.

"You don't seem to be able to see anything from someone's inside. You're always the director, looking on from the outside. Even now. Can't you try, just this once, to see things from my point of view?"

"Your trouble is that you only see things from the inside. Your inside; no one else's."

They were going to hurt each other again. Jonny was determined not to. He went into the living room, but he didn't pick up the ringing telephone. He didn't want things to end badly with Emmy. God knew, he didn't want them to end at all.

"Good-bye," said Emmy, putting on her jacket.

"I'll drive you to the airport," he offered.

That would save her having to park her car in the lot and have a friend pick it up. "Okay. Thanks."

They drove in silence most of the way. Emmy didn't want to go over any of it again, and Jonny wanted to crawl into a black hole and cease to exist.

The Santa Ana winds drove down from the desert, choking him. The heat grew intense as he drove toward Hollywood after dropping off Emmy. He had an appointment with Dom at four-thirty. He'd already gone so far over budget filming *Flaming Forest* that the APG board members had decided to pull out of the project.

"I tried to persuade them to let you finish," said Dom, looking cool and fresh in his enormous, air-conditioned office. "But you've filmed practically seventy hours and you say you're not even half way through? What on earth are you shooting?"

"I exaggerated," said Jonny desperately. "I really am almost done."

"I'm really sorry this happened. I know what the movie means to you."

"Yeah, well . . ." Jonny looked out the huge picture window at the smoggy peaks of downtown Los Angeles. Dom had been made a vice president and his new office was twice the size of the last one.

"I'm worried about Mom," Dom changed the subject. "Have you talked to her lately?"

"No. What's the matter with her?"

"Dr. Goodman says she's lost a lot of weight and has trouble breathing. She won't admit a thing to me."

"I'll give her a call."

"Maybe you could visit her for a few days. I'm so swamped here I'm not going to be able to go for a while." When Jonny didn't respond, he added, "She's taking Penny's disappearance very hard. Feels that she failed her."

"I can't go."

"Why not?"

"I just can't."

"You okay?" asked Dom.

"Yeah . . . I gotta get going."

Dom walked him to the door. Depressed, he thought how

strange it was that, despite the fact they were brothers, they couldn't talk to each other. They might have been from different planets.

"By the way, Toni and I have put off the big day. Her parents are still too upset about Violet's death to deal with a big wedding in September."

"You must be relieved," Jonny said with a laugh.

"Sort of . . ." Dom laughed too.

The brothers looked at each other. Jonny's eyes were full.

"What's wrong?" said Dom, gripping Jonny's shoulders.

"She's gone—Emmy's gone . . ."

"Oh, no."

They weren't from different planets after all, Dom realized, putting his arms around him.

"I'm so sorry . . ."

Jonny cried.

CHAPTER TWENTY-FIVE

PENNY, she said to herself, gazing at her reflection in the bathroom mirror. *Penelope.* Then she whispered softly, *Lark.*

Lark . . . Lark. *Lark.*

It was her name now. One's name reflected one's being. What did that mean about her? What kind of person was Lark?

She did not know. Sometimes she felt as though not only her face was to be made over, but her entire being.

What would Dom think about that?

Dr. Bellamon had taken more than a superficial interest in her. He was amazed at what appeared to him as her very poor sort of education. European politics were a mystery to her. While she appreciated art, she knew little about it. She had read no Shakespeare, no John Milton. She had never even been to a play.

"We'll have to rectify that," he told her and bought tickets to various West End performances in London.

More than once she asked him why he was doing so much for her, but he always put her off with a joke or a story. She remembered what he'd said that first night—about trusting him, even if she didn't understand—but she found that she never entirely could. He was approximately the same age as Justin Groome, and she was always on guard against him, in spite of the fact that he had made no physical overtures to her.

Even when he showed her how to hold the tennis racket, he barely touched her.

He encouraged her to read more than she ever had before. She read the autobiography of Isadora Duncan and letters written by Robert Louis Stevenson and a life of Garibaldi. These people who had led lives of such courage and adventure instilled in her a feeling that what she was doing was brave and exciting.

During the long summer evenings he talked about news stories of interest and explained political events. Together they examined portions of plays or poems which she did not understand. During the day she sometimes accompanied him to London and he dropped her off at the Victoria and Albert or the British Museum. She spent entire days looking at the paintings and sculptures and on the way home was thoroughly quizzed by Dr. Bellamon on what she had seen. On weekends, when he was not at his London office or performing surgery at the hospital, he taught her how to play tennis on his grass tennis court. Sometimes they played croquet.

Yes: Her entire self was being made over.

Could one's soul be remodeled also?

She scrunched her eyes shut tight. Dom would be interested in these questions, she thought unwillingly. They would discuss the philosophical nature of one's being as it related to one's body and to one's name. Dom would remind her that she was a person before all this happened.

That was the hardest part: remembering one's old self, the person she'd been before her father died. She had been popular and lively and always in trouble. She was the one who brought the joints. She'd gotten drunk at parties from the time she was thirteen. *A liar—a thief—a slut—*

That was the Penny before Dom had arrived on the scene.

It occurred to her that she had begun to change long before the disaster to her face. Susan had already shown her how education could be enjoyed, she had taught her to appreciate art and music, and she had given her a thorough grounding in movies. The night of her graduation Penny had looked lovely. Jonny had said so—and others too. She had already begun to

look sophisticated. She had started on a course which Dr.
Bellamon was simply continuing.

This was no sudden transformation. It was part of growing
up.

And she had fallen in love, too. Despite the heartbreaking
certainty that she would never see Dom again, she still felt
richer for loving him.

Lark opened her eyes again. She felt stronger now. More
real. She had substance. *I was, I am, I will be:* The key was in
realizing the continuity of her life. It was there for the finding.

But it wasn't easy. As autumn set in she remembered vividly
the previous fall, when she had spent so much time in the
cozy kitchen with Susan. She went through periods of loneliness and confusion, interspersed with the anticipation of having her face look normal again. She had nightmares; on several
occasions she awoke sobbing for Susan. When she cautiously
mentioned the bad dreams to Dr. Bellamon he assured her
they were normal.

"You have undergone a profound shock. Your subconscious
is finding ways of dealing with it."

It was during her periods of depression, when she was overcome with a homesickness so intense it hurt, that she wondered most suspiciously about why Dr. Bellamon was doing so
much for her. Nobody did anything for nothing, especially
not someone they'd never seen before. And yet he seemed so
detached and he was always unfailingly polite.

One afternoon in late October they were returning from a
walk in the forest when Dr. Bellamon asked her, "Why do
you lock your door at night?"

She was startled that he knew she locked her door. Had he
tried to come in?

"Do not worry," he added. "I have not tried your door
myself. Sara told me you unlock the door in the morning to
let her in when she brings you hot chocolate. I am merely
curious. Are you still afraid of the people you ran away from
in the United States? I assure you they will not find you here."

She walked silently, squinting at the low, cool sun. Finally she said, "I was raped once. I've never gotten over it. I guess I'm afraid of it happening again."

He nodded. "I had a feeling it was something like that."

"You did? How?"

"You shudder if I so much as accidently touch your sleeve." His eyes darkened. "Rape is a terrible thing. Did you have psychiatric counseling after it happened?"

"No. I haven't told anyone except you."

The sun disappeared behind a thick gray bank of clouds and Lark felt a few drops of rain on her bare head. Dr. Bellamon was looking at her with such angry puzzlement she was confused. "I had no idea . . ." he murmured, as though he were trying to figure something out.

"I don't think about it very much anymore." Lark shrugged.

"You may lock as many doors as you wish if it makes you feel any better. But," he added, "we will try to unlock the ones with the bitter secrets."

The rain grew heavier. They hurried back to the house. Lark wondered why he was surprised at learning something about her that he did not know.

CHAPTER TWENTY-SIX

O N a windy November morning, Lark was finally released from the hospital after a week of surgery and another two weeks of recuperation.

Despite the bruises and mild swelling, she was stunned by the transformation to her face. Dr. Bellamon took her out to celebrate.

"Pleased?" he asked as he drove.

"I still can't believe it." She craned her neck to look at herself in the rearview mirror. "Is that me?"

"I think it is more you than your previous face was. The broad forehead shows your intelligence. The mouth tipped up like that denotes your sense of humor. Your eyes seem wider and more innocent."

"And I love my nose! It's so straight—and I don't see a single freckle on it. And my teeth!" She grinned at herself.

"The dentist did an excellent job, I agree."

She settled back in the seat. "Why do you say I look more like me now than I did? You don't really know what I looked like before."

He smiled. "I have a fairly good idea."

He took her to lunch at Gravetye Manor, a huge mansion made of Sussex gray stone, adorned with pointed, Gothic windows. The long driveway was lined with ancient oak trees.

Inside, they were shown to one of three comfortable waiting rooms. They sat in deep leather chairs in front of a roaring fire. Dr. Bellamon ordered Almacenista sherry for them both. Lark wanted to wander around and examine the hunting trophies and paintings on the walls, but she was intimidated by the formality of the place. At a nearby table a party talked gaily about their exploits at the morning's fox hunt.

Lark turned her attention to Dr. Bellamon who looked as elegant as anyone else there.

"I feel as though I've come to the end of something, now that my face is so different. I can't go on staying with you, for one thing."

"I agree that you have to get on with your life. The first thing to do is to procure new identification. It is difficult, but not impossible."

He explained to her how it was done. They would find the name of someone who had died as an infant around the same year that she herself was born. Then she had to go to the department of records and get this person's birth certificate. With that in her hand, she could legally change her name from the infant's to Lark Chandler. After that it would be no trouble to apply for a passport, a driver's license, a bank account, and even credit cards.

"You are going to be English from now on. Properly English. You will have to work on your accent. We will make up an ironclad story about your upbringing. The English are ruthlessly cunning about analyzing accents. You must never slip into an Americanism when you are in public."

"I see." She hesitated. "What if I want to go back to the United States some day though?"

"Do you, Lark?"

She sipped the sherry, thinking for the first time about her long-term plans. She glanced up to find Dr. Bellamon still studying her. "I haven't given a thought to what I'm going to do after my face is fixed!" She laughed. "I really was taking it one step at a time, just as you said I should. But I think that before I die I may want to clear up some business I left behind in the States." Unwillingly, she conjured Justin Groome's face in front of her. "I may not feel strong enough to face it for years and years, but at some point I think I will go back."

"Then you will go back," he asserted, as though he could see her future. "Whether for love or for revenge, who can say as yet? Time will tell. But in the meantime you will be English."

A waiter in black tie came over. "Your table is ready, sir."

He led them to a table near a window. The wind scattered brown leaves from the nearby oak trees. Deer wandered delicately about the lawn.

The menu had items that thrilled Lark: venison, pheasant, rabbit, pigeon, grouse.

"I don't know if I can bear to eat a deer," she said with a laugh, glancing at them out the window. But she ordered it anyway.

Looking up from her plate, she found him gazing at her with an expression of such pride that she blushed. Then she realized he was proud not of her so much as of his handiwork. Confused, she looked down again.

"What are you thinking?" asked Dr. Bellamon.

"I was wondering who Dr. Smith is," she replied.

"I do not know who Dr. Smith is. Tell me."

She related the story of the man in the doctor's coat who had given her Dr. Bellamon's address. "When I first came to you, I felt almost as though you were expecting me," she said. "Were you?"

He raised his hand in denial. "I found your case very interesting, just as your Dr. Smith said I would. He was probably a doctor I had met at a plastic surgeons' convention. I am afraid I really do not remember." He changed the subject abruptly. "I want you to pay attention to the wine we are drinking. It is one of the finest Bordeaux to be had. 'Latour à Pomerol'—a nineteen seventy-five vintage. Study the label a moment."

She did so, giggling. "Are you going to turn me into a wine connoisseur as well as an art connoisseur and a tennis player?"

"Perhaps not a connoisseur, but every properly educated woman should have some knowledge of wine. The sherry we had earlier was an unblended variety that is quite exceptional. I hoped you would have remarked on it."

She hadn't even finished it. "Sorry. I'll try to notice next time."

A few days later at breakfast he handed her an envelope. "There is your birth certificate," he said.

She opened it curiously. There was her name: Lark Chandler. Her new birthday was March 15. She glanced up with a twinkle.

"I hope I remember that."

"The ides of March," he said. "It is easy to remember."

"The what of March?"

"It is the day Julius Caesar was betrayed and murdered. You must have been taught about that in school."

"I hope it's luckier for me," Lark said. "I like being twenty-one. But can I lose a few years when I turn thirty?"

"For the rest of your life people will say 'She doesn't look her age.'"

They both laughed.

"Now you can apply for a passport, a driver's license, and so forth."

"I can hardly believe it!"

"When you decide the time is right for you to return to the States, you will have two options. One is to apply for a green card, or, at the least, an H-One or H-Two visa, which will give you limited permission to work in the United States."

"And the other option?"

"Is to marry an American citizen."

"Yuck," she said. "I'm not marrying anyone."

He looked grave. "If it is the terrible tragedy of being raped that—"

She interrupted. "It doesn't have anything to do with that."

"With your beauty it will not be difficult to find a husband."

"Yuck," she repeated.

"Did you have a boyfriend when you left the States?" asked Dr. Bellamon.

She shook her head.

He left her soon afterward to go to his office. "I will see you tonight at supper," he told her as he went out the door. "We can discuss it further then."

After he'd gone, Lark stared at the certificate in her hand.

Her mythical parents' names were on it: Derek Chandler and Elizabeth Chandler, *nee* Buckly. Birthplace: London, England.

She really was someone else. Penny had gone, vanished, never to return. She was Lark Chandler now.

"Are you all right, miss?" Sara had come in the room to clear the breakfast table.

"I'm fine," Lark looked up with a smile.

In the beginning she had tried to make friends with Sara, for she didn't think Sara could be much older than she. But Sara scrupulously stuck to her role of maid, politely refusing Lark's invitation to have a cup of coffee together or to play tennis. Lark decided she was a bore. But she was surprised at how quickly she got used to being waited on by Sara. She was already practically addicted to the cup of hot chocolate she was brought each morning.

"Being rich may not make you any different," she decided, putting on her wool jacket and Dr. Bellamon's Wellingtons. "But it sure makes life nicer."

She went for a long walk. The clouds were black. Yellow lights from the stores in the village streamed onto the wet sidewalk, even though it was only midmorning. It looked as though it would rain at any minute. The low branches of the hawthorns lining the sidewalk brushed her head, giving her the sensation of walking through cobwebs. She passed some Victorian semidetached houses and glanced in the bay windows. What lives went on in there? Images impressed themselves on her brain like the fingerprints of someone squeezing her arm. A couple was sitting on a couch watching television. An elderly man was reading a book by a gaslit fireplace. Some people were laughing around a kitchen table. A small girl looked solemnly out the window.

They could all have been her.

She climbed up a slope of dying ferns and gorse bushes. Ahead of her was the wide green; beyond that Ashdown Forest.

It began to drizzle but the oaks and ashes and yew trees protected her. Even the silver birches, trembling under the light drops, helped keep her dry.

She walked beside a meandering stream.

I need money first of all, she thought. *That means I need to get a job. I also have to get my own apartment, 'cos I can't go on living with Dr. Bellamon. He's done too much for me already. It'd be weird to stay there any longer. When I've saved enough money, I'll pay him back what I owe him. After that I'll think about going back to the States. Eventually maybe I'll be able to prove my innocence and expose Groome. But how? How?*

First, though, was the problem of getting a job. Unemployment was high in England. She had read the statistics in The *Guardian* the other day and it had depressed her.

She turned away from the stream and headed out of the woods across a golf course. It had begun to rain steadily. No one else was out.

Something would come up. Right now she simply wanted to be outside in the wind and rain, surrounded by the fairy-tale green of Ashdown Forest, free from the ties of the past. Free even from Dom. What had he said to her when her father died? *You'll never forget this, but you will get over it.* Well, she would never forget Dom, but she some day would get over him.

Right now it was exhilarating to realize that no one in the world knew where she was at that moment. She felt freer than she had ever felt before.

Only when the rain thickened and began to soak through her jacket did she turn and head back to Dr. Bellamon's house.

CHAPTER TWENTY-SEVEN

THAT evening at supper, Lark said, "I want to get a job."

Suppers at Dr. Bellamon's house were formal, scrumptious affairs. He had a remarkable chef, Jean Bodot, a Frenchman who was married to Betts, his nervous housekeeper. During the week his maid, Sara, served supper.

"That is a good idea. I think we should also find you your own flat. You will heal more quickly, emotionally I mean, if you exercise your independence." Too many times he had seen his patients become emotionally dependent on him well after they had recovered physically. "As long as you were not going out very much not many people knew you were staying with me. But now we have to think of the proprieties as well."

"I know."

"There is a pretty little bed-sitter in London that a friend I know is giving up. It is near Kensington, and it rents for only three hundred pounds a month. I think you should take it."

"I'll need a job to pay for it."

"I am giving a dinner party next week. It is an annual thing for me—a holiday party for my closest friends. I am hoping one of the guests may give you an idea about the sort of work you might be interested in."

"Oh, great."

"One more thing," he went on, "I want you to start calling me Carl. 'Doctor' is not necessary now that you are no longer my patient."

"All right—Carl."

"About your identity," Dr. Bellamon said, after Sara had served them custard trifle. "We have to figure out where you are from. I am afraid we don't have time to really cultivate your English accent, and besides, there is always the chance that you might slip."

"I'm pretty good with accents," Lark said, "but I wouldn't want to risk it."

"Here is one possibility: You were born in London, as the birth certificate shows. Your father's business transferred him overseas and you lived several years in the States."

"Yes." She took up the story eagerly. "He was an account executive at a big shoe store that exports shoes. We all moved to New York City when I was twelve or so. I really liked it there and I've always wanted to go there to live."

"Shoes!" He laughed.

"Why not?"

"Where are your parents now?"

"They were killed in a car accident three years ago. I've been getting my college degree at New York University."

"What sort of degree?"

"How about movies? I know a lot about them."

"Fine."

"This is fun. But do you think anyone might try to catch me out?"

"I doubt it. Still, you'd better have your answers ready. As for how you met me—I am an old friend of your father's. You have known me ever since you were a baby."

Lark moved into her new apartment—she couldn't get used to calling it a flat, although everyone else did—that weekend. There was not very much for her to move. With the money she still had left, she had bought a pair of jeans, some shirts and underwear, and a lambswool sweater. She rarely took off the sweater. Wool was the only material that could keep out the damp cold of English autumn. She had kept the running shoes. When she went out, she dressed as inconspicuously as possible, but even in jeans and a baggy sweater, heads turned as she passed. With her long dark hair cascading down her back, her intense Prussian blue eyes, and the beautifully sculpted face, everyone who saw her was struck by the notion that they had just glimpsed someone rare and special. Her understated clothes only emphasized her exotic beauty.

Unused to the sound of the traffic, Lark hardly slept the first few nights in her new apartment. She sat by the window, looking down at the street that bubbled with lights and noise, sipping herb tea and making up stories about her past.

Carl dropped by for a visit some days later. It was Sunday. Lark had bought a mattress, some white cotton sheets, and two wool blankets, but that was all. The little bed-sitter looked barren. There weren't even curtains in the windows.

"I turn out the light when I get undressed," she said in response to Carl's shocked question. "I don't need curtains."

"You certainly do. This place looks like a cell. You should have seen it when Anna lived here. I was not aware the floor was made of wood, it was so covered with her belongings."

"I like it this way." And it was true. Lark liked the sparseness. She had hung her few clothes in the built-in closet, which had four shelves inside for things like underwear and socks. It was all she needed.

Carl checked out the cabinets over the sink. Empty.

"Aren't you planning to eat?"

"I have to get some kitchen stuff," she admitted. "I was hoping I might pick something up at a thrift store."

Carl smiled. "You mean a charity shop. I can probably spare you a spoon and a saucer or two. I will ask Betts to look into it. I have come to remind you that my dinner party is on Saturday. Clive, my chauffeur, will pick you up in the limousine so you will not have to take the train."

"Who will be there?"

"A producer, the president of a modeling agency, an actor, journalists—people like that. I'm hoping that someone will be able to help you get a job."

"That'd be great."

Carl looked pleased. "I have a feeling you enjoy parties?"

"I used to," she admitted. "But this party will probably be very different."

Unexpectedly, Carl swayed and started to fall. Lark grabbed his arm as he sat heavily on the mattress.

"Are you all right?"

He looked pale. "Yes . . . yes." He breathed deeply. Lark was not convinced that he was all right, but she didn't know what to do. She couldn't even offer him a glass of water since she had no glasses. But he pulled himself together. "I want to talk about what you ought to wear to the party. I think it should be red. You are slender enough to wear something tight fitting. Leave your shoulders bare. You will also need a coat: I think camel hair. If you go to Harrod's, you will find something that will suit. Charge it to my account. Will you do that?"

"I can't," she protested. "You've done too much for me."

"Nonsense. Consider it an early Christmas present."

Still she hesitated. She was about to refuse again, when she met Carl's eyes. She could have almost sworn he was pleading with her to accept the gift.

"Okay. Thank you very much." She was concerned about him. "Now, don't you think you'd better go home and lie down?"

He ignored her.

"Yes," he said, kindly, "a red dress is the best thing for you just now. It will get you in the holiday spirit."

Chapter Twenty-Eight

LARK was excited about Carl's dinner party. She knew the zinfandel dress was perfect as soon as the saleswoman at Harrod's brought it out. It was sleek and clingy and she bought ivory stockings and wine-colored high heels to match. Then the coat. It was the first one she'd really owned. On the farm she'd just had a duffel jacket. Susan had loaned her a trench coat when they'd gone into New York, but somehow they'd never gotten around to buying a real coat for her.

Carl's limousine was going to pick her up at six but Lark was already dressed and ready to go at five. It was raining again—it rarely wasn't raining in England, she decided. The summer past had been the wettest summer of her life. Still, she loved the rain. It wasn't like the depressing, heavy sheets that swept the countryside in upstate New York. English rain was magically delicate and pretty—just enough to make one feel fresh and clean.

Lark had met Clive, Carl's chauffeur, a few times before. He was getting his bachelor's degree in film at the University of London. Like Sara, he kept a polite distance from her.

"How's school going?" asked Lark from the backseat.

"Very well, thank you, ma'am."

"Did you know I went to film school in New York?"

"Did you, ma'am."

"I'd think we'd have a lot to talk about."

But to this remark Clive did not even respond. Really, the lower classes in England were as snobbish as the upper classes,

Lark thought with disgust. How Clive would laugh if he saw her cleaning the hennery!

"Where do you come from?" she asked.

"Norfolk, ma'am."

"Where's that?"

"In the north, ma'am."

He was too stuffy for words.

"You must have your udders full, going to school full-time and working for Dr. Bellamon as well. When do you get any time off?"

"Beg pardon, ma'am?"

Lark gave up trying to talk to him. When they arrived at Carl's house, Clive held open the car door.

"Good evening, ma'am."

"Bye. Don't get your feathers plucked."

"Beg pardon, ma'am?"

"It's just an expression."

She skipped up the marble stairs to the front door and rang the bell. Carl opened the door himself and surveyed her with pleasure.

"Perfect," he murmured, as he helped her off with the camel hair coat and saw the zinfandel dress. "You make me feel very proud. You are simply ravishing."

She knew that he was complimenting himself as much as her. Carl pulled her hand through his arm and led her into the living room. Men in black tie and women in bright dresses were grouped around the room. The room was festively decorated with sprays of juniper, rose hips, and holly.

"Sherry?" offered Carl.

"Yes, please."

A corpulent, red-faced man came over.

"Now where has Carl been keeping you a secret? Hello, I'm Charles King. It's a pleasure to meet you."

Lark said, "Hi," and stuck out her hand. Catching Carl's frown she quickly added in a British accent, "It is such a pleasure to meet you."

"Charles works for the *Sun* although he likes to deny it," said Carl, handing Lark the glass of sherry. "And this is Jack

Adler, who makes television documentaries. Did you watch the one last week on the African elephant?"

"I watched it and I wish I hadn't," broke in a small, round woman with a mauve taffeta gown which emphasized her roundness. "I cried for hours afterward. Those poor beasts! I collected every ivory thing in the house and shut them all away. I'll never buy ivory again."

"That was the purpose of the documentary, wasn't it, Jack?" said Charles King.

"I thought it was a pretty good film," Jack responded mildly. He was a fair, mustachioed man, probably in his early forties. "Of course, Bettina here would cry if I'd made a film depicting the hard life of the poachers."

"I would not," the woman called Bettina protested indignantly. "Those men are animals."

Charles laughed. "So are the elephants, my dear."

"Anyway," said Carl, "the only reason you think they are criminals is that Jack portrayed them as such. But those poor poacher blokes just think they're making a living."

Charles winked at Lark. "Don't you think journalists are a breed apart? They claim to simply state the facts. But actually one can slant someone's emotions with merely a quote here, a photograph there, an adjective somewhere else; leave out other information and one has built a solid case for whatever cause one supports."

"I don't particularly admire your journalistic techniques then," retorted Jack. "I consider everything I do to be completely unbiased. I present the facts exactly as I see them."

"Oh-ho, I don't believe that," broke in another woman. She was taller than Lark, and so slender she looked as though she might break in two. She wore a skintight jumpsuit made of shiny emerald green spandex, and an enormous green bow in her red hair. "I saw the documentary you made last year on the MP from Worcester—what was his name? Anyway, the poor bloke got on your wrong side and you went after him like a shark."

"I saw that too," said Carl. "He seemed a harmless enough fellow until you got your claws into him. Wasn't it a simple case of adultery?"

"I didn't make that documentary, a colleague did," said Jack. "But I disagree that there was any vindictiveness involved. Henry Smartt was running on a platform of ultraconservative morality. He was against abortion, even in the case of rape or incest. Then we found out he was having a—ahem—a thing going with a young girl, not yet of age. We called it rape, merely a technicality, of course, since the girl seemed to be as enamored of him as he was of her. But we certainly weren't going to let him get away with it."

"Is he married?"

"Not anymore."

"Dinner is served," announced the specially hired butler.

Carl said, "Jack, take Lark in, will you? Charles, you have got Isabella over here." She was the girl in spandex. He paired off the rest of the guests and they entered the dining room.

Lark had never seen the long dining table set so formally. Spode china and crystal gleamed on the crimson linen tablecloth. Red candles glowed in heavy silver candlesticks placed in the center of the table, with silver bowls of small white roses spaced down the middle. A chandelier sparkled overhead. Delicate fragrances emanated from the soup bowls already in place, the china covers on top of each bowl keeping the soup hot.

When the guests were seated, the butler began removing the tops to the lemon soup.

Jack was seated on Lark's right, Charles on her left. Jack drew her attention to him first.

"How is it that we've never met before?" he asked. "It seems such a pity."

She smiled. "I've been attending college in the States," she replied in her best British accent. "I was studying film at New York University."

"Ah, you're interested in film?"

"I'm interested in making documentaries." She smiled into his eyes, wondering if he could help her get a job. His eyes were silver. "That's why I wanted so much to meet you tonight."

He seemed flattered.

"Do you live in London?" he asked.

"Yes. I have a flat near Kensington."

"I live in St. John's Wood. Been there for years."

The soup plates were removed. Charles, on her other side, compelled her attention. "Isabella lives in Kensington as well. Have you two met before?"

"No."

Isabella, seated on Charles's other side, had turned to Carl.

"She's a model," Charles told Lark. "I assumed you were one too, and that you knew each other."

"I'm not a model!" Lark started laughing as though the idea were preposterous, but then she remembered her face.

"It's not such an outrageous mistake." Charles laughed too. "But I suppose you're an actress and you think modeling is very déclassé."

"Not at all. It's that I can't act! No, I've been studying film at college in the States. I want to be behind the camera, not in front."

"Really? I always feel a girl with a face as charming as yours should give us the pleasure of seeing it as much as possible."

"Really," she said.

The next course was brought out, a coq au vin cooked in Chambertin which, Lark made a mental note, was also the wine they were drinking.

Jack turned back to Lark. "Where are you working now?"

"I just graduated. I'm looking for a job."

"It's not easy to get work without experience."

"It's not easy to get experience without work," she volleyed back.

"That's true," he said, laughing. "Where do you see yourself five years from now?" He regarded her with a cool, interested gaze.

She longed to say: I don't give a damn where I am five years from now as long as Justin Groome is in prison and Penelope Houten is vindicated.

"I'd like to make television documentaries," she said brightly. "Particularly documentaries of political personalities, like the one on that member of parliament you were talking about earlier."

"I'm surprised you didn't say you want to be an actress. You certainly have the face for it."

"Oh, I can't act for the world."

After the crême brulée (served, Lark noticed, with a '78 Coutet Sauterne), the guests retired to the sitting room for coffee and liqueurs. Bettina, in the mauve gown, came to sit next to Lark. She had very yellow hair, a pink complexion, and a sharp twinkle in her light blue eyes.

"Charles says you're not an actress. What are you then?"

"I just left school. I'm looking for work in television."

Bettina gave a mock groan. "You and the rest of the world. I'm glad Charles and I are both newspaper people. He's the gossip columnist and I'm the news editor at the *Sun*. People always think it should be the other way around, since I'm such a gossip, but Charles is more of a gossip than even I am. We've both been there for years; in fact, we met there. I was only a secretary when I started."

"I didn't realize Charles was your husband."

"Oh, yes, we've been married for twenty-five years now." She lowered her voice. "Tell me the truth and I swear I won't breathe a word to anyone: Is Carl responsible for"—she waved her hands melodramatically—"for how you look?"

Lark laughed and said, "Of course," in such a way that the word was ambiguous.

"Whenever I see one of his creations I'm almost tempted to put myself in his hands. But I'm too cowardly. Besides, I'm fond of my face, funny looking though it is."

"I was fond of my face too," Lark responded slowly. "I was in a bad accident. I didn't have any choice."

Bettina nodded sympathetically. "That does make a difference."

The guests began departing shortly after one o'clock. Jack offered to drive Lark back to London and she accepted. He'd be better company than boring Clive, the chauffeur.

"I hope you had a nice time," said Carl, when she told him Jack had offered her a lift home.

"Oh, I did. You can quiz me on the wines you served tomorrow."

Jack shook Carl's hand.

"Thanks so much for having me, old chap. Brilliant supper. Charming guests. Flattered to be invited."

Once outside, Lark breathed deeply. She had drunk more wine than she should have and the cool air felt good.

"My car's over here," said Jack.

He unlocked the passenger door of a white Jaguar and held it open for her.

"Are you going to be in town for Christmas?" he asked as he started the engine.

"Yes."

"It's a deadly time of year, isn't it? Everyone pretending to be jolly and inside they're bloody miserable. The most prominent aspect of Christmas is loneliness. I've always felt that."

"Don't you have family to go to?"

"I have parents who live in Kent. My sisters and I will probably pop down for a day or two and visit. But the whole thing's a sham, really. I'd rather stay in town and get drunk than have to face an evening of watching telly with the Pater."

She didn't know what to say.

"Where's your family?" he asked.

"My parents are dead. I haven't any brothers or sisters."

"I'm sorry."

But Susan and Dom and Jonny and Emmy would be at Dogwood Farm.

"Blow." He put out a hand and turned her chin so that she had to look at him. "I didn't mean to upset you."

"I think I had too much to drink."

"What did you mean when you told Carl he could quiz you about the wine?"

"He's trying to make me a connoisseur." She chuckled.

"You couldn't have a better teacher. Carl's a very special bloke."

"Yes, I know."

The streets were practically empty. London seen in the middle of the night was different from the noisy London of the day. This was almost like a scene from a *film noir*.

"It was fun." She sighed, thinking of the party.

"Especially since you were there. How did you meet Carl, anyway?"

"He was a friend of my father's. We've always been close."

"Funny that I haven't met you before. Carl and I have been friends for years."

"As I said, I've been out of the country."

At length, he drew up to the front of her apartment building and turned off the engine.

"I'd like to see you again," he said. "May I call you?"

She'd been hoping he might help her get a job. It hadn't occurred to her that he might be attracted to her. She cursed her stupidity.

"You're seeing someone else?" His silver gray eyes regarded her with calm curiosity.

"No, it's not that."

"I'm not asking you to go to bed with me. Let's have lunch sometime next week. I'd like to see you again, that's all."

"Okay."

He got out. Lark reached for her door handle, but before she could open the door she realized he was coming around to her side to open it for her. She would have to get used to courtesies like that. Even Justin Groome, on their outings in the country, had never opened the car door for her.

When she got out, Jack reached for her hand. Automatically, she pulled it away.

"Good night," she said quickly.

"Good night."

He waited in front of his car until she was safely inside the lobby of her apartment building.

CHAPTER TWENTY-NINE

CARL telephoned the following afternoon. Nursing a slight hangover, Lark had stayed in her flat. It was a good day to stay in. The weather had turned cold, and even the two layers she wore under her wool sweater barely kept her warm. The central heating in the apartment building was a joke.

"How are you feeling?"

"Great, especially considering all the 'seventy-nine Rousseau Chambertin I drank."

He laughed. "Good for you."

"How are you feeling? I thought you looked tired."

"I am quite well, thank you," he said dismissively. "Did Jack take you home all right?"

"Yup."

"Try not to say 'Yup.' It is very American. Did he say anything about helping you find a job?"

"He wants to take me to lunch."

"I see." Pause. "Do you like him?"

"He's okay."

She practically heard Carl thinking.

"You are very young to get seriously involved with a forty-year-old man who has been married twice," he said at last.

"He's been married twice?"

"Yes. Not that I am saying anything against Jack, mind you. He is a fine fellow, and perhaps he will be able to help you find a job." His voice hardened. "It is you I am worried about. You are still finding your identity. You are elated, but you are also anxious. You are not ready for any sort of emotional involvement."

"I need a job," Lark pointed out, annoyed. "If Jack can help me get one, that's fine with me."

"Fair enough. But give yourself a chance to find your feet before getting emotionally involved with anyone." Carl softened.

"I hardly think that lunch will be all that emotional."

"Have lunch by all means."

Jack called later that evening. "Rested?" he asked, assuming she knew who he was without identifying himself.

"Yes. Are you?"

"Not in the least. I've been at work all day."

His voice was low and intimate, his accent was Cambridge. She liked the way he talked. She curled up on the mattress and smiled into the receiver.

"You work on Sunday?" she asked.

"When we're under deadline."

"Oh, of course."

"Are we still on for lunch? I wondered whether you were free on Wednesday."

"Let me check"—Lark snuggled up to a pillow—"Yes, I seem to be free."

"Why don't we meet at my office? That way I can show you around the place. You might find it interesting."

"I'd love that."

He gave her the address and asked her to come at noon. Lark replaced the receiver, smiling contentedly. She had a feeling Jack would come through with a job.

The offices of Stafford Productions were situated on Charlotte Street, just off Tottenham Court Road. At noon on Wednesday Lark pushed open the wrought iron gate, walked up a stone path, and entered the four story, redbrick building. A receptionist asked her to sit down and wait for Mr. Adler.

"You can leave your coat in this closet."

Lark took off her camel hair coat. Under it she wore a slim-fitting, black wool skirt with a slit up the back. An Irish linen blouse peeked out from a close-fitting jacket cardigan made of sage green mohair. She glanced at her reflection in the mirror inside the closet door. No one would ever guess that she had purchased her clothes from an Oxfam shop. Even the black pumps on her feet were secondhand. Her hair was slightly mussed from the wind, but it looked nice that way. It was swept away from her face, and clasped in back with a black bow.

She looked really great. It surprised her all over again.

She closed the closet door and sat down in an armchair. Jack appeared moments later.

"Hello." He took both her hands in his and clasped them warmly. "You look exactly as I remembered."

She extricated her hands. "Why would I look any different?" But he seemed different to her. At the party she had been so buoyed by her idea of becoming a documentary film-maker and making an exposé of Justin Groome's life that she hadn't paid attention to him. But now he seemed more real. His silvery eyes responded to her smile.

"I'll show you around first, shall I?" he offered.

"Sure." She heard herself sounding too American again.

"This is the viewing room, where we can watch the films that have been made. And here's the edit lab. Conference room—oh, excuse us." He closed the door quickly. "I didn't realize there was a meeting going on. Come upstairs and meet Andrew. He's one of our executive producers. If you want to get a project done, all you need is his backing and it's as good as sold. Andrew, I want you to meet a friend of mine. This is Lark Chandler."

Jack punched him in the ribs and grinned at Lark. He was older than Jack, unshaven, with dark circles under his eyes. He wore suspenders over a blue shirt that was stained with sweat.

"Excuse my appearance," he apologized to Lark. "We're working on a deadline. I haven't gone home in two days." He glanced at Jack. "Last time I saw you, you looked in bloody worse shape than I do. Did you arrange for a session with your makeup man?"

"We wrapped at eight o'clock this morning," Jack pointed out. "Plenty of time to go home, have a shower, dress, and show up for lunch. I advise you to do the same. Or won't your wife let you in the house looking like that?"

"Get out." He grinned at Lark. "Not you—you can stay, if Jack will let you, which I don't suppose he will." The telephone rang. He waved good-bye to them as he picked up the receiver.

They moved on. "Do you work well with deadlines?" Jack asked, as they went into his office. Large windows overlooked the street below. A stiff wind was blowing the clouds across the sky, showing patches of deep blue in between, but rarely any sun.

He motioned her to an orange overstuffed armchair.

"Absolutely," Lark replied, crossing her legs. "I've never missed a deadline in my life."

He shrugged into a Harris tweed jacket. "Sometimes when you say things, I can't tell if you're making them up or if you're being sincere. Are you hungry? I made reservations at the Savoy for one o'clock. It's almost that now."

They took a taxi, although it was less than a five-minute drive. Their table overlooked the Strand. Lark refused a cocktail, but she did drink some of the wine Jack ordered. She could tell it was a Bordeaux, but it wasn't as good as some of those she had had at Carl's house.

She asked him about the documentary he was working on now: the seventies. He responded at length, almost as though he were trying to impress her, and not the other way around. Yet it was Lark who wanted a job—if there was one to be had at Stafford Productions.

She hadn't thought about how their lunch date would end, and she was surprised at its abruptness. They had left the restaurant and were standing in front on the windy sidewalk.

"I'll put you in a taxi here," said Jack.

"Thanks for the lunch and showing me your office," she said. Then he bundled her into the taxi, gave her address to the driver, and closed the door. He waved through the window.

Lark leaned back, disappointed by the sudden end to the pleasant afternoon. And she felt discouraged by the fact that nothing had been said about her possibly working at Stafford Productions.

But Jack called again just two days later.

"Sorry I didn't get back to you sooner. I was asleep all yesterday. Catching up. Most of the people at work were, even though it was Thursday. We have odd schedules. I hope that's something you can live with."

"Sure." She *had* to stop saying "sure."

"I got a chance to talk to Andrew about you, though. Told him you were looking for a job."

Lark held her breath. "Yes?"

"There's an opening you might be interested in, although it isn't working in the documentary field. Still, it's a start."

"What is it?"

"Reading unsolicited manuscripts. Your job would be to evaluate them. The pay is rotten, and for the most part the scripts are rotten, but you'll learn the ropes. I hope you'll take it."

She was thrilled. "Of course I'll take it. Thank you so, so much. When do I start?"

"I don't see that there's much point in starting before the New Year. Christmas is next week, and the office closes between then and New Year's. Would Monday the fourth suit?"

"That would be fine."

"I'll be out of the city till then. Do you have any plans for New Year's Eve? I could take you around to some parties."

"That sounds great."

"Good. I'll call you when I get back to town then."

"Okay."

When she'd hung up, she paced the small apartment, feeling excited. Her first job. It seemed incredible. She would actually be making money. What did he mean by the pay being "rotten"?

She had to think seriously about clothes. She couldn't wear the same black skirt every day. She wondered if anyone noticed that her outfit looked a little worn?

It made no difference anyway. She could not afford to spend money on clothes. She would go back to the Oxfam shop and see if she could find some outfits that, with a little sewing here, and adjusting there, would look okay. Sometimes just dry cleaning a blouse made it look like new.

She called Carl to tell him the news.

"I have a job," she said when he answered.

"So Jack came through," he said. Then, almost to himself, "Maybe it's not such a bad thing, after all."

"Bad thing!" Lark yelled. "It's fantastic!"

"Careful, my dear. You sound distinctly American. Now, tell me about this job."

She gave him the details.

"It sounds as though it might work out," he said.

"I hope so."

"I am glad you called," Carl said after a pause. He sounded uncomfortable. "I have been meaning to tell you that you are going to be on your own for Christmas. I will be in Wales with friends. Will you be all right?"

"Of course," she said at once. What was Christmas, after all? She and her father had barely noticed it.

Only last year it had been fun. Really fun.

"I'll be fine," she said, less convincingly.

"I will see you once again before I leave. I have a gift for you. Also I have a ticket for a performance of Handel's Messiah at St. Paul's on Christmas Eve. You will enjoy going to that."

"You don't have to do that."

"But I want to."

When he had said good-bye, Lark stared out the narrow window at the wet street below. Susan and Jonny and Emmy and Dom would be together at Dogwood Farm, with their friends coming and going, bringing gifts, keeping secrets, kissing under the mistletoe, laughing, singing . . .

No doubt they had forgotten her.

Sometimes living a lie would be lonely. But she had expected that.

On Christmas Eve it snowed. Lark decided to wear blue jeans and a violet cashmere turtleneck to the concert. The cashmere was Carl's present to her; she had opened it early. A form-fitting cashmere skirt went with it: perfect for work.

She took the underground to St. Paul's for the concert. The streets were slippery with slush, and she was glad she was in her running shoes and jeans instead of the red dress she had half debated wearing. Why bother to dress up? She would be alone for the evening.

The almost empty bus let her off near St. Paul's and she crossed the snowy square. Inside, an usher showed her to her seat. To her dismay it was right in the middle of a row near the front. Several people had to stand up to let her pass. That meant if she wanted to leave early she couldn't do so without making a scene.

The seats on either side of her were empty. She studied the program for a while, then looked around the enormous church. The dark cupola overhead was so high it seemed part of the night sky, but bright lights flooded the nave where the seats were rapidly filling up. It was very damp and she was glad of the cashmere.

The lights began to dim.

As they did so, a man pushed his way down the row, heading for the vacant seat beside her. Lark glanced at him as he sat down.

He was handsome, in a dark, haggard way. He met her eyes with a friendly twinkle.

Coolly, she turned away. Then did a double take.

She was sitting next to Jonny Whitfield.

CHAPTER THIRTY

"STOP blaming yourself," Dom urged his mother for the hundredth time. "You did everything you could."

But the emptiness of the house at Christmas had thrown Susan into an acute longing and depression that made her talk incessantly and self-reproachfully about Penny. Justin Groome was sick of hearing about her, but he hid his irritation well.

"It's hard to believe a young thing like that could vanish without any sort of help." He stared into the fire. "Her face looked ghastly. Anyone who saw it would remember it."

"She didn't look that awful!" protested Dom. "Besides, she was last seen getting on a bus to New York City. There are seven million people there, and most of them look worse than she did."

"I hired a private investigator," Justin addressed Susan. "I'd hoped he'd have more luck than the cops."

"We hired one too," Susan sighed.

"You heard about the credit card, then?"

"The one belonging to the patient in the hospital? Yes, but it wasn't necessarily Penny who stole it."

"Ahem. It was most likely Penny. She has a talent for that sort of thing. She even stole my credit card once."

Dom and Susan stared.

"I didn't want to mention it back then, since I didn't want to get the poor girl into trouble. She used it to get tickets to some damn concert. Naturally I caught up with her there. I thought I frightened her enough so that she wouldn't try it again."

Dom saw how the information shocked his mother. "It probably wasn't Penny who stole the card at the hospital," he said quickly. "According to the cops, there'd been a suspicious-looking character, dressed as a doctor, hanging around. He probably took it. The only purchase made on the card after it was stolen was for a plane ticket to England which was never picked up."

"And anyway, why would Penny go to England?" added Susan, getting up to prepare dinner.

The house wasn't decorated as it had been last year for Christmas. There was a tree, but it wasn't very big and even the decorations seemed wistful. Emmy wasn't there, of course, and Jonny was abroad somewhere. Dom was only able to visit for a couple of days. He had been made president of the American Production Group in October. The job offer had not come as a surprise, for his predecessor had been neither popular nor too successful. But what had come as a surprise was the amount of time his job took. He hadn't been home since August and here it was already Christmas.

"When are you going to see Toni?" asked Susan on the afternoon of Christmas Eve. Justin had left to spend Christmas with friends at his Long Island house. He had tried to persuade Susan to go with him; she had refused. Dom knew she still hoped Penny might show up.

"Tomorrow. We're meeting at her place."

"You're still engaged?"

"Yes."

"I don't mean to pry, but you never talk about her. So I was wondering."

"We mean to set a date," said Dom. "But it's hard to see my way clear to a free weekend for a wedding, much less a honeymoon."

Susan looked concerned. "You're not sacrificing your personal happiness for the sake of your work, are you, Dom? It's a terrible danger for a man in your position."

"I know. I don't think I am. I love my job."

"If Toni moves to L.A. to be with you, I feel pretty sure

that Marianne could take over Whitfield Communications without any problem. She's been there almost as long as Toni. She's bright and very ambitious."

"That's good to know. I was going to suggest starting a West Coast branch. Toni would be ideally suited to do that."

"Yes . . ." Susan sounded doubtful.

"You don't think it's a good idea?"

"If Toni wants to do it, I'm all for it. But I have a feeling that once she's married she won't want to devote so much time to her work."

Dom laughed. "Are you kidding? She's almost as much of a workaholic as I am."

"She's a perfectionist," corrected Susan. "She wants to be good at everything she does. But if that means choosing between being a good career woman or a good wife and mother" —Dom flinched—"she'll give up one of them, rather than do two things not quite so well."

Dom changed the subject. "Are you sure you don't want to move back to New York? It seems so lonely up here now."

"It's only lonely because Penny's not around. But I still have my old activities and my friends. I like it here."

"Dr. Goodman says—"

"Dr. Goodman has been worrying about me for years," interrupted Susan. "I feel fine. Don't worry so much about me."

"But even I've noticed you're having trouble breathing."

"I'm getting older. I just have to take things easy."

Dom gave up. Their Christmas was quiet. On Christmas afternoon he drove to New York City.

Toni met him in her apartment, looking stunning as usual, this time in a white suede miniskirt with a matching jacket, an absinthe silk scarf, and forest green suede boots. A white felt hat shaded her jade eyes provocatively.

They went to dinner at Le Relais on Madison Avenue near Toni's apartment. Snow lay in piles in the gutters, but the sidewalks were clear. They were seated at a table near a window strung with little white lights.

"Drink?" Dom asked Toni.

"I'll have a screwdriver."

"Two screwdrivers," Dom told the waiter. "And let me see a wine list."

"How's Susan?" asked Toni.

"She says she's okay, but she looks frail. She still misses Penny, of course." He regarded her speculatively. "She thinks that if you moved to L.A., Marianne would be able to take over Whitfield Communications."

Toni reached to his side of the table for a piece of bread and he glimpsed the lacy edge of her bra. She wasn't wearing a shirt under the jacket.

"What do you think about that?" she asked.

Dom smiled at her. "I've been wanting you to move in with me for practically a year."

"I know."

"But you're the director of your own company. Working for someone else is not going to be easy."

"You're not going to move back to New York, are you?"

He was silent. "No," he said at last.

"Well, then."

"There's also the possibility of opening a West Coast branch of Whitfield Communications."

"I know. I've thought about that myself. But I don't think I want to."

"Why not?"

Toni looked out the window. She didn't want to say she hoped that soon after their marriage she would get pregnant and be able to devote her life to Dom and their children—at least for a few years. She had a feeling Dom would shy away from even thinking about children. Once they were married it would be different. "Too much pressure," she offered. "I'll have other priorities."

Dom smiled at her again. "You'll be great at whatever you do."

Toni thought about last Christmas and her eyes softened. It had been an emotionally difficult year, but once she and Dom were married everything would be better. She loved him so very much.

Dom reached over to take her hand in his. "There's something on your mind. What is it?"

"I don't want to move in with you unless we're married. I've said that before."

"Okay." He paused. "When do you want to get married?"

"How about this winter? It'll have to be in New York, since that's where all my friends are."

"Are you thinking of a big wedding?"

"No, of course not. There wouldn't be enough time to prepare for it. We could have the ceremony in a snowstorm in Central Park and then go to my apartment for the reception. Something like that?"

Dom laughed. "I doubt your parents will let us go that far, but I'm all for it. The snowstorm idea sounds dramatic enough to suit you." He lifted his glass. "To us, Toni."

"To us."

As they walked back to Toni's apartment up Madison Avenue, Toni snuggled close to him. He slipped his arm under the mink coat.

"I love you," Toni whispered. When he didn't respond she moved away. "Do you still feel the same?"

"Me? Oh, yes."

"You sound so detached." They reached her apartment and entered the brightly lit lobby. Toni greeted the doorman. In the elevator she asked, "You haven't met someone else?"

"No, it's not that," Dom replied. "I wonder how happy you'll be in Los Angeles. You seem like such an East Coast type of girl."

She snuggled up to him again. "Time will tell. Let's not spoil tonight thinking about the future. I've missed you so much."

He bent his mouth to hers and began kissing her. Kissing Toni was always something of an adventure. She was remarkably able to move from one erogenous zone with her lips and tongue, and before you knew it both of you had your clothes off. This is what happened now. Somehow they managed to leave the elevator, and the next thing Dom knew they were in her living room. Toni stood before him in her stockings, garter belt, push-up bra, and G-string, wreaking havoc on his brain and body.

CHAPTER THIRTY-ONE

AS soon as Lark's initial surprise subsided, she was overtaken by a fury almost as intense as that she felt for Justin Groome. Jonny had seen what happened the night of Violet's death, and he had abandoned her to take the blame. She could never forgive him for that.

What the hell was he doing, sitting beside her? Surely Carl could not have arranged it. Why would he? If he knew who she really was, he would have said something to her before now. But if he hadn't arranged it, how was it that she was sitting next to Jonny Whitfield? It seemed too monumental a coincidence!

She was hardly aware of Handel's music. Long before she was ready, the audience was clapping, the brilliant lights were going up for the intermission, and Jonny was grinning at her.

"Pretty awful." His teeth were straight and white, his smile as charming as ever.

"I'd say it was awfully pretty."

"You would?" He glanced at the empty seat beside him. "I met up with a girl who gave me this ticket and said she'd meet me here. Think it was a brush-off?"

"I can think of cheaper ways to get rid of you."

His maple-sugar eyes sparkled. "Hell, it's no great loss. I hardly knew her." He looked past her to the empty seat on her other side. "What happened to Mr. Right?"

"Mr. Left, you mean." She met his gaze steadily, trying not to show any anger. The last time she'd seen him Groome had been pistol-whipping him. And then he'd scuttled off to California and left her to take the blame for Violet's murder. Incredible.

"Let's blow this joint before they start cackling again up there on stage," said Jonny. "If I have to hear the 'Lalahooia Chorus' one more time I think I'll puke."

In spite of her fury, Lark couldn't resist the invitation. She longed to know how Susan was—and to hear about Dom. The lights were starting to dim and the conductor came out amid enthusiastic applause. Jonny was already in the aisle, waiting for her.

She stood up and pushed past the knees, apologizing. When she reached Jonny, she realized she'd left her coat in her seat. Groaning, she whispered, "I forgot my coat."

"I'll get it."

Unembarrassed, Jonny went back to her seat, ignoring a low grumble of annoyance. He returned, triumphant, and helped her on with the coat while they stood in the aisle.

There were low cries of "Down, down."

Winking at her, Jonny took his time. Lark wanted to sink through the floor.

"Damn assholes," he said loudly as they went outside.

The snow fell lightly; just enough for effect, not enough to accumulate. Jonny flashed her a smile and held out his hand. "I'm Jonny Whitfield."

"Lark Chandler." She forced herself to shake his hand, then released it almost right away.

"Where should we go?" Jonny said. "It's Christmas Eve. Half of London is closed."

Lark didn't answer. She could hardly believe she had agreed to go anywhere with Jonny Whitfield.

"How about a pub?" he suggested.

She shrugged. They started walking down the street. Jonny wanted to know where she was from—he couldn't place her accent—and she gave him the story she'd made up about going to film school in New York.

"I'm in the film business," Jonny said disconsolately. "Take it from me: stay away. It's a racket."

"I'd like to go to Hollywood sometime. But I'm mainly interested in making television documentaries."

"Television's a racket too. Believe me, you're too young and innocent to get started in that field."

"How do you know I'm young and innocent?"

"Your face says you're young and your eyes say you're innocent."

"My eyes lie. I'm actually a liar, a thief, and a slut."

"Sounds good to me. Where do you live?"

But she didn't tell him. She was chilly by now, and was glad when they finally found a pub called The Swan. Inside, the rich burgundy and amber hues of their drinks reflected glints from a blazing fire. They were soon warmed thoroughly. The place was crowded. Jonny and Lark were pressed against a wall near a frosted, diamond paned window. Jonny didn't seem to mind the crush, but Lark felt claustrophobic.

"What are you doing on your own on Christmas Eve?" asked Jonny. "Where's your family live?"

"Dead," she replied briefly. Then, "How come you're not with your family?"

"I'm trying to set up a movie deal here. It'd be bad timing to go back just now."

"Businesses pretty much close up over the holidays," said Lark. "Surely there isn't much you can do here until after New Year's?"

"True, but I don't feel like flying back to the States just for a week. My mother lives on a godforsaken little farm and she has a friend visiting whom I can't stand. And my brother— who can't stand me—will be there with his fiancée. I guess I wanted an excuse not to be there."

"Oh."

"What's the matter?" asked Jonny. "You look sick."

"So your brother's getting married." She sipped her ginger wine. "When?"

"Who knows. He's put it off as long as he can."

"Why does he put it off? Doesn't he love her?"

"Love?" Jonny snorted derisively. "Give me a break."

"Why's he marrying her?"

"People always say there's one reason to get married, and a

million to get divorced. I say it the other way around: There's a million reasons to get married and only one to get divorced." He sighed deeply.

"How come you're not married?"

"My wife left me."

She wasn't surprised. "Where did she go?"

"New York, I think."

"You mean you don't know?"

"I'm not sure."

"You haven't communicated at all?"

"What's there to say?"

"You could say you're sorry you were such a louse to her."

He cocked his head. "That's a funny thing to say. How do you know it was my fault she left? Maybe she was the louse."

She met his gaze head-on. "I can tell that you were the louse."

Jonny's dark eyes were somber. "I got this weird feeling when we met back at the church that you didn't like me."

She turned away.

Watching her, he gave a mock sigh. "I've always been told I'm such a charmer."

"A charming louse, granted."

"What else can you say about me on such short acquaintance?"

"Let's see—here, give me your hand."

He gave it to her willingly. She turned it palm up and pretended to examine the creases.

"You're incredibly talented. Something of a genius, as a matter of fact." He looked pleased. "But your career's been kind of bumpy. Lots of ups and downs."

"You're very good at this."

"Aren't I? Okay, let's see. Now, that's funny. I've never seen one of these before."

"What's that?"

"It's a guilt line."

"A guilt line?"

"You feel real guilty about something you did once."

"I can't think of anything."

"It may not be something you yourself did. It may be something you covered up or lied about."

"Where's this line?" he asked.

She pointed to a tiny crease near his pinky.

"Gee whiz. I didn't even know it was there. What else?"

"I see a fear line."

"A fear line!" Jonny's laugh was troubled. "What are you talking about?"

"There's someone you're afraid of."

"I thought you were only supposed to say positive things when you read someone's palm."

"I'm so sorry," she said coldly. "These things just popped out at me."

Jonny withdrew his hand. "Let's go outside. I bet Kensington Park looks real pretty in this snow."

"It's closed at night."

"Then we'll sit in Trafalgar Square or walk along the river. That coat's warm, isn't it? Come on."

They went outside. It was still snowing, but lightly.

"Where does your mother live?" asked Penny as they walked. She had been longing to ask about Susan.

"Upstate New York."

"Do you see her often?"

"Not enough. I stopped in for a few days on my way here."

"Is she okay?"

Jonny laughed. "Don't tell me you could tell from my palm that my mother's ill!"

"Is she ill?" Lark asked anxiously.

"Yes, but how did you know?"

"I'm psychic." They reached the Thames and stopped to lean over the stone railing, watching the boats steam up and down the river. Lights reflected off the rippled water and Tower Bridge in the distance was studded with lights too. Trying to keep too much emotion from her voice, Lark asked, "What's wrong with her?"

"The doctors think it's her heart. I think it's stress."

"What sort of stress is there in upstate New York?"

"You'd be surprised." He fished in his coat pocket and handed her a small box. "Merry Christmas, Lark."

She blinked. "How on earth——?"

"I bought something for that bitch who stood me up tonight. I figure you might as well have it instead. As a matter of fact, I think they'll suit you better."

Inside the box was a pair of art deco earrings, flashing with diamonds and sapphires. She decided they couldn't be real.

"They're real," said Jonny, "so don't lose 'em. They were going for a song at a place in the Burlington Arcade. I was picking up something to take Mom, and I couldn't resist these as well."

"I can't believe it."

"So, you see, I'm not really a louse."

"Well, thanks." She felt uncomfortable.

"Why do you want to make documentaries?" asked Jonny, sensing her embarrassment and changing the subject. "I'd think you'd want to be an actress. You've got the face and the bod for it."

"I can't act."

"Who cares about that?"

"I'd care."

"I never understood the appeal of making documentaries. I was in the middle of shooting a great movie about the razing of the Amazon forests. It's got lots of documentary type stuff in it, but it's also got a good plot. I'm a fiction man, myself. I go crazy over good stories, good characters, and great scenes."

" 'Was' in the middle of shooting? What happened?"

"The damned producers backed out just before I finished. Said I was taking too long and spending too much. The usual baloney."

In spite of her bitterness, she felt sorry for him. "I'd like to make documentaries with good stories and great scenes. Docudramas, in particular."

Jonny snorted again.

"What are you doing in London?" she asked.

"Trying to drum up business. I've got a terrific idea for a new movie."

"What's the story?"

"Have you heard of a model called Maria Benton? She was pretty well known in the eighties. Youngest model on several fashion magazine covers. She became a huge success overnight. Then some sordid facts began to emerge about her life: Her stepfather abused her, her boyfriend used to beat her up, her husband married her for her money and then abandoned her. She got involved in drugs and later turned to prostitution. Her life was in all the scandal papers for months."

"What happened to her?"

"She was beaten to death by her ex-boyfriend. Supposedly her husband was at home at the time and did nothing to save her."

"It sounds horrible. Why would you want to make a movie of her life?"

"It's not of her life, it's of a character's involvement with the three men: stepfather, boyfriend, husband. I made up the story itself. I just took the idea from reading about Benton."

"I think it would be stronger as a docudrama. People love to think they're learning something when they're watching television."

"I was thinking of this as a feature movie."

"Maybe that's your problem," Lark answered absently. "It's too depressing a story for a feature. But as a TV movie it's perfect. Especially if it was presented as a slice of a real girl's life."

"You may have something there. But I hate television. Everything's rewritten by damn committees. Then if the editors don't destroy a concept, the ads do."

Lark was getting cold. "I should go home."

"You live alone?"

"Yes."

"Why?"

"I like it."

He put his arm around her. Hastily, she pulled away. "What the hell are you doing?"

He looked confused. "Hey—it's Christmas Eve. We're both on our own—I just thought—"

"Forget it," she snapped, walking away from him.

He hurried to catch up with her. "What's the matter?"

It troubled her, how she still reacted to a man's touch. She felt it as an ugly current, signifying harm. But she said to Jonny, "I'm in love with someone else."

"Oh." He seemed nonplussed. "So am I. Does it make a difference?"

"It does to me."

He shrugged and smiled kindly. "Well, let's find you a cab. You look chilly."

When they finally were able to flag down a cab, Lark softened enough to offer to share it with him.

"So are you going to tell me your great guilty secret?" she asked as the cab drove off.

"I should never have let you look at my hand!" he wailed.

"Well?"

"It's this: I'm a drunk."

She was disappointed. "The line on your hand says it's a more serious kind of guilt than that."

His eyes narrowed. "Does it?"

She looked away. "Maybe it has something to do with Emmy."

"How'd you know my wife's name was Emmy?"

"Why—uh, you told me."

"Did I?" He leaned against the back of the seat. "We all do things we're horribly sorry about," he said slowly.

"Tell me what you're most sorry about."

"There're too many things, and they're all on a par."

"There must be something in particular. I don't mean drinking or gambling or being a lousy husband—but someone you betrayed or something that you did against every sense of honor."

"Why must there be?"

"Uh—why? Well, we all have something like that."

"What's yours?"

Lark hesitated. She wanted to give Jonny no inkling of who she was and yet she longed to hear him say he was sorry for what he had done to her. "I let someone down once," she said slowly.

"I have something sort of like that," Jonny said, just as slowly. "A kid I know was accused of something she didn't

do. I know she was innocent and I didn't do anything about
it."

"Why not?"

"Mostly 'cos I'm a coward."

"What happened to the 'kid'?"

"She disappeared."

"No! Murdered?"

"I hope not!" Jonny looked aghast. "I think she just ran
away."

"But she might have been murdered! That sounds exciting."

"You're a gruesome little thing, aren't you? God, I'm beat."
He closed his eyes again. "Who's this guy you're in love
with?"

She didn't answer.

The cab pulled up in front of her apartment building. Lark
stared at Jonny, thinking that it would take a week, at least,
before she could even begin to sort out her feelings about this
meeting.

"Here's my card," said Jonny, fishing it out of his pocket,
but then he took it back. "I moved—I forgot. This card's
obsolete. If you phone that number you'll get my brother, not
me." He carefully began crossing out the information.

"You sold your house to your brother?"

"He was the only person I knew who could afford it. I
needed the money sort of in a hurry. I'll write down my hotel.
I'll be here another couple of weeks. Maybe we could get
together again before I go."

"Maybe."

"How about New Year's?"

"I'm busy New Year's."

"Well. Thanks for your company. Maybe we'll do a movie
together sometime."

"Maybe."

A quick handclasp, and she got out.

CHAPTER THIRTY-TWO

"LET'S stroll around the office first," said Jack. "I'll introduce you to some of your colleagues. We're all quite informal here."

The woman in charge of development, where Lark would be working, was a large-busted, long-haired woman called Nellie. She wore thick glasses and had a booming voice. When Jack left Lark alone with her, it took a few minutes for her to feel comfortable. But before long, Lark felt she had made a friend. The offices did seem informal, yet underlying the casual "cheerios" and friendly handshakes was an atmosphere of efficiency and urgency.

There were two other people in the basement offices doing the same thing as Lark. Margaret and Rob worked part-time. Margaret was an aspiring stand-up comic and Rob was an actor. The three made friends quickly. They called her "Malarky" and teased her about how hard she worked. Sometimes they all went to a pub after work or to a movie. It was nice to have friends her own age again. Lark's office was windowless. Margaret and Rob pasted photographs of their families and funny posters to try to liven up their cubicles, but Lark's remained as bare as it was when she first arrived. They tried to convince her to bring in photographs of her family.

"They're all dead. Who wants pictures of dead people on the walls?"

"Then put up a poster."

"Waste of money."

"How about if we mailed you a postcard? Would you put that up?"

"Depends if I liked the picture," she said, laughing.

Right from the beginning Lark loved her job. She enjoyed reading scripts, even the bad ones—and there were plenty of those. She didn't have to be at the office until nine-thirty but she usually worked late, staying at least until six-thirty. Sometimes she was so engrossed in a script that she took it home to read. More than once Nellie passed along some compliment that had filtered its way down to her from the "Upper Floors," as they were called.

No one but Lark took the unsolicited submissions seriously. She read each one carefully, and filed away in her mind its positive features, and the poorer aspects that made it fail.

She loved the work, it was true, but she was also grateful to have something that kept her from thinking about the past, and Susan, and her extraordinary meeting with Jonny. Most of all, she was grateful to be able to focus her attention on something other than her haunting yearning for Dom. In spite of what she had read and heard about time being a cure for just about anything, time had done nothing to soften the longing she still felt for him. Her encounter with his brother had reinforced this. She knew she would never see Dom again, but when she was alone in her flat he was in her thoughts constantly. Where was he, just now? Was he asleep? What was he wearing? What was he thinking? Sometimes the image of his face floated in front of her totally unexpectedly, and it took all her inner resources to overcome a passion so intense it took her breath away.

No, she did not mind staying late at the office.

Carl continued to be her closest friend and advisor in London. He was interested in every aspect of her life, giving her affectionate encouragement and advice. He urged her to see a therapist in order to resolve not just the adjustment to her new face, but to deal with having been raped. But Lark refused.

"I don't trust anyone," she declared firmly. He seemed disturbed and she softened. "I don't mean I don't trust *you.* I've told you more than I meant to tell anyone. But I can't share any more with you—or anyone else. That life ended. The girl died."

He shook his head. "The girl did not die," he said quietly. "You will discover this for yourself when you are called upon to find her."

"She'll never be found," Lark vowed. Then she determinedly changed the subject and flashed him an affectionate smile. "By the way, when is my education going to be complete?" Carl was as generous as ever in taking her to shows, in encouraging her to read the newspapers, and helping her understand the political situation.

He was taken aback by her question. "I hope my own education will never be finished, and I hope yours won't be either. That is the trouble with Americans. You think your education is over once you graduate."

"But eventually don't you think you'll know all there is to know? I'm beginning to feel like I do already."

"There is always more to be learned."

"Why do I get the feeling you're grooming me for something? Have you discovered that I'm a long-lost princess who eventually has to return to her country and her people?"

He smiled at her. "Sort of."

"Are you grooming me?"

"Later you will look back and say I was grooming you," he said, and his voice was sad. "But remember this: I did it for your sake also."

"I don't know what you're talking about," she complained.

"I am talking about the fact that you are a very special woman with a great deal of untapped potential. I hate to see human beings wasted in this world. There are too many rubes. Bah. I do not want you to be wasted."

"Well . . . thanks." She added impulsively, "It's hard to remember that I owe you so much. I really do feel as though we're related in some way."

"I am glad about that. For the time being let us forget that you owe me anything."

She had been at work three months when she came across a screenplay that engrossed her as no other script had so far. It was called *Autumn Purple,* and it was about the effect of a father's suicide on his family. It brought tears to her eyes, and it made her laugh out loud too. The script needed a rewrite, but she was impressed enough to recommend a second reading.

After describing the plot, she finished her report by writing: "*Autumn Purple* is one of those rare screenplays that entertains, informs, and has an emotional depth in just the right combination. It has humor and yet it is deeply moving. It's also topical, since suicides, especially of heads of families, have become sadly frequent in recent years. Naturally the script needs to be rewritten and some of the plot restructured, but I strongly urge a second reading: A television movie made from this script would be a terrific success."

On the strength of her recommendation, Nellie sent the manuscript upstairs for another reading, although she had no great expectations for it. Some weeks later, she stopped by Lark's office.

"Mr. Cavendish wants to see you," she said in a puzzled voice. "He's our vice president."

"What does he want to see me about?"

"I don't know. He's on the top floor. His secretary will show you to his office."

Lark's first thought was that someone had discovered she lied about her degree in film. She was shown into Mr. Cavendish's office. He sat behind his wide desk and waved her to a chair.

"You must be Lark Chandler," he said, staring at her, his chin in his hands. "How odd that we've never met."

"We are on different floors," she pointed out, not bothering to add that there was very little interchange between the basement readers and the executives on the fourth floor.

"We were a bit taken aback by your rave report on *Autumn Purple*," he said, glancing at the manuscript in front of him. "It's very unusual to find something like this that's unsolicited."

"I was surprised too."

"We got a second opinion, as you suggested. It agrees with yours. I wonder how many people would have spotted the potential in this particular script."

"Oh, I think most people would have," Lark answered. "You can tell by the structure, by the dialogue, that it's a very professional job. With some rewriting—"

"That is what I'm coming to," interrupted Mr. Cavendish. "We'd like to give you a chance at tackling a rewrite of *Autumn Purple* yourself. Since you view it so favorably, we feel you might know just how to proceed."

She was dumbfounded. "I'd love to," she said, quickly. "I do have some ideas for it."

"You're a writer yourself, aren't you? Jack mentioned you had a screenplay or two up your sleeve."

Where on earth had Jack gotten such an idea? Lark recovered and said, "Yes, I do." She would stay up all night writing one.

"You'll need a word processor to get to work on this. I've spoken to Andrew about moving you temporarily to the office next to my secretary's. There's a computer in there you can use. It's got a screenplay program installed so that will make it easier for you. What sort of computer do you use at home?"

"I don't have one."

He was shocked. "But you said you're a writer! You do know how to use one?"

She hated saying that she didn't. She nodded and then qualified the nod by saying, "It's been a while, though. I'll stay late tonight and refresh my memory."

"Very well. Ann, my secretary, will set you up. Here's your baby . . ." He handed her the screenplay. "We look forward to seeing what you do with it. Good luck."

Ann took her into the neighboring office which seemed to be unoccupied except for a smallish monitor and keyboard on the desk. The printer was on the neighboring table.

"This is where it turns on," Ann explained, "and here are the programs you can use. You'll want the screenplay one, won't you? Here it is. We may as well put it in now. There. Here are all the instruction books if you need to look up anything." She glanced at her watch. "I'll be here till six if you have any questions."

"Thank you," said Lark, sitting down in front of the black and amber screen.

Things had happened so quickly she could hardly believe it. It wouldn't be too hard to learn how to use the machine, would it? It looked just like a typewriter. Not that she could type all that well, but at least she knew the basics.

She picked up the instruction booklet and got to work.

CHAPTER THIRTY-THREE

FOR six weeks, through the damp, chilly spring, Lark wrote and rewrote *Autumn Purple*. She loved working on the script. She showed the first draft to Jack, whose understated praise made her ecstatic. It was completed at the end of May and she eagerly waited for production to start.

When she asked Jack why it was taking so long, he laughed.

"These things can sometimes take years. And it's possible that the film'll never be made. My advice to you is to move on to another screenplay."

"I've asked for one but Mr. Cavendish says he's going to wait and see how *Autumn Purple* turns out."

"Write your own."

"Me? What made you tell him I'd already written a script anyway? I never told you that."

"If you went to film school you must have taken a screenwriting course."

"Oh . . . right."

"In any case, you ought to think about writing a treatment for a screenplay. We're always looking for innovative projects."

"Really?" Her mind began to race. Was it too early to suggest something on Groome?

Of course it was. This was London. What would they care about a flea-bitten congressman from New York?

"I'll think about it," she said, looking up.

Jack was gazing at her, the gray of his eyes almost silver in the fluorescent light of his office. They had become close friends in the five months that Lark had been at Stafford. His reserve somehow reassured her. But just now she glimpsed an ardor behind the reserve that startled her.

She stood up. "I'd better get back to work."

He glanced at his watch. "It's practically seven P.M." He sounded amused. "Isn't it time to call it a day?"

"There are a couple more things I want to get done."

"Let me take you to dinner instead," offered Jack, rising also.

Lark hesitated. They had gone to lunch on occasion, but dinner seemed different. As he helped her on with her jacket, and lightly touched her arm, Lark again felt a scary current coursing through her body. *Watch out.*

If Jack sensed her flinching, he gave no sign. They took a taxi to an Indian restaurant in Knightsbridge. Jack's inscrutable reserve throughout the meal relaxed her again. But afterward, as Jack walked her home, she felt tense again. Finally Jack paused in the middle of the sidewalk and turned to look at her.

"What's the matter?" she asked, stopping also.

"I was going to ask you the same question."

He took both her hands in his and when she tried to pull them away he simply held on more firmly.

"Look around you," he said, gently. "We're standing on Kensington High Street. There are thousands of people going past. I'm a friend, not a stranger. Now, tell me: Why are you afraid?"

Cars honked. A tall, double-decker bus lumbered past. Crowds of commuters pushed past them, annoyed they blocked the sidewalk. And the long English twilight was not yet over.

Lark smiled weakly at Jack. "I'm not afraid."

"Good." His silver eyes regarded her calmly. "Because now I'm going to kiss you."

Lark gulped. "But—"

"It's just a kiss." He half smiled at her. "We're still out

here, on the street, in public. If you get nervous, all you have to do is scream."

Her hands were still firmly held by him, and as his face bent toward her, Lark experienced an odd curiosity. After all, he was right: Nothing bad could happen to her out here in the street. Besides, Jack's expression was so kind. What would it feel like, to be kissed by him?

The kiss was so brief, Lark was hardly aware it had happened. Before she knew it, they were walking again, this time holding hands.

All Lark's tension came sweeping back as they walked the last block to her apartment building, but Jack said nothing about coming upstairs.

"Good night, Lark."

"Thank you," she said. "For dinner."

He laughed, lightly touching the back of her hair. She broke away from his gaze and unlocked her front door. He waited until she was safely inside before leaving. Neither mentioned the kiss again.

Autumn Purple was finally put into production. It took three months of shooting and then another month of postproduction work before it was aired in September. It was met with disappointing reviews and was then immediately forgotten.

Lark was crushed.

"Don't be," Jack advised her. "There are a million flops to every success. No one blames you for it."

But she couldn't help blaming herself. "I'm no good as a screenwriter," she told Carl miserably.

"Your problem is that you are too good. The script you showed me contained subtleties that were lost in the process of filming. In a way you have too much imagination and you take too much for granted. Try to think more like a regular person."

"I am a regular person."

His eyes were impenetrable but kind. "No, Lark, you are a very, very special person. Not just to me, but to a good many others as well."

"Gee, thanks," she said, still feeling despondent. "I don't

know what I'm doing at Stafford anyway. If I'm such a failure I'm never going to get ahead."

"Nonsense," he said. "Who says you are a failure? One project like this one is not enough to judge one's failure or even one's successes. What you must do now is to go on. Find another project to work on. Remember you have a great deal of experience in back of you to use in your writing."

She felt encouraged. "I'll tell you one idea I had that would be perfect for Stafford. I was going to talk to you about it after *Autumn Purple* was the big hit I assumed it would be." She laughed at herself. "But maybe it'd be worth pursuing anyway."

"Tell me."

They were sitting in his drawing room, late one Saturday afternoon, having tea. "Tea" was one of the loveliest of the English customs that Lark had encountered. She looked forward to it every day with pleasure, and had learned how to scorch the teapot with boiling water before putting in the tea leaves, and to pour the milk in the cup before the tea.

The tall windows were open for the September air was mild. The scent of new mown grass, fresh apples, and the warm tea made her feel completely at home. She had been in England over a year, spending much of her time in Carl's large country house, and by now it felt almost as much her home as her apartment.

"Well, it's this." She sat forward in the wing chair. "Last Christmas I met a movie director who was trying to sell a movie about a model called Maria Benton. His idea was to fictionalize the story and make it into a feature. But the thing sounded perfect for a TV docudrama. It has just the right amount of glitz and sordid glamour."

"Maria Benton. I have heard of her."

"Exactly. She's major enough so most people have heard of her, but minor enough so that her story will be something of a revelation. It was pretty ghastly."

"Yes, I see. Who was this director you met?"

"His name is Jonny Whitfield. Have you heard of him?"

Carl smiled. "Almost everyone has heard of him. What did you think of him?"

Lark grinned. "He's actually soft as a grape in spite of his fame. And I got the feeling he really needed work."

"Why not contact him?" Carl poured them both more tea. "If his movie is still for sale, you might be the best producer for it."

CHAPTER THIRTY-FOUR

A few days later, Lark took out Jonny's business card. It would be eight o'clock in the morning in Pacific Palisades.

Should she call?

Might Dom recognize her voice? She'd heard voiceprints were as identifiable as fingerprints. If he sounded like he recognized her voice she could always hang up.

Bracing herself, she dialed the number.

"Hello?"

Toni. Of course. They must be married by now.

"I'm trying to get in touch with Jonny Whitfield," she said in her best British accent. "I understand he no longer lives at this address, but I wondered if you would kindly give me his new telephone number. I'm calling from Stafford Productions in London."

"Just a moment." Toni cupped the phone with her hand but Lark heard her say: "Where's Jonny's number?"

She heard a muffled voice in the background and knew it was Dom's. She closed her eyes, feeling faint. *Dom's voice.*

A moment later Toni was back. "Hello? I have it—just a moment." She gave it to her.

"Thank you so much," said Lark, and hastily replaced the receiver. Her heart thumped wildly.

Eventually she reached for the telephone again. She needed this break. She needed Jonny's movie concept in order to get ahead.

She needed Jonny.

An answering machine responded to her call.

"Hello, this is Jonny Whitfield's answering machine. Leave a question at the beep. *Beep.*"

She spoke hurriedly. "Jonny, this is Lark Chandler. We met almost a year ago, last Christmas. I want to talk to you about that film you told me you were trying to sell here in London, the one about Maria Benton. I'm working at Stafford Productions now, and I have a feeling there might be some interest in it, if you haven't done anything else with it in the meantime. Give me a call."

The next day Jack took her to lunch at the Savoy and she told him her plan. He encouraged her to pursue it, but advised her against having too much faith in Jonny Whitfield.

"He's a boozing, ambitious overspender. But there's no question his movies are excellent."

Lark swirled the wine in her glass. She had a strong intuition that there was more on Jack's mind than work.

"Lark."

She looked up. "Yes?"

"I want you to come to my flat after lunch."

She drew in her breath. "No."

"I'll call the office."

"No."

"I do understand," he said quietly. "You're in love with someone else. You think you'll never care for me the way you care for this other man. He's hurt you so badly you can't bring yourself to trust anyone. Carl's told me enough to help me understand." He looked serious. "I still want you to come to my flat."

Strangely enough, Lark was not as reluctant as she'd thought. The memory of the last time they'd kissed so fleetingly on the street had lingered. It was true she would never love a man as she loved Dom, but did that mean she could never desire a man either?

Jack's flat, just off Parliament Square, was large and spacious, with tall picture windows overlooking Westminster Abbey and the Houses of Parliament. It had started to rain on their way there, and now huge drops spattered against the glass. Lark stood looking out, feeling nervous.

Jack came to stand behind her and wrapped his arms around her waist.

"Do you want to talk?" he murmured.

She shook her head.

"You're a very beautiful woman. I adore long hair." He kissed it. "I adore blue eyes." He turned her so she faced him and he kissed her eyelids.

She stood motionless, feeling curious but only half-alive.

His mouth trailed down her cheek to her mouth. His tongue gently pried open her mouth. Lark felt her body grow rigid.

Jack drew away. He was laughing. "Now, now, my dear. This won't do at all."

"I'm hopeless, Jack. I really am. I don't know what to do."

His arm around her, he led her to the sofa. "That's nonsense. You don't do anything when you make love. You simply enjoy yourself."

"I can't," she whispered.

He laughed again. "You most certainly can—and will."

They sat down. Jack drew her into his lap and kissed the side of her head. "You don't have to do a single thing," he murmured. "Don't think about anything. Just feel—can you feel this?" He kissed her ear.

"Yes."

He massaged the back of her neck. "Can you feel this?"

She nodded.

"That's all you have to do. Just feel. Can you feel this?" He drew a line along the bridge of her nose.

She smiled.

"And this?" He outlined her mouth.

He kissed her, and this time when she tasted him a ripple of excitement coursed through her.

"That's my girl," murmured Jack. He unbuttoned her blouse.

Lark felt increasingly eager. Her fear that at any moment she would be jolted into frigidity diminished with every ca-

ress. Her body responded to Jack even if her heart was locked
away.

The rain spattered more loudly against the window. The
sound was soothing. Lark slid into a realm of physical sensation under Jack's gentle eroticism. He slipped off her blouse,
and then he eased off her skirt. He unfastened her bra, and
continued to caress and play with her body.

He laid her on the sofa. Lark's eyes flickered open and she
watched him undress and reach for a condom in his jacket
pocket. When he came to her again, he whispered.

"All right?"

She nodded. She received him with a low gasp. For a moment she thought she was drowning.

"That's my girl," said Jack, tenderly. "My brave girl. Do
you feel this?" And he lightly ran his finger along the bridge
of her nose again.

Lark smiled, relaxing. It felt good, being held in a man's
arms like this. She sensed the wonder of such a unity, the
perfect match between a man and a woman. Shyly, she stroked
his back, as his movements became more intense. She savored
the sensation of his rhythm and let herself be carried with it.
It was easier than she'd expected. There was nothing to it,
really. The sensations were already there, building.

"Lark—" gasped Jack.

He slowed after a while, sweating and holding her tightly.

"All right, my girl?"

She nodded, smiling into his eyes. "Yes, quite all right
now."

But that night she dreamed of Dom. They were standing
beside a lake, shaking hands good-bye. They turned away
from each other, walked a few yards, then both turned back
simultaneously and rushed into each other's arms, clinging as
though they would never let go.

Lark awoke, her heart pounding, her face wet with tears.
Jack had his back to her and she gazed at it in bewilderment.

Would she carry this love she felt for another man with her
to the grave, she wondered? Did one ever outgrow something
like this? Surely it would come to an end eventually, or be
replaced by something else?

But in her heart she knew there would always be an emotion painfully strong when she thought of Dom. She might never see him again, but he was a part of her, and he would remain a part of her for the rest of her life.

CHAPTER Thirty-Five

S EVERAL days passed before Lark went home with Jack and they made love again. It was even easier this time, and afterward she tried to tell him how grateful she was. He cut her off.

"Forget it, love. I don't want your thanks."

"Why not?"

"Would you like it if I told you how grateful I was to you for making love with me?"

"No."

"This is to do with how much I like you, and I hope you like me. It has nothing to do with gratitude."

Still, she felt grateful. She did not love Jack, but he inspired passion in her, and desire. Their lovemaking sessions became more exciting and she looked forward to them more and more. Sometimes she spent whole weekends with him. They even paid weekend visits to Carl at his Sussex house. Lark couldn't figure out what Carl felt about her relationship with Jack. He never spoke of it.

It was amazing to realize she had been in England for almost a year and a half! The chilly autumn winds swept across the downs, cheering and invigorating her.

Jonny's phone call came in the middle of the night when she was sound asleep.

"Lark? It's Jonny. I just got your message—been out of town—no one passed it on to me. What's your news?"

"Just a moment." Lark laughed. "Let me wake up."

"Christ, is my timing off? Why'd I think it was the middle of the morning there? Of course, it's the middle of the night—"

"That's okay." She sat up and gathered herself together. Her clock said three-thirty. "I just wondered if you had ever got some interest in your project about the model—Maria Benton."

"No. I gave up on that one."

"I think I can get some interest where I work."

"Where's that?"

"Stafford Productions. I'll give you the address."

She heard a kind of amazed silence then Jonny said hurriedly, "Let me get a pencil . . . Okay, I'm back. I can't believe this. How'd you remember who I was?"

"Don't be silly. Okay, here's the address. Send it as soon as you can."

"Only thing is, I want to direct it. I'm not willing to give it up on any other terms."

"It'd be great having your name on the credits."

Jonny laughed. "That's nice of you. Do you really think they might be interested?"

"Maybe."

"I can't believe it. But I'll send the treatment off anyway. Can't hurt, can it?"

"No, it can't hurt."

The treatment arrived, special delivery, within two days. Lark read it over carefully. She was sure the thing could be successful—if it were done as a docudrama. She just wasn't sure whether Jonny would agree to that.

She showed the treatment to Jack, who passed it along to Andrew. At the next development meeting, *Maria Benton* was at the top of the list for discussion.

Lark was ready with her pitch. Some of her listeners had tears in their eyes as she described some of Benton's story. She ended by saying, "Jonny Whitfield would direct. It's his project."

"I know of Jonny Whitfield," said Andrew dryly. "He's an alcoholic sponge. He's gone over budget on every project he's ever worked on. We wouldn't be safe letting him near this thing."

"Don't worry," Lark said rashly. "This thing means a lot to him. He'd be fine."

The upshot of the meeting was that Lark was to write a draft for the screenplay and show it to Jack. If he liked it, they would discuss it again.

She telephoned Jonny from her office that afternoon.

"They want me to write a screenplay," she told him, excitedly.

Jonny was annoyed. "But the screenplay's already written. Why'd they want you to do it?"

"Oh! I didn't realize you'd already written it. I thought you'd just gotten as far as the treatment."

A silence followed, and she knew that he was suspicious.

"I don't want to lose control of this thing," he said after a moment. "Initially all I wanted were investors so I could put the project together myself."

"I understand that, but it didn't work." She was disappointed in his reaction. "I had enough trouble convincing the big shots in the company that you'd be able to stay on the wagon long enough to direct the damn thing."

"Okay, okay. Don't get huffy. Let me think."

She waited, then broke in on his musing. "Look, why don't you send me the screenplay you wrote? If it seems right, I'll pass it along. If not, maybe you could come to London and we could work on it together."

"That's a good idea," he said at last. "I'll be there this weekend. See you." He hung up.

Thinking about the project long and hard in the next few days, Lark got more and more excited. Working with a famous director—even if he did have a reputation for alcoholism and absenteeism—would be a feather in her cap.

Jonny telephoned from his hotel in Belgravia on Saturday morning.

"I'm here," he said. "Can I come over?"

Her apartment still had only the mattress on the floor. "Maybe I should come there," she suggested.

"Fine. I'm waiting."

She wore navy blue corduroy pants and a large Aran cardigan which she had splurged on earlier in the fall. Her usual thriftiness with regard to clothes was beginning to pay off. She already had over five thousand pounds in the bank.

She took the underground to Belgravia. The hotel receptionist telephoned up to Jonny then waved her to the elevator.

Jonny looked disheveled and hung over. His collar was open, his shirttail hanging out. He grinned and waved a glass filled with what looked like a Bloody Mary in front of her.

"Want one?"

"We're here to work," she said, irritated. She snatched the glass from his hand. "Excuse me."

Before he realized what she was doing, she had poured the contents down the sink.

Jonny sank onto the bed in amazement. "What the hell?"

"No drinking while we work. If I'm able to sell this thing there'll be no drinking while we're shooting either. I'm serious about this, Jonny. It means a lot to me. If you want to work on it with me, fine. If not, we'll pay you the standard fee for a treatment and say good-bye. It's your choice."

"Okay," he said sullenly.

"Where's your manuscript?"

Jonny pulled it out from his suitcase. "Here. Why don't you look it over first and then we'll discuss it?"

She sat down at the desk. Jonny stretched out on the unmade bed and appeared to go to sleep. Lark was a quick but thorough reader. She saw at once what needed to be changed, what was exactly right, what needed to be filled in.

Within an hour they were sitting side by side at the desk. Jonny took notes and argued. Lark argued back.

Oblivious to the passing time, they stayed there until past midnight. When, exhausted, Lark staggered home, she was elated.

The thing would work. It had to.

Chapter Thirty-Six

"**H**OW friendly are you with this Jonny Whitfield fellow?" asked Jack.

They were lying in his wide bed late one Sunday morning in early December. Cold snow blew against the large windows.

"We have a business relationship."

"How long have you known him?"

"Over a year. We met last Christmas. Why?"

"You know he's married?"

"He's actually divorced now."

"You know he's an alcoholic?"

"Yes."

"I'll grant that he's a genius, but he's also a mess. He's gone way over budget on every movie he's ever touched."

"Not this one. I'm going to keep tabs on everything."

"How do you know so much about him?"

"I—I read the papers. He's told me some stuff himself."

Jack lazily stroked her breast. "Don't you think it's about time you told me a bit more about yourself?"

"Like what?"

"Who is this fellow you're in love with?"

She was silent.

"Don't want to talk about it?"

"I'm sorry."

"I'm in love with you, Lark." His voice was low. "I fell in love with you that first night we met. I expect dozens of men

have told you that, for you have a face that any man would fall
for. But I wanted you to think that I was different. That I
really cared. Cared enough to wait for you to care too." He
took a deep breath. "I want to marry you."

"I can't marry you." Her voice was strained.

"And that fact has nothing to do with Jonny Whitfield?"

"No, it's nothing to do with Jonny."

They were silent, then Jack shook himself. "How about
some breakfast in bed? I'll make eggs and toast. And don't
think I'm giving up on you. I'm going to ask you again, never
fear."

Lark lay back against the pillows. She knew that practically
all the women in the crew were head over heels in love with
Jonny, the irascible, tousled, charming director. She wasn't
surprised that Jack assumed she had fallen for him too.

Jack reappeared in the doorway. "Will you spend Christmas
with me? We could go away for a few days."

She was tempted. "Where?"

"I was going to suggest going to Ireland. I have a good
friend who lives in a town called Sneem. He'll be charmed to
have visitors. Why don't I give him a ring?"

"Ireland." Lark sighed. "It sounds lovely. I can't get away
for more than a few days, though."

"Then that's all we'll go for," promised Jack.

CHAPTER THIRTY-SEVEN

BY the following spring, filming for *Maria Benton* was almost complete. Lark had been given the title of associate producer, and although she knew the title was more honorary than practical, she took it seriously. She felt responsible for every aspect of the production. The production coordinator, a young man just out of film school, was supposed to locate sites, make sure the actors got to the sets on time, and arrange for refreshments for the crew. But Lark was almost always ahead of him. The production coordinator found her officious. Everyone else thought she was wonderful.

They thought so especially with regard to how efficient she was in dealing with Jonny. He did not have a single drink during the entire three months. It wasn't easy for Lark, but she kept their arguments about his drinking private so that no one knew how much she dogged him. Several times she intercepted an order for a bottle of scotch he'd sent out for. On occasion she even had to follow him into a pub and persuade him to return to the hotel with her.

Jonny disliked her interference and threatened to quit on more than one occasion.

"Go ahead," she replied calmly. "We can always find someone else to direct."

"One damn drink isn't going to make a difference."

"You know that it's never just one damn drink. If you get drunk you get hung over, if you're hung over you're late for work, and if you're late for work, the budget gets screwed up, and if the budget gets screwed up, I'm fired. So forget it. I'll get you some ice cream instead."

"Blah."

While they were working, Lark hardly saw either Jack or Carl. On the few nights she had off she usually went home to sleep. Most days she was up by five and in bed after midnight. She lost weight and circles formed under her eyes, but she didn't care.

"I'll catch up with sleep when this is over," she reassured Carl on the phone. "I don't have time right now."

Not until the night of the final wrap did she allow herself to relax. Jonny took her out for dinner. She was so exhilarated she barely blinked when he ordered a scotch.

"I'm allowed now, aren't I?" He grinned mischievously at her.

Sighing, she ordered a Watney's. Jonny changed her order to a bottle of Dom Perignon.

"I can't drink a whole bottle!" she protested.

"The waiters will finish it in the kitchen. Give them a treat." Jonny downed his scotch and ordered another.

"Did your brother ever get married?" asked Lark.

"Yes, about a year ago."

"Are they happy?" She didn't *sound* anguished, did she?

"Sure—why not?"

"I just wondered." She sipped the champagne.

"What made you do this?" he asked.

"Do what?"

"Put your heart and soul into one of my projects."

"Probably because I felt it was my project. I know you wrote it and directed it, but I produced it, virtually. It was my first major sell. It had to be a success. In order for it to be a success I had to put my heart and soul into it."

"That sort of makes sense," said Jonny. "But you don't seem to me to be the cut-throat asshole film producer type of guy. What exactly are you after?"

She wanted to say "Revenge," but she didn't. Not yet. Not as long as there was any chance that she might be tried and convicted as Penelope Houten, murderer, and sent to prison for a crime that Justin Groome had committed. She didn't trust anyone—especially not Jonny.

And yet, the better she knew him, the better she understood him. And forgave him, too. In some way, he was as much a victim of Groome as she was. Eventually, he would be the one to help her get Penny Houten vindicated. She felt somehow certain that, in the end, he would come through for her.

She decided to voice a decision that had been steadily growing in her heart all through the cold, wet winter. "I want to move to the United States."

"Oh, yeah? Why?"

"Because I have some ideas in mind for more docudramas, along the same line as *Maria Benton*."

"You mean of celebrities?"

"And politicians."

"What's wrong with making them here?"

"There are certain people I have in mind."

Jonny nursed his drink. They ordered dinner, and Lark thought he hadn't been paying attention to what she'd been saying.

But then, out of the blue, he interrupted something she was telling him about living in London.

"I don't think I've told you how grateful I am to you for making this possible," he said. "I was practically on my last legs when you called me."

"I didn't know that. I just knew you'd described a good idea."

"I'd like to repay you somehow."

"You already have," she said sincerely. "By doing your best with this. That's all I wanted."

He appeared not to have heard. "I could get you a job in the States," he said. "My brother is president of American Production Group in Los Angeles. They're always looking for people like you. I wonder if we could arrange for an H-One?"

"What's that?"

"It'll allow you to work for a company in the States without a green card. APG would have to say you're indispensable to them and that sort of bullshit. You'd only be able to work for them, no one else. H-One visas come in useful in hiring foreign actors or actresses."

"Oh." Her heart was thumping. "Might . . . your brother's company be interested in making docudramas like *Maria Benton?*"

"Dom's pretty innovative. We'll show him *Maria* and I think he'll be impressed. I'm flying back in a couple of days and I'll talk to him about it. I'm sure there's a way we can work this out."

The irony of it made her want to giggle hysterically.

"I'm not sure if it's the best thing," she managed to say.

"What? Oh, now you're nervous. Brace up—Hollywood's actually just a lot of tinsel covering the same old floorboards. You'll make it big there, I promise."

Chapter Thirty-Eight

CARL waited until after the edit was finished before he invited Lark out to celebrate too. He picked her up at her apartment on Saturday evening. She had slept practically solidly for two days straight. Now she felt refreshed and eager.

"Where are we going?" she asked as they left the city streets behind.

"Gravetye Manor."

"Goodness. What are we celebrating?"

"Your birthday," replied Carl equably. "The ides of March, remember?"

She groaned. "I'd forgotten. Is it really my birthday?"

"You'd better remember it, my dear, unless you want people to wonder."

"This is really nice of you." She leaned back against the soft leather seat.

"I understand Jack wants to marry you," said Carl after she'd caught him up with what had been happening on the set of *Maria Benton*.

"Did he tell you I'd turned him down?"

"Yes." Carl looked gravely at her. "But he thinks you will change your mind."

"I won't," replied Lark.

"What are your plans?" he asked. "Do you want to remain at Stafford?"

"No." She paused. "When I first came to you for help I was

so scared that I thought I'd never want to return to the States.
But lately I've begun to change my mind."

"This change of heart has nothing to do with Jonny Whitfield, has it?"

She didn't answer right away. The truth was that it did
have a lot to do with Jonny. More and more frequently she
found herself longing to be able to confess to Jonny who she
really was. She would love for him to be able to tell Susan that
he'd seen her and she was fine. She knew she wouldn't do it,
because she couldn't trust Jonny not to tell Justin Groome.
But the longing made her realize that she was, in some
strange way, still trapped by her past, despite her new identity.

As the car wound up the long drive to Gravetye Manor, she
felt more strongly than ever that she would never truly be free
until Penny Houten was vindicated and Justin Groome was in
prison. The only way that would ever happen was by returning to the United States and confronting him.

The car was parked. Carl had already gotten out of the car;
now he peered back inside.

"Are you all right, my dear?"

"Yes."

She climbed out and they entered the magnificent hall.
They were shown to a corner table near the blazing fireplace.
Carl ordered wine, but he hardly touched his glass. When he
wasn't looking, Lark glanced at the label.

"Mmm . . . Chateauneuf-du-Pape," she murmured, sniffing the glass. "I would say perhaps a seventy-nine—no,
eighty. Probably Chateau Fortia."

"Excellent," said Carl, so approvingly that she didn't have
the heart to tell him she'd sneaked a look at the label.

"Have you been sick?" she asked. He had lost a lot of
weight.

"I always had to watch my weight," he replied. "This is
something of a relief."

Lark was concerned, but if Carl didn't want to discuss it,
there was nothing she could do. He had always shied away
from personal questions. In spite of their closeness, she knew
little more about him than she had when they had first met.

Except she knew he preferred Kandinsky to Paul Klee and Samuel Becket to Jean Cocteau. And she knew he liked a Mercedes Benz better than a Jaguar.

She asked, "How did you decide to get into plastic surgery?"

He replied with a question of his own: "How did you decide to go into the television business?"

"I have no idea how it happened."

They both laughed.

"I still don't know why you've been so nice to me," she sighed. "I don't see you bringing your other patients to Gravetye Manor."

"Ah, you do not know where I take my other patients." He eyed her affectionately. "But, please, no more of this 'patient' business. Let us admit that you can no longer be considered my patient. We are fast friends now."

She smiled, but a vague premonition troubled her. It was clear Carl had something else on his mind.

It wasn't until they were driving back to Carl's house in the chocolate Mercedes that Carl said, "You didn't answer my question earlier. About Jonny."

Lark started. "I'm sorry. Jonny? No, my wanting to go back to the States has nothing to do with him."

"Forgive me," said Carl, "but Jack mentioned you are in love with another man. Naturally, I am curious."

She laughed. "It's not Jonny, if that's what you're wondering."

"A man you left behind in America?"

They were stopped at a red light and, glancing at him, Lark found his questioning eyes fixed on her.

"I can't talk about it," she said.

"I understand."

"But you asked about my plans. Jonny Whitfield thinks he could get me a job at American Production Group in Los Angeles. He has connections there."

"Ah. So." He sounded pleased. "It is just the right move for you to make."

"Have you heard of the American Production Group?"

"It is a well-known company." He drove faster. "Doesn't Jonny Whitfield have a brother who works there?"

"Yes." She swallowed. "Dom Whitfield is the president."

"When will you go?"

"Nothing's definite. Jonny just said he'd try to fix me up with something. Everyone knows how unreliable he is."

"But if a job offer comes through, you will take it." It was a statement, not a question.

"I haven't definitely decided anything."

"I would like you to take it."

Lark regarded him curiously. He stared at the road ahead.

"Why?" she asked.

"I want you to meet Dom Whitfield."

"Why?" she repeated.

He smiled. "I want him to see you as you are now."

Lark's face went white. "I don't understand."

"Lark, dear," he said, very softly, "you do not really believe I would have done so much if you were a perfect stranger?"

She could hardly breathe.

"Let us wait until we're home," suggested Carl, as he turned off the motorway. "I will explain there."

"Are you kidding?" shouted Lark.

Carl looked amused. "You have wondered from the beginning why I took such a special interest in you."

"You said it was because you liked me."

"I do like you. I like you much more than I expected to."

"So I was right—you were expecting me that first day I arrived in London."

"You are very bright. I am surprised I was able to convince you so easily that I had no motive besides that of helping you."

"I forced myself to be convinced. I needed you to fix my face."

"And I need you now."

They reached his house. He pulled up in front, not bothering to park in the garage. "Let us go in."

In the living room Carl went over to the window, drew open the curtains, and stood looking at the darkened lawn outside. The room was cold without a fire.

Lark sat tensely on the edge of an armchair. "Well?"

"I am going to tell you a story. It is the story of three friends. They were at Harvard University together. One was in law school, the second in business school, the third in medical school. Yet they were close friends because they had been roommates as undergraduates. They were also all in love with the same woman."

"Oh, boy," Lark muttered sarcastically. But she was rigid with suspense.

Carl came to sit in an armchair across from her. "Each did his best to win her. In some ways she loved them all equally. But in the end the lawyer won her. He had moved to Washington and become a shooting star in the field of politics. It seemed he was successful at whatever he did. He married her. His name was Steve Whitfield."

Lark was so jittery she shot out of the chair and began to walk back and forth in front of the darkened fireplace. Carl appeared not to notice.

"The other two friends also moved to Washington. The doctor became a well-known plastic surgeon. The businessman turned to politics."

"Justin Groome," breathed Lark.

"Yes. Steve's marriage to Susan had strained the friendship between the three men. Or perhaps life itself strained it. Justin did not do well in the world of politics, in spite of strong family influence and pressure. Steve, who came from nowhere and had nothing, always did a little better. When they finally ran against each other for election to Congress, there was very little liking for each other left." Carl paused. "The doctor continued to love Susan as much as he ever did.

"One day Justin Groome came up with a plan that would leave Susan free for the doctor and the seat in Congress would be made free for himself. The idea was to help the House Un-American Activities Committee lay a trap for Steve. He tried to get the doctor to help him. The doctor had come to the States from Eastern Europe and was still trying to get American citizenship. Groome promised he could get it for him if he participated in this business. He also swore that Susan would never find out what he had done. The doctor refused. But

Justin went ahead anyway. On the basis of various taped recordings and secret testimony that he gave, Steve was ruined professionally. About a year later, he committed suicide. Justin had not expected that. He had expected Susan to divorce Steve when he was accused of being a Communist. But she stood by him right to the end.

"A year later Susan got engaged to the doctor. They were very much in love. But the day before they were going to be married, she broke off their engagement. She had been told it was the doctor who was responsible for Steve's suicide. The doctor left Washington and he never saw her again."

Lark sat down again.

"Justin Groome convinced her of this lie. He thought he could have Steve's wife as well as his seat in Congress. The doctor was determined that he never would. He made sure he knew everything she was doing—without her knowing. His love for her turned into a kind of obsession. He discovered she was going to have a child—his child. Oh yes, men and women slept together before their wedding nights back in those days too. Steve's son was ten years old at the time. Her second son was born in New York City some months later."

Lark knew what was coming even before he said the next sentence. She had known it ever since he had begun the story.

"She named him Dominic. He was a bastard, but she never revealed his father's identity—not even to him. That much I know. Of course, I was the doctor. You already guessed this."

"Yes," she said, her voice filled with pity.

Carl's face was unnaturally pale. "You see why I have devoted so much time to you, and why I want you to take the job that Jonny has promised you. You must take it. You will take it."

"No, I don't see," she tried to sound calm in the face of his fervidness. "What do you want me to do?"

"I want you to meet Dominic, to make friends with him. I want you to make him fall in love with you . . ." She started to protest and he dismissed her objections with a wave of his hand. "Yes, I know he's married, but that won't matter. I want you to make him give you his all, his entire trust. If he trusts you, and then you tell him about me, he will accept me as his father."

She shook her head. "It's impossible."

"Impossible, no! It is the only way! I want my son to know me before I die. To acknowledge me as his father. It is the only wish I have left."

"It's impossible for me to do this," she repeated. "Why don't you talk to him yourself? I'm sure he'll listen to you without my acting as an intermediary."

"The truth is," Carl replied more slowly, "I do not know how much his mother told him. But even if she told him nothing, you may be sure she will repeat Justin's lies to him, if she finds out I have been seeking out her son."

"If he believed what Justin said, nothing I could do would make a difference anyway."

"If you made him trust you, if you persuaded him—"

"I can't do it. I have my own reasons, believe me. This is something I can't do."

A silence ensued. Carl seemed to relax a little, but it was the posture of a cat about to spring. For a brief, strange moment Carl reminded her of Justin Groome. She shivered.

"You have to do it," Carl said, his voice low and emphatic.

"I don't have to. Even for all I feel I owe you, I don't have to do this." She tried to sound casual, but it didn't work.

"Then I have not made myself clear. I have been watching Susan—through various means—ever since Dominic was born. I have watched him grow up, oh, not me personally, but I have minions who have watched him and reported to me. I watched him take care of his mother. I watched her move to the country. And I watched you, too, Penelope Houten. I know everything about you. I know about your farm, and how your father died. I know that you are an accused murderer. I can ruin you."

She shrank back.

"I do not mean to frighten you," he went on. "I do not want to ruin you. It is just that there would be no point in my telling you secrets if I did not know a few of yours. It keeps us both safe from each other."

"The doctor who came to me . . . Dr. Smith . . ."

"He was no doctor. He was a man I hired to speak to you. And naturally I arranged for you and Jonny to sit together at the concert on Christmas Eve. I hoped you two would become friends. I have been very patient up till now."

"What good would it do you to betray me?"

"You want freedom from your old identity; I want Dominic as my son. Together we can win both these things. We are not playing chess here, exchanging a pawn for a pawn, or a knight for a knight. We are in league together. I have created you anew. I have made you more beautiful than you ever dreamed. Now you must do something for me."

"I'll pay you for my face. I swear it. I always meant to."

"Will you pay me for the time I counseled you? For the lessons I gave you in art and music and theater and politics? No—no, my dear, our relationship is far more binding than that of mere financial payment. I have made you into a cultivated, sophisticated woman of the world. When he meets you, Dominic will feel life is not worth living without you. I know my son."

"Why on earth didn't you tell Susan the truth—that it was Justin who destroyed her husband?"

"In the beginning I was too angry, and after I left I felt there was no point."

"No point!" exclaimed Lark, astounded. "No point in telling Susan the truth about a man she thinks is her friend? You're nuts!"

"She trusted Justin's word without giving me a chance. It still seems incredible to me that she did that, while she said she loved me. There can be no love that is not based on trust."

"You should have at least tried to tell her. Let her make up her own mind."

"And you?" he said, sadly. "Why didn't you tell her?"

"About what?"

"Am I wrong in assuming that it was Justin who raped you?"

Lark stared into the black fireplace. "I guess I understand what you mean," she said finally. "In a way I almost blamed Susan for letting it happen. I certainly blamed her for trusting him."

"So you see."

"But I still can't do it. Dom's married and to me that does mean something."

He waved a hand in the air. "This makes no difference."

"It makes a difference to me." She paused. "I wish I could help you, but I can't. You chose the wrong person."

"Nonsense. You will help me. You do not want to give up everything you have struggled so hard for simply because of a principle, do you? It would be a waste of your life. A terrible waste. A murderer would find it hard to get any sort of work in television while she was in prison—or in the gas chamber."

She shivered again. "I'm innocent, as a matter of fact. Didn't you find that out too?"

"Then why did you run away?"

"Maybe I'm a coward. But I'm an innocent coward."

"You cannot prove your innocence?"

She was silent.

"Or can you?"

"One day I will prove it."

He looked at her strangely. "I have a feeling there is something I don't know about you."

She shrugged. "Anyway, I can't believe you would actually ruin me like that. You're a decent human being. I can see that you are. You've been decent to me."

"Yes, up to a point. But I'm also ruthless. Do not underestimate me."

They gazed at each other. Lark knew she was at this man's mercy. She knew she would try to meet Dom, and to do what Carl requested. She had to, or else Carl would reveal her true identity to those from whom she was hiding.

Because in the shadowy recesses of her mind, to where she constantly shoved him, lurked the great grim figure of Justin Groome. She wasn't afraid of being accused of murder.

She was afraid of him.

Chapter Thirty-Nine

LARK'S flight for Los Angeles left Heathrow Airport on a Monday morning in late summer. She had with her one suitcase, her birth certificate, a British passport with an H-1 visa which had been secured for her by Dom's company, and seven thousand dollars in traveler's checks which she had saved from working at Stafford Productions for almost two years.

Accompanying her was Carl Bellamon.

"Do not be nervous," he'd said when he'd first told her he was going with her. "I'm not going to be an albatross around your neck."

"A what?"

"An albatross." A fleeting expression of annoyance crossed his face. "A symbol from Coleridge's poem, *The Ancient Mariner.* I suppose you have never read it."

"No, I haven't."

"I sometimes forget your background. Remind me to find a copy of the poem for you. Every educated person has read *The Ancient Mariner.*"

"I thought Californians didn't read anything besides menus and matchboxes," she teased.

"But I am not Californian. You have an advantage, my being your tutor. You will impress everyone."

Especially Dom, Lark thought, but neither mentioned his name.

They flew first class; Carl had made the travel arrange-

ments. In spite of what Carl had revealed to her and de-
manded from her, Lark's feelings for him had not changed.
She could not forget his kindness to her. She remembered
Susan's words: "Sometimes you never get over feeling grateful.
Maybe one day you'll understand what I mean."

She did understand now.

Besides, he was sick. She was sure of it, although he refused
to admit it to her. His face had thinned, his hands trembled.
Only two years had passed since they had met, but he had
aged about ten. She had a feeling he needed her as much as she
had needed him when she had arrived in England.

She feared Los Angeles might take some getting used to.
The sprawling city loomed smoggy and sun-scorched in her
mind. Carl had told her that nothing grew there naturally:
even the palm trees had been imported.

"Yuck," she responded. "And everyone's rich, dumb, blond,
and famous. Those who aren't belong to a cult."

He laughed. "You will find Los Angeles more complex than
you expect. Remember that modern myth began in Hollywood. That should appeal to you. And your milieu will be
quite sophisticated. You will not be able to get away with
looking dowdy anymore."

"I never look dowdy!" she flared.

"Some of your charity shop outfits are charming, but they
are not the first word in fashion, you must agree."

She huffily refused to talk to him for an hour, picking
occasionally at the faded blue jeans she wore.

As she gazed out the airplane window, Lark felt homesick
for England. She already missed the gentle, golden rain that
hardly seemed to get anything wet yet made such wondrous
greens. She missed the crooked, cobbled London streets with
their quaint bookstores and welcoming pubs. Already pulling
at her heart were the friends she had made.

Especially Jack. "Maybe you'll never know how much
you've meant to me this past year," she told him before she
left. "In a way you've brought me back to life, Jack. I wish I
could explain it to you. You showed me I had feelings and
responses I didn't know I had. You taught me about myself.

And I know you don't want me to feel grateful, but I am. I wish I could show you how grateful."

"Then marry me," he'd said.

"I can't. I have to take this job."

His long fingers coursed through her hair, as he regarded her with his familiar calm, friendly expression. "I wish you wouldn't go. What if I came after you?"

"Please don't," begged Lark. "It wouldn't work out."

"Perhaps not," he agreed, after a long silence. "But I do love you so."

There were tears in his eyes when she kissed him good-bye for the last time.

Her escape from Northkill had been made in such haste, she hadn't had the time to feel homesick, or to wonder whether she was making the right decision. But here, soaring thousands of miles above the earth on her way to another continent, she had time to think about it. Los Angeles . . . La-La Land . . . City of Angels . . .

She felt she was heading directly into the sticky web from which she had only barely escaped before.

They came in for landing at night. For over an hour Lark watched the cities of the sand gleam out of the desert darkness. Getting ever denser, the lights shook themselves into long, glittering threads of color as they approached the airport. Orange, green, yellow, white, red, but mostly orange to penetrate the fog or thick smog, they sprawled out seemingly forever until they were captured by the dark at one end and the sea at the other.

As the plane drew closer to the runway, the drops of light expanded and twinkled and Lark could see the cars moving below, like dewdrops slipping down fine silver threads of a spider's web. She knew what it was to be a fly.

The runway lights were purple. The braking plane threw her forward in her seat. She braced herself with the soles of her feet and then the brakes eased and she relaxed again, like a fly giving up the struggle as the spider pulls off its wing.

She had landed in Los Angeles.

The first night they stayed at the Beverly Hills Hotel. Lark went with Carl, although she was uncomfortable by his insistence on paying.

"You do not have much foresight in making travel plans," he remarked in the taxi. "What would you have done if I had not made reservations for us both?"

"Slept in the airport," she replied promptly. "And tried to find an apartment first thing in the morning."

"Before you find an apartment in Los Angeles, you will have to find a car."

"I'll find whatever it is I need." Still, she was glad of his company and dazzled by the resplendent strawberry pink hotel with the green and white striped awnings shading the windows.

It seemed Carl had a number of friends in Los Angeles. Many were transplanted Eastern Europeans, like himself. "We'll have no problem finding an apartment for you," he said. "One of my friends will know of something."

"What about you?"

"I have been invited to stay at a guest house of one of my friends. He is a doctor who lives in Beverly Hills. The house will be ready for me next week."

In the morning, Carl rented a car and drove her about. Under the glaring hazy sunshine, Los Angeles seemed a vast, strange maze of one- and two-story buildings, all roads and avenues looking alike. The freeways ran thick with cars and noise and smog. Back in the quiet luxury of the hotel, Lark felt she was in a fantastical oasis. Always, she felt out of place.

She also felt stuck. In London she had been able to walk almost everywhere. In Los Angeles, she was immobile without a car.

Carl soon took care of that. Early the following week he made an appointment for her to take driving lessons. Susan had taught her to drive, but she had had no occasion to drive in England. Now it was imperative that she learn well. She applied herself with her usual vigor and determination and within a week she was ready to pass her test. When she told Carl, he handed her a stunning bouquet of gladiolas and a set of keys.

She loved the brilliant red flowers. But, "What are these for?" she asked, holding out the keys.

"I will show you."

They went downstairs to the parking lot. Carl led the way to a silvery blue Honda Accord.

Lark balked.

"I can't accept this," she said, giving him back the keys.

Carl pressed the keys into her hand. "My dear," he said kindly, "do not take this as a reminder that I want something in return from you. You have been like a daughter to me. I have appreciated your company these past two years more than I can say. Take the car in the spirit it is given. I'd like you to have it."

She reluctantly accepted. "But what about your car?"

He nodded at the chocolate Mercedes parked next to her Honda. "I've always been comfortable with my old car, so I had it shipped out here."

The delicious brown sparkled in the sunshine. Lark laughed out loud with happiness. Everything seemed too amazing. She was going to start work in less than a week. The personnel director at American Production Group had been effusively welcoming when she had called and Lark was eager to start work.

As they headed back to the hotel lobby, Lark said, "I still need to find an apartment. I don't want my address to be the Beverly Hills Hotel when I start work."

"We'll look at the apartment I have in mind for you after lunch. I think you'll like it."

As soon as she saw it she knew it was perfect, just as Carl had known she would. Located in Santa Monica, which Carl told her had the largest English population in the United States, the apartment was on the second floor of a white stucco building, which was ornamented with rounded arches, turrets, and roofs tiled with cinnabar colored slates. It consisted of a hexagonal living room, a small bedroom, an even smaller kitchen, and a terrace from where, if she stood on tiptoe, she could glimpse the Pacific Ocean.

She started work the following Monday. The Hollywood offices of American Production Group were located on Holly-

wood Boulevard near Vine Street. The first few weeks, Lark
drove the surface roads to get to work, for she thought she
would never get used to driving the freeway. But the drive
took too long that way—almost an hour. The freeway took
half that time. And once she had gotten used to it, she found
she loved driving the freeways. It was like being in a Hover-
craft, sailing along a fast-flowing river. She hovered over the
city at sixty miles an hour, glimpsing hardly more than roof-
tops. And yet there were wonderful panoramas: faraway
mountains, sometimes white with snow; the Pacific Ocean
gleaming silver and deep blue, highrises clustered in one sec-
tion of the city, an island in a sea of still, shuttered houses and
green lawns.

In spite of pressure from Carl, Lark avoided seeking out
Dom. She heard his name mentioned frequently: It was inevitable, since he was the president of the company. But they
never met. The company was enormous, and its offices took up
an entire twelve-story building.

Carl took her out every weekend and sometimes saw her
during the week also. He took her to art openings on Colorado
and Melrose, to the Los Angeles County Museum, to the Hun-
tington Library. They went to movies, as part of her job. They
went to concerts and operas at the Dorothy Chandler Pavilion
and plays at the Mark Taper Forum and the Ahmanson The-
atre. He introduced her to his friends: doctors, famous actors
and actresses, museum curators, artists.

The house in Beverly Hills belonging to his doctor friend
was practically a castle, with a six-foot gray wall surrounding
three acres of lush greenery and exotic flowers.

"When you said everything that grew in L.A. was imported
I thought that meant there'd only be scrub brush and some
tumbleweeds," she said, as Carl showed her around the garden
on her first visit. "This is fantastic."

"What do you think of my cottage?"

The separate guest house, into which Carl had moved, was a
six-room villa, draped in wisteria. There were two black marble bathrooms, each one the size of her bedroom.

"Your friends must think a lot of their guests."

She never met them. Carl said they were in Europe for the

summer. They had given Carl freedom to use their tennis courts and kidney-shaped swimming pool. Lark loved to float on the water under the cornflower blue sky, reeling from the heady fragrances of camellias and jasmine, sipping chilled champagne. She thought she truly had come to the end of the world. Southern California seemed a legendary place, where nothing could ever go wrong.

"I'm in love," she told Carl.

He pricked up his ears.

"With L.A. I'm in love with L.A. I feel as though I've finally come home."

CHAPTER FORTY

AS associate producer, Lark was responsible for finding and developing new projects for the studio and working with authors on rewrites. Trent Weston was her immediate supervisor, a short, fair-haired, chubby director of development, whose mild manner belied the nervous perfectionism which he brought to his job.

He had gone to UCLA with Jonny Whitfield and had remained close friends with him, through all the peaks and valleys of Jonny's career. Jonny had described to Trent Lark's part in his "rescue" the year before and even without having met her he felt warmly toward her. The first time he took her out to lunch they talked mostly about Jonny. Trent was worried about him.

"Ever since Dom had to pull the strings on *Flaming Forest* he's been going downhill. You saved his life temporarily with that Benton thing. Now that's over, he's on the skids again."

"Why did APG pull out of *Flaming Forest?*"

"Jonny was taking too long and spending too much money. That's always been his trouble. He has no understanding of what goes into financing a movie. Once he's behind the camera all he can think of are these great ideas he has."

"But if they're so great, he should be allowed to make them!"

"In Hollywood, movie-making comes down to one thing: the bottom line. None of Jonny's mammoth projects has ever made money."

"But some of them are classics."

"Who cares? History, maybe. But in a place like Holly-wood, Jonny's a king without a kingdom."

"Couldn't APG hire him to do something for the time being?" suggested Lark. "What about *Razzle Dazzle?* We haven't got a director for that yet."

"Jonny wouldn't be caught dead directing a TV miniseries like that. He'd rather starve."

"If he's really so great he should be able to shape the televi-sion genre. He could do some good things with that script. Is Jeannette Gold going to star?"

"Yes, and that's another problem. Jonny's shacking up with her at the present. The two have a relationship that's loaded with gunpowder."

That evening, as Carl dropped her off at her apartment after a gallery opening, he said, "You seem happy, Lark."

"I am happy."

"And . . . Dom?"

"I never see him. He works on a different floor. It's as though he's in a different world."

"He is part of your world. You will try to see him."

But Lark was painfully reluctant. She was sure Dom would fiercely resent the sort of interference in his personal life that Carl was suggesting. She didn't want to lose her job. At first she had decided to work in television in order to make docu-mentaries, and eventually in order to get revenge on Groome. But now she knew she never wanted to leave the film indus-try. She was captivated by it: the excitement, the creativity, the famous names, the vast sums of money. No, she didn't want to ruin anything. She wanted to wait.

A little before Christmas, when she'd been at APG for three months, Carl asked her, "Are you going to try to produce something of your own?"

They were dining at Beau Rivage in Malibu. Their table was in a grotto from where they could see the waves tumbling gently onto the white sand below them. It was one of her favorite restaurants.

Lark licked the salt off the edge of her glass of margarita. "I do have some ideas. Want to hear one?"

"Certainly." He hardly touched the grilled red snapper on his plate. Mostly he sipped orange juice.

"It's for a television series along the lines of 'Mystery!' but with a difference. In that series, murder is the central pivot. In my series, the MacGuffin is the romance. The program would contain the same components that make 'Mystery!' so popular: terrific acting, excellent plots, and so forth. But they'd also be funnier and, naturally, more romantic."

"The 'MacGuffin'?" asked Carl. "What is that?"

Her eyes widened. "Don't tell me I know something you don't! The MacGuffin is a term Alfred Hitchcock used. It's the pretext for a plot—the jewels the crooks are smuggling or the secret agent the spies are after. In my stories the romance will just be the pretext for the plot. Exploration of character and relationships will be what the movies will be about. The romance is just a plot device."

"Why is it called the MacGuffin?"

"From a joke. Two men are on a train. 'What's in that package?' asks one. 'That's a MacGuffin,' the other answers. 'What's a MacGuffin?' asks the first. 'It's for trapping lions in the Scottish Highlands.' 'But there are no lions in the Scottish Highlands!' 'Well, then, that's no MacGuffin.' "

Carl laughed. "I like your idea. The romance as mystery."

Carl drove her home. When he pulled up in front of her apartment building, he said, "Have you seen Dominic yet?"

She shook her head, her earlier enthusiasm dissipating.

"I do not have all the time in the world," he said. "When are you going to see him?"

"He's president of the company! I can't just walk into his office and say 'Hi, I know your father.' "

"You are an imaginative girl," Carl said. "I am sure you can do better than that. But I am running out of patience."

"There's the office Christmas party next week. I'll probably see him there."

But Dom didn't show up for the party. Lark was relieved to learn he had gone east to spend Christmas with his mother. Not only was she sure he'd be furious at her interference in his life, but she was also terrified he would recognize her.

Wouldn't she recognize him, no matter what accident had
befallen his face?

"It was heavenly," she sighed to Carl when he asked her
about the party. "Just heavenly."

"Even though Dom wasn't there?"

She flushed. "I don't know what you mean."

"You have a new face, but it is still transparent," said Carl.
"Are you going to see him when he comes back?"

"Yes, I'll figure something out."

CHAPTER FORTY-ONE

OVER Christmas, Lark worked hard on her "Romance!" proposal. Trent was vacationing in Hawaii until the second week of January. As soon as he returned, she gave it to him. He handed it back after barely glancing at it.

"We already tried that some years back. It was a bomb."

"How could it have been a bomb? What did you do?"

"You can look at some of the tapes when you have a moment. Your secretary will show you where they are. No one will touch anything like this again. We lost hundreds of thousands on the project." He glanced at his watch and stood up. "We have a meeting in five minutes. Ready?"

"I'm ready." She was disappointed but not discouraged. Together they went down the hall to the conference room for a marketing strategy meeting.

Afterward, as Lark hurried back to her office (she was always hurrying, it seemed now), she turned a corner and smashed headlong into someone walking the other way. The pile of screenplays and notes she was carrying flew everywhere.

"Excuse me—"

"I'm so sorry—"

Lark reached for a manuscript and the man she had bumped into reached for another. Lark glanced up at him.

Dom was regarding her with the same piercing, tawny eyes that she remembered so well.

"I didn't mean to bump into you." He couldn't take his

eyes off her. "But you did turn the corner pretty fast. In a hurry?"

She gulped air. The edges of his dark hair were gray and there were deeply etched smile lines on the outer corners of his eyes. He looked years older than when she had seen him last.

He handed her the pile of papers he had collected. "I don't think we've met. I'm Dom Whitfield. And you're—?"

He had been regarding her with an expression of such intimacy that Lark was certain he had recognized her. Only now did she realize that he hadn't.

She pulled herself together and held out her hand. "I'm Lark Chandler. I'm fairly new here."

"Glad to meet you."

They got to their feet. Lark clutched the pile of papers in her arms. She felt as though she had been running hard.

She had a wild impulse to ask him how Susan was, how was their Christmas, did he like being married. She thought how surprised he would be if she threw herself into his arms, if she said, "It's wonderful to see you again! I've missed you so much!"

She couldn't help smiling.

"What's so funny?" asked Dom. He still hadn't taken his eyes off her.

"Just something I was thinking."

"I'm putting it together," he said slowly. "Lark Chandler. You're the Britisher who saved Jonny's ass last year."

"Did I do that?"

"That's what I heard."

"Definitely an exaggeration."

"Maybe." He glanced at his watch. "I'd better get going. Trent's expecting me. Nice to meet you."

He moved off down the corridor with his long, unhurried stride. Lark realized she'd better get to her office before her legs buckled.

She closed the door behind her. She had been sure that, when he saw her, Dom would have some suspicion of the truth. But he hadn't. She should feel relieved, and yet she felt disappointed too. If Dom's face were unrecognizable, she was sure she would still know him anywhere.

She sat down and stared at the manuscript that had been discussed at that morning's meeting. The words were dull, the plot undistinguished.

Her telephone rang.

"Yes?" she answered.

It was her secretary. "This is Rosa—Mr. Whitfield's secretary is on the telephone. Mr. Whitfield wants to know if you are free for a drink this evening after work."

"Uh—but I have a deadline."

"Lark," Rosa's Hispanic accent grew severe, "it is Mr. Whitfield."

"Yes . . . yes, I understand. Of course I'll do it."

Rosa laughed. "You sound as though you are dreading it. He is not that bad."

It would look very strange if she refused. Besides, wasn't this the opportunity she needed in order to tell him about Carl? Not tonight, of course. She wouldn't get around to it tonight. But if they became friends, eventually she would be able to tell him.

Rosa knocked on her door a few minutes later and poked her nose in the door. "He will come by at six."

"Thanks, Rosa."

"Are you afraid? He is very nice."

"I wish I'd known about the date before I came to work. I would have dressed up."

"You always look very nice."

"Thank you." But she wasn't as confident as her secretary about how she looked. Today she wore a midnight blue shirtdress she had found at a Salvation Army store. It was flattering but old-fashioned and dull. Even the secretaries at APG dressed like models. Today Rosa was wearing a black leather miniskirt, an orange silk sleeveless turtleneck, stockings, and black high-heeled patent leather sandals. Her sparkling brown eyes were outlined with brown and shaded with blue. Her lips were coral, and the color never seemed to wear off. And jewelry! Practically every finger had a ring on it. Mostly Rosa wore silver and turquoise. A silver cactus was pinned on her blouse.

Suddenly Lark's hand flew to her throat. She was still wearing the gold chain that Dom had given her for her birthday. She had never taken it off. Had he recognized it?

"What is wrong?" asked Rosa.

"Nothing." Of course he had not recognized it. Gold chains were something lots of people wore.

At a little past six she was ready and waiting. She hadn't been able to do any work since five. Might she say something that would make him guess? How could he not guess?

"There you are." Dom stood in the doorway. "Ready?"

For a moment Lark couldn't move. It seemed that the years they'd been apart had merely served to intensify the fierce love she had always felt for him.

Dom did not seem disconcerted by her lack of response. He couldn't take his eyes off her.

"I thought we'd go around the corner to Musso and Frank's," he suggested. "That way we can walk. Okay with you?"

She stood up and reached for her purse and jacket. "Sure."

About three blocks from the office, Musso & Frank's was one of the oldest restaurants in Los Angeles, and one of the most popular. It was already crowded when they walked in, but the waiter recognized Dom and led them to his favorite table in the rear. Dom ordered a vodka tonic; Lark a chablis.

Trying to feel relaxed, but overwhelmed by Dom's presence so near after all this time, Lark looked around.

"Have you been here before?" asked Dom.

"No."

"It hasn't changed since it opened back in the twenties. Probably the same tablecloths. Some of the waiters have been here for forty or fifty years." Dom sipped his drink. "Our family is very grateful for how you helped Jonny out of his mess. Did he ever thank you? He has a way of forgetting to."

"I didn't do much. I liked his idea for a television movie, and I arranged for it to be produced, that's all."

Dom nodded, regarding her intently. "Tell me about yourself. How did you get involved in the film industry?"

Lark smiled uncertainly, then cleared her throat, hoarse with nervousness. "It was sort of an accident."

"Are you happy at APG? Are we treating you well?"

She looked back at him, studying his familiar tawny eyes, the long nose, his firm, sculpted mouth, with an emotion almost akin to amazement. *This is Dom*, she was thinking, *Dom Whitfield. The man I've dreamed about and longed to see again all these years. And now here he was sitting less than three feet away and she could hardly speak.*

"Very well," she managed.

The wine helped. She drank it faster than usual. Looking amused, Dom ordered another.

"What are you working on at the moment?" he asked.

"I just finished the rewrite of *Razzle Dazzle*. It's scheduled for production next month."

"If we can find a director, that is," said Dom. "The woman who was going to direct got a better offer somewhere."

She remembered her conversation with Trent. "Why don't you hire Jonny?"

Dom shook his head. "This is a television movie."

"Does that make a difference?"

"It makes a difference with regard to his attitude." She heard the annoyance just below the impersonal tone. "We haven't got fifty million dollars to spend on this one."

"When we worked on *Maria Benton* in London he didn't overspend by a penny."

"I've heard that miracle was all of your making," said Dom giving her a sudden smile that made her heart soar. She dropped her eyes, flailing against the emotion that filled her. *This is him, the man I love, and he doesn't know who I am.*

"Have you written any proposals for us?" asked Dom.

Lark hesitated. She knew that Trent had been too hasty in turning down her "Romance!" concept, but she didn't want to appear to be going over his head by bringing it directly to Dom.

"I have something," Lark spoke slowly, "that I think the networks would jump at."

Dom's eyes flickered with interest. "What is it?"

"A television series filmed somewhat along the same lines as 'Mystery!' but it would be called 'Romance!' instead."

"We've tried it. It didn't work."

"Let me explain my idea. I'm talking about hour-long shows that combine humor, action, story-telling, and fun, strong characters. I'm talking about movies like *Romancing the Stone* and *Working Girl*."

"*Working Girl* wasn't a romance."

"It certainly was."

"Besides, those were multimillion dollar projects."

"That's just typical overspending. We could bring in a TV movie for a lot less."

"Have you taken a look at the romance package we put together a few years ago? It was a dismal flop. Audiences simply weren't interested. I don't know if romance is dead, but it didn't work."

Lark leaned forward in her chair, her pale face animated. "I'll tell you where you went wrong with your last project. You took contemporary romance novels that have a lot of sex in them and assumed that women were reading them for the sex. You missed the essence of the romance itself. You missed out on all the suspense. You missed out on all the tenderness."

"Then why is the sex in those books so heavy-handed?"

"Compare it to a mystery. Of course the murder is a crucial element of the plot. You may even want to describe the corpse graphically, or show the murder actually occurring, like in the 'Columbo' pictures. But the pleasure one gets out of the story is in watching a sleuth track down the murderer. That's where the fun and suspense is."

Dom smiled at her earnestness. "So you think we were too heavy-handed?"

"Definitely. In order for sex to be romantic in a movie, there has to be a buildup. There has to be subtlety and tension. Otherwise it's the equivalent of a horror movie, not of a mystery."

Dom laughed; Lark joined in uncertainly. *I can't believe this,* she thought.

"I'm interested," he said, after thinking a moment. "But

we were pretty badly burned on our last project. It would be a hard battle to get the development staff interested."

"I've already spoken to Trent. He told me to drop it."

Dom nodded absently. "Have you got some sort of proposal?"

"Yes."

"Send it up to me. I'll see how the thing looks on paper." He glanced ruefully at his watch. "I'd better be heading home. My wife will be wondering why I haven't called."

It was as though a light had been switched off. Lark sank back in her chair, emotionally drained.

He walked her to her car. "Where do you live?"

"Santa Monica."

"I'm in Pacific Palisades."

"Thanks for the drink," she said brightly, unlocking her car door.

"It was my pleasure. I've been wanting to meet the woman who did so much for my brother. Especially when I found out she was so beautiful. See you around."

She got inside; he closed her door and stepped back. Lark put the car in reverse and eased out of the parking lot. Her heart felt as though it were squeezed in a vise. How could he not know her? She was certain that if he had been the one disfigured beyond all recognition, she would still sense him near her. A person was made up of so much more than just their faces! True, she had worked on her voice so that it was lower, and she spoke with a British accent, but didn't he recognize her hands? She would always recognize his hands. Didn't he recognize her *self?*

When she got home she couldn't stop moving. She paced up and down, her heart beating rapidly. She tried to sit and read, but couldn't remain still. She opened her refrigerator, but couldn't eat a thing. All she could do was to go over the evening again and again in her mind.

It wasn't until the weekend that Lark got the opportunity to tell Carl about her impromptu date with Dom. They were lying on lounge chairs by the pool, protected from the sun by a large yellow umbrella. Lark had made them a pot of tea.

Carl was pleased at her news.

"He didn't say anything about seeing me again," she warned him.

"You will see him again."

"Well, yes, but how friendly do you really think we can get? I can't pursue the president of the company!"

"You certainly can pursue him. I guarantee he is thinking about you at this very moment."

"Carl!"

"It is true."

"I won't do it. I can't."

"You will do it. We both know you will do it."

CHAPTER FORTY-TWO

TONI paced restlessly around the enormous living room. The floor was orange terra-cotta, gleaming with fresh polish. The maid spent over an hour polishing it twice a week.

Where was Dom? It was already past ten o'clock. Not that he was usually home before eight in the evening. Still, even after two years she could not get used to these long evenings by herself.

She tried to think back to when she first started feeling lonely. Practically from the day she was married. Certainly by the time she had moved to California after their brief honeymoon. She had given up her job, her friends, her home in order to be with Dom. She had wanted to. He was the knight in shining armor who would carry her off into the sunset.

She hadn't realized how brief sunsets were and how quickly the long, gloomy night set in.

Dom had given up nothing, had not changed in the least for her. He had continued living his life as though she were merely a chair he had picked up at a store, or maybe a book he planned to read—some day. At first his absorption in his work had puzzled her, then it began to sting. She had done everything possible to tempt him home to her. By now she had long given up trying.

They hardly saw each other anymore.

Her new job meant very little to her. She worked for a public relations company in Century City that handled minor movie stars. In her view, the lives of movie stars were not nearly so challenging and exciting as the lives of politicians. Life here didn't seem real. She missed working for Justin Groome.

Depressed, she went onto the terrace. A cool breeze swept in from the Pacific, bringing with it the pungent scent of eucalyptus. At the bottom of the garden the fountain dribbled into a pool: She heard it night and day, day and night.

It was the waiting she couldn't stand. She could take anything, but the waiting.

She picked a novel off the shelf and took it upstairs to bed. It was almost eleven when Dom returned. By this time she was close to tears.

"Hi," he said.

She didn't answer.

"Toni?"

She would have answered, but she thought she would cry if she did. Instead she turned over and buried herself more deeply in the book. She didn't even know what she was reading.

She sensed Dom's annoyance. He went into the bathroom and then back downstairs. A year ago, he would have pressed her to tell him what was wrong. He would have cuddled her and kissed her and made promises to her.

Or was it two years ago? Had this estrangement begun from the moment they got married? It had been so long since he had shown any sort of tenderness toward her she could hardly remember what he used to be like.

The tears poured out between her eyelids. She reached for the light. More and more often lately she'd tried to hide the fact that she'd been crying from Dom. She never used to cry and she hated doing it now. But sometimes she felt as though she couldn't stop. She'd try everything: swimming in the pool, taking a long drive up the coast, telephoning her mother. But the tears wouldn't stop. Even the maid, Benita, had begun to notice.

I have to do something, Toni whispered into the pillow.

But she had been saying it for almost a year, and she still didn't know what to do.

CHAPTER FORTY-THREE

E VERYONE makes mistakes, thought Jonny, staring at the rim of the glass in his hand. From behind him came the wail of a sad popular tune. He didn't care much for the new music. He'd grown up with the rock and roll of the fifties, and nothing could match the excitement it still gave him. Carl Perkins, Little Richard, Chuck Berry. These new kids didn't have it.

Not even the Beatles had it.

The jukebox fell silent. He thought about his mistakes. Playing a game—which was all life was, wasn't it—there were bound to be slips. Where had he made his? He tried to think. He had arrived in Hollywood when he was eighteen. Gone to UCLA. Then movies had grabbed him. They were the greatest love affair of his life. Sometimes he felt suffocated by film-making, but he couldn't give it up. He couldn't stop thinking about movies, planning them, directing them in his mind. He saw everything as though it were a movie.

What a scene that would make.

He'd always drunk too much; maybe he was a drunk. But he didn't have a problem with that. He didn't drink because he had to, simply because he liked to. It wasn't drinking that was destroying him. It was Hollywood. He was too big for Hollywood. Too expensive, too original, too tremendous. He smiled into his glass.

Be that as it may, it didn't solve his current difficulties. Jeannette was getting impossible to live with. But he had no other place to go. He owed a lot of money. He meant to pay it back. All it would take was a single break.

For a man as famous and gifted as he was, he had surprisingly few friends who might help. Friendship in Hollywood smudged imperceptibly into user. "It's about time you used me" was a favorite expression. It showed people were willing and able to do something out of the power of their position. Or it would be almost a sign of friendship when they said: "Whose expense account should we put it on?" or "I've got free tickets . . ." These expressions denoted an extra intimacy. Otherwise one said: "I've got some tickets and can't go tonight." Or, "Let me take you, it's my turn."

Sometimes he'd meet someone and ask him about a mutual friend: "How is he? What's he doing?" "Oh, I don't know. You know he was fired, and I haven't heard from him since. Funny how people just drop out of sight." The invisible connection had been Using and once cut, they had drifted apart like balloons on a summer breeze.

Someone had once asked him: "Aren't you a friend of his?" and he'd answered: "He has no friends."

Now he wondered how many people were saying that about him.

Maybe it was because he had no money. Maybe he had been the one who had been used all these years, not the other way around.

Trent walked into the gloom. He looked tentative, which immediately annoyed Jonny, who ignored him.

It took Trent a moment to recognize him. He was aghast at his appearance. Jonny had been out of work for some time, and hadn't been eating well. He was sallow and unshaven. Dark circles underlined his round eyes. They were pools of black, without a hint of sparkle.

"Hi, Jonny."

Jonny raised a hand.

"Sorry I'm late." Trent pulled up a chair.

"Want anything from the bar?" asked Jonny. "You'll have to get it yourself."

"No, thanks. Look here, Dom will see you. I think he'll

give you the Venice movie. It's a good story; you'll like making it."

"The lovey-dovey script by Thelma?" Jonny sneered. "Give me a break."

"I am giving you a break." Trent held his glass stiffly.

"I don't want a break."

"It isn't Dom's fault that your rain forest project is on the rocks. He fought for it tooth and nail. But you can't argue with fifty million dollars, Jonny. You can't pretend that money doesn't matter. Why didn't you at least try to bring the film in under budget?"

"That wasn't a budget, that was a restraining order."

"Whatever. There are limits, you know. There have to be."

"That movie was going to be the best damned thing I've ever done."

"Let it go. Move on."

"Fuck it." Jonny glared at the table. Then he asked, "How long do they think shooting will take?"

"Two weeks in Venice—not more. The rest here in the studio. Maybe about a month."

"I don't like to be patronized."

"No one's patronizing you."

"Dom thinks I'm desperate. I'm not desperate."

"No one thinks you're desperate, for Chrissakes."

"Of course I'm desperate. You think Jonny Whitfield would direct a goddamn TV miniseries if he weren't desperate?"

"Come on, Jonny. Pull yourself together. You need this break. You've got talent, you've got brains, you'll get back on track eventually. This is just a stopgap. Not everything you do has to be God's gift to movies."

"I like that."

"Come on up and see Dom. He's waiting for you."

Trent stopped at the newsstand downstairs in the lobby and picked up a pack of mints. "Don't take offense," he said, tossing them to Jonny.

As they walked to the elevator, Jonny slipped a mint into his mouth. Trent nodded to half a dozen people in the elevator. Jonny looked straight ahead. He decided not to go through with it. There were other jobs. Somewhere, someone still wanted to work with him.

Trent marched him down the corridor, making him feel like a dog on a string. Beth, Dom's gray-haired, motherly secretary, waved them by.

Dom was on the telephone; he nodded curtly in greeting. Jonny stood awkwardly. At any moment Trent thought he would bolt.

Jonny went to the picture window and stared out over the flat, foggy plain. The cars below seemed purposeful and confident. They were all going somewhere.

Dom hung up the receiver. "All right, Trent. Thanks." He dismissed him.

Reluctantly, Trent left. Jonny gave him something that could have been a snarl or a smile.

The two brothers looked at each other. There seemed to be nothing to say. Each read the other's thoughts as clearly as though they had spoken.

Dom: I'm giving you another break even though you've screwed up just about everything you've ever touched.

Jonny: Fuck you.

Dom: If you'd just put your mind to it, you'd do a good job on this thing. I'm not just giving it to you because I feel sorry for you.

Jonny: Asshole.

Dom: So you want the job or not?

Jonny started, because Dom had spoken these last words out loud.

"What?"

"There are a few conditions attached to the offer." Dom's face was carved in granite. Frozen bastard, thought Jonny. He felt sorry for Toni. "No drinking is the first one."

"What else?"

"No rewrites. Lark Chandler's got the script exactly as we want it."

"Yeah."

"No squabbling with Jeannette and holding up the shoot. You're still an item? Save your tantrums and hysterics for when you're in bed together. Try to behave like a professional."

Jonny drew himself up. It was more than he could bear, having his little brother bossing him this way. "You're an asshole," he said.

"Do you want the job or not?"

"When does it start?"

"Two weeks."

"Do I get an advance?"

Dom's eyes softened. "You look awful, Jonny. Why are you ruining yourself?"

Jonny was silent. It was an easy question to ask by a man seated on the pinnacle of power. But it was impossible to answer.

"Is it Emmy?"

Jonny shook his head. "You haven't been able to convince your damned investors about *Flaming Forest*, have you?"

Dom shook his head. "You went over budget before you were halfway through the movie. You were also way past your deadline. They don't trust you anymore."

"Someone else might be interested."

"I think they would, but not with you as director."

"They're fools."

Dom sighed and took out a checkbook from his desk. "How much do you need?"

"I don't have a cent."

While Dom wrote, he said, "I feel as though I'm throwing this into the trash."

"Do you want to attach conditions to the money I get paid too?" asked Jonny sarcastically.

"I wish I could. Just try not to drink or gamble it all away."

Jonny smiled, but barely. "How will I make it into enough to live on if I don't gamble?"

"Don't you ever learn from your mistakes?" asked Dom.

"Sometimes I think life itself is a mistake," was Jonny's answer. "Thanks." He slipped the check into his pants pocket. "You can get hold of me at Jeannette's if you need me."

Dom nodded. His face was hard again, unforgiving.

* * *

Jonny decided not to drink this trip. They were on their way
to Venice. He felt in charge of his crew, and he wanted to set a
good example. He looked around the airplane, glad that no
one was sitting next to him. Jeannette was in the cockpit,
talking to the pilot. He picked up a thriller he'd been reading
and tried to concentrate.

The bar opened. They were up. Free from the earth and its
cares. He heard the seductive sound of ice, and read the para-
graph again. Everyone was quiet and friendly, not wishing to
show any fish-out-of-waterness. The bar was conveniently on
wheels. He imagined the cooling, golden, refreshing drinks as
it came near.

But no. He would have none of it. The cart drew closer.
The drinks were like precious gems. A vast goldfish bowl of
tamerlaines. White like diamonds.

He forced his mind back to the book.

On the rocks, he heard, *on the rocks.* He could see the delicious
liquid being poured. When the tray pulled up beside him he
decided on just one martini to help him sleep. He'd make it a
double so that he would not be tempted to go back and back.

"A double martini on the rocks," he said firmly. He felt
himself to be a man of decision and unbroken resolves.

When he arrived in Venice he could barely stand. Laughing
and talking, the others helped him onto the motorboat taxi.
He remembered the gleaming reddish wood as he climbed
aboard and the cool spray on his face as the boat sped off.
Then he was helped to his room in the rented *palazzo* on the
Grand Canal. He lay on his bed in a fog. But it was a pleasant
fog. Filming wouldn't begin until tomorrow. He had plenty
of time to recover.

For a while he slept.

He heard a knock on the door. "Come in," he mumbled.

A young girl entered. She couldn't have been more than
fourteen. She was dark-haired, olive-skinned, and smiling.

Jonny waved to her from the bed. He was feeling a little
better. "Hi."

She came closer and set a glass filled with a pink liquid on
the table beside him. Then she took off her worn-out jacket.

Underneath she wore a skimpy white blouse of translucent material. Jonny sat up and took more notice of her.

"Who are you?" he asked thickly.

"My name is Fairusa." Her mouth was wide, small, pearly teeth peeping between cherry-red lips. Her dark eyes were anxious, in spite of the smile.

Jonny cleared his throat in embarrassment. Unwillingly, he realized the sight of the child's seminudity was arousing.

Fairusa came closer. "I am here for your pleasure," she repeated, in husky-sweet baby talk.

Jonny sat on the edge of the bed, his head reeling. The girl snuggled close to him, stroking his thigh. Of course he would not make love to a child. Of course not. He had a shred of decency left in him to prevent his doing that, so help him God!

Somehow the slight creature slipped between his legs as he sat staring at her. As she bent over, Jonny saw the curve of her spine and ran his hand down it. She smiled at him, unsurprised, and handed him the glass.

"What is this?" Jonny asked, his voice shaking.

"A very special drink. You'll like it."

He took a sip and decided he liked it very much.

The girl smoothed his hair from his face. Her young breasts were eye level. Sweating, Jonny pushed her away.

"No," he exclaimed.

She looked hurt and anxious.

"I did wrong?"

He stared at her, hot and angry. "Not you. Me."

She smiled in relief and went back to him. "You can do no wrong," she assured him. "I will do it all."

He groaned out loud, but something in the drink was making him swell dizzily and happily. He was putty in her hands; she could do with him what she would.

A *child*, he thought wildly. *What am I doing with a child?*

But for the life of him, he couldn't stop what was happening.

CHAPTER FORTY-FOUR

DOM gave Lark's proposal for the "Romance!" series to Faith Brown, who was vice president of marketing and development. On her recommendation, it was decided that Lark should attend the next executive meeting and pitch some of the details of her proposal.

Lark was nervous, thought Dom. She wore a gray pinstripe business suit, but it didn't suit her the way Toni's business suits did. Toni could not suppress her sensuality even in the stiff cut of the suits. There was always a slit up the back of a too-tight skirt, or a blouse unbuttoned so that her cleavage showed. When Toni wore business suits, Dom couldn't get his mind off her body.

But Lark looked as though she'd be more comfortable in blue jeans. The clothes she wore were containing and protecting rather than inviting. The discreet suit could have been in fashion in the 1940s, with its broad shoulders and long, slim skirt. Still, she was lovely. It was hard for him not to keep looking at her. There was something indefinably familiar about her. He watched the way she tilted her chestnut head when she was listening, and the sudden animation in her pale face when she spoke.

The meeting began with Faith briefly describing Lark's concept for a "Romance!" series.

"You'll have to explain more fully in what way this "Romance!" concept will differ from our last disastrous project,"

Faith told her, sitting back in her chair. She was fiftyish, blond, blue-eyed, and cool as snow.

Lark cleared her throat. Dom tensed inwardly for her sake, although he made no outward show of emotion. She was on her own, whether he liked it or not. But as soon as she started talking he realized he needn't have worried. Far from being nervous, Lark was enjoying herself.

"Two things, primarily," she began. "A good romance is, first and foremost, a good story. Plot is essential. So is suspense: Will she get the guy or not?"

"Everyone knows those romances have happy endings," interjected Vanessa Bloom, one of the directors of the marketing division. "How can you have any suspense?"

Lark turned to her. "In a mystery everyone knows that the murderer will be found. But that doesn't take away from the suspense of watching it, does it? It's the same in romance. But let me add something here. There's no reason why every romance should have a happy ending. *Romeo and Juliet* sure didn't. Nor did *Wuthering Heights*—not really. Not having a happy ending doesn't make the story any less romantic."

"I thought happy endings were part of the genre," someone Lark did not know spoke up.

"Not necessarily. We need to be different. Your last project made too many stupid assumptions. You bought some books, saw that they had lots of sex and happy endings. You figured that was what people liked."

Dom had started to relax, now he tensed again. She shouldn't have used the word *stupid*. The romance project was a sore point with several people who were present.

"Let's talk about sex first," Lark went on. "You can't be so graphic about it in a television show. Even seeing too much kissing makes an audience uncomfortable. You want to know why? It spoils the romance, that's why. I saw one of your pictures where the heroine and hero jump into bed practically during the first fifteen minutes. There's no tension there. There's no conflict. There's no romance." She grinned. "There's nothing so romantic as waiting."

Some of the people laughed.

"The ending of a romance has to come as a climax," she

finished. "Romances are not simply wine and roses. There must be conflicts and misunderstandings and seemingly insurmountable difficulties along the way. The ending—whether happy or not—shouldn't come just as a period at the end of a lot of sex. It should come as a huge relief or it should make you weep."

She sat confidently back in her seat.

"Any questions?" Dom asked.

"I have a couple of footnotes," Lark spoke up when no one else did. Dom sat back, watching her in fascination. "The actors in those movies were terrible. You thought that getting men and women who were gorgeous was all that it took. But that's not the point. People empathize with unusual looking people too, so long as they're people who can act. 'Mystery!' characters aren't always gorgeous, but they are sympathetic. I don't think many people realize that it takes a really good actor to gaze lovingly into someone's eyes."

"Oh, boy," said Vanessa.

"It's true," Lark insisted. "The other thing is that we'd need a far better opening theme. What you had was too mediocre. You need a melody that's as vividly memorable as the theme from *Dr. Zhivago* or from *Spartacus*. People would turn on their televisions so they wouldn't miss the theme music. And the opening credits should be humorous and sexy, so that men don't get turned off."

Dom glanced at his watch and then at Faith.

"We're running late," Faith took up her cue. "We'll have to go on to the next order of business. But let's think this over. At our next meeting I want everyone's response to this. If there are no objections, we'll probably go ahead with a pilot."

Lark glanced at Dom. He was taken aback by the gratitude in her blue eyes and turned to the file in front of him, trying to concentrate on the next project on hand.

After the meeting he asked her to walk him to his office.

"You're a talented speaker," he said.

"The only reason I was okay in there was that I'm interested in the project. If I care about something, I'm okay."

He smiled. "I think you're okay anyway." He was surprised

to see her blush. It was an odd combination, to have someone so reserved and yet so transparent.

They reached his office. "Come inside for a moment," he said. He closed the door behind her. "Privately speaking, I want you to know that I'm pretty sure we'll move ahead with your idea. Faith's behind it and that's the important thing. We'll start with a pilot and a proposal for the rest of the series. If we can sell that to the networks we're on our way. We won't have invested too much in it if it doesn't work."

"Oh, Dom," she breathed, thrilled.

"One thing that you tactfully omitted to mention was that our other project lacked a coordinator who was interested in romances. We decided to tap the market while it was hot, and we didn't understand what really constituted the market."

She nodded.

"Do you read those things yourself?" he asked curiously.

"I've read *Pride and Prejudice* and *Jane Eyre*."

"But those are classics."

"They were written during a time when there was a lot of pulp being put out too. They were better than the rest. That's always the case. There's a lot of trash being written, but there are great books being published at the same time. I don't think publishers can tell the difference in romances. Look how many times *Gone With the Wind* was turned down."

"How many?" Dom asked with interest.

"A lot. Anyway, you know what I mean."

"If we do go ahead with this, you'll be put in charge. Would that be okay with you?"

"Of course."

He sat at his desk. "Are you free for dinner tonight?" he asked. He knew he shouldn't do it, but he couldn't help himself. "I'd like to take you out."

He watched the reserve slam down across her face.

"I'm busy tonight." She sounded desperate. "I'm sorry."

"That's all right. It's Friday night. I'd forgotten."

"I'd better get back to my office," Lark said.

"See you around," he said.

CHAPTER FORTY-FIVE

D OM was haunted by her. He thought about her constantly. Her blue eyes sparkled in front of him at the oddest times. He wondered how long her hair was: He had only seen it piled in back of her head. He wondered about her apartment, what she did when she was alone. He wondered about her boyfriends. He made every excuse to see her, and the workers on Lark's floor were surprised that Dom was so often seen strolling along their hallways.

But, feeling guilty about his attraction for Lark, he tried to be kinder to Toni. It didn't seem to make a difference. She remained cold and indifferent. Even their lovemaking suffered. It was as though she barely tolerated him.

He stood in the doorway of their bedroom, wet from his morning shower. Usually he left before she was up, but this morning he had heard her swimming in the pool at a little past six. Now she had a magazine in her lap and she kept turning the pages slowly.

"Aren't you going to work today?" he asked.

"No," she replied. "I quit my job just before Christmas."

His jaw dropped. "Before Christmas! Why didn't you tell me?"

"I didn't think it would make a difference to you one way or the other."

"Of course it makes a difference to me! What have you been doing? Did you find something else?"

She shook her head. It had been an impulsive decision to leave her job, but in spite of the boredom of being at home so much, she was relieved. She had stopped doing something she hadn't liked doing. It was a beginning.

"I don't understand." But Dom glanced at the alarm clock on the bedside table. "Damn, it's already eight o'clock. I can't believe you didn't tell me."

He started pulling on his clothes. Dom always looked casually well dressed. Today he chose a burnt orange and brown silk shirt and shantung trousers, baggy and pleated. He rarely wore a tie.

"You're obviously mad about something," he said, as he dressed. "What is it?"

"I'm not mad."

"Then what's the matter? Have I done something wrong?"

She kept turning the pages of the magazine. Her throat felt swollen.

"If I've done something wrong you should tell me what it is."

She managed to say hoarsely, "It's not that simple."

"What do you mean?"

"It's an endless accumulation of things, Dom. I can't pin it down to one thing."

"Then pin it down to a few things. Tell me what's wrong."

"Forget it. I can't. Not when you're like this."

"Like what?"

"Look at yourself!" she cried, flinging the magazine aside. "Listen to yourself! You're angry that I'm upset! You're anxious to get to work! You want me to run down the list of my emotions in a businesslike way, so you can get it over with and run off to your damned office! Well, I'm not like that! I'm not one of your secretaries. And I'm not a two-dimensional floozy in one of your movies. I'm a person, damn it."

Dom stared. "I know you're a person."

"Then why don't you treat me like one? You act as though I'm a piece of furniture!"

He took a step toward her, smiling a little. "When we make love, I treat you like a piece of furniture?"

She was silent. As though he'd won the battle, Dom turned away to get his shoes.

"There's someone else, isn't there?" Toni said suddenly. "I know there is."

"There's my work," Dom said coldly.

"It's obvious there's someone else. Who is she?"

"I have ten million crises to take care of in a single day. If I don't have time for my own wife, you can be damned sure I don't have time for a mistress."

He grabbed his shoes and went downstairs. He couldn't understand his own anger. A year ago he would have gone over to Toni, stroked her and cuddled her, and kissed her tears. He would have whispered reassurances, and then the fight would have ended in sweet, satisfying sex.

He put it down to the fact that he was running late. Toni did have a knack for picking the worse times for a fight. He resolutely did not think of Lark.

"I have to get out of here," Toni told herself after he'd left. "I never thought I'd get this way, just because I'm married. But I'm a changed woman. I'm behaving like every lovesick fool I've ever despised."

She took her coffee outside on the sun-soaked terrace overlooking the stunning garden. A poinsettia tree dropped a few long, crimson leaves onto the wall.

There was no question that it was paradisaical here. But Toni didn't want to be in paradise. She was homesick. February: New York would be sliced by bone-chilling winds, blanketed with dirty gray snow. Her refuge would be in dry, overheated apartments and offices. Perhaps it was mere nostalgia, but she couldn't let go of her longing to go home.

At noon, Toni impulsively dialed Dom's private office number. "Hello, Dom?"

"Hi, Toni. I'm in a conference right now. I'll call you back later."

"Don't bother," Toni forced her voice to sound cool. "I'm just calling to tell you I'm going back to New York. I'm leaving this afternoon."

There was a silence on the other end, then Dom said, "Don't do anything till I get there, all right? This meeting will be over in an hour and I'll come home then. We need to talk."

She hung up without saying good-bye. She was crying again. Sometimes when she broke down like this, without warning, she wondered if she would ever be able to stop.

She went to the mirror. "Stop it. Stop it."

She didn't want to appear puffy eyed and haggard when Dom came home. He had fallen in love with her because she was beautiful and sophisticated and self-confident. How could she have turned into such a weakling?

"Stop—*stop*—"

She pressed a tissue to her eyes as she walked down the cool hall to the kitchen. Benita, the maid, was upstairs working the vacuum cleaner. Toni switched on the coffeemaker.

Dom didn't return until five. "What do you mean, you're going back to New York?" he demanded.

She started crying again.

"Don't start that," he exclaimed helplessly.

"I can't help it—"

"What's been going on with you? You've changed so much this past year. What happened to the feisty businesswoman I married? I was worried that I wouldn't get to see much of you because you were such a workaholic."

"I don't know what happened," Toni replied honestly. "I just know that this isn't working out. I'm homesick. I miss my job. I miss my family. I miss the parties. I miss being taken out. I need affection, Dom. I didn't expect you to change so dramatically simply because we were married."

"I didn't expect you to change either," Dom said slowly. "I thought you'd still be going out to parties and seeing friends. And your work meant the world to you. I guess the more you lean on me, the more I back away. It scares me."

Toni pressed the tissue to her eyes again. "It's as though I've got some sort of crying sickness," she muttered. "I never used to cry."

Dom came over and put his arms around her. "Let's give it another try," he said gently. "We'll go away for a couple of weeks and try to heal the rift, okay? I'll take you to Bermuda. I'm due for a vacation in any case."

This was not what she expected. She started crying again.
"Okay, Toni? Can we try again?"
She nodded. "Okay," she said, her voice muffled in his silk
shirt.

CHAPTER FORTY-SIX

DOM could only take a week off work since they were in the middle of crucial negotiations for a new movie that he wanted to produce. He also wanted to be on hand in case the television movie Jonny was directing in Venice went awry. He didn't trust his brother.

The first night in Nassau they went to a seafood restaurant overlooking the bay. They danced, and talked a little, and drank wine. They were both uncomfortable, but the wine helped.

When they returned to the hotel, there were three telephone messages for Dom. "I'll have to get on the phone for a bit," he apologized. "Sorry."

Toni didn't answer; she wasn't surprised. She went onto the terrace and lay on the lounge chair, gazing at the stars. She felt she was on a date with a man she was overwhelmingly infatuated with, but who was married to someone else.

Dom was on the telephone for over an hour. Toni went to bed. When he finally joined her, she pretended to be asleep.

The next day they went swimming.

Over lunch Toni asked casually, "Did you stop by the desk? You have a bunch more messages from L.A."

"I'll pick them up after lunch."

As soon as the meal was over he went to the front desk. There were two messages from Trent, and two from his secretary.

He called Trent first.

"Glad you called," Trent said. "It seems as though your brother's gone off on another binge in Venice. We're wasting thousands of dollars, Dom. The crew and actors are sitting there waiting for him to come out of it."

"Is there a problem or is he just drinking?"

"He and Jeannette are fighting over the script. They always do, but because we're filming in Venice it's costing us more than we can afford."

Dom thought rapidly. "Lark Chandler's still around, isn't she?"

"Yes."

"Send her to Venice," Dom said. "Jonny might listen to her."

"Can't do it. She's in the middle of working on our 'Romance!' proposal. You don't want to put that on the back burner, do you?"

"It'll only be for a few days. I think it's important."

"All right, Dom. But I think this may be something you have to handle yourself. We're already over budget."

"I know. I'll go there myself too. But I have a feeling Lark might have more success than I will."

"Will do," sighed Trent. "Having fun otherwise?"

"It's okay. Transfer me to Beth, will you? I'll have her make my plane reservation."

When he hung up the phone, he was surprised to find Toni standing in the terrace doorway, listening.

"So much for that," she said quietly.

He sighed. "I can't help it. It's a question of millions of dollars."

"Of course it is."

"Toni—"

She crossed the room and lay, facedown, on the bed. She wished she knew what to do.

"How about if you came with me to Venice?" Dom suggested after a moment. "That way once the crisis has been resolved we could continue this second honeymoon."

She wanted to say "It's too late" but she didn't want it to be too late. "Okay," she said.

CHAPTER FORTY-SEVEN

TRENT tapped on Lark's open office door.

"Happy Valentine's Day," he said, tossing a pink-ribboned box of Perugina chocolates on her desk.

Lark wrinkled her nose.

"What's the matter?" asked Trent. "Don't you like chocolate?"

"I love chocolate. But there's something about Valentine's Day that makes my stomach turn. Wasn't St. Valentine stoned to death?" She opened the box and offered him one.

"Whatever it was, it happened a long time ago. Now all that's left of the story are the chocolates. Succumb to hedonism, Lark. You're in L.A., now."

"Mmm. These are good."

"A problem's come up," said Trent. "We need your help trying to get Jonny Whitfield back on track. He's been in Venice for the past ten days, supposedly filming *Razzle Dazzle.* It appears that so far they haven't had more than a couple of full days of shooting. He's claiming that it's Jeannette's fault, but our understanding is that he's as much to blame as she is. It was an impossible combination, having him as a director and her as the star."

"What do you want me to do?"

"Dom wants you to go there. If it's a question of rewriting the script for Jeannette, you're the best person we have."

She was excited at the prospect of going to Venice. "When do you want me to go?"

"First thing tomorrow. Phone down to our travel agent. Tell her I authorized the trip, since Dom's away."

"No problem."

"Dom'll probably show up there too, by the way."

Lark flew first to Milan, then changed planes for the short hop to Venice. Her flight arrived at Venice Airport at ten o'clock in the evening. A shuttle bus took her to the cavernous train station which fronted onto the Grand Canal. Her taxi was a *vaporetto*, a sleek motor launch which skimmed along the gorgeous waterway to the *palazzo* where Jonny was staying, along with the stars of the show and some of the crew members. Trent's directions had been explicit and simple: Just go halfway up the Grand Canal and stop at the pink *palazzo* on your left. But Lark had not been prepared for the marvel of the short ride. She could hardly believe the splendor of the crooked old buildings illuminated along the shimmering waterway. Each had its own wood landing at the front door, decorated with poles painted in colorful spirals. Other *vaporettos* plied the watery main street, making waves as hers had done. Water buses crisscrossed from side to side, stopping only for a minute to disgorge passengers and take on another noisy, standing-room-only, crowd. Clusters of gondolas strung with lanterns were paddled by singing gondoliers, the sound of "O Sole Mio!" bouncing off *palazzo* walls.

When they reached her destination, she saw the pink facade of her *palazzo* was spotlit, reflecting itself in shattered bits of color in the dark water. A half-moon shone over its shoulder.

She was greeted at the door by an elderly manservant who showed her to her room on the third floor. Inside, the high ceilings were painted in bright colors *a la Tiepolo*. Blue skies were filled with whipped cream clouds upon which floated fat baby angels, flowers, and large butter and cream, half-naked women and men, wrapped in loose gowns of golden satins and pink silks. The bed was an old four-poster, shrouded in heavy burgundy drapes.

Two tall, narrow windows overlooked the Grand Canal.

"May we bring you something to eat or drink?" inquired the Italian servant. "The meal is finished in the dining room, but we can make arrangements for you."

"No, thank you. I think I'll go straight to bed."

"*Buona notte.*" He bowed himself out the door.

Lark was too tired to face Jonny that evening. It was important that she be psychologically strong when she spoke to him. Besides, it was already eleven o'clock. She undressed and put on her terry-cloth dressing gown. But she couldn't sleep. She sat by the window, looking out over the broad canal at the gondolas, water taxis, and busy *vaporettos.* Shimmering light reflected from the water onto the underside of a bridge.

Am I really here? she wondered. *In Venice?*

With all her heart she wished she could share her first experience of the magical city with Susan.

In spite of the time difference and being up late, the next morning she awoke early. Sunshine poured into her room. She dressed quickly in black corduroy pants and her green mohair sweater. Before leaving, she took out the art deco earrings Jonny had given her for Christmas. She hoped they would remind him of how much they had accomplished together on *Maria Benton* and would encourage him to do his best on *Razzle Dazzle.*

Taking her copy of the screenplay, she went down the wide, marble stairs and followed the sound of voices that emanated from what turned out to be the dining room. Its French doors overlooked the Grand Canal, and the shimmering light reflected on the dark wood beams and equally dark window frames. The crew had already gathered at the round tables, or were helping themselves at the buffet table which was set with an "American breakfast." Silver trays offered porridge, crisp bacon, scrambled eggs, toast, rolls, coffee, tea, along with silver pots of jams, whipped butter, and fresh yoghurt.

A few people from the office saw her and waved. She smiled back and poured herself a cup of coffee from the sideboard.

"Where will I find Jonny?" she asked a young woman who was serving herself some eggs on a croissant.

"He's in there," the woman pointed.

Lark went over to a massive wood door leading to a sunny parlor adjoining the dining room. A group of people were standing around Jonny. He was doggedly drinking a glass of bourbon and arguing.

Lark knocked on the open door and walked in. "Excuse me, Mr. Whitfield. May I talk to you a moment alone, please?"

Her sharp voice silenced everyone.

"Well, hello there," Jonny said. "I like your earrings."

Lark turned to the rest of the group. "This will only take a few minutes."

With relief, the tired group filed out of the small room.

"How'd you find me?" Jonny said.

"I was sent here." She took the bottle from his hand and set it on the windowsill. "What do you think you're doing?"

He laughed hollowly. "I'm trying to create something from the shambles. You should see what that cat Jeannette wants me to do with the lousy script."

Lark sat beside him on the gold brocade couch and set the script on her lap. "Let's study the problem. I'm sure we can work it out."

"Not with that bitch, we can't. The goddamn prima donna thinks she can tell me what to do with every goddamn line. I've had it with her."

"If the changes she wants aren't good ones, and she refuses to follow the script, she'll have to be fired," Lark said calmly, not at all sure if this was possible.

Jonny screamed with laughter. "Fire Jeannette Gold! We'd have to start impeachment proceedings at least a year in advance. Wouldn't that be a riot? I'd love it!"

"Let's see. Where exactly is she making changes?"

Jonny calmed down enough to find the scene they were working on. "It's already taken a week," he grumbled. "Everyone comes down on me for overspending, but it's her fault we're balled up here. God!"

"Describe the changes she wants," insisted Lark.

It took the better part of an hour to work out a compromise. Jonny was finally appeased.

"It's nice to see you again," he said when she got up to leave. "Where are you going now?"

"To talk to Jeannette Gold."

"Good luck. How're they treating you at APG?"

"Very well." She grinned. "Thanks for setting it up for me."

"You're losing your English accent."

"That happens. I'm going to tackle the prima donna now. Get a cup of coffee, will you? Maybe something to eat?"

"I'll get coffee," he promised.

He stood up, a little shakily. But he felt confident enough to go on with the movie. After all, he was Jonny Whitfield.

Lark was shown upstairs to Jeannette Gold's suite on the third floor. Jeannette was lying on a couch, watching an Italian movie on television.

"Who are you?" she asked when Lark knocked and entered.

"Lark Chandler. APG sent me to try to straighten things out here. May I come in?"

"If you'll listen to the changes I want made in the damned script. I'm the one who has to say them."

"I appreciate that, and we want the dialogue to sound natural."

Jeannette sat up. Her head was a halo of gold, falling over vivid green eyes. The thick pancake makeup she wore for the shoot couldn't disguise the fragile beauty of her heart-shaped face. She would be a perfect Caroline in the movie.

"You look perfect for the part," said Lark, admiringly. "I knew when I first heard you were interested that you were the one person who could really carry it off. It's a difficult role."

Jeannette smiled sweetly. "Well, thanks. I've been bossed around by that tyrant for so long I'd forgotten I was appreciated."

"Oh, you're appreciated all right, don't worry about that. We wouldn't have had one of the best directors in Hollywood direct you if we hadn't thought you were worth it, and the movie worth it."

Together they went over the changes that she and Jonny had agreed to. Jeannette wanted to add a few more of her own; Lark appeased her as much as she could.

When, two hours later, they emerged arm in arm, a cheer went up from the waiting crew. They were soon back outside, ready to start filming again.

The February sun sometimes disappeared behind the whipped cream clouds, then with equal suddenness it would shine out in all its splendor, warming the patient crew. Props

and lighting were already set up near a stone bridge spanning
a narrow back canal. The soft grays and oranges of the buildings reflected in the green water lapping below. Because there
was no traffic, the city was enveloped in a silence and tranquil-
ity which was occasionally shattered by a raucous water truck.

Lark stuck around for a while, watching, before she remembered she hadn't eaten breakfast. She left the set and wandered
down a narrow street, looking for a restaurant.

It was damp and chilly; she was grateful for her wool
jacket. She crossed and recrossed the tiny stone bridges which
spanned the network of canals, walking carefully up and down
their wet, stone steps and along the uneven cobbled streets.
People passed her, talking, laughing, sometimes calling
loudly. She stood for a moment on one of the little narrow
bridges, sunk in wonder.

"I wondered when I'd bump into you again."

He had come up beside her so quietly she hadn't heard him.
It was as though he had been there the entire time.

"Hi, Dom."

"You don't seem surprised to see me."

"Trent mentioned you might be here." They stared at each
other. Lark tried to smile casually, but failed. Dom leaned
toward her; briefly she thought he might touch her and she
trembled violently.

But all he said was, "I hear you've worked your magic on
my brother and the prima donna already. How do you do it?"

"Just by being reasonable. It's not as if anyone wants to
really sabotage this movie."

"Sometimes I wonder. Where are you going now?"

"To grab a bite to eat."

"Come on, I'll take you out."

La Madonna restaurant was hidden down a tunnellike cob-
blestone street off the Grand Canal. It was noisy and crowded.
They sat across from each other at a small table, occasionally
bumped by hurrying waiters and busboys.

"You're nervous," Dom said, placing a warm hand on top of
her cold ones. She realized only then she had been tearing a
cocktail napkin to tiny pieces.

She stared at the large, tanned hand that covered hers and

felt hers tremble again. *It's Dom*, she thought all over again. *Dom's hand. He's touching me.*

She caught her breath. "I guess I am."

"Why?"

"I have a big responsibility ahead of me."

"You mean my brother? That won't be a problem for you. I was just talking to him. He's already promised he'll stay off the booze for the rest of the trip."

The waiter came over. Dom released her hand and Lark cradled it in her lap for a while, marveling that he had touched her. While he studied the menu she took the opportunity to recover herself. He ordered liver *a la Veneziana*; Lark chose *linguini a le vongole*, the house specialty. Sipping Italian Merlot and talking to Dom about *Razzle Dazzle*, Lark forced herself not to think about Toni.

"He thinks the world of you," said Dom suddenly, when their plates had been cleared.

Her mind was so completely on Dom that she didn't grasp what he meant.

"What?"

"Jonny," he said. "He's crazy about you. You saved his ass once and now he's elevated you to the status of a goddess."

Lark flushed. "Oh. I really did very little."

Less belligerently, Dom continued, "Jonny has charisma, there's no doubt about it. He can charm the pants off a nun. But he has problems. Alcohol is only one of them."

"You don't have to tell me this."

"Don't misunderstand. I'm not bad-mouthing my brother. As a director he's a genius. I'd be the first to admit that. But with women—well, he's hurt a lot of them in the past. I'd hate to see you be another one of them."

"My relationship with Jonny is purely professional."

"Let's stop for coffee on the way back to the set. It's nicer outside."

They found a small cafe with three tables out front overlooking a small piazza. They sat outside, even though the sun had once again gone behind clouds, leaving them in a damp mist which occasionally thickened into something near rain. They decided to ignore it.

"Maybe it'll go away," Lark said. "I can't bear to go inside. It's all too lovely."

Dom ordered cafe espresso, *correcto*.

"It's with brandy," he explained. "It'll warm us up."

"Sounds good."

"I don't know why I'm bothering to warn you about Jonny anyway. You can probably take care of yourself. But what is it about you that makes a man want to throw his coat into a puddle so you won't get your shoes wet?"

They both laughed.

"Too late." She lifted a wet shoe for his inspection. "Anyway, I'm actually pretty tough."

"Then your face disguises that toughness really well."

"Doesn't it?"

They were silent. Lark's hair grew curly from the damp. Neither made a move to leave.

Suddenly Dom said, "I'm married, you know."

Their eyes locked. In his she suddenly saw the ardor that smoldered behind the piercing intelligence of his tawny eyes.

The look was like a kiss.

Lark dropped her eyes first. She was grateful Dom did not suggest they leave yet, because she did not think she would be able to stand.

They stayed on in silence until the drizzle turned to steady rain. Then, without speaking, they got up and made their way back through the winding streets to the set. They walked separately, but inclined toward each other, as though they were talking, which they were not.

CHAPTER FORTY-EIGHT

TONI had known it would be like this the moment they arrived in Venice. Dom was surrounded by actors and crew. If he wasn't talking to someone there, he was on the telephone talking to someone in Los Angeles.

Even though she had known it would be like this, it made her sick at heart.

Alone, she explored the old city, wandering along the winding main street, jostled by the midmorning crowds. The bustling thoroughfare had no cars, bikes, or trucks—just people. Some, the Venetians, she guessed, hurried. Others walked as if in a dream, a slight smile on their rapt faces. They would stop suddenly, seemingly for no reason, making others bump into them. Then Toni would see the facade of a church, all arches, statues, and sooty curlicues, that had arrested them. She detoured around the tourists, her heart too heavy to be lifted by overweight saints in dirty marble.

On the steps of the great loggia overlooking Piazza San Marco she looked around at the glittering shops and elegant restaurants. Today the square was canopied with gray piles of clouds, backed by silver light. Pigeons flew about, catching bits of corn from interested tourists.

Directly across from her rose the church of San Marco. Golden domes bubbled from its top like maple sugar boiling in springtime. The facade was ablaze with color. Over the front arches, four large bronze horses galloped fiercely into the

silver sky, pulling the church as though it were a chariot of
God.

Toni circled the piazza under the shelter of the loggia, looking at the exquisite glasswork in the stores. When she reached
the opposite side, she entered the Doges' Palace. The church
had once been the private chapel for the doges, the nobles who
ruled Venice when it was the foremost sea power of the world.
Each vast room was more resplendent than the last. The ceilings were painted with energy, filled with floating figures and
giddy piles of clouds. The Venetians brought the sky inside,
and outside made it their ceiling, Toni thought.

But even the rows of portraits along the walls depressed
her. The vast, empty rooms once held all the nobles of Venice.
Now, flattened into paint, they seemed merely a gallery of
vain and pompous men.

She turned off to follow the footsteps of the lover Casanova.
She had read about his tempestuous life. She went across the
Bridge of Sighs, up some dark, damp steps into a tiny prison
cell right under the roof. It would be freezing in winter, and a
furnace in summer. Casanova had been an adventurer, a wild
man, full of fun and mischief. How had he survived for years
in this dreadful cell? He had taken months to dig a small hole
in the roof, then had escaped over the tiles and into a waiting
gondola.

Her love for Dom was like a prison, too, but one from
which she had no will to escape. She could not leave him.

She went back outside into the midday mist.

She left the piazza. It was too square. She needed ups and
downs, circles and spirals, and loop-the-loops. She wandered
the back streets, up the slippery marble steps, over the little
stone bridges, then down to the winding back lanes of the
city. Some streets were so narrow people couldn't even open
an umbrella.

She ate a prosciutto and lettuce sandwich at a stand-up cafe
espresso bar, jostled by hurried businessmen shouting their
orders, smoking their acrid cigarettes. *"Scusi, signora, per
piacere."* They ignored her except to push her out of their
space. She leaned against the high counter, looking out at the
street. It began to drizzle. She ordered a *gelato* and coffee,

waiting for the rain to stop. It still had not wholly cleared when she paid the bill and walked on, heading vaguely back to the hotel.

As she wound her way through the mostly empty streets, she saw a couple seated at an outdoor cafe, talking earnestly. The large red and white umbrella did not wholly keep them dry, and yet they did not seem to mind.

Toni felt a pang at the intensity of the relationship. Time was when she and Dom had been as oblivious to their surroundings as this couple were. A host of memories flooded her. Taking the Staten Island ferry in a snowstorm. Picnicking in Tanglewood on a summer evening. Making love on a Nantucket beach. The time they had flown to Paris for the weekend—just for fun. They had sat at an outdoor cafe, drinking vermouth and watching the passersby, but always they were aware of each other, crazy about each other. They held hands, just sitting there. They kissed constantly.

Toni brushed away a wash of tears. She hurried past the couple, wishing she had not seen them. It did no good to remember.

She stopped abruptly.

The man was Dom.

She had never seen the woman before.

So mesmerized were they by each other, they had not noticed her. Plunging down the nearest side street, Toni hurried away. Dom had said a countless number of times there was no one else. But then who was that woman?

In her room she took off all her clothes, as though trying to shed the image of her husband with another woman. Shivering from the damp cold, she took a hot bath. Even when she finally emerged, she did not feel warm. She put on leggings and a dust rose turtleneck over a T-shirt, not bothering to dress up. She had no desire to go out that evening.

She did not know what she would do when Dom came home. Should she confront him? Accuse him of lying to her? Or simply ask for an explanation?

Dom came in after dark. He looked preoccupied as usual. He took off his trench coat and glanced at Toni who lay on the wide bed, reading.

"I think it's going to turn out all right," he said. "A friend of Jonny's is here who's been able to reach him before. What a mess, though. Is there anything to drink?"

Toni usually ordered cocktails for them; she had not thought of it tonight. She shook her head.

"Are you okay?" Dom asked. "You're not dressed for dinner."

You're Toni Sumner, she told herself. Attractive, successful, wealthy, with a family who loves you, clients who respect you, and friends who enjoy being with you. What does this man do to make you forget all that? Pull yourself together.

"I'm not hungry," she said.

"I'll be in the dining room if you change your mind," Dom said.

After he had left, Toni did change her mind. Mostly she was curious about the woman. Who was she? Where had she come from?

She dressed carefully, knowing that dinner with the crew in the dining room would be a magnificent affair. Dom ate like a king without seeming to realize it. He took it for granted. It was one of the natural perks that came with power. She chose a burgundy stretch velvet bodysuit and made up her face carefully. It was a trick she had learned a long time ago: if you're depressed, make sure you look your best. Otherwise you feel worse.

The woman was there, seated between Dom and Jonny. She wore a sweater the color of spinach fettucine and not a hint of makeup. Yet despite her lack of interest in her own appearance she outshone everyone else in the room. Her curly dark hair was swept back from a wide brow and wrapped around her head in two French braids. Her mouth was full and sensuous. Sapphire eyes surveyed Toni as she approached.

Toni could have sworn that the woman recognized her. Had Dom described her in such detail? Then the woman looked away and the moment passed.

Dom found another chair for Toni and introduced her to the rest of the party.

"This is Lark Chandler, from England," he said. "She's one of the latest additions to our staff."

Toni nodded politely, but she felt again that strange sense of recognition on the part of the woman. Her smile was guarded but friendly. Toni sat on the other side of Dom. She ordered mineral water.

"Feeling better?" Dom asked her.

"A little."

Jonny was talking to Lark. "It went well this afternoon, don't you think?" he said.

"Absolutely. Keep it up, Jonny."

"How long will you be staying?"

"I'm not sure. As long as I'm needed, I guess."

"You're definitely needed," Jonny flashed a disarming grin. Then he spoke across the table to Toni. "You're looking ravishing tonight, Toni. Going places?"

"I hope so," Toni answered lightly.

Dom spoke to Lark in an undertone. Jonny saw Toni throw her husband a look of such suffering that he felt jolted. It was a look he had sometimes seen on Emmy's face.

"Hey, Dom." He tried to shift Dom's attention away from Lark. "How long will you and Toni be staying?"

"I'm not sure yet. Probably not more than a day or two. I don't think I'm really needed here. And there're mountains piling up back in the office."

At which point Toni quietly slipped away and went outside.

It had stopped raining. The stores were closed up, but the streetlights lit the way. She didn't know where she was going. She walked for a long time. Eventually she ended up on the old Accademia bridge, looking at the restless green water below.

A hand touched her shoulder.

"Hey, Toni."

It was Jonny. He was a little drunk but he looked kindly at her.

"Hey, Jonny."

"I think you need a drink."

He took her to Harry's Bar on the Grand Canal. They sat at a booth. Jonny ordered scotch; Toni had one too.

"You hadn't met her before?" asked Jonny.

She shook her head.

"It's just a passing thing," Jonny said.

"How do you know that? When has anything Dom became involved in been 'just a passing thing'?"

Jonny was silent.

"How long have they known each other?"

"Not long. There's nothing going on between them. Dom wouldn't screw you over like that. He's not like me."

"You mean they haven't slept together? What does that mean? Nothing. They're head over heels in love. Both of them."

Jonny was unable to deny it.

"I can't give him up," Toni whispered. "I love him too."

"And he loves you. He'll soon realize that. This is mere infatuation."

They sipped their drinks.

"I can't bear this anymore," Toni said abruptly. "I have to leave him."

"Oh, no, Toni!"

"It isn't fair to either of us if I stay. Let Dom decide on his own what he wants to do. If he wants me, he'll come after me."

Jonny shook his head. "It's only the fact that you're around that keeps him aware that he loves you too. If you leave he'll forget."

"What kind of love is that? I want something deeper, more lasting. I don't want to force him to hang on to me."

"But that's not how it works."

Toni knew he was remembering Emmy's leaving him. She felt she understood Emmy now. She longed, with sudden, desperate energy, to be out of Venice, away from Dom's film world, away from the telephone calls, the arguments, and away from the anguish of losing him.

"That's the way it works with me. If a man doesn't care about me, he can go screw himself."

"Where will you go?" asked Jonny.

While she thought over her reply, they ordered another round of drinks.

"I'm going back to New York," she said at last. "I'll talk to your mother about getting involved in Whitfield Communications again. If that's not feasible, I'll get another job."

"You may find it's not the same. 'You can't go home again' and all that shit. Are you sure you want to do it?"

"No, I'm not sure." But the more she thought about it, the more definite she became. She had to get out of Dom's life before she turned into a mere shell of her former vibrant, energetic self.

"But I'm pretty sure," she said.

CHAPTER FORTY-NINE

LARK called Carl as soon as she returned to Los Angeles.

"How was the trip?"

"It was fun," she sighed. "Venice is so beautiful."

"Was Dominic there?"

"Just for a few days. His wife was there too."

"You must have had several opportunities to talk to him."

She didn't answer.

"Have you made any attempt to speak to him about me?"

"Carl . . ." she said hesitatingly, "it's impossible for me to get so close to him I can tell him about you in such a way that he'll want to see you. You have to do it yourself."

"I cannot. Have you forgotten what will happen if you don't?"

"No, I haven't forgotten." But she couldn't believe he would actually tell people who she really was. At heart, Carl was kind—one of the kindest men she had ever met.

"Well?" he persisted.

If she did talk to Dom it would be out of gratitude to Carl. It was a small thing to do for a man who had done so much for her.

"I'll speak to him. I promise."

"Thank you, my dear." Carl cleared his throat. "Have you thought about telling Penny Houten's story to a reputable newspaper? If you find a principled reporter you need not fear that they will reveal their source."

The suggestion sent Lark's head reeling. She was stunned the thought hadn't occurred to her before. And she knew just who she could tell her story too: Emmy Elson, Jonny's ex-wife.

"Lark?" said Carl.

"It's a fabulous idea," said Lark. "I can't believe I haven't thought of it myself."

"Good."

They said good-bye, Lark promising to visit him the following day. Trent had mentioned that Emmy was the editor of *Monday Week* in New York City. Lark was too nervous to call from her apartment for fear of being traced, so, a few days later, she went to a public telephone box and dialed *Monday Week,* using a lot of change. A secretary was unwilling to put her through to Emmy when she gave her name as Mary Smith.

"Tell her I have some information about Congressman Justin Groome that she might be interested in," said Lark, in a rush.

To her delight, Emmy came on the phone right away. "Hello? This is Emmy Elson." Her voice was low and husky, and Lark conjured up an image of her immediately—rich auburn hair, quizzical eyes and her innate serenity.

Lark had wrapped a silk scarf around the receiver, hoping that would disguise any familiar tone to her voice. "I have some information that you might be interested in about Justin Groome. I'm a friend of Penny Houten's. As you may know, she's still in hiding."

She sensed an excited pause, and then Emmy replied, "Yes? I'm very interested."

"You'll try to verify what I tell you, of course. But the main part of the story you're going to have to take on faith, I'm afraid."

"Why don't you begin at the beginning?" Emmy said patiently.

"Okay—it's this. Justin Groome is a murderer. He murdered a young woman named Violet Sumner back in nineteen eighty-five. He murdered her because she was blackmailing him, threatening to tell people that he had raped her. At the time of the murder, he pinned the blame on Penelope Houten, whom he had also raped. Let me tell you exactly how it happened."

The conversation lasted the better part of an hour. Emmy Elson asked sharp questions and elicited more information from Lark than she had originally intended to share. But Lark was glad to unburden herself of the truth. Afterward, elated, she went to the King's Head Tavern and treated herself to a special dinner of fish and chips. She felt giddy with excitement. If the truth emerged, if Justin Groome were convicted and punished for his crimes, then one day, some day, she could go home again.

It wasn't easy to find a copy of *Monday Week* in Los Angeles. In the second week of April she discovered it at a newsstand on Las Palmas in Hollywood. She found no article about Groome, and she was disappointed.

When she went to her apartment that night she began putting together an idea for her docudrama about Justin Groome. It would be along the lines of *Citizen Kane*, but modern, a bit of "Dallas" thrown in, combined with a reverse *It's a Wonderful Life*. Justin Groome would be the one who was shown what life would be like had he never been born, and see the happiness and good fortune that people miss out on because of his selfishness, cruelty, and greed.

She was pleased with the idea. When it was finished, she would show it to Dom. He might not like it, considering Groome was a family friend. He might not believe it. But at least he would have read another side of the story. And he might like it enough to want to produce it.

Time was getting short. People were continually being hired and fired in this industry. If the "Romance!" series flopped, would she be fired? Possibly. But at the present she was in a strong position to present her idea for the docudrama.

For the next few nights she did not leave the office at all while she rewrote and revised the film treatment.

CHAPTER Fifty

EXCITEDLY, Emmy Elson played back the tape recording of their conversation. The woman's story confirmed many suspicions she had about Groome. While she was still married, Jonny had dropped macabre hints about him. Emmy guessed that Jonny was both contemptuous and terrified of Groome, so for several months now she had wanted to learn more about the congressman.

Not for a moment did she wonder who the woman was who had called her. Of course it was Penelope Houten. Only Penny could know so many details about what had happened. Only Penny would want this story made known to the public, in order to vindicate herself.

Emmy wondered where she was now. Far away, she hoped, and safe.

The first order of business was to do some follow-up interviews on the basis of what "Mary Smith" had told her. She would enlist the help of Marcia Collins, her assistant editor. Marcia was the best interviewer on the paper and she was as trustworthy as a donkey. She was also ambitious and would jump at the chance to work on a story of this magnitude.

Emmy herself would contact Susan Whitfield. Susan would probably not be of much help, considering how she had taken Justin Groome's word for what had happened. Still, there might be something there.

She supposed she would have to talk to Jonny as well.

Since moving back to New York Emmy had immersed her-

self in journalism. She felt *Monday Week* belonged to her. It
was fast becoming reputable, nationally acclaimed. It had
been a challenge to combine a weekly leisure paper with one
that reported political stories, both local and national. But it
had worked.

Emmy wasn't ambitious in the way Jonny was. She was
committed and often her commitment bordered on obsession.
But her work was an end in itself, it wasn't a stepping-stone
to something greater. She didn't understand that kind of ambition, just as she didn't understand the pleasure a mountain
climber might have in scaling increasingly challenging
heights. The mountains were pretty much the same, weren't
they, even if they were bigger? Sometimes she thought that
Jonny must see the emptiness in his life as he constantly
grabbed for something bigger and better. It was as though he
never paused to appreciate what was in his hand at the present
moment. He didn't understand that life was an end in itself,
not a means to an end.

She shrugged off thoughts of Jonny, annoyed with herself
for getting sidetracked. She'd have to get in touch with Dom,
and with Justin Groome. She'd be stirring up old ties, old
associations, associations she'd much rather put behind her.
But a job was a job, and a story was a story. She might not be
ambitious, but publishing a good story gave her immense
satisfaction.

First she would pay a visit to Susan Whitfield.

Susan looked tired. There was a tightness to her mouth and a
sadness in her eyes that had not been there the last time
Emmy had seen her four years earlier.

They gave each other a warm hug.

"I was so surprised when you called," Susan said, taking her
into the sunny kitchen. "It's been a long time."

"Yes, it has. I've missed you."

"I was sorry we drifted apart when you and Jonny split up."

"Me too."

"Can I make you some tea?"

"I'd rather have coffee, if you have it."

While Susan was making it, Emmy sat at the kitchen table,

looking around. She remembered the room vividly, the wide, wood shelves with the gleaming pewter, the wood stove. Mild April sunshine filtered in through the open windows. The room did not look changed and yet it seemed different.

"So you're writing a story on Justin Groome?" Susan said. "I don't know that I can help you much. I don't do any work for him now."

"I wanted to ask you about some background information," Emmy replied. She reached in her purse and took out a notebook and a pencil; at the same time she switched on the minicassette player she always carried in her purse. "Do you mind? It helps to keep me accurate."

Susan shrugged.

"You've known Congressman Groome for how long?" asked Emmy.

"He was at college with my husband. We've been friends ever since."

"He's had a lot of relationships with women in that time, hasn't he?"

"He's quite a ladies' man, yes."

"And he never married."

"No, Justin never married."

"Are you aware of any special relationships—a special woman whom he might have wanted to marry?"

"He's often spoken of wanting to marry me," Susan said with a laugh. "I never took him seriously."

"Why not?"

"I just never did. I didn't want to marry again in any case."

Emmy nodded. "He was very close to Violet Sumner some years back. Did you know her?"

"Not very well. You remember that Toni, her sister, used to head up my company before she married Dom. That's how I met Violet."

"I see."

"I don't seem to recall that Violet meant more to Justin than any of his other girlfriends. As I said, he's quite the ladies' man."

"Can you tell me how long he knew Violet?"

"Let me see—they probably met when Toni came to work

for me at Whitfield Communications. That was about six or
seven years ago. Violet was still a teenager. Justin didn't get
interested in her until later."

"Do you know that for sure?"

Susan poured Emmy a cup of coffee. Every movement she
made was graceful, but suddenly her hand shook.

"What do you mean?"

"I heard that Congressman Groome grew very fond of Violet almost right away."

Susan's eyes narrowed. "She was only fifteen or sixteen at
the time they first met. I don't understand your question."

"Would you say that Violet was basically a naive, spoiled,
unintelligent sort of girl?"

Susan frowned again. "I suppose so. Certainly she seemed
that way next to her sister. Toni was very protective of her."

"Why do you suppose anyone would want to murder a
naive, spoiled, unintelligent sort of girl?"

Susan sat down. "What are you getting at?"

"Doesn't it seem odd to you?"

"It was an accident. You're trying to stir up old accusations
against Penny, but you won't get anything out of me. Penny
was a dear, dear girl. It's absolutely incredible that something
like that should have happened. She was as much a victim as
Violet."

"Oh, I wasn't talking about Penny," Emmy spoke soothingly. "I know she didn't kill Violet. I'm trying to find out
who did."

Susan opened her mouth to continue her protest, then shut
it again as Emmy's words sank in.

"What do you mean, you know Penny didn't kill Violet?"

"It stands to reason, doesn't it? She hadn't even met the girl
before that night. Justin Groome insisted it was jealousy, but
from what I understand, Penny could hardly tolerate
Groome's presence. It was unlikely that it was jealousy."

"Penny and Justin were good friends, actually."

"They were?"

"Oh, yes." But Susan was remembering something.

"What are you thinking about?" prompted Emmy, watching her.

"Just something Penny said when she was in the hospital."

"What was it?"

"About Justin. She said he'd killed Violet, and her dog too. She told Dom the same thing. But then when the police came to question her, she clammed up and wouldn't say a word. So we assumed she hadn't been telling the truth."

"So instead you believed Justin Groome's version of what happened that night."

"I guess the fact that Penny ran away kind of confirmed her guilt."

"It's possible she was intimidated into keeping her mouth shut."

"It's possible, I suppose." Susan was far away in time. "But that means that Justin—I can't even think of it, Emmy. It isn't possible."

"Let me backtrack a moment. Groome is quite a ladies' man, you say. Have you been aware of his affairs with younger girls?"

Susan looked sickened. "I forgot I'm talking to a reporter," she said. "I was thinking of you as a friend, as Jonny's wife."

"I understand."

"Justin's an old, old friend of mine. If you're trying to get me to say something that might incriminate him, you're on the wrong track. I can't help you."

"I'm not looking for anything incriminating—just for general background information." But she knew she'd gotten as much as she could from Susan. She put away the notepad and sipped her coffee. "Do you like living here?"

"It's lonely, but on the whole I like it."

"You miss Penny, don't you?"

"Very much."

"Are you worried about her?"

"Terrified. I feel so sure that if she was all right she'd let me know somehow." Tears stood in her eyes.

"What do you think could have happened to her?"

"Whenever I pass through Times Square when I'm in New York I ask myself that same question."

They were silent.

"Susan . . ." Emmy said hesitantly. "I wouldn't worry too much. I have a feeling she's okay."

"Do you?" Susan looked at her. "Have you heard from her? Is that why you're writing the story?"

"I got a call from a woman called Mary Smith. She told me things only Penny could have known."

"And she said that Justin did these dreadful things?"

"I'm afraid so."

"Well." Susan looked deeply distressed. "Even if it was Penny, she could have made up the whole story. She had a marvelous imagination."

"Would you say she's a liar?"

"She's been known to lie on occasion."

"To you?"

"No, not exactly."

"To Justin?"

"Yes."

They looked at each other.

"I know what you're thinking," said Susan. "That Justin's poisoned me against her."

"Has he?"

"Maybe he's tried to. I guess I just don't know about Justin anymore."

Emmy realized it wasn't the kitchen that felt changed; it was Susan. She seemed smaller, and all her old vivaciousness had gone. "How's Jonny doing?" Emmy changed the subject, feeling sorry for her. "I'd like to talk to him about this too."

"I gather he's in bad shape."

"Do you know how I could get hold of him?"

"I'm afraid I don't. Dom might know."

But Dom didn't know either.

"Mother said you might call," he told Emmy when they spoke the following week. "It's nice to hear your voice. How have you been?"

"I'm fine, thanks."

"Are there any questions you want to ask me for your story? I'm as anxious as anyone to find out the truth. I never believed that Penny could have done something like that. And then Jonny kept dropping hints that got me wondering."

"Me too," said Emmy.

"He always seemed so guilty, although I'm pretty sure he didn't pull the trigger. He was knocked out. But he acted guilty nonetheless. And he never could bear to hear Penny's name mentioned after it happened. I think he was relieved when she ran away. You know how Jonny never likes to face bad situations."

"Yes, I know."

"I can't help you much more than that. You don't . . ." he asked this hesitantly, ". . . have any idea about Penny's whereabouts, have you? She's the one who really could give you the story."

Emmy laughed. "She already has. I'm just trying to follow up on the details, get verification and so forth. It's kind of important for me to get Jonny's side of the story."

"You've spoken with Penny!" he shouted. "But when? Where?"

"A few weeks ago. I don't have any idea where she was calling from. And she didn't tell me it was her. I only guessed."

Dom drew a deep breath. "So she is alive."

"If you run into Jonny, please let him know I want to get in touch with him, will you? Let me give you my telephone number."

Dom wrote it down and said good-bye. He stared at the telephone after he replaced it, then he remembered he had someone in the office with him. They had been in the middle of a discussion when the phone had rung. He looked up and met Lark's eyes.

"Sorry for the interruption," he said.

She cleared her throat. "That's okay."

"Are you all right?"

"Just fine."

Dom stood up. "Could we finish this tomorrow afternoon? I don't think I can concentrate right now. You've got enough to go on for the present, haven't you?"

"Yes. But I'll be in a meeting until four tomorrow. Let's make it Thursday morning."

Dom glanced automatically at his appointment calendar and gave a curt nod. He reached for the phone again. "I'll see you then."

Lark practically fled from his office.

Chapter Fifty-One

IT was late when Emmy returned home after a long day at the office. The spring night was unusually warm and muggy. Her apartment was on Perry Street, a four-story brownstone, of which she owned the top two floors. The very top floor she used as the living room and kitchen. Through a large skylight she could see the Empire State Building. Her bedroom, an office, and a guest bedroom were on the floor below.

After opening all the windows and changing into shorts and a T-shirt, Emmy went to the kitchen to make herself a cup of coffee and a tuna sandwich. The doorbell rang just as the water boiled.

"Who's there?" she spoke into the intercom.

"Jonny."

Emmy started to say "Jonny who?" but she pressed the buzzer instead.

A few moments later he stood in her doorway, regarding her with an expression she'd never seen in his eyes before: uncertainty.

He gave her a crooked smile. "I thought you were going to say 'Jonny who?'"

"I was." She stepped back to let him come in.

Jonny shrugged out of a wrinkled jacket. Only then did Emmy realize how thin and haggard he looked. There were purple pouches under his eyes.

"Nice place," he said, glancing around.

"You look awful. Want something to eat?"

"Sure."

"How about a tuna sandwich?"

"Emmy . . . Emmy." He shook his head. "You're not still eating tuna? Don't you have any compassion for the poor dolphins?"

"Don't worry; it's albacore. Coffee too?"

He nodded. When she returned to the living room with the sandwich, Jonny was stretched out on the couch. He sat up, looking guilty.

"I'm more tired than I realized," he said. "I just came from my mother's house."

"How is she?" Emmy handed him the plate.

"She's okay. She told me you wanted to get in touch with me."

"I did."

"Said you're writing a story on Justin Groome."

"That's right."

Jonny looked serious. "I wouldn't, if I were you."

"No, I don't suppose you would."

"He's ruthless."

Emmy shook her head. "I'm not afraid of him."

Jonny toyed with the sandwich. "I guess I'm not hungry. It's so strange to see you again." It had been two years since she had left him.

"It's strange to see you."

"I've missed you."

"Have you?" Was he going to try to charm her again? "Would you mind if I asked you some questions about the night of Violet's death? I need some verification for certain things I've been told."

Jonny rubbed his eyes, tiredly. "I won't be changing my story at this late date," he said.

"I wouldn't expect you to. Still, you always hinted that you weren't telling the whole truth about that night. I had a feeling Justin Groome had probably warned you not to."

Jonny looked at her.

Emmy reached in her purse and took out her notebook. "Let's do it another way," she suggested. "I'll tell you what I understand happened that night. All you have to do is say yes or no. That's fair, isn't it? And I won't use your name in the article, of course. But I need confirmation of my source."

Jonny nodded slowly.

"Okay." Emmy sat up and spoke briskly. "As I understand it, this is what happened. Justin Groome and Violet Sumner were arguing about something. You and Penny overheard them. Penny inferred from the argument that Violet was blackmailing Justin. Perhaps he had raped her—or seduced her, whatever you want to call it—when she was younger. She was threatening to tell the press unless he paid her off.

"You and Penny left quickly, not wanting to hear any more. You were drinking—surprise, surprise. Penny was drinking too. Suddenly Justin found you. He seemed angry at finding you both there. He grabbed Penny and you jumped up to defend her. He punched you.

"Violet showed up. Justin grabbed Penny again. You tried to reason with him. He punched you again. Penny threw herself on top of you, protecting you. Then Groome took out his gun and shot Violet."

"I didn't actually see that part," Jonny said slowly.

"No, but Penny was clinging to you. The dog jumped to her defense. Groome shot it."

"How do you know all this?"

"It's true then?"

"You've spoken to Penny. You must have. Where is she?"

"It is true. Why didn't you say anything before, Jonny? Why did you let the girl take the blame?"

"You know why."

Emmy looked sadly at him. She loved him still, this cowardly, ambitious, ex-husband of hers. Had Groome threatened to expose some sordid story of his past if he told the truth? And Jonny, desperately trying to raise money to make his masterpieces, had had to decide between his own career and the fate of a young girl he hardly knew?

"He would have killed me," said Jonny.

"I wish you'd eat the sandwich."

He took another bite. "Did you talk to Penny?"

"I don't know where she is, if that's what you want to know."

"No, not really. I just wondered whether—she's all right. Groome bashed in her face pretty badly. She must feel terrible."

"I suppose she must."

They were both silent.

"Well . . ." said Jonny at last.

"Well . . ." said Emmy.

"It's such a surprise to see you. You're doing okay?"

"Yes, I really am," she answered.

"That's good."

"Where're you staying?"

"Tonight? I don't know."

" 'Cos I have to get some sleep."

"Yeah . . . I know . . ."

"You can crash downstairs in the guest room, if you want."

They looked at each other.

"Okay, I will. Thanks."

She took his plate and cup back to the kitchen.

Given enough time, people said, even the past becomes bearable. But that's only a manner of speaking. If you allow yourself to dwell on the rosy beginnings of your affair, and then you let your mind drift down into the bleak anguish you felt toward its end, it wasn't so bearable. If you remembered the laughter which you thought would have no end, and then you remembered how it turned almost imperceptibly into angry cries and accusations and finally into chilly, lonely resentment—then it wasn't so bearable. If you thought of Hollywood's effervescent promise of happiness and success, and then recalled its ultimate flatness and betrayal, no, nothing was bearable when you thought of all that.

Emmy didn't want Jonny back in her life—even for a short time. Even if he offered her stability, security, a family—the things for which years ago she would have given the world—she would never let him back into her life.

She went back to the living room. Jonny was where she had left him.

"Good night," she said.

"Good night."

Chapter Fifty-Two

WHEN Toni returned to New York, she tried to immerse herself in her old life-style. But the fast-paced social life which she'd remembered as being so exciting, now seemed frantic. The parties she had missed were insipid. She found it difficult to confide in her old friends as she used to. Even visiting her parents in Connecticut was not as pleasant as it used to be. They felt strongly that she should return to her husband.

But Dom had not even tried to get her to return.

Justin Groome was delighted to see her again. He was sympathetic about her separation from Dom and encouraging about her future. After several extravagant, supportive lunches, Toni began to feel guilty she had once called him a barracuda in a goldfish bowl.

"What about getting your old job back?" Justin suggested.

"I doubt Marianne would be happy about that."

"Between you and me, Marianne isn't capable of running the business as you were. I've already mentioned to Susan that I'm looking around for another PR company to handle my senatorial campaign."

"You're kidding!"

"Susan was upset, naturally. But if you were to take your old job back I'd definitely reconsider. Why don't you give Susan a call? Talk it over with her."

"I'll think about it," said Toni.

Justin looked grave. "Susan's been distant toward me lately.

I don't get to see her as often as I used to and I guess she's resentful. At least, that's what I think is the reason. If you talk to her maybe you could find out more."

Toni telephoned Susan that afternoon.

"Toni, dear. How nice to hear from you. Where are you?"

"In New York."

"Is Dom with you?"

Toni was annoyed and surprised that Dom hadn't told Susan about their separation. Did he think she might change her mind?

"Dom and I are separated. Didn't he tell you?"

"Oh, no. No, he hasn't said a word. I had no idea." Susan was upset. "How did this happen?"

Toni said wryly, "I'm still trying to figure it out myself."

"Oh, my dear."

"Susan, I need to talk to you about Whitfield Communications."

"If you want your old job back, I'll be delighted. I have a feeling Marianne will be too. It was too early to hand the reins over to her."

Toni gave a sigh of relief. "Thank you. I kind of need something to do."

"Good. Why don't I come to the city next week and the three of us can have a meeting? We'll need to catch you up on what's been happening."

Toni didn't mention what Justin had said about Susan's reserve toward him. She saw a lot of him, particularly after she was reestablished in her old job as director of Whitfield Communications. He convinced her that he wouldn't succeed in his campaign without her help. His appreciation of her helped boost her confidence, but it didn't assuage her inner feeling of emptiness. She didn't cry as she had when she was in California, but she did spend a lot of time alone, more than she ever had before.

"You need to have an affair," Marianne told her. They had taken their sandwiches to Paley Park on Fifty-third Street, since it was another warm spring day. Toni was grateful for the miniature oasis and spent many of her lunch breaks there. She loved the flow of the waterfall, a smooth wall of water pouring down the back wall, the trees just putting forth their leaves, the sense of shelter.

"I don't think so," she answered Marianne. "I think what I need is a total renovation done to my co-op. I need a fresh start." Her parents had used it on occasion while she had been gone; now she had moved back in.

"Aren't you going back to Los Angeles?"

She didn't know. If Dom came after her, would she go back? If one night he rang her doorbell and he was standing on her threshold, and he said, "I can't live without you, Toni. Come back to me," what would she do? She closed her eyes, imagining it. For a moment her heart beat faster.

But Dom would never do it. He would wait for her to come back to him, not the other way around.

"I don't think so."

"I'm sorry. Divorces are hard."

Divorce.

"Let's not talk about it. Let's talk about what I should do to my co-op. It needs a lot of work."

"I know a contractor who worked on my brother's place. He did a good job. Want his number?"

"Sure. I think I'll put marble in the bathroom, for a start."

"A marble bathroom! That sounds wonderful."

"And I've always wanted built-in shelves in the living room. It would give it the look of a real library. I'd like something unusual too, maybe have the shelves marbleized."

"It'll be expensive," Marianne warned.

Toni shrugged. "I hardly spent any money the past two years. I might as well splurge now."

She called the contractor. Arrangements were made to start with the bookshelves in the living room.

She gave her key to the contractor, and then went to visit her parents in Connecticut for a few days. When she returned on the following Monday, she found the living room in shambles. Dust sheets covered the furniture which had been pushed against the walls. A workbench was in the middle of the room, and a dusty man, stripped to the waist, was using an electric saw. The noise was like the sound of a dentist's drill only ten times louder.

Toni groaned. The carpenter glanced up, nodded coolly, but didn't turn off the saw. His face was lean and dark, and for some reason he reminded Toni of a wolf. He went back to his work, ignoring her. His ebony back gleamed with sweat.

She picked her way past him and went into the bedroom. Taking off her jacket, she tossed it on the bed, then went into the bathroom.

The sound of the saw ceased. When she went out again the man was packing up his tools. Toni gestured unhappily at the living room.

"When will you be done?"

He shrugged. "I'll be back tomorrow. Maybe two weeks more."

It was the first time he'd spoken, and Toni was arrested by the musical lilt of his voice. He had a strong French accent. She looked at him more carefully. His black arms were like trees, his thighs in the tight jeans were lean and muscular. She wanted to go on talking to him.

"What time will you be here tomorrow?"

"In the morning." He finished putting away his tools. His indifference bothered her.

"Would you like a beer before you go?" she asked.

He looked at her with more interest. But, "No, thank you," he said. "I had better be going."

"What's your name?"

"Pierre."

"I'm Toni. Where are you from?"

"Haiti." Pierre finally smiled at her. "Perhaps I will see you tomorrow?"

She nodded. When the front door closed behind him, Toni went into the kitchen and poured herself a drink. She would get her life back together, she vowed. Without Dom.

A moment later she burst into tears.

CHAPTER FIFTY-THREE

J ONNY stayed with Emmy for a month. He caught the flu which prevented his departure right away. After he was better he kept saying he was going back to Los Angeles. But he didn't seem to have the energy.

Summer came early that year; there were hot, sticky days even in May. On one Saturday he and Emmy took the D train to Coney Island where they got off and hurried through the tacky, crowded amusement park to the boardwalk, as though by hurrying they might find their way back seven years to a golden stretch of sun and sand on the beach in Malibu.

It was so hot they went swimming right away. Floating lazily on the mild waves, Jonny closed his eyes and dreamed up images to keep away his incessant longing for a drink. The most vivid image was their opulent garden in Pacific Palisades. He could almost smell the orange blossoms. He was in the swimming pool and Emmy waved deliciously from the terrace. He remembered the way she used to dance down the red tile stairs to the lawn, her auburn hair glinting, her brown legs shining with oil and sun. They made love in the pool while the sun went down. Emmy was laughing at something he said. She was always laughing back then. They used to make love everywhere. On the lawn. On the balcony. On the kitchen floor: he'd lie back, the white tiles always sparkling clean. Emmy's skin, pressing down on top of him, was as cool as the floor beneath him. "Supper's ready," she'd say when the moment came. Sometimes, if they had friends staying or if the maid was upstairs in the bedrooms, he would gently put a hand over her mouth to suppress her cry. It was lovely to watch her, like that.

"Why didn't you tell me that APG canceled the *Flaming Forest* contract?" Emmy floated on her back, tickling the waves with her toes.

"I heard about that the day you left. I didn't think you'd give a damn."

"I probably wouldn't have," she agreed.

Their separation had wrought changes in her that confused him. He wished she still wore the pieces of golden fabric that she'd tie tantalizingly at all the right spots instead of the staid black one-piece. He wished she laughed more. He wished they were lovers.

"Do you ever think about the house?" he asked suddenly.

"In Pacific Palisades?"

"Yes. We had such wonderful times there."

Her eyes closed. "Funny," she said, "I hardly remember you there at all."

"What do you mean? I was there all the time."

"No, you weren't. You were never there." But she added, almost apologetically, "It was a gorgeous house though. Does Dom like living there?"

She opened her eyes and found Jonny regarding her curiously. "What do you mean, I was never there?"

"I don't remember your being there at all. Isn't that strange? Because you must have been there occasionally."

"It was more than 'occasionally.' "

"Was it? Funny that I can't remember. I remember being there alone."

After a while Jonny said, "I never understood why you were upset about my affair with Jeannette. It wasn't my first one, you know."

"I know. Affairs were as necessary as breathing to you."

"Almost as necessary," he joked.

Emmy started diving into some friendly looking waves.

"I can remember the day I first thought about leaving you," she said, stopping to catch her breath. "You weren't happy with the color of Jeannette's hair in one of your pictures. Some

of the crew were over at our house. You took them all outside
and showed them your new Porsche and said you wanted her
hair exactly the same gold."

Jonny laughed. "What amazes me is not that you divorced
me, but that you could marry me in the first place."

Emmy dived again and turned a slow somersault underwa-
ter.

"Is it true, Em?" he asked when she emerged.

"What?"

"That you married me just because I was a great director?"

"Were you a great director?"

"You didn't answer my question."

"If I told you it was because I loved you you'd misunderstand anyway. You assume that loving someone is the same as
using them."

"I loved you when I asked you to marry me."

"That's what I mean."

"I don't understand."

She shrugged.

"Are you saying I used you and you didn't use me?"

"Nothing's so cut and dried as that. Maybe I used you too.
Maybe one only loves the people one uses. How do I know?"

"How did I use you?"

It was her turn to laugh.

"I remember loving you," replied Jonny soberly. "I remember making love and being in love. I had affairs, but I never
loved anyone the way I loved you."

Emmy started swimming to shore. Jonny followed.

"You must be very upset about this," he said.

"About what?"

"Me. Where I'm at now."

"Not really."

"Ah, then you're glad. This is revenge for you."

"No, it's not that either."

He was silent, then he said, "I'm still the same guy you
knew back when. I have the same dreams and ambitions I did
when I was eighteen. But at fifty they seem ludicrous. Why is
that? At eighteen everyone thought the world of me, although
I hadn't achieved anything. But now I'm considered a failure,

simply because I didn't keep churning out stupendous movies year after year."

"If I am upset it's for your sake, not mine. It's a shame you had such bad luck. Although you did ask for it, with your drinking and all."

He heard her, but pretended not to. They toweled themselves dry and lay down side by side on the sand.

"What artist do you know can churn out great things constantly, through an entire life, from their eighteenth year to their eightieth?" asked Jonny. "There have to be lapses, moments or months or years when they struggle with writing blocks, poverty, illness, frustration . . . boredom. Shouldn't society forgive those lapses? No one can be great all the time. It's not in human nature. But that doesn't mean a man's a failure, for God's sake." He grew impassioned. "I don't feel like a failure. Given the chance, I could create my greatest piece of work. I know I could. But no one's going to give me that chance. If you're an artist and you're down and out in this world, you're out."

"That's Hollywood."

"Not just Hollywood. Society in general."

"Well, society wasn't established by or for artists. It was established by politicians for the masses."

"And they're very different," said Jonny.

"No, they're not," she said, missing the point again, he thought. "People in politics face the same problem. So do people in business. And in sports it's even worse. You're only as good as your last home run. Society measures everyone by their most recent successes and failures. Why should artists have special treatment?"

Jonny sat up with a sigh. He had pitied her back then for not being a great artist and for not understanding art. His art, in particular.

"Life is so damned screwy," he said.

"I think it's normal."

A flying Frisbee almost decapitated him. He scrambled after it and cheerfully tossed it back to three teenage girls playing near the water's edge.

"It's screwy," he said, lying down again.

"Okay, then normal is screwy." She closed her eyes to the sun, listening to the squeal of sea gulls.

It was strange that she felt life was normal, Jonny thought. Sometimes it seemed so screwy to him he thought he should twist his head right around and set it back on properly. He liked that idea. Maybe he'd try it in a scene. Done right it could get a laugh.

"I'm working on a new screenplay," said Jonny.

"Are you?"

"I can see you don't believe in me either anymore."

"Sure I do."

"You'd probably think it's too depressing for a screenplay. But the jokes are pretty good."

"I know; your jokes can always make me cry," she said.

Jonny looked pleased. "That's the best kind of joke."

They ate fried clams and drank Cokes. Both of them would have preferred beer. They walked along the wide, wood-planked boardwalk. Later Emmy went swimming again. Her hips swayed alluringly as she walked. Her long legs were pale and smooth. Jonny lay on his stomach so no one would notice his hard-on. But he felt sorry for her. One tends to only pity those one uses, he thought. If she was right about him, that meant he pitied those he loved, too.

"I'll be going back this week," said Jonny, when she came back.

"Okay."

"I really appreciate your letting me stay this long."

"That's okay."

He put out a hand; she took it. "You're being so cool to me," he said in a low voice.

"I'm protecting myself," she replied. "That's all."

The sun sank into a muddy haze on the edge of the sea and people started packing up their things to leave. Emmy and Jonny stayed on. Mostly in silence they watched the sea darken. Both of them wondered what the other was thinking, but neither asked because they already knew.

Jonny wanted her to ask him to stay. And that was the last thing Emmy was going to do.

Chapter Fifty-Four

IN the middle of August the first article about Justin Groome was published in *Monday Week*. Lark was so excited she could hardly contain herself as she read it. But its contents disappointed her. There was no mention of Penny Houten or of Violet Sumner. It was all information she had only vaguely heard before: about Justin Groome cheating on his law school entrance exams and his powerful family hushing up the scandal. Justin Groome failing the bar exam three times. Justin Groome using his family's influence to avoid being drafted into the Korean War.

Disappointed. though she was, Lark was encouraged too. This was the first in a series of articles. Maybe Emmy was setting him up, so that the final allegations would come as a scandalous climax to the saga of Groome's unscrupulous career.

"You have been looking extraordinarily perky lately," remarked Carl. "Has your good mood anything to do with the recent article in *Monday Week?*"

"How do you know about that?"

"I read the papers. Naturally, I'm interested in anything pertaining to Justin Groome."

Carl had not brought up the subject of Dom since her trip to Venice. Lark saw Dom so infrequently now, she felt farther than ever from being able to tell him about his father.

A few weeks later a second article was published in *Monday Week,* this one relating to Groome's shady connections with

corrupt businessmen and how he allegedly bought his way
into office. But still there was no mention of Penny. All summer long the allegations were reiterated in other national and
New York newspapers and magazines.

It wasn't until September that Groome's alleged rape of
Violet and of Penny were described. And later in the month
the entire story of Violet's murder and Groome's role in it
came out, exactly as Lark had told Emmy it had happened.
Groome's popularity ratings began to slide. Lark was gleeful.
Things were definitely starting to happen.

Filming began that fall for the pilot for the "Romance!"
series. There was little more that Lark had to do with it. She
had been at APG for a year. She made the final touches on her
treatment about Justin Groome and decided to show it to
Trent first. If he liked the idea, it would be discussed at the
next meeting. If the staff went for it, it was unlikely that Dom
would veto it, in spite of the fact that Groome was a family
friend.

She gave it to Trent before leaving the office, knowing that
it might take a month before he got around to reading it.

Just a week later, however, he buzzed her intercom and
asked if she could come into his office.

"I'll be right there."

Trent was seated at his desk, his back to her, staring out the
window. He swiveled around when she knocked on the open
door.

"Come on in. Have a seat."

"Hi, Trent."

"I read this with interest. Docudramas are hot right now.
And the man makes a juicy subject. But I'm worried about
the libel aspect. He's denying all these allegations, you know.
And he's running for the Senate in next year's election. He
wouldn't like this at all."

"He's not meant to like it."

Trent eyed her curiously. "Do you know him?"

She shook her head, regretting the personal tone in her
voice. "But look at what he's done! He's a villain!"

"An alleged villain. Until he's tried and convicted, he'll go on denying these allegations. And if he's tried and released, it'll make us look like fools."

"In *Monday Week*—" began Lark.

"*Monday Week* likes a good story as well as anyone. But they use the word *alleged* throughout the article."

"Couldn't we use it in a disclaimer at the beginning?"

Trent looked thoughtful. "I'll tell you what I'll do," he said at last. "I'll have Dom take a look at it. He has a good feel for this sort of thing. I have a feeling he'll veto it right off the bat, but you never can tell. Anyway, it's the best I can do."

"That's a lot. Thanks, Trent."

"It's a terrific treatment," Trent said before she left. "I always thought you had something like this in you, but even so I'm impressed."

Back in her office, Lark felt depressed. She had a feeling Dom was going to be far more concerned with a probable lawsuit than he was about telling the world about Groome's *alleged* crimes.

She was right. A few days later Dom stopped by her office. She was eating an avocado sandwich while sorting some mail, and felt at a distinct disadvantage being caught with her mouth full.

"Don't you have time to get out for lunch?" Dom asked, looking perturbed.

"Not today." She swallowed the mouthful and wiped her hands on a napkin, hoping her gladness at seeing him wasn't too evident. "Hi, Dom."

Dom closed her door and pulled up a chair. "It's two-thirty. Aren't you eating lunch kind of late?"

"I didn't realize how late it was."

He changed the subject. "I came to talk to you about this." He placed the manuscript on her desk. "It's impossible, Lark. I know you're going to be disappointed, but we can't produce a film like this. I happen to know Congressman Groome, and it's not something he'd let me get away with. He'd sue the pants off APG."

"But we might win the suit."

"By the time we won the suit we'd have been dragged

through so much shit that no television station would work with us again."

"Why, though, if it's true?"

"That's the problem. There's no way any of this stuff can be proven. It's an amazing theory, and I read it with great interest. As I said, I happen to know Groome—and I also knew the girl you wrote about. Penelope Houten. I'd do anything I could to help her prove she's innocent. But none of this has been proven. Until it has, it's libel."

Lark bit her lip. "What if I could prove that every word in that screenplay is true? Would you go ahead then?"

"If it could be proved, he'd be in jail. The reason he's not in jail is that it can't be proved."

"I think . . ." Lark said uncertainly, "I think that Emmy Elson, who wrote the articles, is trying to track down Penelope Houten. She could tell whether or not that part of it was true."

She glanced at Dom and saw a flicker of pain in his eyes.

"Give that idea up," he said gently. "She's not going to find her."

"Why not?"

"As I said, I knew Penny. She used to live with my mother. When she disappeared we all tried to find her. So did the police and later the FBI. None of us were successful. Emmy believes she's spoken to her but she can't be sure."

"She might come forward if she had the opportunity to vindicate herself and place the blame where it belongs: on Justin Groome."

"You really believe this stuff, don't you? You don't think *Monday* just got hold of some rumors and blew them out of proportion?"

"No, no, *no.*"

He regarded her curiously. "You seem to care as much about this project as you did about your 'Romance!' series."

More, much more, Lark cried inwardly. She waited for Dom's decision.

"I'm sorry," he said at last. "I don't see how we're going to do it. It's an excellent story, though. If Groome were already convicted and behind bars I'd say go ahead and write the screenplay without a moment's hesitation."

"But it's a docudrama like this that will get him put behind bars."

"No, a prosecutor does that." He stood up and gave her a heart-stopping smile. "I'm sorry I'm the bearer of bad news. I hope you'll get to work on something else and show it to me. You know I'll look at whatever you propose."

She was too disappointed to respond politely. "Thanks, anyway."

He regarded her a moment longer, as though puzzled by her, then he left.

Lark picked up the treatment and threw it across the room.

CHAPTER FIFTY-FIVE

TONI stood at the door of Justin Groome's penthouse, welcoming guests. The cavernous living room had been transformed for the occasion. This was Toni's first major fund-raising event that she had orchestrated since she had returned to Whitfield Communications. She had rented straight-backed silver-painted folding chairs and provided an elegant buffet of teas and coffee, biscuits, buns, cakes, and assorted cheeses. A sumptuous bouquet of fuchsias, irises, and golden-rod splashed against the window.

"It will save the room from looking like a meeting hall," Marianne had said when they planned the occasion.

"Or keep the fools from falling out," Toni had answered dryly.

Always, at the back of her mind, were the scathing allegations she was reading in the newspapers. Whenever she looked at Justin she would ask herself: Could he have raped my sister? Could he have murdered her?

It seemed impossible, and yet she couldn't help wondering.

"Welcome," she said to a small group of precinct leaders from Connecticut. "Thank you . . . yes . . . just go ahead and get a drink over there at the bar. You may take a plate to your seat if you choose."

The words were like a litany.

The lines thinned.

She felt someone's eyes on her and grew uneasy. She had had this feeling lately of being watched, and she didn't like it.

She decided to duck out now and return to her apartment. There was no reason for her to listen to Groome's speech one more time. Dwight, his press aide, was more than capable of mediating the question and answer session if Groome wanted help. He would be annoyed that she wasn't there afterward to help get rid of the press, but she didn't care. Her career was beginning to mean less to her now than it had when she had been married to Dom.

The afternoon sky was a bright October blue, the wind brisk. She was glad for her mink coat as she walked the ten blocks to her apartment.

The Haitian carpenter was there, working on her new library shelves. She had put off the renovations during the summer, not wanting to live on a job site. But Marianne had persuaded her to finish them now that it was fall. Toni kept forgetting about the work being done. It was as though she did not really live there any more. She had been away too long.

But, staring at the carpenter, she felt a jolt in her chest and wondered if the real reason she had put off the renovations was that she was afraid of her attraction for him. He nodded a greeting.

She asked, "How much longer will you be?"

"Till five." He went back to his work.

Toni took off her coat, hung it carefully in the closet, and went into the kitchen. She poured herself a glass of orange juice. After a moment she added a splash of vodka. She heard the carpenter hammering in the living room and visualized his powerful hands on her back, holding her, calming her. Why did she feel in need of calming? She tried to put him out of her mind. Just because she found herself missing Dom very much, didn't mean she was going to start hankering after every man she saw.

She felt the tears threatening. Sometimes lately she wondered if she were heading for a nervous breakdown.

"Excuse me," the man stood in the doorway. "I need to ask you a question about something."

Composing herself, she went with him into the living room.

He paused before speaking, looking at her with concern.

"What's your question?" she asked sharply.

"This shelf," he asked. "You specified for it to be shorter than the others, but I don't know if you realized that the others would be touching this edge of the window. It will throw the aesthetics off."

She studied the shelf he was discussing, but she was more conscious of the veins running through his large, dark hands which held the shelf, and the muscularity of his bare arms. He wore a red T-shirt with the arms torn off and faded blue jeans. She suddenly imagined him naked and had a vision of herself running her finger through the sawdust on his body, making a pattern that circled and spiraled on his thighs, his flat, hard belly. She shook herself and found him regarding her with an amused expression.

"Fix it however you think best," she said awkwardly.

"Fine." He glanced at his watch and turned to put away his tools. She gazed at his hands as they gripped the tools, imagining them on her breasts. She felt her nipples harden, then, as he reached for an old blue sweater, she realized she was cold.

"Toni . . . May I call you Toni?"

She nodded, savoring the sound of her name spoken in his low, resonant voice. He pulled the sweater over his head, then said, "I am going to a friend's art opening later. Would you like to come?"

Toni's eyes widened. "Sure," she said, surprising herself. "Where is it?"

"In the East Village."

The East Village! Toni was disconcerted that anyone would invite her to an art opening in the East Village. Why, she rarely even went to openings in SoHo. Her art gallery friends were all Madison Avenue or Fifty-seventh Street people. Fur coats, champagne, and caviar, that sort of thing. An East Village opening would not be her style at all.

Yet she almost felt Pierre had invited her as a dare. She couldn't resist.

"I'm going to go home to shower and change," said Pierre. "I'll meet you at the gallery. It's on Avenue C and Eleventh Street."

The feeling that she was being challenged intensified. Was she really willing to find her own way to the heart of Alphabet town to meet a virtual stranger? Was loneliness driving her crazy? Of course she wouldn't.

"Okay," she heard herself saying.

At seven-thirty Toni's cab pulled up on the corner of Avenue C and Eleventh Street. A group of scruffy looking youths wearing black jeans and black leather jackets were hanging around outside, holding plastic cups or drinking beer out of bottles.

Toni wished she'd changed into pants before coming. She felt conspicuous in her short skirt and fur coat.

She paid the cab driver, got out and heard some low murmurs of "Shame." A pale girl with short, peroxided hair brushed the sleeve of her coat with her hand.

"Poor old minks. I wonder how much they suffered before being murdered and made into this thing."

"I'd guess they're at least fifty in that coat," said a man in disgust.

"More like sixty."

"What?" Toni was not used to any stranger touching her coat, and it had never occurred to her that her gorgeous fur might stir any emotion other than envy.

"And a hundred trash animals." The girl with the peroxided hair stared accusingly at Toni. "Did you know for every sixty minks that are trapped, a hundred more animals are accidentally killed by the traps and tossed out? Dogs, deer, cats, rabbits—"

Toni pushed her way past the girl, wishing she hadn't succumbed to Pierre's ridiculous invitation. This was no place for her.

The loft was jammed with people. Toni felt everyone was staring at her gorgeous fur coat and thinking how cruel she was. Defiantly, she snuggled into it.

Where was Pierre?

She made her way to the bar, looking for something to drink. There was no bartender; just a white Formica table with white jug wine and plastic glasses on top. The wine wasn't even chilled. Grimacing, Toni turned away. She couldn't drink that stuff. Finally she spotted Pierre. He was talking to a giant woman dressed in orange and green stripes. She had one round, gold earring in the side of her nose and several smaller ones in her ear. When she spoke something glittered on her tongue and it took Toni a moment to realize her tongue had been pierced also.

Pierre glanced up, met Toni's eyes and came over.

"There you are. Are you enjoying yourself?"

"Not particularly."

"What do you think of the art?"

She hadn't noticed it. Now she glanced around the walls at the huge white canvasses. What looked like white rubber hoses were artfully attached in large squiggles. She shrugged. "Nothing. Are they yours?"

"No, a friend of mine. Do you want to meet her?"

"Is she the pierced one you were talking to?"

Pierre smiled. "You have pierced ears," he pointed out.

"I draw the line at tongues, though."

"My friend draws the line at nipples. But this does not stop her from piercing her tongue—and her clitoral hood."

"Ugh."

"We all have our own boundaries." He took her arm and guided her to the door. "I feel women should be free to do whatever they wish to their bodies. But personally I cannot say I enjoy seeing any sort of mutilation." He smiled again. "Even pierced ears."

"But that's different!" she exclaimed.

"Is it?" They stepped outside. "Come on, I can see you are not interested in the art. We can get something to eat."

Gratefully, she allowed herself to be escorted onto the street. Pierre kept stopping to talk to people, often in French which she did not understand. It seemed he knew everyone in that place.

When they were finally alone and walking west past burned out, abandoned buildings on Eleventh Street Toni asked, "Where are we going?"

"To my loft."

"I thought we were going to have dinner."

"I can cook if we are hungry."

Toni had never met anyone like him. It was as though he were doing exactly what he wanted to do, with no thought of trying to impress her.

"Are you afraid? I am really a very nice person." Pierre's brown eyes twinkled at her.

"No. Just puzzled. I mean, you hardly know me. Why would you take me back to your place?"

"It is the best way to get to know you," was his easy reply.

His loft was on the Bowery. It was one large room, with some of the area given over to a wide, low platform bed. A television set was on a scratched wood coffee table, with three ill-matched straight-backed wooden chairs placed around it. The rest of the space was given to plaster and wood sculptures. Toni slipped out of her coat and left it on a pile of boxes near the door, then wandered among the sculptures, bewildered. They were too strange to really like, but they had form and—something else. Something undefinably moving.

"You're an artist," Toni said.

"Not really. I am a carpenter. I do those for a hobby."

Pierre stretched out on the bed, watching her through half-shuttered eyes.

"Come here," he said, patting the bed beside him. "I want to hold you."

Uncertainly, Toni went over to him. He put his large arm around her and settled himself more comfortably. Toni closed her eyes.

Absently, Pierre stroked her hair. They lay in silence for a long time. A restful peace filled her. She felt she belonged. It was quiet in the loft. The sound of some drunks arguing outside on the street seemed very far away. She heard the faint ticking of a clock. The refrigerator turned itself on.

"What are you thinking?" asked Toni at last.

His eyes were closed, but he smiled. "One of the paintings in the show was of a ship. I was thinking about that. I have a dream, Toni. As soon as I have saved enough money I plan to buy a sailboat and sail about the Caribbean. It won't take much. I can make expenses renting it out, me as captain. This city stinks. I was thinking about that."

"Oh."

"I came here to make some money. Did I tell you I come from Haiti? It's the loveliest country in the world. But it's a hell to live in. I've seen things that would make your blood turn cold. They did mine." He paused.

"Oh, Pierre."

"I came to New York to start a new life. But it's the damndest city. There's money to be had, and I have made good friends. But it stinks. How can such wealth be in such close quarters with such poverty? Does it not break your heart to walk past people sleeping in the streets? Don't people know how much good could be done with the money that is spent on a single meal at a restaurant? I thought America was more civilized."

Toni didn't know what to say. She was one of the wealthy ones.

He still stroked her hair. "What about you?" he asked.

"What about me?"

"Why are you sad?"

"I'm not—am I?"

"It's funny," Pierre said after a while. "You're everything I don't like about this city. You're wealthy, gorgeous, probably heartless too. But there's something about you I feel drawn to. Just as I feel drawn to New York."

She didn't know whether to feel stung or flattered.

He shifted his position so that he was looking down at her, regarding her sleepily. "What is it about you that I like?"

"I don't know."

"I think I know. There is a Toni inside somewhere that is longing to get out. I am determined to find her. Maybe it is that. I can never resist a challenge. New York is a challenge too."

His work-roughened finger traced her eyebrows and ran down her cheek to her lips. She closed her eyes. She felt his finger on her throat, outlining her collarbone.

"Look at me," Pierre whispered.

She opened her eyes.

Pierre's mouth met hers. His tongue pried open her teeth. Her tongue met his cautiously. They gazed at each other as he explored each of her teeth, the roof of her mouth, under her tongue, the tip of her tongue.

Toni's breathing was ragged.

Pierre's hand moved up her leg. She saw the surprised delight in his eyes when he realized she wore stockings instead of panty hose. He grew hard, pressed against her thigh. She felt his hand on her pelvis, on her stomach. Then it lightly brushed between her legs and she shuddered deeply.

"Pierre—" she breathed.

"Ssh—"

Toni had never lain so passively when she was making love. But Pierre had her pinioned so she couldn't move. She didn't want to move. She felt a little delirious in spite of the fact that she had had nothing to drink.

Pierre tugged her cotton sweater over the top of her head. He left the satin and lace bra on, smiling.

"Pierre—" she said again.

He kissed the skin around the lacy material. "Mmm?"

But she didn't say anything else. She wanted him so badly it hurt. She wanted to tell him she loved him, but it was absurd. How could anyone fall in love on a first date? But she was crazy about him. She wanted to give him all of herself, not just her body.

Pierre found the zipper on the side of the short black skirt and slid the skirt down over her thighs. She wore her champagne panties, matching garter belt, sheer stockings. Pierre lifted himself up so he could gaze at her in wonder.

"I think I've finally met my ideal woman," he murmured.

This she could respond to. "I think I've met my ideal man."

"Don't move," he ordered. "Stay there."

He rose and stood next to the bed, still gazing at her. He unbuttoned his shirt and took it off. His bronze chest was broad and muscular, his stomach hard. He unbuckled his belt and unzipped his fly. In a few moments he was entirely naked. The muscles under his dark skin rippled sensuously as he opened a small drawer in the bedside table and took out a box of condoms. Toni couldn't take her eyes off him.

She still wore her high heels; he took them off, one at a

time. He lay down beside her. His movements were so leisurely, and yet so sensuous too, that Toni wondered whether
their lovemaking might last all night. Or perhaps all year—or
for years and years. There was a timeless quality to everything
that Pierre did.

Toni always wore her panties over her garter belt. Pierre
was able to slip them off without difficulty. He left the belt
and stockings on.

His gaze was as sensuous as his touch.

A finger traced a spiral inward to a breast, finding its way
under the filmy material. After a while, Toni felt him un-
hooking the bra from the front and easing it off her. She was
trembling with excitement. She wished he would hurry up,
but she wanted the experience never to end.

"Please . . ." she begged at last. "Please."

When he mounted her he did it with unstudied calmness
and control. He sank into her with a groan. Toni groaned too.

Their fever intensified. Toni had never felt such fullness,
such intensity of sensation. She cried out a little, then bit her
lip, then she cried out his name. She was rocked in a storm.
There was only her and Pierre, out on some ocean, somewhere,
nowhere, only the two of them in the whole world.

When it was over she was sobbing. Panting, Pierre rolled
off her and embraced her. Neither of them spoke. Toni's sobs
faded after a while and she drifted off to sleep. Even as she
slept she knew that Pierre's arms were around her, holding her
as though he would never let her go.

Chapter Fifty-Six

AT four in the morning Toni got up to get dressed. Pierre's eyes flickered open.

"I have to go," she said.

"Go where?"

"Home."

He sat up and pulled her back beside him. "I don't like that," he murmured, his face close to hers. "I think part of making love is sleeping together too. Why do you want to leave?"

"I have to be at the office by eight."

He lifted her wrist and squinted at her watch. "It's only four o'clock."

"But I have to change and shower and exercise and—" she was weakening.

"I think you have had plenty of exercise tonight, and I have a shower you can use. And why not wear the clothes you were wearing last night? You looked lovely in them."

She thought he might begin caressing her again and they would make love, but he didn't. He wrapped his arms around her, nestling her to his chest. Sighing, she drifted to sleep again.

She got to the office by eight-thirty, feeling light-headed from lack of sleep. She had managed a hasty shower and cup of coffee at her apartment, but she still felt dazed.

As Toni entered the lobby in her office building, a woman sprang forward.

"Excuse me, are you Ms. Toni Sumner?"

"Yes, I am."

"I'm from the *Monday Week*." She flashed a press card in front of Toni's eyes. "I have some follow-up questions for the series we're writing on Congressman Groome. His secretary told me I should talk to you."

Toni called for patience: It was important for Groome's sake that she maintain a smiling persona for the media.

"Yes, just at present Whitfield Communications is handling all Justin's requests for interviews." Toni glanced at the elevator.

"I want to ask you some questions about your sister, Violet Sumner."

Toni's guard went up, as it had whenever she had been approached by a reporter in the last few weeks. The woman looked back innocently. Her eyes were large, bottle green. Her mouth was pale, her hair like straw.

"Yes?" said Toni.

"Your sister was killed at a party several years ago."

"That's correct."

"What are your personal feelings about the allegations that Congressman Groome killed her?"

"They aren't true, of course. Why don't you come upstairs and I'll go over the story with you?"

"Thank you."

In the elevator they had nothing to say to each other. Toni's thoughts kept wandering to Pierre, asleep on his wide bed, his muscles relaxed . . .

The elevator stopped. Toni unlocked her office door. "Give me five minutes, will you? I just need to check on a couple of things."

"Sure."

The woman did not sit; she looked around Toni's reception area, as though there might be something there that would give away secrets.

As Toni hung up her fur coat, she remembered the girls' remarks about the minks at the art opening. She wondered if they really used sixty to make a coat.

She smoothed her hair, repainted her lips, and put the coffee brewer on. Her secretary would not be in for another twenty minutes.

"All right, you can come in now," she called through the open door.

As the woman entered, Toni asked, "What did you say your name was?"

"Marcia Collins. You have a nice office."

"Thank you, Marcia. Won't you have a seat?"

Marcia sat down and leaned inside her purse. Instinctively Toni knew she had switched on a tape recorder, although she also brought out a pad and pencil in order to take notes.

"Now, then, how exactly can I help you?" asked Toni briskly.

"I'm very interested in discovering more about Congressman Groome's relationship to your sister."

"Congressman Groome is one of New York's most eligible bachelors, as everyone knows. He's successful and personable. My sister was very fond of him and they had a wonderful friendship. The circumstances under which she died were very unfortunate. Another girl, Penelope Houten, was jealous of Violet. There was a fight and it seems Penny accidentally fired the gun which killed Violet."

"I've been trying to locate Penelope Houten. Do you have any idea where she might be?"

"None at all. Her face was badly disfigured in the fight and she was in the hospital for several weeks. Just before she was going to be released and stand trial, she ran away."

"Do you think she might have been murdered?"

"Good heavens, no!" Toni was shocked. "What makes you ask that?"

"It seems that she was the only one who witnessed Violet's death. Besides Congressman Groome, that is. I wanted to speak to her personally and get her story."

"She wasn't a witness. The police say she was the killer. Maybe unintentionally, but the killer nevertheless." It had happened three and half years ago, but Toni still hated thinking about Violet's death. "I'm sure it's all in the police reports. But it happened years ago. Don't you have more current topics of interest for your readers?"

A shadow of a smile crossed Marcia's face. "Oh, I think our readers will find this very interesting."

"Why do you suspect Congressman Groome?" Toni couldn't help asking.

"Doesn't it seem strange to you that two young girls would be so enamoured of an old, not very attractive, pompous politician? Your sister must have taken you into her confidence a little. Did you really feel that she was in love with Justin Groome?"

"Violet was too young to be in love with anybody."

"And yet there was something between them."

"Justin may have swept her off her feet. Not every woman goes for the *Gentleman's Quarterly* type. Justin can be remarkably charming."

"Still, it seems strange. They met when Violet was fifteen or sixteen and the relationship continued for five years. Did you feel, during those five years, that Violet was happy?"

Toni frowned. She couldn't honestly say that Violet had been a happy person, but it had never occurred to her that her unhappiness had anything to do with Justin Groome. "I wouldn't call theirs a 'relationship' when my sister was only fifteen. They were just friends."

"Oh," said Marcia Collins, scribbling away. " 'Just friends.' I see. We've heard allegations that Congressman Groome started an affair with her while she was underage."

Toni automatically denied it. But she was remembering something. There had been a night, a long time ago, when Violet had come to her apartment, unable or unwilling to return to their parents' house in Middleton after a day trip to New York. She had been hysterical but she hadn't said why. Toni had put her to bed, called their parents, and assumed it was just a fifteen-year-old's mood.

Justin Groome had telephoned the next day, asking after Violet. Apparently they'd been together the night before. Violet had been upset, he had reported. Thinking back, it was as though he'd been trying to elicit information from Toni. Had Violet said anything about him?

Toni must have reassured him. When she'd hung up the telephone, Violet was standing in the doorway.

"That was him, wasn't it?" she'd said.

"Justin?"

She nodded. Then without another word Violet went into the shower. She'd already taken two, one the night before and one earlier that morning. But nothing Toni said or did could get another word out of her on the subject. Toni had given up trying.

Toni shrugged off the memory. It had happened so long ago —and Violet's mood could have had any number of explanations.

"I don't know anything about that."

"Were you close to your sister? Would she have confided in you if she had been raped?"

Toni jumped nervously. "I believe she would have," she said in a strained voice.

"One possibility is that once Violet came of age she threatened to tell people that Congressman Groome had raped her. It would have been devastating to his career."

"You mean she was blackmailing him?"

"She always needed money, didn't she? She dropped out of college and was never very good at holding down a job." When Toni didn't speak, Marcia continued. "We understand that Penelope Houten was raped by Mr. Groome."

"As I've said before, I don't know anything about that," Toni said slowly. "Whenever I saw them together they seemed to be friends."

"It's possible Congressman Groome felt that being blackmailed by an emotionally unstable young woman like Violet was too much of a threat. So he killed her. He also took care that Penelope Houten would be jailed, or at the least, discredited so that no one would believe her if she accused Mr. Groome of raping *her*."

Toni shook her head again. Surely it was beyond the realm of possibility.

"I've read those reports already," she said uncertainly. "I never heard anything so crazy."

"There's a lot left unexplained. For one thing, the police

report containing Penelope Houten's supposed confession has been destroyed. At least, it can't be found, if it ever existed. Mr. Groome claims he heard the confession, but no one on the police force in Northkill has any recollection of it. That in itself is strange, don't you think? And why do you suppose she disappeared?"

"Maybe she was too scared to stand trial."

"Maybe she was murdered by the real murderer."

"Her body was never found."

"It's possible that she was terrified of being murdered herself, having witnessed your sister's murder. We're merely exploring possibilities, you understand."

Toni forced herself to smile. No matter what her own doubts were, she still had a job to do. "You're on the wrong track. Congressman Groome is a model to his community. He's kind, humorous, compassionate, and a decent human being. I'm sorry you've been to so much trouble for nothing."

"Oh, not for nothing at all," protested Marcia, her voice bland. "It's been very interesting."

Toni wondered what she had found interesting.

"There's nothing in the story," she reiterated, as she escorted Marcia into the reception area. "But if you have any other questions, do feel free to call me."

"I will indeed. Thank you for your time."

When Marcia Collins was gone, Toni asked the receptionist to send in her secretary, Kathleen, as soon as she arrived. Alone again, Toni paced around her large office. She knew Emmy Elson was the editor of *Monday Week*. Emmy had a reputation for scrupulous reporting.

Kathleen tapped on her door within a few moments.

"Check into the background of a reporter called Marcia Collins, will you?" asked Toni. "She works at the *Monday Week*. First get me Mr. Groome on the phone."

It was a full half hour before Toni was put through to Congressman Groome.

"Toni? Is something wrong?"

"There might be. You know how damnably these rumors are affecting your campaign."

"Hell, is there another one that jerk's spreading?" Con-

gressman Groome's rival, Timothy Marshall, had already un-
veiled some shady actions of Groome's which had cost points
in the polls.

"It might be his doing. I don't know about that. Someone
from *Monday Week* was here this morning asking more about
Violet."

Silence.

"Justin? Are you there?"

"Yes."

"She says . . ." Toni swallowed, "that you raped Violet
and then killed her because she was blackmailing you. And
that you raped Penny too."

"She can't get anything on me. Penny confessed to Violet's
murder."

"She's tried to get hold of that confession and it's gone."

"What do you mean, it's gone?" Justin sounded distracted.

"Vanished. No one remembers there ever having been a
confession except for the one she gave you while she was still
in the hospital. They've got only your word saying you didn't
do it."

"Oh, but that's absurd. Innocent till proved guilty, remember?"

"Tell that to the papers," said Toni, still wondering.

"How'd you handle it?"

"As best I could. I have a feeling I wasn't able to shake her,
though. Be prepared for a visit."

"Damn," said Groome. "Once these blasted rumors start
there's no telling where they'll end."

"I know."

"Did she . . ." Justin paused. "Did she mention Jonny
Whitfield?"

"Jonny? No, I don't think so. Why?"

"Did she say where *Monday Week* got hold of the rumors?"

"I didn't ask." Toni frowned. "Emmy Elson, Jonny's ex-
wife, is editor of the *Monday,* though."

"I know."

"She left Jonny a while back. As far as I know they haven't
kept in touch."

"I wonder about that," Justin said grimly. "Thanks for letting me know. And tell me if anything else comes up."

"I will."

Groome hung up the telephone. "Damn," he exploded. "Damn, damn, *damn.*"

CHAPTER FIFTY-SEVEN

E MMY Elson sat on a bar stool in her favorite Irish bar near her office on Eighth Avenue and Fifty-sixth Street. It was dark, dingy, and almost always empty, unless there was a football game on. She said she would meet Groome here, and here she was, and he was late. She was annoyed. She ordered a Coke.

Groome entered the dimness and came right over to her. His wide jaw seemed heavier, the pouches under his eyes puffier. "It's been a long time, Emmy Elson."

"Yes, it has."

"Mind if we sit at a table?"

She slipped off the bar stool and picked up her drink. "This one's pretty private," she said, leading the way to a booth.

When they were seated, Groome waved at the waitress. "Bloody Mary, please." He turned to Emmy. "I can't say that I'm happy about the articles you've been printing about me. I want to discuss them with you."

"We did our best to get an interview with you before now," Emmy replied politely.

"I usually let my press secretary or my media consultant handle requests for interviews. But here I am now, ready to respond."

Emmy smiled faintly. She took out a notepad and a pencil from her purse. "Let's begin at the beginning. Did you have an affair with Violet Sumner when she was underage?"

"No."

"Did you have an affair with Penelope Houten when she was underage?"

"No. But I will admit that she was very attracted to me."

"Were you being blackmailed by Violet Sumner?"

"No."

"Did you murder Violet Sumner and try to frame Penelope Houten for the murder?"

"No."

Emmy set down her pencil. "That's all," she said, lifting her eyes. "Thank you very much."

"You could destroy me just by printing that I deny all that. Where did you hear it?"

"My sources are confidential."

"You must have spoken to Jonny about this article?" asked Groome.

"Naturally."

"Is he the one who told you these slanderous lies?"

"His quotes are in the articles," Emmy soothed him. "They basically match yours."

"He didn't say anything else, off the record?"

Emmy stared at him blandly, without answering. Justin could tell she didn't like him.

"If Jonny didn't tell you those lies, there's only one other person who would," said Groome sourly.

"Who?"

"Penelope Houten herself. She's the only one who stands to gain anything from seeing me in trouble."

"What would she have to gain?"

"She'd be declared innocent—she could come out of hiding."

"How well did you know Penny?" asked Emmy, conversationally.

"Not terribly well. I used to see her when I visited Susan upstate. You know she adopted the kid."

"I'd appreciate it if you gave me your version of what happened the night of Violet's death."

"Certainly. I'd been invited to Penny's graduation party. Penny . . . well, I don't really know the details. All I know is that she confessed to the murder when she was in the hospital. I think Penny was jealous of Violet. She was very fond of me, you know. Not that I think she planned to do anything to Violet. It was an accident, I'm sure it was. I'm sure she didn't mean to do it."

Emmy waved at the bartender to bring her another Coke. "What happened then?"

"Penny ran away. She never stood trial for the murder. She simply vanished. I assumed she was dead after this long, but now these articles have started to emerge I'm beginning to wonder. You're sure you haven't been in contact with her?"

Emmy shook her head. "You say Penelope Houten confessed to the murder," she said after a moment. "But I haven't been able to get either transcripts or videotapes of that confession. The police in Northkill don't remember her confessing to anything. They remember her refusing to answer any questions. So does Susan."

"Really?"

"Why did you say she confessed to the murder?"

"She pulled the trigger," insisted Groome. "I saw her do it. Her prints were on the gun."

"You could have placed the gun in her hand after she was knocked out."

"But that's just a theory of yours. Jonny could have done the same thing."

Emmy nodded. "But it's a question of motive. Jonny had no motive to kill Violet."

"Nor did I!"

She didn't answer.

"If you print any more of these lies I'm going to sue."

"I'm surprised you haven't already."

Groome finished his drink. He was thinking hard. It was more important for him to get hold of Penny than it was to sue *Monday Week*. If they didn't print the story, some other rag would get hold of it. Penny would see to that.

"Look," he said, changing his tone. "If we could just get hold of Penny, we'd be able to verify all the facts. You have a fine reputation as an investigative reporter. I've looked into your background, and I know a lot about you. You were responsible for tracking down and locating those two missing kids, when the police failed. That was pretty impressive."

"It was a long time ago."

"Still, you have a knack for that sort of thing, I would guess. How would you like the job of finding Penny? It would be in both our interests."

"How do you know she's still alive?"

"There's never been a death certificate filed on her. I checked."

"She may have changed her name."

He smiled unpleasantly. "I'm quite sure she did."

"It's not my line of work. Surely the police are more qualified?"

"They weren't able to find her when her trail was still hot. I have more faith in you. Don't you see what a terrific story you'd have if you were able to hear her side of it, directly from her own lips?"

"It would be a terrific story," Emmy agreed.

"If you found her you could tell her I'd do everything in my power to get her a fair trial. She must be deathly sick of hiding out like this, with no future—and no face. I'd be willing to pay the finest plastic surgeon in the country to fix her face for her."

"It's been a long time, Mr. Groome," Emmy regarded him steadily. "Do you really think she'd want to see you again?"

Justin Groome's blue eyes glinted. "Yes," he said. "I think she would."

Not for the first time since she began working on this story, Emmy felt afraid for Penny. It occurred to her that if she didn't promise to help Groome find Penny he would get someone else who would.

"Let me think it over," she finally said. "I have no idea if I'll be successful, of course."

"I understand that. I'm willing to pay for the time you put into your investigation, plus all expenses. It will remain confidential." He glanced at his watch. "I have another engagement. Here's my card. Give me a call as soon as you hear anything."

"Good-bye, Mr. Groome."

He reached over to shake her hand. His smile was brilliant and friendly. Emmy smiled back.

"Good-bye for now," he said.

Groome's next appointment was in the Oak Room at the Plaza. He walked there, the wind stabbing at his greatcoat like sharp icicles. He could smell snow, although it was still early November.

Miguel Garcia y Reyes was there ahead of him. Groome had never yet known him to be late for an appointment. He liked that. It gave him a sense of security.

Groome sat down with a cool nod, wondering whether Miguel already knew why he had made this appointment. Sometimes Miguel had an uncanny way of knowing in advance what Groome wanted.

"I'm anxious to find a young woman," he started in at once. "Her name is Penelope Houten. I knew her many years ago."

"Ah, yes."

Groome looked at him sharply. "What do you know of her?"

Miguel lifted both hands, palms out. "Nothing, I assure you." He was a large man, with thin, transplanted orange hair, and brown eyes that always seemed to be smiling. Groome imagined what it would be like to have Miguel's hands around his throat while those brown eyes smiled.

"I am very busy on projects of my own," Miguel said slowly. "There has been a great deal of bad publicity about our rain forests in Amazonia. The sympathy is for the Indians now. I hear you, too, sympathize with the Indians."

"Pah," snorted Groome. "That was a speech I was making to college kids. I tell 'em what they want to hear."

"So you have not turned your back on the fine work that ITTO is doing?"

"Not in the least." Groome's mind was on other things, but he forced himself to attend to Miguel. He needed him. "The ITTO consists mostly of timber producers and consumers, and if I become senator they are important constituents of mine."

"This is true. Still, I have a great deal of work to do to make sure the livelihood of hundreds of people is not threat-

ened. The TFAP wishes me to speak to them next week. So I
do not know if I can help you just now."

"I'm sure you are very busy," Groome said impatiently.
"But I'd pay you well for this."

Miguel sighed.

"Tell me everything you know of this girl," he said, taking
out a pen and a small notebook, "and I will try to find her."

Chapter Fifty-Eight

"**W**ELL?" asked Carl, grimly.

Lark avoided his gaze. They were dining at the City restaurant, and she could barely hear Carl above the noise of conversation.

"I haven't pressed you because I understood your scruples about the fact that Dominic is married. But he is separated from his wife, Lark. There is no reason for you not to try to get close to him."

"Those are just rumors."

"Are they?"

"I'll tell him, Carl. I've promised, and I'll keep my promise."

"But why are you shilly-shallying like this? What are you waiting for?"

She changed the subject, as she tended to do when Carl brought up mention of Dom.

"I'm thinking of leaving APG."

"Is that so? Why?"

"A treatment I wrote was turned down. I want to find a company that will produce it. I think I have to go to New York."

"Rubbish." His gray eyes were stormy. "Does this treatment have anything to do with the life of Penelope Houten perhaps?"

Lark glanced around nervously, hoping no one had heard.

But the resonant buzz of conversation blended and obliterated what they said.

"I urge you to reconsider," said Carl. "You are in a strong position now at APG. Eventually you may meet someone who will be interested in your story. If you move to New York you will have to start all over again. There is no hurry to find a producer for the screenplay."

"I feel as though there is."

When she had told Trent she was thinking of resigning, he was horrified. "You're crazy! We haven't even tried to peddle the 'Romance!' series yet. If it takes off you could be vice president in less than a year. Where do you mean to go? What do you mean, New York? New York doesn't have the opportunities we've given you here in Hollywood. What's the matter with you? Are you nuts?"

"It's personal," was all she could say. "There's something I have to do, and I realize I can't do it here."

"What do you have to do?"

"It's personal," she repeated.

The news that she might leave swept around the office. Everyone was surprised and shocked, particularly since the "Romance!" series looked so promising.

A few days later her phone rang.

"Yes?"

"Beth, Dom Whitfield's secretary, is on line two," said Rosa. "He wants to know if you're free for lunch today."

"But I'm taking you to lunch," said Lark.

"We can easily do it another day."

Lark was torn. But she'd already had to reschedule her lunch date with Rosa twice. "Tell her I'm already tied up."

Rosa sounded as though she were going to argue, but Lark had hung up. A moment later the phone rang again.

"Dom Whitfield on line two." Rosa was laughing.

"Thank you." Lark took a deep breath then pressed line two. "Hello?"

"Lark, this is Dom. If you're busy for lunch, can you join me for a drink after work instead? I have a proposition to make."

She wondered if she'd ever get used to hearing his voice again. "Okay."

"Come up to my office around six."

"Okay," she repeated.

When she'd replaced the receiver, Lark buried her face in her arms. Now that Dom and Toni were separated she felt her relationship with Dom had subtly changed. He made no attempt to hide his attraction for her. It would not be long, she was certain, before he asked her out not just because she was a business associate.

And she? Well, she wanted to tell him about Carl being his father. She had promised Carl, but she had a feeling Dom would be furious with her for interfering in his private affairs. Perhaps he wouldn't even believe her.

Lark lifted her head and tried to focus on the treatment for a miniseries on her desk. She wanted to put all the Whitfields out of her mind. Her love for Dom was a ferocious, all-consuming passion underlying everything she did. The books she read, the clothes she wore, the films she saw all were with him in mind. He was a part of her.

But Susan was relegated to another part of her consciousness, one she rarely ventured into. It was too painful to think about Susan.

At six o'clock she went upstairs. Dom was in his office, pacing impatiently while he spoke on the telephone. He exuded a controlled energy, almost seeming to vibrate with angry enthusiasm. As soon as he saw her, he ended the phone conversation abruptly and hung up.

"Thank you for taking the time to see me," he said, and she felt guilty for having turned down his lunch invitation.

She tried to smile naturally. "No problem."

"Ready to go?"

"Yes."

As she followed him to his sage green BMW in the parking lot, Lark reflected that if marriage had not seemed to make Dom happy, neither had his separation from Toni. If anything, he looked even more haggard. There was a hollow look in his eyes, and very little warmth left. He seemed tense too;

she sensed the tension in his hands as he shifted into gear and maneuvered the car out of the practically empty lot.

She longed to ask him what had happened to the black Spider he'd had in New York.

"I'm taking you to a place on Sunset called Angelo's. Been there?"

"No."

"The waiters there know me, and I very rarely bump into colleagues or anyone I don't want to talk to."

She nodded. A silence fell. She wracked her brain for something to say but clanging in her brain like a fire bell were the words "I love you—I love you—I love you." She was half-afraid if she opened her mouth those words would come out.

Dom did not seem to mind the silence. Certainly he made no attempt to break it. He left the car in front of the restaurant for the valet to park. Once inside, the maitre d' seated them at a booth. Dom ordered a vodka tonic. Lark asked for a glass of house red.

"It's Santiago, a Chilean cabernet," the waiter informed her.

Lark's wine education had not extended as far as Chile, but she nodded. She turned to find Dom's eyes fixed on her and she dropped hers again. There must be something she could think of to say!

"I hear you're thinking of leaving us," said Dom.

She looked up again. "I'm still just thinking about it."

"Do you have any plans?"

"I'm thinking of moving to New York. I'd like to work with a network television station."

"You'd make more money if you stayed with us."

"Probably. I'm not really interested in that."

"No, I didn't think you were. But have you thought about the question of your visa? As long as you're in the States you only have permission to work for us."

Her face fell. She had forgotten that legally she was still a British citizen. Dom gestured at the waiter to bring him another vodka tonic.

"Lark, you've been an enormous asset to APG. In the year you've been with us, you've been responsible for two of our major successes. And you've been no end of help on the set of *Razzle Dazzle.*"

"Thanks, but really I—"

He held up a hand to stop her. "I know, I know. I've heard about your modesty, in addition to all your other talents and graces. I'm not asking you to stay on as associate producer. But I am asking you to wait until we see how the 'Romance!' series turns out. If it's a success your future is secure in Hollywood. You can write your own ticket."

"Not necessarily," she said slowly.

"I know what you're thinking," he said, surprising her. "You want to get that Groome thing onto the airwaves so badly you'd give up your own career in order to try to do it. But you're going about it the wrong way. You need more power in this town, and then you can do what you want. Don't you see?"

Lark regarded him in amazement. This was totally unexpected.

"It's not just because of that," she lied.

"Really?"

Her eyes dropped again. How would their conversation ever get personal enough to allow her to broach the subject of his father? They were miles distant, mere business colleagues.

But then Dom reached over and put his hand on top of hers where it rested on the stem of the glass. Lark felt as though his skin scorched hers. Her heart thumped wildly and she couldn't look at him.

After a long moment, very shyly, she placed her other hand on top of his.

"Dom—" she breathed, barely audibly.

They were interrupted by the waiter bringing their second round of drinks. Dom drew his hand away and picked up his glass.

He cleared his throat. "Look, if you stay, and the 'Romance!' series goes, you'll be its coproducer. That means you'll have virtually complete control over a project that I know you'll enjoy and you'll be good at. Give yourself a year or two establishing yourself as a producer, and a successful one, as I have no doubt you'll be. By that time I'll probably be fired, and my replacement might be thrilled by your Groome script. In any case, you'll be meeting other producers and directors while you're here. If we've turned something of yours down, that you worked on independently, you can still peddle it to another company."

Lark was amazed. His offer to coproduce the "Romance!" series was stupendous, way beyond her wildest expectations.

"I'm thinking, I'm thinking." She laughed, looking up and finding his quizzical gaze fixed on her.

"At least you haven't turned me down out of hand," Dom said. He was looking more relaxed. "Are you hungry? I just realized I'm drinking on an empty stomach."

"Yes, a little."

They ordered hamburgers and a salad. Dom asked for a wine list. He glanced at her.

"Is red still all right with you?"

"Yes. May I see what they have?"

He handed her the wine list, looking amused.

"How about a Côte de Brouilly?" she suggested. "They have an eighty-five Domaine de Chavanne which'll go great with the hamburgers."

She had to choke back her laughter at seeing Dom's expression.

"Fine with me," he agreed.

She gave the order to the hovering waiter.

"Where'd you learn about wines?" asked Dom when he'd left.

"I've always been interested in that sort of thing," she said vaguely.

"What sort of thing is 'that sort of thing'?"

"Oh, you know."

"You have got to be the most evasive creature I have ever met."

They savored the wine until the hamburgers arrived. This time the silence between them felt as natural as breathing.

"Dom," said Lark suddenly, her mouth full, "you know something?" She looked up and caught a look of shock on his face. "What's the matter?"

He shook himself. "Nothing. I just thought—you reminded me of something when you said my name just then. Of someone. It was weird. What were you going to say?"

"Your offer of coproducing the 'Romance!' series never occurred to me. I'm really not prepared to answer you tonight. You didn't expect me to, did you?"

"I guess I hoped you would. But we haven't hit the dessert yet."

"I realize what a compliment it is. I know I'd be a fool to refuse. It's just that—maybe I am a fool."

"I'm sure you're not that. Any decision you make will be grounded in wisdom."

They had zabaglione for dessert with a glass of marsala. But Lark barely touched the drink. She knew she should drive Dom home. He had consumed well over the limit.

"In all my inquiries about you," said Dom, "I've heard nothing about a boyfriend. Do you have one secretly stashed away?"

She shook her head.

"How come I can find out so little about you?"

"There's very little to find out."

"I have a feeling you like being mysterious."

"How do you know I'm not just superficial?"

He smiled at her. "Anyone who orders Côte de Brouilly with their hamburger can not be superficial."

When they finally stood up to leave, Dom gripped the side of the table to steady himself.

"Whoa," he muttered. "I haven't drunk this much since my honeymoon."

"I can drive you home," offered Lark.

"I think you'll have to. But then how will you get home, unless you borrow my car? In which case, how will I get to work tomorrow?"

"We'll work it out. I can take a cab from your place."

"All right, you superficial beauty. I suppose I can explain why your car was left overnight in the parking lot if I have to."

The fresh air braced them. Lark took Dom's car keys, grateful that he wasn't arguing with her about driving.

"Take Sunset Boulevard," he directed.

Lark loved driving along Sunset, especially at night when there was very little traffic. The drive was leisurely and quiet. They spoke little. Twice Lark thought Dom had fallen asleep, but then she glanced at him and saw his eyes, dark and tired, staring straight ahead. Suddenly he asked, "How long ago did we meet?"

"Last winter."

"Funny, it seems like years. You're constantly on my mind, Lark. Your name is on someone's lips at every meeting. Jonny raves about you as his savior. I just can't seem to get away from you." He ended this surprising outburst on a jagged laugh which shook Lark immeasurably.

"The easiest way would be to fire me," she said, trying for lightness.

"That's not what I had in mind."

Her hands gripped the steering wheel. Just what did he have in mind? An affair? She drew in her breath, trying to calm down. She couldn't have an affair with him if he didn't know who she really was. And much as she longed to tell him the truth, she knew she would not dare. She was still too afraid.

Dom directed her up a winding narrow hill road, sparsely dotted with beautifully lit mansions. She pulled into the driveway of the house near the top. The smell of eucalyptus was everywhere. Far below and around Los Angeles spread out before them, a cacophony of lights reflecting the stars overhead. Neither got out of the car.

"It's marvelous," she said softly.

"I know what I said sounded abrupt to you," Dom said after a moment. "But it's true. I can't get you out of my mind."

Dismayed, Lark went on gazing at the twinkling lights. Did he expect her to spend the night with him? Had he taken it for granted, after the way she'd whispered his name like that in the restaurant? Fool, *fool,* she cursed herself. She couldn't get involved with Dom Whitfield. Not to tell him she was really Penny would be a lie he would never forgive her for if he ever found out.

He touched her arm. "Lark—beautiful Lark." His hand cradled the back of her neck, gently turning her face toward him.

She felt she was in a fever. His touch intoxicated her. His *eyes* intoxicated her. She reached wildly for the door handle. "I should get home. I should call a cab."

His eyes narrowed in puzzlement. "You're afraid," he said slowly.

She opened the car door and leapt out. "I'm not—*I'm not.*"

He came up behind her and put his hands on her shoulders rubbing them gently. "There's no need to be afraid." He turned her around so that she faced him. Then he leaned toward her and kissed her on the mouth.

Lark closed her eyes. The lights of the city danced in her head as she felt him tasting her. Her arms went around his neck. She had dreamed of this moment for so many years that now she simply abandoned herself to the joy of the moment. *Dom—Dom—Dom.* He was kissing her. He was holding her, caressing her hair. His tongue moved down the side of her throat. He whispered her name. "Lark—"

But it wasn't her name. Was it? Not to Dom. Not if he knew.

She drew away, her breathing ragged, fear coursing through her again. She gazed around, half-afraid Justin Groome might suddenly emerge from the shadowy rhododendrons that hid the tall fence surrounding the house. She could not tell Dom the truth.

"I have to go home."

Dom looked as though he longed to ask her something, but then he said kindly, "Come inside and I'll call a cab for you."

He led the way down a short flight of tiled stairs to the front door and took out his keys. The door opened into a magnificent living room with a vast picture window overlooking the same panoramic view of Los Angeles that had taken Lark's breath away outside. A coffee colored couch and two armchairs were arranged in front of a fireplace. Lark saw Dom in everything about the room: It personified his taste, his wealth, his understated power.

She paused on the threshold, looking around.

"The house belonged to Jonny until two years ago," Dom said. "I bought it from him as a favor, but now I like it."

"It's very beautiful." But she stayed on the threshold. "I'd better call for a cab."

"Let me make you a cup of coffee first," he offered.

"No thanks. I'd really better go."

He studied her, his head tilted to one side, as though trying to figure her out. "All right," he said at last, and went over to the telephone to dial.

When he'd ordered the cab, he said, "At least come on in and sit down until it gets here."

She felt foolish standing in the doorway and cautiously went over to the armchair. They regarded each other. Lark saw the shadows in his eyes, the weariness in his face, and wondered if his success was really worth the expense of his personal happiness.

She felt another wash of emotion, more complex than the love she already felt for him, and turned abruptly away.

"I can't accept the job offer," she said. "It's impossible."

"What?" Dom sounded confounded.

"Of course I can't accept. I was mad to consider it even for a moment."

"Will you tell me why?"

"Isn't it obvious?" She sounded almost bitter.

His mouth crooked into a half smile. "Because I'm in love with you or because you're in love with me?"

He had said it so casually at first his words didn't register. Then a rosy flush spread over Lark's features. *He had told her he loved her.*

Dom rose and came over to her, staring down at the flush that had suffused her face. "You do love me." His voice was almost awed, as though she had conferred upon him a great honor. "And yet there's something else, isn't there? That's not the reason we can't work together. You're afraid of something."

Lark stared back at him, not answering.

"Won't you tell me what it is? Maybe I can help."

"You can't help."

"But what could it be that would make you turn down the

offer to coproduce the 'Romance!' series?" he said, half to himself.

"I want to accept. I wish I could."

"Then accept." He took both her hands in his and gripped them. "Don't look at it as an emotional entanglement, but as a career move. It might be the most important one you make. Don't pass it up because of something intangible—certainly not because of our feelings for each other. We can't say what might happen. We can't predict. But don't make a mistake regarding something real and tangible, like your career." He added earnestly, "Take the job. We won't be working so closely that it will make life intolerable for either one of us."

They heard a car rumble up the quiet hill and Lark knew it was her cab.

The sound of a cool, self-conscious cough made them jump. Their eyes swiveled to the stairs. Dom dropped her hands. Toni smiled coldly at them. She carried a suitcase in one hand and her purse slung over her shoulder. Her pantsuit was light fawn, a silk material that fluttered around her curvaceous body. She wore high heels. She looked very elegant and chic, and totally in control.

"That was very touching," she drawled. "But watch out what Dom says about that career thing. He means it."

Dom pulled himself together.

"When did you get here?"

"This afternoon. I'm just here to pack my things and get out of your life. I'm not planning to spend Christmas with you. Don't look so stricken."

"My cab's here," said Lark. "I'd better go."

She slipped out of the room before either of them could say anything. Dom and Toni were left regarding each other warily.

"It was time to get this thing settled," said Toni, letting her guard down a little. "I hate having things drag on like this."

"I feel the same way. I did call you."

"Once." She hadn't returned his call. One message wasn't enough.

"Toni."

She went into the hall and set down her suitcase. She did not have to look at him to know his expression, that wary, intense gaze that made her forget everything, everyone on this planet except him—and her.

She knew he was struggling with what he wanted to say. She waited, longing for it to be some word of love.

Finally, he strode to the picture window and stared at the twinkling lights of Los Angeles. He spoke rapidly, "Maybe it was my fault. But I expected something else, Toni. I didn't realize you'd get so wrapped up in me. I didn't realize you'd give up everything, simply in order to be my wife. We're living in the nineteen-nineties. Relationships like that don't work anymore."

Toni's eyes burned. "Be honest with yourself at least, if not with me. You were never really in love with me in the first place."

He didn't deny it. Before he'd met Lark he hadn't known what being in love was like. "I didn't know I wasn't, and that's the truth."

She stared hotly at the emerald green and black Kirman rug at her feet.

"I'm not going to persuade you to stay," Dom went on. "It wouldn't work. But I feel terrible about it, nonetheless."

"Me too."

Dom turned to face her. "I've been a brute to you, Toni. I've known it all along, but I didn't want to face it." He hesitated. "I want you to know that there's been no one else. I mean, nothing's happened. I've been true to you in deed, if not in spirit."

"Thanks for telling me."

He went over to her, looking speculative, a warmth in his tawny eyes that she couldn't miss. If he leaned over to kiss her she'd punch him so hard he'd be reeling, she thought. She narrowed her eyes, warningly.

Dom backed away. "When are you leaving?"

"Now." But she didn't move.

"It's after midnight."

"There'll be a flight eventually."

"I'll drive you to the airport."

"I'd rather take a cab."

They went on looking at each other.

The Russians had a word that had no equivalent in English, remembered Toni. It described the feeling you had for someone you had once loved.

It was the feeling she had for Dom now.

In a few moments she would call the cab company. In a few moments she would say good-bye to Dom coolly and calmly. There was no reason to fight anymore. Not now that it was over.

There was no more reason to cry, either.

Chapter Fifty-Nine

I T was Christmas Eve. Jonny was in Las Vegas. He sat alone at a bar, drinking. Every now and then he lifted his glass to the light to see how much was left, and it would seem for a minute that it was floating in the air.

A man approached whom Jonny had never seen before.

"May I join you?"

Jonny shrugged unwelcomingly. He decided he had never liked dyed, orange hair on men.

"My name is Miguel." The man's brown eyes sparkled. "I do not think you know me."

"No, I don't," agreed Jonny, wishing he would go away.

The man smiled. "We have some business to discuss, my friend."

Jonny's eyes narrowed. "We do?"

The man smiled back serenely. Jonny detected from his accent that he was from some Latin country. He gulped down the rest of the drink.

"Yes." The man spoke quietly but clearly so that no one but Jonny could hear him. "You have spent some time—some amorous time—with a young girl named Fairusa. We have evidence of this. I have the photographs with me. Do you wish to see them?"

Jonny's face paled. *Statutory rape,* he thought, and then, *Oh, no, Emmy . . .*

Then he remembered that Emmy was gone.

"What do you want from me?"

"A favor, that is all."

Blackmail. "How much?" he asked, automatically.

The man looked shocked. "This has nothing to do with money!"

"Well?"

"This film you have been working on. It is about the rain forest of the Amazon, yes?"

Jonny ordered another drink. When it arrived he forced himself to sip it slowly.

"Yes."

"We wish you to bring to us every reel that has been filmed, and you promise not to continue."

"Why?"

"This does not matter."

"This is bullshit. I wouldn't make a promise like that to the president of the United States. Who is 'us,' anyway?"

"This does not matter," Miguel repeated. "Will you bring to us the completed film?"

"I guess you haven't heard, *amigo*," said Jonny, smiling a little into his glass. "There is no film. They've pulled me off the project. I was spending too much money on it."

"The film was almost finished."

"Not quite. Shit, you don't have to worry. It's not going to be released." He glanced up. "Who are you, anyway?"

"I have already introduced myself. My name is Miguel. We both have a common interest in . . . Fairusa."

Jonny turned away again. Emmy, he moaned inwardly. What have I done?

"She seduced me," Jonny said. "Evidently you set me up for it. But I can talk my way out of that. I can hire the best lawyers in town."

"I see." Miguel looked gently reflective. "May I remind you of something? I wish to take your mind back fifteen years. You were in Brazil on a business trip."

Jonny remembered that trip. That had been when he'd first gotten the idea for the movie on the tragic destruction of the rain forests. He had taken a boat ride up the Amazon. And there was a woman . . .

"There was a woman of whom you became very fond."

Now what? thought Jonny.

"You made her pregnant."

"That's not true!"

"It is true. She became engaged to be married, but she had the baby early. Too early. She confessed that it was yours."

"How do you know all this?"

"That woman is my brother's wife."

"Go on."

"She gave birth to a girl."

Jonny waited.

"That girl's name is Fairusa."

Jonny hopped off the bar stool and walked swiftly to the terrace. The cool, desert air felt good, helped to remind him where his skin was. The skin of fire. He put his head in his hands and leaned his shoulder against the wall. Despair filled him.

The stars seemed to crawl over him like hungry ants. He turned and watched the blazing neon lights on the street below. Cars crawled by. Worms eating his festering body, crawling through the holes already eaten in him. His mouth was dry. The wind had died.

Miguel came out and put his arm around Jonny's shoulders in a friendly way. "You take things too hard," he said gently.

"Sure I do." Jonny was aware that the other man mistook despair for weakness.

"You cannot meet our request?"

"There's no way I'll give you what I've already shot. But I've already said the movie's not going to be released. You can tell your big business cronies back in Rio that they can relax."

Some time later he knew he was alone on the terrace. He wondered what Miguel would do. In order to stop the film from being released, would he ruin Jonny's life? *Fairusa* . . .

Well, he couldn't be worse off than he was then, could he? What could some blackmailing sonofabitch from Rio do to hurt him at this late date? His life was already over, wasn't it?

CHAPTER SIXTY

"**H**OW do you suppose Emmy Elson got hold of a story like this?" Toni asked Justin the next time she saw him.

"I have no idea."

"She didn't contact me—the other girl did. Marcia Collins. Did Emmy ever get in touch with you?"

"Yeah. Sonsofbitches, all of them."

Toni regarded him. "You'll sue, of course."

"I don't know what I'll do yet. I'm trying to win an election campaign. A court case right now would take up all the headlines."

Toni was surprised that he hadn't called his lawyer already. It seemed to her that he had to sue for libel simply for the sake of appearances.

Justin was pacing. "Who's behind it?" he said. "That's what I want to know. Who's behind all these lies?"

"A man in your position has made a lot of enemies in his lifetime," Toni pointed out. "You didn't get where you are today by being Mr. Nice Guy."

Justin did not appear to hear. "What's the news of Jonny Whitfield?" he asked. "Has he been in touch with his wife?"

"What difference would that make?"

"He might be out to get me. Or someone might have bribed him into passing on these lies. Do you have any idea what he's been doing lately?"

"He's still struggling to get millions to make his outlandish creations in Hollywood. Fewer and fewer producers will touch him. He's an overspender. I gather he isn't doing too well."

"So he needs money."

"I suppose so."

"But who would pay him to tell these lies?"

"You really think Jonny is making up this stuff about you? Why would he do that?"

Justin glowered. "He doesn't like me. Never has."

"Still, there wouldn't be any point."

"Do you know how I can get hold of him?"

"No."

"Could you call Dom and find out?"

"No."

"You two still aren't speaking?"

"No. There's the telephone. Why don't you call him yourself? It's seven in the morning there. Dom might still be at home."

To her astonishment, Justin did exactly that. He picked up the receiver. "What's the number?"

She gave it to him, regarding him curiously. Why did Justin think Jonny had anything to do with the articles?

"Hello, Dom? Justin here. Listen, I'm trying to pin down Jonny. Got a number for him? No . . . I see." He jotted something down. "Thanks a lot. Hope I didn't wake you. No, no . . . a personal matter. Thanks again. Bye."

"Well?" asked Toni.

"Jonny's in Vegas, gambling as usual."

"What a surprise."

"I think I'll fly to Las Vegas this afternoon and talk to him. You can hold the fort for me here, can't you? The phone's been ringing off the hook again. I told Dwight to tell the press 'No comment' for the time being."

"You'll have to be a bit stronger than that," said Toni.

"In time, in time. First I have to find out what I'm up against."

Jonny was stone-cold sober. He never drank when he gambled. He was winning tonight and he was feeling better.

Fuck Hollywood, he thought. *Fuck the whole damn lot of them.*

The roulette wheel went around and the silver ball spun dizzily into a red slot. He hadn't been concentrating, that's why he'd lost that one. The crucial part about gambling was the concentration. It was a form of kinetic power, to be able to get the ball to land on the right color, or to have just the right card turn up in your hand. You could will that sort of thing, if you concentrated hard enough.

A tap on his shoulder made him jump.

"Justin!" Jonny stood up, annoyed. "What are you doing here?"

"I just flew in from New York. I heard you were here."

"Let's get a drink." Any magic power he had was definitely gone now. He would not win again that afternoon, of that he was certain. "I'll just go cash these in."

Justin waited for him in the bar. He was seated at a table in a corner, farthest from the television which blared over the counter. Jonny ordered scotch; Groome did not drink.

"Know anything about this?" he asked, shoving the front page of the latest issue of *Monday Week* in front of Jonny.

Jonny glanced at it indifferently, then, as the story captured him, he read more carefully. When he was finished he looked up with a broad smile.

"Good God!" he said. "The truth comes out at last. How on earth did you let this slip by you?"

Justin glared. "Are you sure you didn't have anything to do with it?"

"No, but I'll tell you one thing. It's not just the New York newspapers that are after you. Even Hollywood is interested in your story."

"What do you mean?"

"There's a treatment for a screenplay being peddled right now that describes the whole sordid story of your life. It's written as a docudrama, and a very convincing one at that, I understand."

"Are you sure you had nothing to do with this?"

Jonny's drink arrived; he sipped it. "I'm quite sure. What would I have to gain?"

"Someone might pay a good deal for information like this. A lot of people would like to ruin me."

"And I won't deny that I'm one of them. But I will deny I had anything to do with this article."

"I want whoever's been feeding these lies to the paper to deny them immediately. I want the whole thing quashed."

"I'll bet you do. Good luck." He started to rise.

Groome reached over and grabbed Jonny's collar. "Look here, you gloating, drunken, sonofabitch, did you tell anyone these lies? Anyone at all?"

Jonny struggled to free himself. His neck was being squeezed and he couldn't breathe. "No," he gasped.

Groome released him and Jonny collapsed back in his seat. He loosened his collar nervously.

"You never told Dom?"

Jonny shook his head.

"Your mother?"

"No."

"Your ex-wife?"

"No."

"If you're lying to me—"

"I'm not lying, I swear it."

Justin studied him with contempt. "You're a coward. You'd never admit you're lying because you know I'd break every bone in your body if I thought you were responsible for this article."

"For Chrissakes, leave me alone. I tell you I had nothing to do with it."

"All right, now tell me about this screenplay you read."

"I didn't read it—I just heard about it. Someone gave it to Dom to read. He turned it down of course. He wasn't going to get involved in a lawsuit with you, and he was smart enough to realize that's where it would lead."

"Who wrote it?"

Jonny didn't answer.

"Do you want me to force you to answer?"

"No. I don't know who wrote it."

"You're lying."

"I'm not lying," Jonny said miserably. He didn't know why

he was trying to protect Lark, except that he had no wish for her to go through what he was going through himself just now.

Groome regarded him in disgust. "Never mind. I can find out easily enough. Now, you listen to me. I'm going to find out who's doing this to me, and when I do, that person is going to pay. If you're keeping something from me I'll include you in on the payment. And if you find out where this stuff is coming from, I want you to tell me. Is that clear?"

"Jesus, Justin. How on earth would I find out that? I'm not a politician. I don't even live in New York."

"Some of these accusations are things only you know. That makes you my number one suspect. If you're feeding them to someone else, I'm still holding you accountable."

Jonny stared with loathing at the older man. "I hope that's all you came here to say."

"No, it isn't. I'm offering you a chance too. I know you've been kicked off that movie you were making about the rain forest. You ran out of money, didn't you? I'm willing to back you in it, if you help me find Penny. I figure that's a fair deal."

Jonny's jaw dropped. "You'll finance the rain forest project?"

"It's almost finished, isn't it?"

"Pretty much."

"I'd like you to have the satisfaction of finishing it," Groome said pleasantly. "But, as I said, I do need Penny in return."

Jonny hardly heard the last part. "Are you going to talk to Dom about this? Financing the project, that is?"

"Certainly. A few more environmental votes won't hurt me. But you will find Penny for me, won't you?"

"I don't know where she is."

"If you aren't the one spreading these rumors, then she is. I want her found. Your wife must know where she is."

"If Emmy knew, she'd never tell."

"She might tell you."

"No, she wouldn't."

"I don't care how much damned integrity she has, if she

knows where Penny is, I want you to find out." He stood up. "You know where to reach me. I'm counting on you, Jonny."

Jonny didn't answer. Groome's large frame blocked the white glare from the sunshine outside as he passed through the door. Then he disappeared.

Jonny ordered another drink.

He gazed at the article again. The details of the night of Violet's murder were indisputable. Emmy Elson and Marcia Collins—whoever she was—had managed to describe them not only with factual clarity, but with tension and compassion too. Penelope Houten was made out to be a hapless victim who fled because she knew that where Justin Groome was concerned there would be no justice for her.

Incredible. But true, as he well knew.

Jonny pushed away his drink. He was sure Penny was behind this. How confidential were newspaper sources, anyway? Could Groome force Emmy to reveal names? Not physically force her perhaps, but if she were threatened with going to prison for contempt of court, would she reveal Penny's whereabouts?

He didn't think so. Emmy would be willing to go to prison for the sake of a principle. But he didn't know about the other girl.

His fear for Penny dissipated after a short while. His mind was on Amazonia, and the chance he now had to finish the project that was never very far from his heart. Leaving his unfinished drink, he got up and left.

He was headed back to Hollywood.

CHAPTER SIXTY-ONE

"**D**OMINIC is getting a divorce," said Carl.
"Is he?"

It was Christmas Day. Lark was at Carl's house: They were going to lunch at Ma Maison.

"I'm going to put my proposal to you a different way, Lark. I realize I was a little overbearing when we first discussed this. Naturally I have no intention of betraying you. You can trust me on that score." He sat down on a steel-framed kitchen chair. "Will you sit down too? I am tired."

"Carl, I know you're ill." She put an arm around his shoulders, upset by how thin he had grown. Even his face seemed skeletal. "Why won't you tell me what's wrong with you?"

"I am ill," he said. "I have been ill for years. I didn't want anyone to know, but it's getting past the point now where I can hide it."

"But is there nothing you can do? No cure?"

"There was no cure for the plague," he replied bitterly, "except to get rid of the rats that carried the disease."

Anxiously, she sat beside him. "What can I do?"

"You can help me with Dominic. I want my son to recognize me before I die. I want him to know me and to love me. And I have not much time. Help me, Lark! Help me reconcile my son to my existence."

Carl buried his face in his hands. Dry sobs rattled his throat, choking him. His body shook in abrupt convulsions. It was horrible.

Lark knelt before him, tears burning her eyes. Carl loved his son, perhaps as much as she did. And he was dying. She was as certain of that fact as she was of Carl's love.

"I'll tell him," she whispered. "I swear I will."

Carl took out his handkerchief and blew his nose, trying desperately to compose himself.

"I found out I was HIV positive seven or eight years ago," he said. "I was involved in many different relationships in the late seventies and early eighties. Some of them were homosexual. I contracted AIDS shortly before I met you." He paused. "I have told no one else. Only you and my doctor know."

"Oh, Carl—*Carl*."

"It is too late for regrets now. In the beginning I tried all sorts of cures, those faddish things, you know? But I kept getting sick. Each time it was worse. Now I have cancer and it has spread too far for it to be stopped. All I want is to have my son recognize me as his father before I die. And then I want to die gracefully, without any fuss. I will not linger in a hospital."

"I'll help you—I'll do anything."

"Then tell Dominic about me. I know you can do it so that he will listen and feel well-disposed toward me. I know he will trust you."

She would never forget how Carl had helped her in the difficult time after she had run away from home. She owed him her beauty, her security, her success. She would stand by him now.

"All right, I will."

"And you will not go to New York?"

"No. God, *no*. Of course I won't leave you. And I'll tell Dom on Monday."

They stayed there in silence, her head buried in his lap.

"What are you thinking?" he asked at last.

She sighed deeply. "I was thinking what a terrible thing love is."

"Terrible?" he repeated slowly. "No."

"Terrible," she whispered. "Everyone I ever loved has left me. And now you're going to leave me too."

He lifted her face and studied it gravely. His eyes were red-rimmed and watery. "There are some people who did not leave you. You left them."

His face was washed away in a blur of tears. "Susan," she heard herself crying.

"I left her too. I blamed her for something she never knew. It is too late for me, but not for you, Lark. Isn't it time for you to go to her? She would be so happy to know you are alive."

"I'm so afraid."

"Well." There was a long silence. "Only you can fight the battle between fear and love."

Lark thought about what he said for a long time. His words were like a challenge and the challenge strengthened her. She stood up at last and kissed both his cheeks.

"Anyway," he added, "even if the person you love leaves you, or dies, wouldn't you still rather have had the time together, loving each other, than never to have had it at all?"

She considered. When her mother had died she had wished she'd never been born, but now, looking back, wasn't she grateful to have loved and been loved for those first seven years of her life? And hadn't she been glad to have known Susan that last, wonderful year of school? Everyone would die eventually. Did it really make a difference whether it was after two years or ten years or twenty-five years of being together?

She smiled through her tears. "I certainly would rather have loved you and lost you than never to have met you," she said sincerely.

"Thank you, my dear." He stood up. "Now let us go to our Christmas lunch before we lose our reservation."

CHAPTER SIXTY-TWO

THE following Monday Lark took the elevator to Dom's floor. It was the week between Christmas and New Year's and only a few people were in the office. Most were taking their vacation.

Lark had taken no time off since she had started work at APG. Christmas in Los Angeles had not seemed real to her. Even Christmas Eve had been a workday like any other.

"Hello," said Beth when she saw Lark. "Dom's in a meeting right now, but he should get out by four. Do you want to wait?"

"Yes, I'll wait." It was already three-thirty.

"I understand you might be coming to work on our floor."

She still had not given Dom a definite answer, but now she said to Beth, "Yes, I am."

"That's great."

Lark sat down, smoothed her cream corduroy skirt over her lap, and flipped through the latest issue of *Variety*. Beth's telephone rang constantly, destroying her concentration. She kept thinking about Carl.

About twenty minutes later she pricked up her ears when she heard Beth say into the telephone, "Oh, hi, Dom. Are you back in your office? Lark·Chandler is here to see you. Oh, no . . . half an hour or so. Right . . . okay." She hung up and looked woefully at Lark. "I guess I should have dragged him out of the meeting. Sorry. You should have told me it was important."

Lark laughed. "It's not . . . don't worry." She went down the thickly carpeted hall to Dom's office. She knew the way as well as if she had walked down it a hundred times, even though she had only been there rarely.

Dom was pacing impatiently when she entered. He unknotted his tie as he greeted her.

"Sorry you were kept waiting," he said, tossing the tie on his couch. "I would have been grateful for any excuse to leave that meeting. Have a seat."

She sat down. She hadn't seen him since the night three weeks earlier when she had driven him home and Toni had found them together. Would he mention it? He sat on the edge of the desk and smiled down at her.

"Don't look so scared," he said. "I'm really glad to see you."

"I came to tell you that I'm going to stay at APG for the time being."

He took the news with equanimity. "Fine. We already have a couple of bites on the 'Romance!' series. I expect you've heard."

"Yes."

He regarded her quizzically. Gazing back at him, it seemed again impossible to Lark that Dom did not recognize her. Not even after having kissed her had he an inkling!

"Well?" he said at last, interrupting her reverie.

"Well?" she said in response.

"You could have telephoned me about this. Isn't there something else you wanted to see me about?"

She opened her mouth to tell him about Carl, but then closed it again. She hadn't the faintest idea how to begin.

He jumped off the desk and reached for his jacket.

"Come on, let's go."

"Go where?"

"I'm taking you out. You didn't expect that I'd just let you go, do you?"

Lark let a protest die on her lips. Somehow she had to get the courage to tell him about his father.

He stopped at Beth's desk and handed her a file. "Type those up for me, will you? I'll be gone for the rest of the day.

If anything urgent comes up, leave a message on my machine at home."

"Okay, Dom." She smiled subtly at Lark and turned back to the typewriter.

"Where are we going?" she asked as they got into his BMW.

"We'll drive up the coast a little way. I need to clear my head. There's nothing like watching the Pacific for that."

He stopped at a supermarket and bought a bottle of California muscat, a loaf of bread, some cheese, and grapes. "Sitting on the beach always makes me hungry," he said.

When they were in Malibu, he parked the car on the side of the highway. A small cove, protected by jutting rocks on either side, lay at the bottom of a sheer hillside. Lark wished she were dressed more casually. High heels and a narrow skirt were not the best clothes for trying to get down the steep incline to the beach below.

Hand in hand, they slipped and slid down the steep path. Dom carried the picnic bag. Both were laughing when they reached the bottom.

The waves were big today: they pounded against the sand. A cool breeze broke in from the sea. They took shelter near a protective rock. No one else was around, not even the surfers. Sandpipers ran out after the waves as they swept into the ocean and then sped back to safety as they crashed onto the sandy beach.

"They look so human," said Lark. "Like kids playing with the waves."

"Or tiny bicycles."

Dom uncorked the cold wine and filled two plastic cups.

"Cheers," he said.

"Cheers."

"I don't know if you've heard, but Jonny's back on his rain forest project."

"I thought the film had been killed."

"It was, for a time." He paused. "Justin Groome recently offered to put up the rest of the money for it."

"Justin Groome!" exclaimed Lark. "Why on earth would he do that?"

"I suppose he thinks it'll get him some votes with the environmentalists."

"He's never cared about them," Lark said, half to herself. "What do you think he's really up to?"

Dom shrugged. "I didn't think about it at all. I was pleased for Jonny's sake. With Congressman Groome backing him, I'm going to be able to get the rest of the stockholders of the company to support the film too."

"That's good," said Lark, her mind only half on his words. But she didn't like Justin Groome's involvement with Jonny's film. It didn't seem right.

After a moment Dom said, changing the subject, "Toni and I are getting divorced."

She nodded, not knowing what to say.

"It was inevitable, I guess. But even when something's inevitable, it doesn't make it any easier. I thought I'd feel more relieved than I do."

"It must be very hard."

"It was as much of a surprise to me as it was to you to find Toni at my place the other night. I hadn't seen her since we were in Venice."

"I didn't know. I hope she didn't misunderstand."

Dom smiled wryly. "I don't think so."

Again Lark was silent.

"It's mostly guilt, I think," he went on. "Funny, Jonny and I don't get along too well, but I think we're closer in feelings right now than we've ever been. He won't admit it, but he's still reeling from his wife's desertion. He was never the same after that happened."

"He must be happy to be able to finish *Flaming Forest*."

"It'll be hard for him to finish without getting deeper into debt. He has no understanding of budgets, either a film's or his own. He hasn't had any work since *Razzle Dazzle* and he hasn't been doing too well."

"Can't you help?"

"I've helped a lot," Dom said slowly. "How much can I do? Am I supposed to keep giving him jobs that he screws up? Or should I simply write him checks?"

"Your mother—?" she asked tentatively.

"She does her bit. But ultimately Jonny's going to have to pull himself together on his own. The first step will be for him to check into a drug abuse clinic."

"He takes drugs?"

"Alcohol is a drug."

"Oh, right."

"Anyway, the rain forest movie will keep him straight at least for a few months. It really does mean a lot to him." He made another sandwich. "You know something? I still don't know anything about you."

"There's not much to tell. I'm from London. My parents are both dead, I haven't any brothers or sisters, no close ties."

"That sounds as though you've told me your life story, but at the same time I don't feel I know anything about you I didn't already know."

"There's really not much else to tell."

"Aren't you curious about me?"

"What about you?"

" 'Where I came from, who am I, where am I going?' "

Naturally she hadn't been curious since she already knew so much about him. "I'm curious about the girl that you said used to live with you," she said. "Penelope Houten. I wish I'd known you knew her before I wrote the treatment. You could have helped me with her character."

"I thought you captured her pretty accurately. Did you talk to anyone who knew her?"

"A few people. But any additional information is always helpful. Did you like her?"

"Very much. My mother adored her. We were all really upset when she ran away."

"Why do you suppose she ran away?"

"She's not a coward," Dom replied. "But she did have some awful shocks for such a young girl. I think the idea of running away and starting fresh was too much of a temptation to her."

"What about her relationship to Justin Groome? Do you believe the newspaper reports about that?"

"It's so hard to imagine, Lark. You've never met him, have you? He's such a personable, friendly guy. I can't see him being vicious."

"So you think the newspaper stories are made up?"

"I didn't say that. I honestly don't know what to think. If they are true, I can't believe that Penny wouldn't come forward and simply accuse Justin Groome of rape and murder. She's the type who'd want to see justice done."

"Maybe she's too scared."

"Maybe. But I think her relationship with Justin Groome may have been more complicated than the newspaper stories make out. That's why I'm saying that I don't know who to believe. If Penny came forward and stated these accusations openly, I'd believe her. But this furtiveness is so unlike her. It's as though she really wants to hurt Justin, not just get her day in court."

"Wouldn't you want to hurt a man who raped you and then accused you of murder?"

"I'm not explaining it very well. Naturally she'd want him to be punished. But revenge? Revenge implies that there's a more complex relationship than that of a mere victim."

Lark stared at the ocean. "You've thought about this a lot, haven't you?"

"Yes." He took her hand in his and studied it for a while. Lark felt her breathing grow unsteady and pulled it away. Dom looked up and met her eyes.

"I'll drive you home," was all he said.

They drove mostly in silence. Lark was still trying to think of a way to broach the subject of Carl.

She directed him to her apartment building and he parked the car. When he'd turned off the ignition, he turned to look at her again. The smell of eucalyptus and orange blossoms hung in the air.

"Aren't you going to invite me up?" he asked, wistfully.

She hesitated. Was there a clue she had left lying around somewhere that would make him realize who she was? Had she made a mistake somewhere along the way that Dom would pick up on and recognize? But she'd promised Carl.

"Sure, come on up. I'll make you a cup of coffee."

He held her hand as they walked to her building, and in the elevator as well. She thought he was going to kiss her as soon as they were safely inside her apartment, and she grew increasingly nervous as the moment approached. But he released her hand when the elevator reached her floor.

Inside the apartment she took off her jacket and went straight into the kitchen. "What can I get you?" she asked brightly.

"Nothing, thanks," he called from the living room.

She was disappointed; she wanted something to do. Slowly she followed him into the living room.

"How long have you lived here?" asked Dom, looking around.

"A year and a half."

He quirked an eyebrow.

"Why do you look surprised?" she asked.

"It's not at all the sort of place I'd imagined you in."

"Where did you imagine me?"

He was oddly disappointed in her apartment. "I don't know. I just know this wasn't it." He had hoped, he supposed, to get a glimpse into Lark's personality, her home life, her past, her childhood. But there was nothing here. Nothing. Not even a poster on the wall. It might be a motel room for all the personality she had imbued it with.

It almost startled him to think that Lark might have no personality.

She knew what he was thinking. "I warned you I might be a superficial person."

Dom said, "You're not that, but you sure are strange. Not even a potted plant?"

She kicked off her low-heeled pumps and sat on a wooden chair.

"I forget to water them."

"I've never met anyone who has no relatives at all. Not even one, Lark?"

"Oh, I'm sure there's one or two around somewhere. Second cousins or something. I don't know them, that's all."

He had been walking around the room, now he stood in front of her. "May I ask you something?"

"Of course," she said, smiling.

"Why are you so nervous?"

"I'm not. Am I?"

He looked disappointed again. "You're acting as though you have a corpse hidden somewhere in here and you're afraid I might find it." She said nothing. "I think I will take you up on your offer of coffee. Or maybe you have something stronger?"

"Not really. Just beer."

He shook his head.

"I could make you chamomile tea?"

"Okay."

Lark went into the kitchen.

When she returned with the tea, Dom was sitting on the couch.

"Here you go," she said, handing him the glass.

"Thanks," he said, taking it. Keeping hold of her other hand, he pulled her down beside him. She sat tensely on the edge of the couch.

"You intrigue the hell out of me, Lark. Why is that?"

She tried to free her hand. "I have no idea. Tell me more about your family, Dom. Tell me about your mother." She longed to hear about Susan.

"It seems to me you've been turning the tables on me all afternoon. Every time I ask you a question you answer it with one of your own. My mother lives on a farm in upstate New York, south of the Berkshires. I visit her as often as I can."

"And your . . . father?"

"He's dead."

"Oh."

"He died before I was born. He was one of those men who were accused of God knows what during the McCarthy witch-hunts in the early fifties. It ruined his life."

Here, at last, was her opening. She took a deep breath.

"Dom, this is going to seem very strange coming from me, since I hardly know you, but I have something to tell you that's going to shock you. Are you ready?"

Without moving a muscle, she could tell that his whole body tensed. "Yes," he said in a deceptively lazy drawl. "I'm ready."

"Your real father didn't die before you were born. He wasn't married to your mother; they were going to be married, but something happened to break it off. He's alive and he wants very much to see you, and for you to acknowledge him as your father."

There was such a long silence that she wondered if Dom had heard. His eyes were closed, but eventually they flickered open and there was no warmth in them this time. Just a hard, even gaze.

"That's very interesting. I suppose he asked you to be his emissary because he was too cowardly to tell me himself."

"No."

"No?"

"Dom, try to understand."

He sat up, releasing her hand. "I do understand, my dear Lark. I understand a good deal more than you give me credit for. I know about my real father. My mother did not keep secrets from Jonny or myself. She knew that one day a man as selfish and unscrupulous as he would come back for me. I'm only amazed that he waited so long."

Now it was her turn to be amazed. "You know about Carl?"

"I don't know where he lives or what he does. I only know what he did to my mother's husband. I only know that he's a scoundrel, a liar, a user, a manipulator. I only know that I have no wish to see him, nor will I ever have any wish to see him." He took a calming breath. "How on earth did you get mixed up in this, Lark? It seems fantastic."

"I met him when I lived in London. When he found out I was working for you, he thought maybe I'd be able to plead his cause. Won't you at least talk to him?"

"Never."

"Dom, he's dying."

"Darling, we're dying from the moment we're born. It's just that it takes some people longer than others. Dying is no excuse for one's actions."

"No, but it might be an excuse to get the story straight. He didn't do it."

"So he says, anyway."

"Don't you want to at least hear his side of the story?"

"Never. I don't go in for that deathbed sob stuff. He can rot in hell for all I care."

She grew angry. "Do you think your mother would behave this way if she were in your shoes?"

"No, but Mom's closer to sainthood than I am. She has that rare quality of compassion. I haven't."

"Garbage. Of course you have it. I've seen it myself."

"Oh? Where?"

"Anyway, you're the one who's being selfish! You don't even know him. He's kind, generous, thoughtful—"

"Shut up, Lark," he snapped. "You don't know what you're talking about."

She was furious. "How do you know I don't know what I'm talking about? Carl's been like a father to me! He's not a manipulator. He's not a coward. He's made mistakes, but so have you, God knows! You're the most arrogant man in the world if you think you're too good for him!"

Dom seemed taken aback by this outburst. "I didn't say I was too good for him. I just said—"

"I know what you said. You said he's a scoundrel, a liar, a user, a manipulator. You haven't even met him! Talk about pronouncing a verdict before the trial!"

He looked at her. "Were we talking about that?"

"Jesus, Dom. Sometimes you act as though there's ice in your veins, not blood. The man's *dying*."

Dom stood up and paced around the room, as though trying to keep his temper in check. Finally he turned to her.

"I didn't mean to lose my temper," he said at last. "It's not your fault that he inveigled you into doing this. But I don't want to argue about it anymore either. It's making me hot under the collar just thinking about it. So let's drop it, okay?"

She bit her lip.

"I'd better get going anyway," he said. "It's pretty late. Thanks for the tea." He had hardly touched it.

"You're welcome."

"By the way, what's he dying of?" he asked as he went out the door.

"AIDS."

"It figures."

She watched his retreating figure until he turned the corner, then went back inside the apartment. Damn him.

She dreaded calling Carl. She dialed his number slowly.

"Carl, it's Lark. I have bad news." She spoke hurriedly. "I told Dom about you and he doesn't want to see you. It seems his mother has already told him all about you, so he knows the history of your relationship. He feels kind of bitter. I tried to tell him the truth but he didn't believe me."

"Thank you, Lark. I'm sure you did your best."

"I did try. I think he's a real jerk. Maybe you're better off not meeting him."

She heard him chuckle. "Let me know when he changes his mind. He'll probably call you in the next week or so, asking for more details."

"I don't think so. He really didn't want to discuss it."

"We'll see." Carl said cheerfully.

"I'll come and visit you on Saturday," she said. "How are you feeling?"

"A little better today, thanks. It will be lovely to see you, whenever you have the time. I know how busy you are."

"I'll make time for you. Carl . . . I really wish . . ."

"I know you do."

"I told him you've been like a father to me."

"That is the kindest thing anyone has ever said. Thank you."

She gulped.

"Good night, Lark."

She replaced the receiver, wondering at Carl's optimism. She thought Dom was intractable. Still it was better to hope than to despair. Carl hadn't much else to look forward to.

CHAPTER SIXTY-THREE

THE preliminary responses from network television stations regarding "Romance!" were so positive that Lark found herself working night and day to keep abreast of her correspondence, following up on marketing and other concepts, as well as getting to work on the next story in the series. She had decided to make a series within the series and to start with six contemporaries. If they were successful she would go on to six Regencies, then six historicals, and six Gothics.

There was so much to do, she hardly saw Dom at all, and when she did it was within the office confines of a meeting or a hurried conversation on the phone.

She was working on the final draft of the second "Romance!" story when her intercom buzzed. Automatically, she pressed the intercom and continued typing as she said, "Yes?"

"Someone is here to see you," announced Rosa.

"Who is it?"

"Mr. Justin Groome. He says you do not know him and he does not have an appointment but he would appreciate it if you would take the time to see him."

Lark swallowed. But she said, "I'll be out in a minute."

Slowly she got up from her desk and went into the reception area. Justin Groome stood in front of Rosa's desk, bantering with the secretary. Rosa was blushing.

"Here is Ms. Chandler," she said.

Justin Groome turned and held out his hand to Lark.

"Thank you for taking the time to see me. I know you must be busy."

Lark managed a polite smile. She forced herself to shake his hand. He loomed over her, larger than life. In spite of the immaculate pinstripe suit, crisp shirt, gold cuff links, and sweet-smelling after-shave, Lark sensed his dissipation and wondered at it. His jowls seemed heavy, his hard eyes had bags under them.

Would he recognize her?

"My name is Justin Groome," he introduced himself briefly. "I need to talk to you somewhere in private."

"Come back into my office," she heard herself replying, amazed at how relaxed she sounded.

"I'd rather go out somewhere."

Lark glanced at her watch. "I'm sorry," she lied, "I'm meeting someone in half an hour. My office is very private, though."

"Fine, fine," Justin said, but he looked as though it weren't fine at all. She wondered if he wanted to avoid running into Dom.

It was already five-thirty, but most of the staff were still there. She led Justin down the corridor to her office. She wanted to leave the door open, but Justin closed it.

"I hope you don't mind," he said.

"Have a chair," she offered. She sat behind her desk, protected.

Justin stared at her a moment. "You aren't what I was expecting."

She stared back, as coolly as she could. Her eyes were the same color. Would he recognize her eyes?

"What were you expecting?" she asked politely.

"You have quite a reputation in Hollywood. I imagined you were someone older and tougher. You don't seem very experienced."

She waited for him to tell her why he was there.

"Do you know who I am?" he asked suddenly.

She jumped slightly, then realized he wasn't asking whether they'd met before. Cautiously she said, "You're a congressman."

"Yes. Of course you know who I am. I understand you're interested in making a movie about my life. I'd like to look at the screenplay."

"It hasn't been written."

"It hasn't? Then what's this thing that's being peddled around Hollywood?"

"Just a treatment for the screenplay. A few pages outlining the story."

"May I see it?"

"I'm sorry, that's not possible."

"Why not?"

She tried to think why not. The reason was, of course, that he'd hate it. He'd do everything in his power to try to stop the film from being made. "It's not public property yet."

"I didn't expect you'd let me see it. I understand you got most of your facts from some newspaper stories. Is that right?"

"Yes."

"I understand your story isn't exactly flattering."

"The treatment hasn't been sold. The screenplay isn't even written. I don't know how you heard about it in the first place, much less that it isn't flattering."

"Yes, well . . ." He took out a cigarette. "Do you mind?"

"Yes, I'm afraid I do. Let's go into the conference room. No one minds if you smoke there."

He shook his head and put away the cigarette. "Forget it. Let me ask you something. Have you talked to Penelope Houten about any of this? The girl who murdered Violet Sumner?"

So he hadn't recognized her. She took a deep, relieved breath.

"No."

"I've been trying to find her for years. As you know, she disappeared—probably because she was afraid of being sent to jail. If she were to come back and stand trial, she'd be treated fairly. I'd see to that. That's why I've been trying to find her."

"I have no idea where she is."

Justin took out his wallet from his inside breast pocket and handed her a business card. "I wonder if I could ask you to give me a call if you do hear from her? It means a lot to me. I was very fond of little Penny. I hate to think of her hiding somewhere, dreading being found out, and with her face looking so terrible. She'd be much better off if she stood trial and faced the consequences. I'd even pay for plastic surgery once she was out of jail."

"That's a very kind offer."

He looked very hard at Lark. "I really was fond of her. We had something very special together."

"Did you?"

"So you'll get in touch with me if you see her?"

"I doubt that will ever happen."

Justin's hard eyes twinkled. "I'm finding I like you much more than I expected. You're a very beautiful woman."

"Thank you."

"It's a shame that you're so bent on trying to damage my reputation. Under other circumstances I feel we could have been good friends."

"Do you?"

"Yes, I really do." His teeth gleamed when he smiled. "You're not only beautiful, you're obviously talented, self-confident, and brave. I like that in a woman. By the way, why are you so bent on trying to damage my reputation?"

She smiled back. "I wouldn't dream of trying to do any such thing! My only goal is to produce an entertaining show."

"I suppose I should feel flattered that you find my life so entertaining."

"It's been a very full life. You've accomplished a great deal."

"How can I persuade you that the newspaper reports are all lies?"

"I understand you're an extremely persuasive man. You can always try."

Justin Groome stood up. "I have the unhappy feeling that you've already convicted me without a trial. But now that I've met you I'm more determined than ever to vindicate myself and prove to you what a nice guy I really am. I'd like to have your respect."

"How are you going to do that?"

"I have to find Penelope Houten. She'll tell the truth about me."

"How will you find her?"

"I have people working on it. I just hope I find her before you're successful with your screenplay."

Lark smiled. "For your sake, I hope so too."

"Thanks for taking the time to see me," he said.

She came around to the front of the desk and opened the door. Bravely, she held out her hand. He shook it, and held it a moment longer than necessary, as though he liked it too much to let go.

Then he stepped into the corridor. He strode down the hall to the reception area, looking neither right nor left.

It was dark outside. Lark's heart pounded hard. Taking a deep breath, she went to the window and smiled secretly at her reflection. The mask Carl made had really worked. She had hid safely behind it.

CHAPTER SIXTY-FOUR

A week later, Dom entered Lark's office and closed the door behind him.

"I want to apologize for losing my temper the other night," he said.

"I guess I lost mine too. I didn't realize that you already knew about your father."

"I haven't changed my mind about not wanting to see him. But I'm not angry at you. I don't know what it is about you, but I can't stop thinking about you. I go over things you say, the way you say them. I see your smile, your expressions. You're still haunting me."

As if propelled by an invisible, powerful force, Lark went toward him. She knew it was dangerous to push this any farther. She knew that she could not tell Dom the truth about herself until she had been vindicated of the charge of murder. She knew she could not tell him the truth until Groome was safely behind bars—or dead. She knew all this, but she heard herself saying, "I've been haunted by you too."

A flame flickered in Dom's eyes. She stopped three paces from him and they regarded each other as though suddenly they didn't know what to do. The tension was broken abruptly when Lark's intercom buzzed sharply. She turned away to pick up the telephone. "Yes?"

"Mr. Stevens is here to see you," announced Rosa. He was a writer she had made an appointment to see at three o'clock.

"All right, Rosa. Ask him to wait. I'll be right out." She hung up slowly.

Dom was smiling at her. "Let's continue this later."

Continue what? she wondered. But as she watched the warmth in his expression, she knew what he meant. Her heart gave a jolt, torn between ecstasy and despair.

"There's a lot on your mind, isn't there?" Dom said, coming over and taking her hand. "I know you've been keeping something from me. But we'll work it out somehow, I guarantee it. Give me a call when you're through with your meeting with Stevens."

After he'd left, Lark took out her compact. Her hair was pulled back in two French braids from which not a hair escaped. She smoothed it anyway. She needed the reassurance of seeing her face just then. Just before she caught sight of her reflection, she relived the moment in the hospital when she had first seen her face after the "accident." Seeing her face now gave her a shock too, but one that left her feeling more confident.

The meeting lasted for over an hour, and afterward she had to catch up on some memos. Even then she was half-tempted to simply go home, but that would not be fair to Dom. He was waiting for her call. Already it was well after six.

She picked up the telephone, annoyed to see her hand trembled.

"I'm wrapping up my day here," she told him, surprised at how calm she sounded. "How's yours going?"

"I'm not exactly twiddling my thumbs, but psychologically I am. Come on by my office whenever you're ready."

First she went to the ladies' room and freshened her lipstick. She rarely wore any other makeup. Her delicate skin did not require foundation other than a moisturizer and her eyes were already enhanced by the dark lashes. She wore a pale peach cotton suit with an Irish linen blouse underneath. Her ivory pumps were low and comfortable. As she surveyed herself in the full-length mirror she felt that even if her costume were not fashionable enough for a night at the Roxy, it was pretty enough to carry her through this particular evening.

Dom was ready when she knocked on his door.

"Let's go," he said. "We'll take my car."

"Where are we going?"

"To my house. I want you to start liking it."

"You don't have to worry about that." Lark laughed as they headed for the elevator. "I like your house just fine."

On the drive along Sunset Boulevard, they talked mostly about work. But when they began climbing the winding road to his house, Lark fell silent, stunned again by the view. Lights from Santa Monica and the bay beyond sparkled along the edge of the ocean. She breathed in the fragrance from the eucalyptus trees.

Inside the house Dom told her to drop her briefcase, purse, and jacket on a chair in the hall. "I'll fix us drinks. How about something exotic? I could make daiquiris, if you'd like."

"A daiquiri would be perfect."

"The bathroom's through there," he told her. "The kitchen is this way. Maybe you'd like to wait on the terrace where you can see the view."

He guided her along a wide terra-cotta tiled hall which opened onto a balcony. The steep hill fell away below. Dom left her there and she leaned against the stone wall, gazing at the shadowy garden. She could hear a fountain splash quietly. A large eucalyptus rustled in the breeze. She shivered from the faint chill in the night wind. But it was lovely out here. A delicious sweet scent wafted from some flowers climbing the side of the terrace.

Dom came out, two glasses in his hands and a navy blue sweater slung over a shoulder. He put the glasses on the stone railing. "I thought you might be getting chilly," he said, handing her the sweater. "It's big, but it'll work. Here's your drink."

He had changed into blue jeans and an oversize gray sweater. His feet were bare. Out of the formal business suit, he looked younger.

Lark gratefully put on the big sweater. Dom pulled up two lounge chairs and they lay back in them, sipping the fruity drinks. With a start, Lark realized she had never felt as happy as she was just then.

The stars came out, large and solid.

"You're being very quiet," Lark said at last.

"I guess I'm too happy to talk," Dom replied. He reached for her hand and swung it gently like a bridge between them. She closed her eyes to better savor the feel of his hand in hers. *Dom's hand.* It seemed so extraordinary.

"Are you hungry?" Dom asked after a while.

"A little."

"Let's go inside. I can throw together a salad and I have some bread and cheese to go with it. Sorry it's nothing more elaborate."

"That sounds fine."

They ate in the living room. Accompanied by a bottle of Chassagne-Montrachet white burgundy, the light meal was perfect.

"One of these days I'd like to show you my wine cellar. I have a feeling you're one of a very few people who would really appreciate it."

"I'd love to see it."

Lark found she was too happy to eat much. The room was warm and she took off Dom's large sweater.

After a while Dom took Lark's glass from her hand and set it on the coffee table. He was not smiling now. He was looking at her so tenderly Lark felt she would melt. He sat beside her and drew her gently into his arms. He kissed the top of her head. Then he unpinned her hair and started undoing the braids.

"I had no idea your hair was so long," he said laughingly at one point. "I thought this would just take a minute."

Every touch on her skin made her tremble. When her hair was loose and falling around her shoulders, Dom caressed it, then pushed it aside to kiss the side of her throat. She responded by gliding her fingers down his cheek and along the side of his jaw.

I can't believe this, she thought.

He traced a finger along her bare leg to her foot and pushed off the leather pump. Then he trailed his finger up her calf, to the back of her leg, to her thigh.

His hand touched the throbbing pulse in her throat, and unbuttoned the top few buttons of her blouse.

Then he explored the outline of her breast.

"Let's go into the bedroom," Dom murmured. "I want to lie down with you."

To Lark's horror, it was as though she had suddenly awoken from a wonderful dream. She was not melting wax under his sensuous touch; she was frozen.

Dom sensed her sudden, unaccountable tension. His hand lazily circled her collarbone. He made no attempt to get up.

"What's the matter?"

"I don't know," Lark said miserably, sitting up.

"Didn't you know we were going to make love?"

"Yes."

"And you wanted to?"

"Yes."

"What happened to make you change your mind?"

"Nothing. I still want to."

"All right, let's go into the bedroom."

She nodded and they both rose. But as they walked to the bedroom, they knew the spell had been broken.

Dom took off his sweater and lay on the bed in a T-shirt and his jeans. He put his hands behind his head and closed his eyes.

"Tell me what happened," he said. "Trust me a little with something of your life. You've told me nothing—absolutely nothing. Sometimes I wonder if I've fallen in love with an enchanted princess who's going to turn into a statue at some horrible moment. Or who will simply disappear."

Lark stood by the bed, staring down at him. "I've told you about myself."

"You've given me nothing of yourself. I've told you about my childhood, I've dropped stories about my buddies at school, my professors at college, my mother, you know about my father—just endless personal things that add up to a person: me. You've given me nothing. Why?"

"But I have," she protested weakly. "We've talked about my ideas for screenplays—where I'm from."

He sighed in exasperation. "Sometimes it scares me to realize I've fallen in love with you. I mean, what is it about you, anyway? Have I simply fallen in love with a pretty face? Is it possible?"

"It's possible."

His eyes fluttered open and he stared at her. "I don't believe it. There's something more, but you don't trust me enough to tell me. I don't know what it is. I don't know why you don't trust me. But I know that nothing can come of a love affair that isn't based on trust."

It could have been Carl speaking, Lark thought. Might Dom end up like his father, betrayed by a lack of trust? Emotionally drained, she felt close to tears. She had been mad to think it might work. Her past was like a great barbed wire fence saying Keep Away.

She knelt on the bed beside him. She made up her mind to tell him a little.

"You're right," she said earnestly. "There is something I can't tell you. But it doesn't mean that I'm not real."

"And just now?" he asked. "What happened just now that made you freeze?"

It was strange, she thought, that her affair with Jack had not completely eradicated a fear that still accompanied her feelings about sex. But then, Jack had inspired passion in her, not love.

"I was raped once," she said at last. "I don't mean that anything you did or said brought the memory back, but when I suddenly realized what was happening, I started to remember. I'm really sorry. I didn't expect that to happen. I thought I'd buried it."

He sat up. "God, Lark! I'm the one who should apologize. I took it personally, of course." He pulled her toward him and she laid her cheek on his chest. "We'll just lie here. We don't have to make love until you're ready."

"But I am ready," she protested. "I'm not a child. I knew what we were doing. It's just for a moment that I had a lapse."

"I knew you weren't as tough as you make yourself out to be. Faces don't lie."

"Don't they?"

He caressed her hair.

"You mean more to me than anything in the world," he said, quietly. "Just holding you like this is heaven."

He settled himself more comfortably, his arms still around her. Lark nestled against his chest and closed her eyes, feeling better.

"Is that why you care so much about getting Penny's story known?"

"*What?*"

"I mean that you empathize with her? She was supposedly raped too."

"Oh, right. Yes, I suppose I do."

She had no idea how long they lay there. After a while she felt Dom stir. Her eyes opened and met his.

"Beautiful, beautiful woman," he murmured.

She felt a strange sensation just under her skin where his hands touched her. A warm glow crept through her. His body was lean and hard against hers. He felt good, but more than that, he made her feel desirable. *He loved her.*

His lips met hers. Gently his tongue searched her mouth, tasting her.

Dom unbuttoned her blouse slowly, kissing her skin as it became exposed. Lark raked his hair with her fingers.

"I've thought about us being together like this ever since I met you," he said, circling the satiny bra with his fingertip. "It's a dream come true. I never want this night to end."

"It is a dream come true," she whispered.

"I'm going to take your skirt off. Even if we just lie together like this all night, you may as well be comfortable. Okay?"

"Okay."

He unzipped the side zipper and slid the skirt over her hips. She lay on the bed in her bra and panties. Dom took off his shirt then lay back down and took her in his arms again. Every movement he made was calm and unhurried, as though he were afraid of frightening her.

She turned so that her mouth met his, wanting to kiss again. Dom responded slowly, tantalizingly.

He began stroking her very slowly. He unclasped the bra and kissed her breasts, circling inward until he reached their erect centers. Lark strained her body toward him. Every nerve ending leapt under his touch. His mouth moved down her stomach. Her panties came off. His tongue explored secret places at the backs of her knees and around her ankles. The insides of her thighs. His tongue was sometimes hard, then soft, then hard again. Her hips rose to meet him.

The sweet reverberation became a crescendo. She abandoned herself to a rapturous frenzy. She cried out his name. Dom kissed her and kissed her.

"I love you, Dom Whitfield," she told him, when she had quietened. "I have never loved anyone but you, and I never will."

He chuckled and kissed her again.

"You're revealing more tonight than I ever dreamed. In another twenty years I might know you pretty well, don't you think?"

Just then the telephone rang.

Chapter Sixty-Five

SWEARING, Dom sat up and reached for the receiver. Lark put a hand on his long back, stroking it wonderingly. Then she felt it stiffen, and his shocked voice saying, "She's there now? When did this happen?"

Lark tensed.

"I'll be there as fast as I can," Dom spoke into the receiver. "Tell her to hold on."

He hung up and turned to Lark.

"It's my mother. She's been taken to the hospital with a heart attack. They'll be giving her a bypass operation tomorrow. I have to go to her."

Lark's mouth fell open.

"Are you okay?" he asked.

"Yes." Her voice sounded calm, didn't it? "I'm terribly sorry."

Dom stood up and reached for his trousers. "I have to call the airline. I don't know how long I'll be gone. Jonny's in Brazil and he won't be able to make it back, I'm sure."

"Dom," the words came out in a rush, "take me with you."

"What?"

"Please," she said. "It means an awful lot for me to . . . meet your mother."

"Well," he hesitated, "I think she'd like to meet you too. But she's seriously ill. It's not the best time."

"I understand that. But I still want to come."

"You won't mind if it's awful? I'll be spending most of my time at the hospital. I won't be able to entertain you."

"I wouldn't expect you to."

"Then I'd love your company," decided Dom. "It would make all the difference in the world."

They took a flight out of Los Angeles airport early that morning. By the time they arrived at Northkill Hospital the operation was over. Susan was in intensive care, recovering. Dom went in to see her alone.

Lark wandered around the hospital, reliving the weeks she had spent there as a patient so long ago. In a way it was good to be back. It gave her a tangible sense of her past. She really had been a person before she became Lark.

Dom joined her a while later.

"I'd like to get a cup of coffee in the cafeteria," he said. "Then I'll see Mom just once more before we go. We'll stay at her farm tonight. It's only half an hour's drive from here. You'll like it."

Lark was relieved that Dom was distraught about his mother's operation, for it saved her from his scrutiny.

After their coffee, Dom went back upstairs. This time Lark accompanied him.

Susan's face was gray as death. A tube ran into her nose, and needles were inserted in her arms. Her lovely face was wrinkled and slack. Lark gripped Dom's hand.

"I've been told it's all routine," he said, his eyes full. "She's doing well."

Lark was unable to speak. Letting go of Dom's hand, she crossed the room to Susan's bedside.

"Susan," she whispered.

Susan's eyes flickered open. Her eyes met Lark's in surprise, and then she actually smiled. "Penny," she managed.

Tears streamed down Lark's cheeks. "I'm sorry . . . I'm so sorry . . ."

"I always knew you'd come back." Susan's whispered voice was raw. "But, darling, what took you so long?"

Growing aware of Dom's presence right behind her, Lark made a superhuman effort to stop crying. Wiping her eyes, she stroked Susan's hand.

Dom appeared not to notice Lark's emotion. He said, "You've come through with flying colors, Mom."

Susan glanced past Lark at him. "I never knew one could feel so much pain and live," she murmured. "But now I've found Penny again I understand the reason." Then she sank into unconsciousness again.

Inside the rented car, Lark blew her nose. Dom blew his too.

"I'm sorry I put you through that," he said.

"Please . . ."

"She mistook you for Penny Houten."

"I know."

"Mother still hopes she'll come back one day."

Lark felt stricken. She should not have abandoned Susan, not for any reason. And now what should she do?

As they drove along the road toward the farm, she looked around at the familiar countryside as though she were in a trance. Snow covered the fields. The graceful silver birches, majestic maples and solid oak trees were etched in black against the lead gray sky. She thought she recognized each tree as she passed; recognized each lamppost by the side of the road. Snow was piled on the roof of the farmhouse and blanketed the yard. It looked desolate.

At some point she would have to face her past. She had always known that, merely tried to put it off for as long as possible. But now here she was, plunked smack in its middle.

She slept with Dom in his room, but when he had fallen asleep, Lark slipped out to see her own old room. It was exactly as she had left it. Her clothes still hung in the closet; her teddy bear was on her bed; the mystery novels on the shelf. She walked around and around, the slanted floorboards creaking beneath her bare feet. She gazed out the window at the dark garden and the snowy fields beyond. *I am here*, she kept thinking. *I am finally here. I have come home.*

The next morning they were both haggard and exhausted.

"I guess neither of us slept too well," Dom said ruefully. "Would you like to stay here while I go back to the hospital? There's no reason you have to come too."

"Okay." She was afraid that in the twilight zone of recovering from the operation, Susan really might recognize her and give her away to Dom.

She spent the day trudging through the snowy fields and exploring her old haunts. She thought longingly of Georgia, her retriever. Shivering and pink cheeked from the cold, at last she went back inside the house and made herself peppermint tea.

Dom got back at six. He'd bought a large pizza and a bottle of Chianti.

"My mother wants to see you tomorrow," he told her, uncorking the wine. "She was upset that you weren't with me today. I explained to her that you were my girlfriend, and told her your name and everything. But she has this weird idea that you're really Penny Houten. I spoke to the nurse about it, and she said that kind of confusion isn't unusual. Would you mind coming with me tomorrow?"

Lark hesitated. But, "No, I don't mind," she said.

Susan was already out of intensive care and in her own room. She still had an IV, but the tubes were gone from her nose and she was conscious. She smiled at Lark.

"Hello, dear," she said softly. "I'm so glad to see you."

"I'm glad to see you too."

"Isn't it strange that I'm here now, instead of you?"

Dom stepped up to her. "Penny was in the hospital here before she disappeared," he explained in an undertone.

Lark nodded. "Dom," she said breathlessly, "would you mind if I talked to your mother alone for a few minutes?"

He looked taken aback, but reluctantly agreed. Left alone, Lark sat on the edge of Susan's bed. She knew there was no point in pretending.

"Why did you leave us?" Susan asked.

"I didn't have a choice."

"We all have choices."

"Let's not talk about it now. You're not strong enough to hear the whole story. I'll tell you when we're home. But, please, Susan, Dom doesn't know."

"Of course he knows."

"He doesn't know. And he mustn't. I can't tell you why

just now, but I promise I will later. But please don't tell him.
Please."

Confused, Susan closed her eyes. "All right," she murmured.

Lark went to get Dom. From then on Susan scrupulously
referred to her as Lark.

They brought Susan home a week later. Their time away
from their jobs was running out, and both could only stay a
few more days. Dom arranged for a nurse to come and live
with Susan, and promised to come back at the end of the
month.

Susan was relieved to be home, although she was upset by
how haggard she looked. She had lost none of her vanity.

"I have to go to the beauty parlor."

"Not yet." Dom laughed at her. "We can stand the sight of
you like this for a while longer."

That night, after Dom had gone to sleep, Lark went to
Susan's room. She knew she was having difficulty sleeping.
The light was on and Susan was sitting up in bed wearing a
quilted blue bed jacket. "There you are." Susan smiled.
"Want to put another log on the fire? It's chilly."

Lark did so, then curled up on the foot of her bed. She wore
Dom's flannel dressing gown over her T-shirt and sweatpants
and felt perfectly warm.

"Tell me what happened," asked Susan. "We were all so
devastated when you ran away. You knew we'd all stand behind you."

"I was afraid."

"And you're no coward. Of what were you afraid?"

Lark whispered his name: "Justin Groome."

Susan had sat forward to hear her reply, her eyes glittering
in anticipation. With Lark's answer she sank back among the
bedclothes, looking dazed. "I prayed it wasn't so. And
yet . . ." she trailed off, then took Lark's hand in hers. "Tell
me what happened. Tell me everything."

"The night of my party I saw Mr. Groome murder Violet.
When I was in the hospital he said if I ever tried to change his
story about my doing it he'd kill me too."

Susan gripped her hand. Her lips were tight. "Go on, dear. There's more, isn't there?"

"He raped me." Lark said this in a monotone. "We were in New York and he told me you were going to meet us at his apartment. He raped me, then I came back here by myself."

Susan's brow was furrowed, trying to remember. "My memory has grown so poor," she murmured unhappily.

"You told me you'd meet me at an art gallery. He showed up instead and took me to his apartment."

"I think I remember. I was very angry with you."

"Justin Groome told you I hadn't shown up at all. You were worried about me, not angry."

Susan's eyes were full. "But why didn't you tell me what had happened?"

Lark gazed into the fireplace. "I wanted to. You can't imagine how badly I wanted to. But I couldn't. There were two reasons really. The first was that I was scared. It was my word against Justin's, and he was such a great friend of yours. You said something yourself about him once: Justin can convince anyone of anything. He would've convinced you I was a slut. That it was my fault. I didn't want anyone to know what had happened."

"Especially not Dom," said Susan softly.

"Especially not Dom," Lark agreed.

"I don't think that's fair. We always trusted you, dear, right from the beginning."

"It would have been my word against Justin's," she repeated.

"We both would have believed you," insisted Susan. She looked terribly small and frail, surrounded by a mound of pillows, the flickering firelight casting odd shadows on her face. "What was the second reason you didn't tell me?"

Lark hesitated. "It's complicated to explain. I don't know if I can make you understand without hurting you. But in some strange way I blamed you for what happened. He was your friend. I felt you should have known about him, and you should have protected me from him."

"But how could I have known, if I wasn't told?"

"I guess I felt that if you really loved me, you would have known." Lark stared at the fire. "You would have trusted me."

"But you didn't even give me the chance to trust you!" Susan cried. "You didn't give me the chance to decide for myself who was telling the truth, you or Justin."

Lark sighed. "That's what Carl said." She turned to regard Susan.

For a moment she thought Susan hadn't heard. Then her eyes widened and she sat forward, clutching the blankets. "What?" Her voice was cracked and strained, and Lark was suddenly afraid Susan might have another heart attack.

Lark stood up. "This is too much for you to hear all at once. I forgot how sick you've been. I'll tell you the rest tomorrow."

Susan shook her head. "Sit down," she ordered, her voice still strained. "For God's sake, tell me how you came to mention Carl's name."

Uncertainly Lark sat back down. But she knew that Susan would not rest until she heard the whole story. She decided to tell her as quickly as possible.

"This is what happened: While I was in the hospital a stranger gave me Carl's business card and told me he was a plastic surgeon who'd be glad to fix my face up for free. I guess I didn't want to think about why he'd do this—I assumed maybe he was merely interested in my kind of accident. I made it all the way to London to see him. Carl was extraordinary. He didn't tell me the truth about himself until a couple of years after he'd fixed my face. He told me he'd been keeping in touch with everything you'd been doing ever since you broke off your engagement."

"But why—" Susan gasped for air.

Lark stood up again. "I'll get you a glass of water," she said anxiously. "Or tea, maybe?"

Weakly, Susan shook her head. "I want to hear everything."

"He did it because he loves you. He always loved you. He wants Dom to know him, to acknowledge him as his father." Lark was really worried about Susan now. She wasn't sure if it would be best to leave her and tell the rest of the story in the morning or whether Susan would suffer more not being told everything now.

"Justin was behind the plot to ruin your husband, not Carl. They were running against each other for Congress and Justin figured that was the only way he could win. Carl had nothing to do with it. He would never hurt anyone."

"Carl never said a word to me," whispered Susan.

"Yes, he did. He said the truth may never be known, and it all boils down to a question of faith in someone one loves." After a moment, she added, "He said that just because one doesn't understand doesn't mean one shouldn't trust, especially the person you love."

But Susan disagreed vehemently. "I wasn't even given the chance to understand! He didn't say a single word against Justin! Was that fair? Was it fair that you didn't? That you let me go on thinking he was my friend?"

Lark shook her head. "No, it wasn't fair. I'm sorry, Susan."

"But how could he do it?" cried Susan. "How could you? Didn't you want to protect *me* from him?"

"I'm sorry," Lark repeated, anxiously. "I'm really sorry."

Susan lay back against the pillows, exhausted. "Now what?" she asked. "What have you told Dom?"

"I told him about Carl. Dom absolutely refuses to see him."

"I'll have to talk to him about that," said Susan weakly. "And what have you told him about yourself?"

"Nothing."

"So you don't trust him either."

"I don't trust Justin Groome. If he found out who I was, he wouldn't let me live a second longer than he had to."

Susan shook her head. "Dom would not tell Justin." When Lark didn't respond, she asked, "Don't you think he'll believe you?"

There was a silence. "I'm not sure," Lark said at last.

"Not sure!"

"He didn't believe me back when it happened."

"None of us were sure about anything. You refused to talk to any of us about what happened."

"By the time I could talk to you, Justin had already visited me in the hospital and threatened to kill me if I told the truth."

"He must have threatened Jonny too," Susan said, almost to herself.

"Why did Dom leave like that?" Lark couldn't help asking. "He went back to California without even waiting to see if I was okay."

"He had a job to go back to," Susan reminded her gently, "and also a fiancée. At that time you were more of a sister to him than a lover."

"I was never a sister to him. And if he ever finds out I'm Penny—"

"*When* he finds out," corrected Susan.

"He'll hate me for lying to him about who I am."

"Yes, a little. But he'll never hate you as much as he loves you. And I know he would believe whatever you told him about Justin."

"Even if he believed me, that wouldn't help me now. He'd probably feel that I should stand trial and try to be vindicated of the murder charge."

Susan looked at her. "Well?"

"As long as Justin has the power he has now, I haven't a prayer in court. He wouldn't *let* me be vindicated, not if it means ruining his career, his life. I know he wouldn't."

Susan reflected. "Dom wouldn't force you to do anything you didn't want to do."

"I don't know about that."

"Anyway, you can't marry a man with that kind of secret at your back. Both of you will always feel betrayed."

"We haven't even talked about marriage."

"It's just a matter of time, believe me."

The two women regarded each other. Susan stretched out her frail arms to Lark, enfolding her in them. Lark lay with her cheek on her chest.

"You'll never know how much I missed you," whispered Susan.

Lark couldn't speak.

"Excuse me, am I interrupting?"

Dom was standing in the open door, looking at them, puzzled.

CHAPTER SIXTY-SIX

LARK sat up hastily. Susan looked at Dom. Neither of them answered.

"Girl talk?" he said.

"Sort of," said Susan. She turned her face away from him, exhausted. "What time is it?"

"Two o'clock." Dom went over and stroked his mother's forehead, looking bewildered.

Lark got to her feet. "Good night, Susan." Her voice sounded choked. "Sleep well."

"Good night, dear."

Dom remained behind, but not for very long. When he entered his bedroom, Lark lay in bed, her back to him.

"You seem to have gotten close to my mother awfully quickly."

"She's like that," said Lark, awkwardly. Then she added, "She's okay, isn't she?"

"Just exhausted, I think. Been talking to her for a while?"

"Not really," lied Lark. "I thought I heard her and I went to her room to see if she needed something."

Dom climbed into bed and nestled up to her back, cradling her stomach. "You're cold." He kissed the back of her neck. After a moment he said, "She said you told her about Carl wanting to see me."

Lark froze, waiting for some sign of anger from him. "Yes."

"Well," Dom yawned sleepily. "We'll talk about it later."

His breathing became even. Lark lay awake, relishing being

held by him. She still felt amazed that they were together like this, in her old home, where she'd had so many dreams of being held by him just like this. She knew Susan was right and that she should tell Dom the truth about herself. Safe in the old farmhouse, safe in his strong arms, she felt as though no harm could come to her.

The sky was starting to pale when she heard a thump from outside in the hall. She was on her feet in an instant and out the door.

Dom sat up, staring after her sleepily. "What happened?"

"Susan!" cried Lark.

She lay on the threshold to her bedroom, looking like a pile of crumpled clothes. Lark knelt beside her, frantically calling her name.

Dom pushed her aside and lifted Susan in his arms. As tenderly as if he were carrying a baby, he laid her back on her bed.

Lark stared helplessly, then dashed downstairs to the telephone. Even while she dialed Emergency, she remembered Dom using the same telephone when her father had committed suicide almost five years earlier.

But Susan could not die. Not now!

"We need an ambulance at Dogwood Farm," she gasped into the receiver. "I think my mother's had a heart attack. Please come quickly." She gave directions to the farm, and an ambulance was promised within twenty minutes.

She went back upstairs. Dom was stroking his mother's forehead. He looked up when he heard Lark in the doorway.

"I can't imagine what happened," he muttered.

Guilt coursed through Lark. She thought she would faint. It was her fault, of course. She had kept Susan talking for hours, in the middle of the night, just when she'd most needed to rest. She'd surprised and shocked her. What a fool. What an *idiot!* If Dom found out, he would think she had killed his mother. Not on purpose, of course, but obviously the shock of learning who she was, and the truth about Justin and Carl, had been too much for her.

The room swam before her eyes. She clutched the doorjamb, then swung away. The hall dipped and sloped and she felt she was sliding down it.

A strong arm guided her into Dom's bedroom.

"Lie down," he said gently. "I don't want you collapsing on me too."

Lark sat on the edge of the bed, feeling sick. "Is she going to be all right?"

Dom looked sober. "I don't know. How soon will the ambulance be here?"

"Twenty minutes."

"I don't know," he repeated.

Lark looked up in dismay. "What do you mean, you don't know?"

"She's still unconscious. I don't know what went wrong."

"It's my fault," Lark choked out. "I shouldn't have gone on talking to her last night. I should have made her sleep. I shouldn't have told her anything. Oh, God . . ."

Dom shook his head. "I know what my mother is like. If she wanted the chance to talk to you, it would have taken a mountain of willpower to say no. I'm sure this had nothing to do with you. Who knows? Maybe she had a premonition of some sort that this might happen, and wanted to get to know you as well as she could before——" He stopped. "And also to hear about . . . my father."

But Lark wasn't comforted. "Why doesn't the ambulance come?" she groaned.

Dom went back to his mother. Soon afterward the ambulance arrived. White-faced, Lark looked on as Susan's limp body was loaded onto a stretcher and taken downstairs.

"I'm going to follow in the car," said Dom, shrugging into his coat. Lark looked after the departing ambulance, torn. Did he want her with him or not?

"I don't know what to do," she said.

Dom gave her a hug. "Would you be able to get some sleep if you stayed here? You look as though you could use it."

She shook her head, clinging to him.

"Then grab your coat. I'm selfish enough to want you with me just now. Better bring a book too. It might be a long day."

But Lark didn't want a book. At the hospital they were told to wait. There was still no word on Susan's condition. Dom paced the waiting room. Lark sat with her face buried in her hands.

"Mr. Whitfield?" They both looked up. A doctor came over. "I'm so sorry. We did everything we could. We won't know exactly what went wrong until after the autopsy."

Lark buried her face in her hands again.

"I'd like to see her," said Dom, hoarsely.

"Certainly." At the door the doctor glanced back at Lark, who had not moved, and asked, "Does your sister want to come too?"

"She's not my sister."

"Oh, excuse me. I was told Ms. Whitfield was her mother."

Dom went over to Lark. "I'm going upstairs."

She got up. "I'll come too."

"You don't have to," he said, regarding her worriedly.

"I want to."

They followed the doctor, holding hands hard.

Susan might have been asleep, if it weren't for an odd stillness that surrounded her. Lark knelt by the bed, too moved for tears.

"I'm sorry, Susan," she whispered.

Dom remained standing. Lark felt something wet fall on her arm and looked up.

He was silently crying.

CHAPTER SIXTY-SEVEN

IN Toni's dreams, Pierre became inextricably confused with Dom. She would laugh and laugh in those dreams. *It feels so good to laugh again,* she thought. *I'm so relieved I'm able to laugh.*

But when she awoke her face would be wet with tears.

At the office she was efficient, hard, friendly. At parties she was sophisticated, gregarious. Only when she was alone in bed was she unable to keep her emotions at bay. She stayed later and later at the office.

She hadn't heard from Pierre since the night they had made love way back in October. The renovations in her apartment had long since been completed. But even the variegated marble in the bathroom left her feeling depressed and unsatisfied.

She tried to concentrate on Groome's campaign strategy, but it was an uphill battle. The polls were reflecting the newspapers' stories about him and nothing Toni did could counteract their effect. Besides, she was growing increasingly tired of Groome.

A month passed: the bleak, frigid month of February. Then late one Friday evening when she was still at her office, Pierre telephoned.

"Hi, it's me."

She took a breath when she heard his low, French accented voice. "Hello, me."

"Are you busy?" he asked.

It was after eight o'clock and there was no reason for her to stay any later, except that she hadn't wanted to go home. "Well . . ."

"I thought perhaps you would like to visit. I've missed you."

"Have you?"

"Yes."

"Then why haven't you called?"

"I did telephone. Your secretary told me you were in California." He paused. "I didn't know you were married."

"We're getting a divorce."

"You should have told me."

She was silent. Rain spattered the black office window. Everyone else had gone home.

"I'd like to come over," she said at last.

"Good."

Hard, cold, slashing rain made it difficult to find a taxi, but she managed at last. Traffic was heavy. She dozed a little on the way downtown.

Pierre kissed her and drew her onto the bed with him. He was watching Arsenio Hall on television. There were no lights on in the loft, only the illumination from the screen.

Toni felt better as soon as she lay down beside him. She couldn't explain it: why the messy, dirty loft with hardly anything beautiful or pleasing about it seemed so peaceful to her. She closed her eyes and leaned her head against the back of the bed. She didn't even mind the television being on. It felt restful not to have to talk. Pierre handed her a glass of seltzer water he was drinking and laughed at something Arsenio Hall was saying. Toni sipped from his glass. She knew Pierre was as aware of her presence as she was of his, although he acted so casually toward her. That was part of the peacefulness in being with him.

"All right," he said, when the show was over. He switched off the television with the remote. "That is all for tonight. Is it still raining? You look wet."

"It's pouring out."

"Come with me. We're going to put you in a hot bath."

In the long, claw-footed bath Pierre washed her back and

breasts with soap. He worked on each toe, each finger. He turned her over and massaged her back and buttocks.

Toni shuddered with pleasure.

He stroked the inside of her thighs, and Toni began to moan. Dom was forgotten, and Groome was forgotten, and her office was forgotten, and New York City was forgotten: She was aware only of Pierre's rough, calloused hand that caressed her so gently.

He helped her out of the bath, wet and dripping. She undressed him. On the wide bed she got on top of him and they began the rhythmic, rocking, age-old dance all over again.

"That got rid of some of your tension," Pierre remarked when, exhausted and content, they could do no more than lie entwined in each other's arms. "You were as strung up as a cat when you got here. What is the matter?"

"Work, I guess. This smut campaign is making Justin Groome behave very oddly. I've never seen him so cold and vindictive. Wants us to start our own antismut stuff on Tim Marshall. Trouble is, we can't find anything bad about him. He has an advantage being so young. Frankly, the more I find out about him, the more I like him. I think I may even vote for him."

"So quit and work for him instead."

She laughed. "It's not so simple. Groome is still our biggest client. He could break me in a second if he thought I was disloyal."

"Not good," said Pierre. "You should never be so beholden to a man. I don't trust him."

"Oh, Justin isn't a man to be trusted! He's simply someone to use and be used by. That's always been our relationship, and it always will be."

"I'd tell him to go to hell."

"I'd love to."

"These things I've been reading in the newspapers about him," Pierre said slowly. "Are they true?"

Toni was silent.

"Are they?" he insisted.

"I don't know."

"Toni, look at me." He was propped on one elbow, gazing

down at her. "This girl who was murdered was your sister.
Don't you ever talk about her?"

She shook her head.

"Why not?"

"I can't bear to," she whispered, closing her eyes against a
sudden, violent wave of tears.

He held her tightly. After a while he said, "If I were to ask
you to sail with me around the Caribbean, you'd tell this
Groome fellow to go to hell, wouldn't you?"

"Probably," she managed.

They stayed in bed all the next day. It was still raining out,
and they ordered in food when they got hungry. Mostly they
made love and watched movies on Pierre's VCR. Toni didn't
even call her answering machine for messages. She thought
she might actually be happy again one day.

The funeral service for Susan Whitfield was brief. Jonny flew
in from Brazil, looking exhausted, his eyes red-rimmed. He
seemed unsurprised to find Lark with Dom.

At first Lark wasn't going to stay for the funeral. Dom
couldn't understand why not.

"We've been together this whole time," he said, looking
hurt and indignant. "Let's see it through together."

Lark didn't want to tell him that she was afraid of seeing
Justin Groome again. She didn't want to give Justin the least
suspicion of her true identity, and attending Susan's funeral
would surely seem suspicious to him.

"Who will be coming?" she asked evasively.

"Most of the village. It seems my mother was popular with
everyone. I don't think too many people from New York will
make it. Not Toni, if that's what you're wondering. Marianne,
who works at Whitfield Communications, will represent the
firm."

"No one else from New York?"

He suddenly understood. "Oh, you're wondering if Justin
Groome will be here? No, we didn't invite him." He flashed
her a smile, the first in a couple of days. "I would have
thought you'd be longing to meet him, just to see what he's
really like."

"I feel I already know what he's really like." But Lark said she'd stay.

Susan was buried in Northkill cemetary. The reception was held at the vicar's house, because Dom and Jonny had decided they couldn't handle the logistics of having a reception at the farm. If Lark had not been so stricken by Susan's death she might almost have enjoyed the reception. She gravely shook hands with her old friends, Billy and Mary, and even Graham was there with his arm around a girl Lark did not know who carried a baby in a sling.

"What'll we do with the farm?" said Dom, when the three of them, Dom, Jonny, and Lark, were finally alone in the warm kitchen later that night.

"I guess we'll sell it," said Jonny, hopefully.

"I don't think we should do that yet," said Dom uncomfortably.

"Why not?"

He didn't look at Lark. "I still feel it's really Penny's house," he said slowly. "I'd hate to think of her coming back and finding not just Susan gone, but the farm as well."

Not arguing, Jonny poured himself another bourbon. Lark went over to Dom and wrapped her arms around his neck. "I think you're the nicest man I've ever met," she said into his ear.

Dom smiled at her.

But Lark could not get over her feeling of guilt, that she in some way had caused Susan to have another heart attack. Nothing Dom said could cheer her.

On the airplane flying back to Los Angeles Dom tapped the *New York Times* that was on her lap and said, "Here, Ms. Miserable. Let's split it." He showed her one of her favorite California cabernets, a Heitz Cellar "Bella Oaks." The flight attendant uncorked it. "It seems incredible that you grew so fond of my mother in such a short time," said Dom, conversationally as they sipped the wine. "You seem even more upset about her death than I am."

"I shouldn't have kept her up talking like that."

"Don't keep blaming yourself." He was worried about her

and decided to get her thinking about something else. "You know, you haven't been very straight with me."

"What do you mean?"

"About your past."

Lark looked stricken.

"There's no record of your going to NYU film school. No one's heard of you there. Sorry, but I can't believe you were ever unforgettable."

"What on earth made you look into it?" she said at last.

"It was a long time ago, when we first met. I was curious about you, not suspicious. Why'd you lie?"

"To get a job."

"I love you, Lark. But I can't go on loving a phantom. I need a woman with substance—I need to know who you really are, what you're really like."

"What I am is here and now. What does my past matter to us? It's all behind—"

"You're looking at life as if it were a piece of tape. You think you can snip off an end and keep going. But life isn't like that: It's more of an accumulation, like a bundle that keeps enlarging. The contents of the bundle make up each of us."

"That's very poetical."

He gave up.

"By the way," he said casually when they were eating lunch, "you can tell that man who claims to be my dad that I'll drop by to say hello sometime."

She looked at him in amazement. "Oh, Dom! It'll mean so much to him."

"I don't know why he wants to see me, but I'll do it, and I'll try to be gracious about it."

Lark pressed his arm gratefully. "That's so wonderful."

"What does he do? He used to be a doctor, right?"

"Right."

"But what sort? He's not still practicing, is he?"

"Not anymore."

"Tell me whatever you can about him, so I'm prepared. How did you two meet?"

"Mutual friends," she said vaguely.

"There you go, Ms. Evasive." But he didn't sound annoyed. "Forget I asked."

She was relieved he didn't press her. She knew she should follow Susan's advice and tell Dom the truth, but she wasn't ready. The article she had been reading in the *Times* said that Groome was under siege. The polls showed him floundering several points behind his rival.

It made him increasingly dangerous.

CHAPTER SIXTY-EIGHT

"I want you with me when I see him," said Dom once they were back in Los Angeles. "Is he in the hospital?"

"Yes. I'll go with you. He's really a nice guy, Dom. You'll like him."

"Don't tell me who I'll like and who I won't like."

"It's just that I know you're nervous about this."

"Well, you're just making me more nervous."

When Lark told Carl that Dom was coming to see him she was surprised at his calm reaction: "I'm very glad, of course. But I knew he would, if you asked him to."

She had told Carl everything that had happened in Northkill. After he'd gotten over the initial shock of hearing about Susan's death, Lark told him it was her fault she had died. The autopsy had discovered only that the new valve in Susan's heart had failed. But Lark knew it had failed because of her.

Carl had been unsurprised by the fact that Susan had recognized her.

"She was always so open and so aware," his voice broke. "She only made one serious error in her life that I know of."

Lark didn't need to ask which that was. She knew it was her friendship with Groome.

She brought Dom the following Saturday.

"Here he is," she said.

The men looked at each other.

"Hi," Dom said. He might be nervous, but he didn't look it.

Carl looked composed too, but Lark knew he was too moved to speak right away. Dom sat in the chair by the bed.

"I'm sorry you're ill," said Dom. "If there's anything I can do, you'll let me know?"

"Yes, I will."

Dom's gold eyes were compassionate. "I'm sorry it's taken us this long to get together. It should have happened years ago."

"Yes, perhaps."

There was an awkward silence. Lark stood with her back to them, gazing out the window.

"I'm sorry about your mother," said Carl.

"Me too."

"I longed to see her again. It would have made me feel so differently, to see her, to talk to her, only once—only once before—" He spoke so softly they could hardly hear. "My damned pride."

Dom cleared his throat. "I don't actually know what happened between you and Mom. She told me only what Justin told her, and that was years ago. Lark says he was lying. Would you tell me the truth?"

Carl gave a smile that lit up his entire face. "I have wanted you to hear it ever since you were born."

"Lark would have told me, if I'd let her." She turned around and Dom held out his hand to her. She went over and stood behind him, draping her arms over his shoulders. He played with her ringless fingers while Carl told his story.

"I felt so bitter toward your mother when I discovered she believed Justin Groome's story," he finished. "She broke off our engagement and only *then* asked for an explanation. She was angry and upset, but I could not forgive her. If you have not experienced a bitterness of the magnitude I felt, I pray to God you never do."

"I've experienced it," said Lark, understandingly.

Dom went on playing with her fingers but he said, "It seems to me a lot of heartache could have been avoided simply by talking things over. Talking's a wonderful thing. Or even writing a letter. Just some form of communication, explaining things. I'd hate to be kept in the dark like my mother was."

"If I had my life to live over," said Carl, "I would do it your way. I would have spoken out."

"Thanks to Lark, at least my mother found out the truth before she died," said Dom.

"Yes, thanks to Lark." Carl regarded her gratefully. But Lark couldn't look at either of them. She drew away from Dom.

Carl looked tired. Dom gripped the thin, bony hand that lay on top of the blanket.

"It's not too late for us to be friends," he said. "I'd like to come again."

"And I would like to see you again." Carl's eyes were full. "Bless you, my dear boy."

In the car, Lark said to Dom, "You know something? You're a really nice guy sometimes."

He laughed. "Here," he tossed her a package. "More proof that I'm a really nice guy."

"What's this for?"

He looked askance. "Lark, love, you'd better remember when your birthday is or people will think you made it up."

She stuck out her tongue at him and opened the package. Inside were gold earrings, a bracelet, and a necklace, all incorporating the mischievous-looking cupid with his bow and arrow that had been chosen as the logo for the "Romance!" series.

Lark was thrilled, not just by the gift but by the growing popularity of "Romance!". Suddenly she was, not a household name exactly, but a name people working in the film industry could definitely recognize.

Jonny was back in Brazil, shooting *Flaming Forest*. Groome had spoken to Dom about the deal, and Dom had managed to persuade APG's board members to let the film be completed. But Dom was perplexed by Groome's involvement in the project. Even for the sake of the positive publicity he would get from environmentalists, it seemed unlike him to jeopardize his standing with the business and banking communities by supporting a film like *Flaming Forest*.

"Besides," as he told Lark when they were driving back to his house after a late day at the office, "Jonny doesn't have any idea how far money goes. He spends a million dollars as though it were a hundred. His sets are so elaborate they cost the moon, and he has a thing for using hundreds of extras—all of whom have to be paid. I'm concerned that instead of using Groome's million to wrap up the movie he's going to get carried away with some new highfalutin ideas."

"Who's the editor?"

"Roger Grigio. He's worked with Jonny before. They drive each other crazy, but they understand each other. He's with Jonny now, in Manaus. He's an excellent editor, but Jonny's already shot more than a hundred hours. Roger's going to have to edit them down to two, or three at the most."

Lark groaned.

"I want the film released by June," said Dom. "I know the board won't tolerate another extension."

"Is Jonny on the wagon?"

"As far as I know. I'm thinking of taking a few days off and going down there. I want him to wrap up the shoot. He sees this project as a monument to ecology. If the movie is five hours long, or even ten, he doesn't care. Jonny's never cared about box office sales. But Roger knows what's needed." He glanced at her. "Want to come to Brazil with me? I'd like to talk to Roger and see how he's doing at the edit lab in Manaus. And you do have a way with Jonny, as we both know. Also, you might enjoy seeing something of the rain forest while it's still there. We'll be gone a week at most."

"It sounds great," said Lark. She was still unused to Dom's casual travel plans. She knew he was wealthy, but even so the Amazon seemed a long way to go just for a few days. She remembered how she used to think New York City, just two hours from Dogwood Farm, seemed like another planet.

They arrived in Rio de Janeiro on Friday morning and went to the Copacabana Palace Hotel. The wide, busy street was directly below their balcony. A strange, distinctive path made of black and white stones in an undulating wave pattern separated the road from Copacabana Beach. Rich, golden sand curved in a perfect crescent from mountain to mountain at each end.

The beach was already beginning to fill with sun worshippers, glistening copper skin, many of them bare breasted, almost all of them, men and women, wearing scant, barely visible G-strings.

"Why do they bother to wear anything?" Lark said, laughing.

"It's sexier than being naked," replied Dom.

Wearing complimentary hotel bathrobes, they ate breakfast on the terrace: black coffee, croissants, and papayas almost a foot long, with fruity, peppery seeds. Lark sat on Dom's lap, her back to the sun, kissing him in between juicy bites of papaya.

"I can't stand this anymore," groaned Dom at last.

"What?" asked Lark, hurt.

"You. You're driving me crazy." He kissed her chin, licking off the drips from the papaya. "Let's go inside."

"Carry me," ordered Lark.

Staggering, he carried her into the room and dumped her on the soft bed. It bounced gently beneath her weight.

"I hope I didn't get a slipped disc," said Dom, falling on top of her.

She chuckled, running a long finger along the muscles in his bare arm. "I doubt it."

Their robes had fallen open. They lay, skin against skin, looking deep in each other's eyes.

"It's okay," Lark whispered at last, as though reading his thoughts. "I'm really okay now, Dom."

His eyes glowed. He took her tenderly, as conscious of her pleasure as of his own. "My Lark . . . my very own." He nibbled the side of her throat and her ear.

"So beautiful . . . so sexy . . . my own . . ."

Lark closed her eyes and murmured his name.

"Open your eyes," he ordered.

She did so. "Why?"

His expression was filled with ardor. "I want to watch you. Your eyes are so beautiful. So expressive." He caressed her more gently, then with a firmness that left her gasping.

"Keep your eyes open." He laughed.

"Oh, Dom."

He got on top of her, slowly, stroking the hair from her face. It was as though there were no barriers between them. They were one—one body, one soul. Lark wrapped her legs around him. They still watched each other, sweat forming beads on their foreheads and upper lips, their expressions growing increasingly dazed.

Lark came first, but she didn't close her eyes. Dom was right after her; he collapsed on top of her.

He started to shift almost at once, but she held him still.

"Don't move," she asked.

"I'm too heavy."

"No, you're not."

"Sure?"

"I'm sure."

The next morning they flew to Manaus, where Jonny's crew was filming. The trip took almost five hours: Lark was amazed by the hugeness of Brazil. They flew over thick blankets of jungle, then they reached areas that had been decimated by loggers and farmers. She had been aware of the disastrous plundering of the rain forests, but until she had actually seen it, she had not realized the enormity of the tragedy. In ugly patches the forest had been razed, leaving scarred dirt in its place.

"If Jonny can capture how awful this is on film, more power to him," she said with feeling.

"That's the trouble with Jonny," agreed Dom. "It's hard not to be on his side, even when he's ruining the company."

The wide Amazon flowed below, thickly opaque.

"I wouldn't want to fall into it," said Lark, admiring it. "Isn't it infested with piranhas?"

"They aren't the worst of it," replied Dom, but he refused to tell her what could be worse than being eaten alive in a single gulp.

Manaus was an old European-style town, with its own opera house which had been in existence since the last century.

"I can't imagine ladies in their crinolines and men in their top hats attending the opera way out here in this jungle!" exclaimed Lark, mopping her brow. "It seems surreal."

Their hotel was off the main square, not as glamorous as the Copacabana Palace, but blessedly air-conditioned.

They rented a jeep that afternoon. Jonny was filming in the jungle, under a thick roof of tangled trees. No sun penetrated the dense verdure. There was not a glimpse of the sky. Just endless wiggly plant life, the hum of strange insects, otherwise an eerie silence. The emerald light cast everything into one-dimensional shadow.

Jonny was much too involved in filming to pay attention to Dom and Lark. When Dom told him he wanted him to wrap up the filming so that the movie could be premiered in June, he laughed agreeably.

"There's not much to edit. We'll be using most of the footage. Sure the movie can be released by June. No problem."

"How many hours have you got so far?"

"I guess it's pretty long."

"Come back to L.A. and help Roger with the edit," Dom urged. "The sooner the movie's released, the sooner more people will know more about the destruction of the rain forest. That's what you want, isn't it?"

Jonny looked into the emerald distance. "That's not all I want," he admitted. "I want to make a great movie."

"It's bound to be great," Lark put in. "But you know that editing is just as important as shooting. Do you want to leave that entirely in Roger's hands?"

"No!"

"Then wrap it up here and come back with us."

"A summer release is nothing to sneeze at," added Dom. "We're planning a benefit to go along with the premiere. A thousand dollars a plate."

Jonny said he'd think it over.

As Dom and Lark drove back to Manaus through the sultry evening air, Dom said, "It's called the rain forest, but in some places the trees are so thick overhead that rain never reaches the ground."

"I've heard that sometimes a whole new layer of forest grows on top. That would explain the darkness."

"Strange place."

"But wonderful. I can understand Jonny's fascination."

They emerged from the jungle at last. As they drew up in front of their hotel, Lark suddenly stiffened.

"Good God!" she exclaimed.

Dom followed her eyes with his own. Justin Groome was coming toward them.

"Dom! Just the man I'm looking for! Jonny said you might fly out for the weekend and I was looking forward to seeing you again."

"Hi, Justin." Dom turned off the ignition and got out of the jeep. "What are you doing here?"

"Vacationing in Rio. I heard that the Whitfield brothers were shooting in Manaus and thought I'd pop up and say hello. Let me buy you a drink."

"This is Lark Chandler," Dom introduced her coolly. "Lark, this is Justin Groome."

"We've already had the pleasure," Justin said, shaking her hand.

Dom looked surprised. They went inside the hotel. It was a relief to be back in air-conditioning. In the bar they ordered piña coladas and sat at a table overlooking the square. The sun was setting and it was still broad daylight. But within a few minutes it was dark. Dusk was brief in the tropics.

Lark took the first opportunity to escape to their room. She sat on the edge of the wide bed. If Groome had not recognized her before, it was unlikely he would now. She forced herself to relax.

A knock on the door made her leap to her feet.

Dom entered. "It's only me," he said mildly.

"Hi."

"Sitting in the dark?"

She switched on the light.

"So that's the man you want to crucify in a docudrama," he said, sounding amused. "Where did you meet him before?"

"He came to the office in January. He'd heard about my movie idea and wanted to talk me out of it."

"He did?" Dom frowned.

"Where is he now?"

"Still downstairs. Jonny came in and joined us so I left him to do the entertaining." Dom kicked off his shoes and lay on the bed. "I guess those newspaper articles are getting to him. He's looking for Penelope Houten. He's sure she's the one behind the stories about him and he wants to get hold of her."

"I'll bet he would."

"I told him I hadn't seen her, although I'd like to find her as much as he would."

"So would the FBI, I would guess."

"Are you hungry?" he asked. "We can go down to dinner any time you're ready."

"Is he joining us?"

"I got out of it, thank goodness. I told him we were on a sort of prehoneymoon honeymoon here."

Lark turned to smile at him.

"Anyway, he wanted to talk to Jonny," added Dom.

"Poor Jonny," said Lark. "Do I have to dress for dinner? No jeans allowed?"

"Oh, I don't know," he said lazily. "You look great in jeans."

"Thanks. But I think I'll put on something cooler." She went into the bathroom and had a tepid shower. When she emerged, wrapped in a towel, Dom was still lying on the bed in the same position as when she had left. He seemed deep in thought. Lark went to the closet and took out a midnight blue miniskirt and matching silk blouse. Dom watched her dress, but his tawny eyes gave her no clue as to what he was thinking.

They ate downstairs in the hotel. The restaurant was candlelit, with fragrant, yellow freesias in bud vases on each table. A pianist played soft jazz at one end of the room. Dom ordered bouillabaisse as an appetizer; he handed the wine list to Lark, who suggested a Pouilly Fumé.

"You never did tell me where you learned so much about wines," he said.

"Your father taught me."

"Did he? Why?"

"He felt every educated woman should know about wine."

"What about things like cheese and caviar?"

"I know more than I did, thanks to him."

"Where did you meet him? You never really told me."

"In England. He and my father were good friends before my father died."

"Tell me more. What did your father do?"

"Sold shoes."

"And your mother?"

"She . . . made hats."

"Where did you go to college?"

"I didn't. But no one would've hired me if I admitted that."

"True enough." He smiled. "Anyway, I can't say I'm sorry you lied, since I guess I wouldn't have met you if you hadn't."

"Why are you asking me all these questions?" she asked after a moment.

"I really want to ask you about Justin," Dom said slowly. "I was surprised you'd met him before. Why didn't you tell me?"

"I think you were out of town when it happened."

"You just met him that one time?"

"Yes."

"Why do I have this weird feeling you two know each other pretty well?"

"I know *about* him," she corrected.

Dom was gazing into his wineglass. Now he looked up and asked, "Who raped you, Lark?"

She flushed scarlet. Did he know? If he didn't know, then why was he asking? The blood pounded in her head. She didn't know what to say.

Finally Dom said, "Still don't want to talk about it?"

She cleared her throat. "It was someone like Justin Groome," she said slowly. "Someone rich and powerful and who had an uncanny ability to convince anyone of anything. I couldn't tell anyone because I knew they'd believe him over me. I was seventeen years old."

Dom held her hand on top of the table. "Thanks for sharing that with me. It must be very hard to talk about."

She nodded, feeling like a traitor. After dinner they went to the lounge. A band played old jazz favorites and a few couples danced cheek to cheek on the shiny floor. Dom ordered cognacs before taking Lark onto the dance floor.

For a while she forgot everything but the fact that she was dancing in his arms.

When they sat back down, Dom said, "I never imagined that I'd want to marry anyone as much as I want to marry you."

"Is that a proposal?" teased Lark.

"No," he replied. "It's a statement of fact. I can't propose till I'm properly divorced."

And I can't accept till I'm out of danger, thought Lark.

"I always believed that anyone who wanted to get married must be an idiot," mused Dom. "But I finally understand why they'd want to."

"Why do you want to?" asked Lark.

"Life wouldn't be worth living without you," he replied somberly.

She remembered Carl saying that that was how Dom would feel, once he met her. How had he known?

"What are you thinking now?" he asked.

"That you still hardly know me. How can you feel this way?"

"That's what puzzles me too."

CHAPTER SIXTY-NINE

MEANWHILE Jonny was having a thoroughly unpleasant evening with Justin Groome. It had begun with two many martinis, and by this time Jonny was fighting drunkenness while trying to convince Groome that he did not know where Penny was.

"Are you sure, Jonny?" asked Justin. His face seemed flabbier and his eyes smaller. Jonny found him repellent.

"I swear it," he replied. "How would I know? I barely knew her, and just when we were beginning to be good friends I let her down without a word of explanation—letting everyone think she was guilty of murder."

Groome's small eyes were marble-hard. "I was willing to finance this movie only if you produced Penny for me."

"But I don't know where she is."

"Did you ask Emmy?"

"Penny's gone, Justin. She ran away four years ago."

"She's somewhere around, nonetheless. I know she is. I'll find her. And when I find her, she'll wish she'd never been born."

Guilt washed over Jonny. If he had stood by Penny, together they might have been able to bring Groome to justice.

But he had been a coward. He stared at Justin.

"For her sake, I hope you never find her," he said. "I'm not behind the media campaign, Justin, but by God, you deserve every difficulty that's coming your way. There are no secrets between us. I know the truth, and you know that I know it.

Just because I'm a coward doesn't mean we have to pretend to each other. You're a bastard, and you disgust me."

Weaving, he made it to the front entrance. Outside, the sticky, sultry air struck him like a slap in the face. He began sweating profusely.

"I hope you won't 'disappear' too," Groome said in his ear. "If I find out you've been holding out on me——"

Jonny turned and walked quickly away. He felt physically ill from the encounter.

Justin Groome flew back to Rio the next morning, but he only stayed in Brazil a few more days. He was finally convinced that neither Dom nor Jonny knew Penny's whereabouts, and also that neither of them was behind the leaks to the paper. As soon as he returned to New York, he went to his office and telephoned Toni at Whitfield Communications.

She was just closing up the office for the weekend.

"I need to see you," said Groome. "Come to my office."

It was already five o'clock on Friday evening.

"Must it be now?" she asked. "I'm meeting Pierre at eight and I want to go home first."

"It's important," said Groome, and hung up.

Toni went to his office. Justin was alone.

"I realize that there's only one way to stop this media campaign from ruining me," he began at once. "And that's to find this girl, Penelope. I know she's behind these insinuations that I murdered Violet. She's determined to ruin me. But I won't let her. She must be found and stopped."

Toni was sick and tired of Groome's obsession with finding Penny. Personally, she was convinced the girl was dead. No one really just disappeared off the face of the earth like that. Besides, if Penny really did think Groome was guilty, why didn't she simply come forward and accuse him?

But it was Toni's job to be diplomatic, and so for an hour she humored Groome in his schemes and plans, while despising him more and more with every passing minute.

"Even if we did find her, how do you propose to stop her from telling reporters these stories?"

"I'll find a way," said Justin in so ominous a tone that Toni actually shivered.

"Well, I've done my best," she said. "The only person who claims to be closest to the 'source'—which may or may not be Penny, for all we know—is Emmy Elson. And she wouldn't betray her source if her life depended on it. She's not the type."

"Damn her. Damn them all. Don't you have any suggestions?"

"Yes, I do. Drop this feud you're having with a nonexistent girl you met a few times many years ago. Forget her. Go on with your campaign in a realistic manner. You're slipping in the polls."

"Screw the polls. There must be a way of tracking her down. I have five private investigative agencies working on it, and not one of them can come up with a single clue, except to suggest that we check all the plastic surgeons who were practicing in the country the year she disappeared. Bah!"

Toni glanced at her watch. It was already after seven o'clock. She was tired of talking about it.

"I've got to get going, Justin. The day's over. Maybe I'll think of something over the weekend."

"The day's not over till we resolve this."

"What is there to resolve? We'll keep going as we are. You keep looking for her, I'll keep working on defending you to the press." She stood up. Even the plush office she had been so proud to visit when she first started at Whitfield Communications seemed ostentious and phony now.

"If you walk out on me now, you're fired," Justin said angrily. "A meeting isn't over until I say so."

As Toni looked at him, she knew she had come to a crossroads. The vision of sailing around the Caribbean on a yacht with Pierre sank through her like cool, refreshing water. They had talked about it again the night before. Pierre had been trying to convince her to sell her co-op. He had sold the lease to his loft. He wanted to leave New York unencumbered. Already Toni had given up a lot since she had met him, and everything she got rid of made her feel lighter and stronger, not weaker. Her sporty red Mazda was gone. She had even

sent her mink coat to an animal rights activist group to be
used in their demonstrations against fur.

The only thing Pierre was adamant that she not give up
was her intoxicating underwear.

He wanted to leave that summer. In fact, Toni was pretty
sure he would go without her if she decided to stay. There
were no halves to Pierre. And he wouldn't want a woman who
only gave him half of herself.

But her career still held sway. She had given it up once
before to live with Dom, and the experience had been a disastrous one. In the year she had been back at Whitfield Communications she had regained her independence and her self-
confidence.

She did not want to lose that again.

Besides, she still loved her job. She had built it up, day by
day, piece by piece. Justin Groome had played on her ambition.

Perhaps it was about to play itself out. Pierre had said,
"Tell him to go to hell," and she had been shocked, because it
showed he did not understand how deeply she cared about her
career.

Nonetheless, she thought of saying it now.

Justin was saying, "I have a hunch that Dom bastard knows
where the kid is. He was pretty cool to me last time we saw
each other. Maybe Dom is the one in cahoots with the Elson
bitch."

"If Dom truly thought you murdered Violet and that you
put the blame on Penny, he wouldn't resort to smear tactics to
punish you. He'd move heaven and earth to make sure you
saw your day in court."

"Bah!"

Toni hesitated a fraction longer. Her mother and father
would be devastated. Her friends would be shocked.

But Pierre seemed to be standing just behind her shoulder,
a rock, a foundation upon which to build a life that might be
far less hollow than her present one.

"Good night, Justin."

He glared. "I meant it. If you leave now, you're fired."

She braced herself, as though to plunge into an icy lake high in the mountains. The water would be shockingly refreshing.

"Go to hell," she said calmly, and walked out the door.

CHAPTER SEVENTY

LEFT alone, Groome stared after Toni, but he was not really seeing her. He was so obsessed with his search for Penny that he was not aware of his world crumbling around him.

There was a good chance that Penny had had plastic surgery. How she'd been able to afford it puzzled him, but if she hadn't had her face changed, surely the FBI would have found her by now.

He thought back. As he remembered, the FBI was pretty sure she had left the country. But how? How? She had made a reservation for a flight to London, using a stolen credit card, but the ticket had never been picked up.

Had she found some other way of getting to England?

Why England?

He knew a plastic surgeon in London. Carl Bellamon had been part of the triangle that included Steve Whitfield and himself. He had drifted away after Steve died.

It was unlikely Carl would know anything about a nobody like Penelope Houten. He was one of the most prestigious plastic surgeons in England. Penny could never have afforded him, even if she had heard of him.

Still, Carl might give him a lead. They had been close friends once. Maybe he had forgiven him by now.

He picked up the telephone again.

"Operator, I want to call England."

When he managed to get through to Carl's home—realiz-

ing it was early on Saturday morning there—a woman's voice
answered. "Hello?"

"I'm looking for Carl Bellamon," said Groome, wondering
who the girl was. In the past, he'd suspected Carl of being
gay.

"I'm sorry, Carl doesn't live here anymore. He's moved to
California."

"Do you have a number where I can reach him?"

"May I ask who's calling?"

"Justin Groome, an old friend of his from New York."

"Oh—long distance. One moment, please." He heard
something banging, and some shuffling. It amazed him how
clear these international telephone lines were now. When he'd
been younger it had taken hours just to get a connection, and
once he did he had to shout over the static. "He's at Mount
Sinai Hospital in Los Angeles. I don't have his phone number
on me just now."

"Is he sick?"

"Carl is a patient there, yes."

"Thanks a lot for your help. What's your name?"

"Isabella. I'm staying in his house while he's away."

"Thank you, Isabella. I'll tell him I spoke with you."

At Mount Sinai Hospital, Groome waited for the elevator to
take him to the second floor where the terminally ill were
situated. It was also Carl's floor. Groome hadn't told Carl he
was coming. He watched a strikingly beautiful woman walk
through the front doors and approach the elevators. She
looked vaguely familiar, then he recognized her as Dom's girlfriend, the one who was trying to get an unflattering television show made about him. What was she doing there?
Instinctively, he ducked around the corner, out of sight.

The woman got in the elevator; the doors closed.

Groome watched the light, then ran for the stairs.

Panting, he reached the second floor. She was walking
along the corridor, her back to him. She turned into a room
and closed the door. Groome followed.

Outside the closed door he read the name: Bellamon.

He stared at it. How did Dom's girlfriend know Carl? Was it merely a coincidence?

Perhaps.

Or perhaps she'd found out that Carl had known Penny and she was trying to track down more information for her screenplay?

In any case, he didn't want to talk to Carl with anyone else there. He went back downstairs and paced restlessly in the waiting room. Through the glass partition he could see the visitors coming and going.

When Lark finally left, Dom was with her. Groome frowned, wondering. So Dom knew Carl too, did he?

Could this, too, be a coincidence?

He watched their backs as they walked across the lobby. Lark's gait was so familiar, Groome caught his breath. One could always wear a mask, he remembered, but there's no disguising oneself from the back.

He felt giddy from excitement.

He waited until they were safely out the front door and then he went back upstairs. He knocked on Carl's door and looked in.

"May I come in?"

A wasted, old man lay on the bed. He looked up without any interest. Then he struggled to sit up.

"Justin!" he exclaimed.

"Hello, Carl. Glad you recognized me. I heard you were here and thought I'd drop by for a visit. Not feeling too good, eh?"

"I cannot believe it is you."

Justin Groome stared at the sick man. "I can't believe it's you. What are you doing here?"

"Dying. What are you doing here?"

Groome pulled up a chair. "Now that Susan's dead I thought we could be friends again," he began.

Carl's eyes narrowed. "No, what are you really doing here?"

"Ahem. I'm trying to find a woman who disappeared about five years ago. She was a dear friend of mine. We have an idea that she may have undergone plastic surgery—and also that

THE BRIGHT FACE OF DANGER

she might have gone to England. We hoped you might be able to help us trace her."

Carl sank back into the pillows. "I am sorry, but even if I were able to trace this woman, my files and my records are completely confidential. You understand this, I am sure."

"Of course. I expected you to respond like that. But we may have something to discuss anyway. I know you're sick, for instance. It's possible that I might be able to help you."

"No one can help me now."

"But there are many advances being made in medicine. New drugs are being tested daily."

"I am aware of that. I have tested more than my share."

"There are certain drugs that I may have access to that you haven't. I'm not promising anything, mind you. I just wanted you to know that it's possible we could reach an agreement."

"Even if you could get me a miracle cure, I do not believe I could help you," said Carl, coldly. "I do not go into the details of my patients' history with them. If the girl wanted a new identity no doubt she came to me under an assumed name."

"I thought we could rummage through your patients at the time she disappeared. You could describe the nature of the injury—"

Carl was beginning to feel tired. He well knew who Groome was trying to find and why. "Get out of here."

Groome was angry. "You'll regret this."

"I am too old and too sick to care. I have got more things to regret than making bargains with crooks."

For a long moment the two men regarded each other with hatred borne from many years. Then the door opened and Lark walked in.

"I forgot my briefcase," she began, then stopped short at the sight of Groome. "You!" she exclaimed.

Groome stood up, staring at Lark. For a moment there her blue eyes had been extraordinarily like someone else's he knew. In them he saw a familiar expression of shock and fear.

He smiled pleasantly at her. "I recognize you," he said and noted with satisfaction that her face went white. "You're Dom's girlfriend. How's the screenplay going?"

"Fine, thanks."

"I'd better be going," said Justin. "Nice visiting you, Carl. Maybe I'll see you again." He turned back to Lark. "Unless I can drive you anywhere?"

"No, thanks. Dom's waiting for me outside in the car."

"Give him my regards. I'm only in town briefly, so I may not have a chance to call."

Groome left.

She went over to Carl's bed. "Why did he come here?"

"Looking for you."

"But why did he come to you? How could he know?"

"I do not know." Carl was certain that Groome had recognized her. "I do know that you should watch yourself very carefully from now on. A man like that is ruthless."

"You think . . . ?"

"Without a doubt."

She picked up her briefcase, trying to conceal her fear. "You're exhausted. I'd better go. Good night, Carl."

"Good night."

She shied from every shadow as she ran to Dom's car on the street. She jumped inside and hurriedly locked the door.

"Lark! Are you okay?"

She sat, trembling. Then she fell into his outstretched arms and broke into strange, dry sobs.

When Groome returned to his hotel room, he dialed Emmy Elson at the *Monday Week*. Her secretary put him through to her right away.

"How are you?" he said, affably.

"Very well, thank you."

"Do you know a girl called Lark Chandler?" he asked.

"No. Why?"

"You've never heard of her?"

"No. Who is she?"

Groome didn't know what to make of Emmy's reply. Could she be lying? He didn't know how to pursue this line of questioning.

"She's Dom's new girl. She's written a treatment for a

movie about me. I'm afraid a good deal of it is based on your articles."

"Oh, dear. I'm so sorry. No, I've never met her."

"Thanks anyway. Sorry to bother you," he said.

"Any time," said Emmy, very politely.

Justin Groome replaced the receiver, thinking hard. He wasn't sure any longer.

But he was almost sure. He thought of the English girl who had answered Carl's telephone in London. If Penny had gone to London, she would have left a clue. Something, anything. He would start his search there.

CHAPTER SEVENTY-ONE

LATE one afternoon Lark was getting ready to leave the office when she received a long-distance telephone call.

"My name is Miguel Garcia y Reyes." The man spoke with a strong Latin accent. "I was recently speaking to someone about a film I understand you are interested in making about a Mr. Justin Groome."

"Yes?"

"It is possible that I may be able to help you get the financial backing needed to produce this film. The subject interests me."

"How did you hear about it?"

"From Walter Arnim. He has a copy of the treatment and he loaned it to me."

Walter Arnim was an actor Lark had met recently who asked to look at the treatment.

"I'd like to meet you and talk it over," said Lark. "When would be a good time?"

"Unfortunately I am presently busy here in Soubriquet, in the south of France. Would it be too much trouble if I invited you here as my guest? I will fly you first class to Paris with a connecting flight to Marseilles. This way we can discuss arrangements at leisure."

"I'm much too busy to take the time off."

"You could come just for the weekend."

"I suppose I could." She was torn. "I'll have to think it over and call you back."

"I hope you will not think it over for too long. I have a feeling we would both benefit from a meeting."

"Give me a telephone number where I can reach you," said Lark. "I'll call you back this afternoon."

When she'd hung up, she buzzed Rosa on the intercom and asked her to come to her office.

"I just got a call from a man who claims he's a film producer interested in something I've written. I have no idea if he's legitimate or not."

"What is his name?"

"Miguel Garcia y Reyes."

"Portuguese?" suggested Rosa. "Or perhaps from Brazil? I have not heard of him. Is he in Hollywood?"

"I don't think so. He was calling from France. Walter Armin gave him a copy of my treatment. He might know more about him."

"I will see what I can learn."

The phone rang. Lark picked it up.

"Hello? Oh, hi, Dom."

Rosa slipped out of the office. Lark told Dom about the telephone call.

"You aren't really thinking about going?" he said.

"Of course I'm thinking about it. But I haven't made up my mind."

Dom was suspicious. "It sounds farfetched."

"I know it does. But it might be legitimate."

"If you definitely want to go, I guess I could go with you," said Dom, reluctantly.

"Could you? That would make all the difference. Okay, I'll call him back. Would you be able to leave next Friday?"

"Yes, that'd be fine."

After she'd made the travel arrangements with Miguel Garcia y Reyes, Lark gave a little pirouette around the office. Maybe soon the movie would be made and millions of people would learn the truth about Groome. The newspaper reports had started the ball rolling. She would send it crashing into the wall.

"What did your friend say when you told him I'd be coming too?" asked Dom later that night.

"He seemed surprised. I don't think he liked it. But he didn't object."

"Good."

Dom had to go to San Francisco on Tuesday for a conference. "I'll fly back Friday morning and meet you at the airport at noon. The flight's at two, right?"

"Yup. That sounds fine," said Lark.

For some reason, security was extra tight at the San Francisco airport on Friday morning. Many flights were delayed, including Dom's.

"What's the problem?" he asked the attendant at the ticket counter.

"Heightened security alert, sir. These things happen."

Dom decided to telephone Lark from the departure gate and warn her he was running late. He tossed his carry-on suitcase onto the conveyor belt and strode through the security check. As soon as he was through, a security guard grabbed his elbow.

"One moment, sir," she said politely.

"What the hell?"

"We need to check something. Come over here, please."

Firmly gripping his arm, she led him to another counter. Two more security guards appeared. One of them opened his suitcase and rifled through its contents. He pulled out a .32 Smith & Wesson.

"Does this belong to you?"

Dom stared. "No."

"You don't have a license for it?"

"I have a forty-five at home," he said. "It's registered. But I've never seen this gun before."

"You'll have to come with us, I'm afraid."

Dom wasn't worried: A man in his position would eventually be believed. Trouble was, it might take a few hours.

"I have to be in L.A. to catch a plane to France at two o'clock," he said. "I tell you, I've never seen the gun before."

"Did you leave your bag unattended at all since you arrived at the airport?"

"It was on a seat while I grabbed a cup of coffee. It was

within sight the whole time, but I guess I wasn't watching it. Someone must have put it in my bag."

The security guards were polite but firm. He was unable to board the flight.

"I have to make a telephone call, then," he said, annoyed. He hoped Lark hadn't yet left the office.

He was taken to the security office. A police officer stayed with him while he made the call.

"Rosa? Has Lark left yet? Good. Oh, well, pull her out of the meeting. This is important."

"I'm sorry, but the meeting is in Bel-Air," replied Rosa. "She said she would drop by the office afterward, though, before going to the airport."

"I'm still stuck in San Francisco. I'm not going to make that flight I said I'd be on. Ask her to try to get us on a later flight, will you? You could take care of that."

"Certainly," said Rosa.

"Hold on a minute." He glanced at the police officer. "Do you think this might take more than a few hours?"

"It might."

"Rosa? Transfer me to Beth, will you?" He waited. "Beth, Dom here. I'm still in San Francisco. I may need a lawyer within the next few hours. Get hold of Steve Collier for me, will you? Tell him to be ready to fly up here. I damn well don't want to spend the weekend in jail."

"What happened?"

"I'm not exactly sure, but I have a strong feeling that someone does not want me to go to France with Lark this weekend."

The meeting in Bel-Air went overtime. Lark had to go straight to the airport afterward. Her overnight case was in the trunk of her car, so there was no need to go to the office.

In the first-class ambassador lounge she was given two telephone messages. One was from Rosa, asking that she call. The other was from Dom.

" 'Been held up at the conference,' " she read. " 'Won't be able to go with you. Have a good time anyway.' "

She was disappointed. She telephoned her office, but Rosa

was not at her desk. She decided to leave a message for Dom
on his machine.

"Hi, Dom, it's Lark. Sorry you're not coming with me. I'll
call when I get there and give you the phone number. I'll be
back on Monday."

The flight to Paris was as exciting as the first flight she had
ever taken. Lark could never get enough of flying. She stayed
at the George V for the night, where Mr. Garcia y Reyes had
made a reservation. The next morning she took an Air France
flight to Marseilles. The small plane flew low over the rich
patchwork of fields and villages. Then she saw the fabled azure
of the Mediterranean, and soon the great harbor of Marseilles.

Mr. Garcia y Reyes waited for her on the tarmac. Friendly
brown eyes beamed a welcome at her.

"My car is this way."

Outside the terminal was a dusty jeep. And sitting in the
front seat was a gorgeous, red-headed woman who looked
strikingly familiar.

"Hello, Lark!" the woman waved.

Lark gaped. It was Isabella, the model she had met at Carl's
dinner party in London years earlier.

"Hello!" Lark exclaimed. "I didn't expect to find you here.
What are you doing?"

"Visiting. Isn't this the most gorgeous place in the world?
Hop in."

She made room for Lark in the front. Rattling along the
coast road, which soon turned into a bumpy unpaved lane,
Lark asked, "How do you two know each other?"

"Mutual friends," replied Miguel. His thin orange hair
flapped in the breeze.

"Everyone knows everyone in this part of the world," Isabella added gaily. "It's heaven."

They passed under a large windmill, its flags turning slowly
in the warm, slow breeze. Lark was agitated.

"It just seems like such a strange coincidence."

"These things do occur," said Miguel.

"We're staying in the most gorgeous house you've ever
seen," Isabella chattered brightly. "You'll love it. It's full of
movie people—actors and actresses and so forth. I was so sur-

prised when Miguel told me you were coming too. We heard through the grapevine that you were doing pretty well in Hollywood."

"I guess I am."

"I've been staying in Carl's house ever since he left. Doesn't he mean to sell it? I keep expecting to hear from him about that."

Not sure how much Isabella knew of Carl's illness, Lark replied vaguely, but she was reassured to hear Carl's name mentioned.

They climbed a steep hill, leaving the harbor behind. Gazing below, Lark had the sudden unwelcome image of Justin Groome's face looming just under the surface of the ocean. She blinked uncertainly and the image vanished.

"Here we are." Miguel pulled the jeep to an abrupt stop. "Welcome to Soubriquet."

Lark shrugged away the thought of Groome and turned to look at the house. It lay on an outrock of land which jutted into an aquamarine ocean.

"Pretty."

A grizzled-haired man came out to get the bags. He nodded at Lark without speaking. Isabella took her arm as they entered the garden and crossed a wide patio. A glass-topped table, several chairs, and large yellow umbrellas were set up in one corner. Bougainvillea and azaleas splashed magenta and pink on the low walls.

Once inside, high ceilings and thick stone walls made the house cool and quiet. But despite the serenity of the place, a chill stole over Lark as she stepped inside. She stood for a moment in the hallway, wondering what to do. Isabella peered back into the hall.

"Coming?"

"Yes."

Lark followed her up some wooden stairs and along a narrow hall.

"Here's your bedroom," Isabella announced, opening a door.

Lark looked around the whitewashed room. A polished wood desk, a closet, and a narrow bed were the only furnishings. Isabella threw open a window. In the distance Lark could make out Soubriquet harbor and the sparkling sea curving toward it.

"You must remember how you met Miguel," said Lark, turning to Isabella.

"I was with a friend in Cannes. One meets people here, that's all. He's very nice."

"When did you get here?"

"A few days ago. What's the matter?"

Lark said uneasily, "It just seems so strange. Is there anyone else staying here too?"

"Of course. It's a full house. You'll meet them all for drinks later."

"Who's here? Tell me their names."

They heard Miguel shouting for Isabella from downstairs.

"Sorry, I've got to go. I think it's time for some skinny-dipping. Want to come?"

Lark shook her head.

"We all get together for cocktails at around five. The others are dying to meet you. The bathroom is at the end of the hall, if you want to take a shower. Not my standard of luxury, but I put up with it for the sake of being here. Isn't it marvelous?"

She left. Lark went to the window and gazed outside. Late afternoon sunshine flooded the garden below. No one was about. Nothing could be more peaceful.

The shower turned out to be merely a showerhead that came out of a peeling wall. There was no shower curtain, only a drain in the middle of the slightly dipped floor. Everything —including the towel Lark had unpacked—became soaking wet when she turned on the shower. Despite that, she enjoyed the lukewarm water that sprayed the little room. Feeling refreshed, she made her way back to her room to dress.

She had not brought much. Besides her traveling suit, she had blue jeans, a white silk blouse, and sandals, and a light jacket for the evening. She was pinning up her long hair when Isabella opened the door and poked her head in.

"Need any help?" she said. "Miguel sent me up to check."

Lark didn't like having her privacy interrupted. "No, thanks," she said.

She couldn't help staring at Isabella's costume, however. Bits of transparent green chiffon barely covered her breasts and hips. Even on the beach, with a bathing suit underneath, the dress, if it could be called that, seemed practically obscene.

Isabella was gazing in equal dismay at Lark's outfit. "You're not going to wear jeans, are you?"

"Why not?"

"We're in Soubriquet."

"I didn't bring anything else."

Isabella grabbed her hand. "Come with me," she ordered.

Lark tried to protest, but Isabella's grip was surprisingly strong.

"Miguel would die with embarrassment if you showed up in jeans. I have just the thing for you."

They went into her bedroom. Colorful clothes lay everywhere. Uncertainly, Lark waited. She did not want Miguel to die of embarrassment because of her.

"Here it is," Isabella held up a translucent, pale blue minidress, threaded with gold. It would leave most of her midriff exposed, and a good portion of her breasts, too, Lark surmised.

"I can't wear that." Lark was firm but polite.

"Try it on. You can't tell until you've tried it on."

"Sorry—"

"Everyone dresses like this in Soubriquet. You probably won't even be allowed into the discotheque in jeans, nice as they are."

Lark was finally persuaded. She tried on the skirt. The sheer material clung to her thighs, the waist was low, resting on her hips. The translucent top lifted her breasts, and left her back and midriff bare.

The outfit did transform her, Lark admitted to herself, looking at the mirror. The gold threads in the material highlighted every curve, every gesture she made.

"I can't wear this," she protested weakly.

"Now your hair," said Isabella. "Buns aren't allowed here. Let me help."

Deftly, she unpinned Lark's hair.

"It's grown terrifically long since I saw you last," she said admiringly. "The men here go crazy over long hair. You're lucky." She took her brush and smoothed the thick waves. "Let's buck up. The others are already outside."

From the patio they heard the sound of voices. Isabella and Lark emerged through the glass doors, girlishly holding hands. The thick azalea bushes almost hid the group from view.

Almost, but not quite. One of the men sat facing the house. He was leaning back in the chair, laughing at something someone was saying. His long legs were stretched out, crossed at the ankles. He cradled a drink on his large stomach. He wore a red shirt, unbuttoned to his chest.

As he looked up at their approach, his eyes clashed headlong with Lark's.

Lark pulled back on Isabella's hand, but Isabella held on tight.

"What's the matter?"

"I don't believe this," Lark said in a low voice.

"What? Frank's a photographer. You'll like him. Leila's another model, but she wants to be an actress. You met Miguel already. And that's Justin. He's into politics in the States."

Lark swallowed, but she had to go forward. She had to pretend this was nothing more than a coincidence.

After all, perhaps it was.

CHAPTER SEVENTY-TWO

"HI, everyone!" Isabella sang out.

Miguel looked around and whistled. "There you are at last," he teased. "How is it that you can take so long to put on so little?"

"It takes a lot of work. Lark, let me introduce you. Frank, Leila, Justin. You'll be bumping into all of them at one time or another, probably in the shower since we all have to share one."

Lark smiled, not seeing them. From somewhere nearby she heard Justin's voice.

"Hello, Lark."

She forced a reply. "Hello, Mr. Groome."

"Justin, please."

"Do you two know each other?" asked Isabella.

"We've met a couple of times," said Lark.

There was a moment's silence, then Frank cleared his throat. "Have a seat, you two. We'll need another chair. I'll get it."

Tensely, Lark took the chair that Justin held out for her. She was aware that Isabella, who had taken Frank's vacated chair, was chattering with Leila, but she herself could think of nothing to say. She was certain now that the entire trip had been set up by Justin Groome.

From somewhere behind the roaring waterfall of fear that cascaded through her brain, she sifted out Justin's voice and realized he was addressing her.

"What would you like to drink, Lark?"

She gave a slight jump.

"I'll have a glass of mineral water."

"Anyone else for refills?" he asked, looking around.

Everyone wanted one. Justin disappeared into the house with the glasses.

Lark turned to Leila. "I hear you're a model?"

"Yes. I hear you're a famous movie producer."

"Not exactly." Every instinct told her to flee. But she had no idea how to get to Soubriquet village, much less to the airport.

Frank returned with the extra chair.

"And then we'll go dancing," Miguel was saying, giving Lark a significant smile. With an effort, she turned her attention to him. "Do you like to dance, Lark?"

"I haven't danced in a while."

Justin returned with the tray of replenished drinks. Briefly, their fingertips brushed as he handed her a glass. Her fingers suddenly felt boneless and she hastily set down the glass. She felt she had been branded.

"We'll go to Jackie O's," said Isabella. "It's still the classiest discotheque in town. But that won't be till later. We still haven't decided where to go for dinner."

Lark sipped her mineral water and sneaked a glance at Groome. He turned to her at the same moment and snared her glance.

"It's been quite a while since I saw you. How have you been?"

"Fine, thanks."

"How is Dom?"

"Good. He's at a conference just now."

"That man works too hard."

"Yes, he does."

She couldn't seem to tear her gaze from his. His eyes seemed harder; you could hardly tell they were blue anymore. It was as if they were of an inorganic material, like plastic. You had to have a soul in order to have color in your eyes, she thought. He had put on weight, but he had always been a large man and he still carried his weight well.

Recalled to her surroundings by Isabella's laughter, Lark dropped her eyes and tried to smile at a joke she'd missed. Her gaze wandered around the garden, to the dusk-enveloped hill behind the house. How could she escape? A cool breeze made her shiver.

Justin leaned over and placed his warm hand on her bare arm. "Cold?"

She shrank from his touch. "A little. I'll get a jacket."

Alone in her bedroom she tried to think what to do. From her suitcase she took a miniature shoulder purse. This she crossed over her shoulder so that it was secure. It was small— barely passport size, and not very noticeable. Inside she put her money, credit cards, passport, and plane ticket. She dared not leave them in the house in case they were stolen and she was trapped in France.

Then she went downstairs to the living room to telephone Dom. With some difficulty she made the operator understand she wanted to call the United States.

Dom didn't answer; when his answering machine came on she debated what to say. She had the uncanny feeling someone was listening to her. She knew she had to be careful.

"Hi, this is Lark calling from Soubriquet. Just wanted to let you know I arrived safe and sound. I bumped into an old friend I knew from London, called Isabella. And someone else you know is here: Justin Groome. I'll be back Monday morning, I hope."

"Making a phone call?" Justin's voice came from the door.

"I promised Dom I'd call when I arrived."

"I think the others have decided on a restaurant finally," said Justin. "The most traumatic decisions you'll have to make while you're here is which beach to go to during the day and which restaurant to eat at in the evening. In between, you'll have to slip in a few movies and a few discotheques."

"Oh, I'm only here till tomorrow."

"I hope we can persuade you to stay longer than that." He set the tray on a side table. "Let's join the others."

The rest of the group were already piling into the jeep. Lark was crushed between Frank and Justin in the backseat.

"The restaurant is right on the waterfront," Justin told her.

"Soubriquet has everything—from international cuisine to the tiniest, family-owned cafe. This place is in-between."

"The food is out of this world, though," added Isabella from the front seat. "Freshly grilled shrimps. The best octopus imaginable. You'll love it, Lark."

Lark was fond of seafood, but once they were seated and had been served, she could hardly taste the dishes in front of her. She was trying to figure out how she could get safely to the airport.

After dinner, for which Justin Groome paid, they drove to Jackie O's, a discotheque situated on the far side of the harbor. Lights from the busy cafes flickered on the dark water. Justin paid the cover charge for them all at the door. Evidently this was his party. Inside, the mirrored walls seemed to spin under the effect of the whirling colored lights. The dance floor was crowded.

In spite of the crush, Justin managed to find them a table. The others sat down, but Frank wanted to dance. Lark obliged him.

When they returned, Miguel and Isabella were dancing. Frank asked Leila to dance and Lark was left alone with Justin.

He moved to sit beside her. "What would you like to drink?"

"Nothing, thanks."

He snapped his fingers at a waitress. *"Un Pernod."* When the waitress returned with it, Justin stood up. "Let's go outside. It'll be quieter."

Lark hesitated. "I like it here."

"You'll like it out there also," he said inexorably.

Outside on the wide terrace Miguel and Isabella were sitting at a metal table, kissing. Justin walked over to the far balcony wall and placed his glass on the wide stone top. When Lark was beside him, he put his hands on her waist and lifted her up. She began to struggle wildly before she realized that he was merely settling her on the wall where she could sit comfortably.

His expression was amused.

"You didn't seem very surprised to see me," Lark tried.

"But I was surprised to see you. I had no idea you'd be here."

"No, I didn't think you did."

"Who is Miguel?" she asked, conversationally. "How do you know him?"

"He's a friend. Sometimes he does a favor for me; sometimes I do a favor for him. He's from Brazil."

"So you're the one who made the arrangements for me to come here."

"Yes."

"Why?"

"I want to talk to you about your screenplay, of course."

"We could have talked about it in Los Angeles or in New York. You've spent a lot of time and money getting me over here."

He chuckled. "As I said last time I saw you, under different circumstances I feel sure we could be friends. There's something about you I find very attractive." He added, "You're a very beautiful woman."

"What is it you want from me?" she asked.

"Naturally, I feel misrepresented by your idea for a screenplay. I want to talk it over with you."

Miguel and Isabella had stood up. Isabella glanced at Lark and surreptitiously gave her a "thumbs-up" sign. Lark was half inclined to laugh hysterically.

"Did you ever get in touch with the girl in your screenplay?" asked Justin. "The one who killed Violet Sumner?"

"Penelope Houten? No, as I told you before. She disappeared after the murder and no one's seen her since. Some people think she's dead."

"Do you?"

"I have no idea."

"You must have some idea."

"Why must I?"

He looked amused. " 'Lark.' Where did the name come from?"

"It was my grandmother's."

He looked so disbelieving, she dropped her eyes.

"Anyway, it suits you. Everything you do is a lark." He ran a finger along her cheek and she flinched. "You seem afraid of me."

"Afraid of you! Why should I be? I think you're being terribly nice to me."

"I wish you wouldn't use that word *terribly*. It sounds peculiar." His hand cupped her chin. "A nice chin," he said. "And lovely cheeks. And a perfect nose. Interesting."

She shuddered. He let her go.

"Are you cold?"

"A little."

"We'll go back in in just a minute. But do you realize what would happen to my career if your treatment were made into a movie that was broadcast on television?"

She didn't answer.

"I think you do. Do you think it's fair to try me and convict me in this way, without a shred of proof? All you have, it seems, is the account of a newspaper woman. What if I were to tell you that every line in your treatment is a libelous, slanderous lie?"

"It would be a terrible thing to ruin your career if it weren't true," Lark allowed. "But Emmy Elson at the *Monday Week* seems certain of her facts. I wouldn't have written this if I didn't have a lot of faith in her ability as an investigative reporter."

"Emmy Elson—yes. Do you know her?"

Lark hesitated. "Yes."

"She's a friend of yours?"

"I don't know her real well. But we have spoken."

Justin's lip curled slightly.

"Then how is it that she says she's never heard of you?"

Chapter Seventy-Three

RRITATED and exhausted, Dom didn't get back to Los
Angeles until late Friday evening. Jonny lay on the couch
in the den, watching television. He was staying at Dom's
house while *Flaming Forest* was being edited.

He jumped up when he saw Dom. "Did you hear what
happened?"

Dom's heart clutched. "What?"

"The vault was broken into at APG!"

Dom started to breathe again. "Is Lark okay?"

"Who?" Jonny looked amazed. "Dom! The vault was broken into. Someone was trying to get hold of the negative of
Flaming Forest!"

"Oh, no. Did they get it?"

"No. I was a bit nervous about it and I thought it should be
kept somewhere real safe. So I moved it here a few weeks ago.
It's downstairs in the basement."

"Who'd want to steal it?"

"I know some people who'll do anything to stop the release
of the film."

"You do?" Dom was distracted. "Did Lark call?"

"There's a message on the machine for you." Jonny seemed
disappointed that Dom wasn't more impressed by his clever-
ness and foresight.

"Thanks." Dom dropped his jacket on the back of a chair
and went to his telephone answering machine. When he re-
wound the tape, he discovered no message was there.

He went back to the den. Jonny was laughing uproariously at something on the television.

"You seem to have erased the message," he said coldly. "Do you happen to remember what it was?"

Jonny was contrite. "Did I erase it? I'm sorry. Let me see— she was sorry you couldn't go somewhere with her. I think she said she'd be back on Monday."

Dom's voice was ominous.

"Did she say where she went?"

"No. I think she assumed you knew. Gosh, I'm sorry I erased the thing."

Dom dialed Lark's apartment. No answer. He was too anxious to vent his anger on Jonny. It was too late to do anything that night. First thing in the morning, however, he tracked down Rosa's home telephone number.

"I'm really sorry to bother you on a Saturday," he told her, aware that he had woken her up. "But I need to find out if Lark got the message I left yesterday."

"I guess we missed each other," replied Rosa. "She did not come back to the office. I left a message at the airport for her to call me, but when she called back I was not at my desk."

"So she didn't get it?"

"No. Sorry."

"Okay, Rosa." He hung up, debating whether or not he should go to France. It was possible that the trip was on the level. But he had an uneasy feeling about Lark. If Justin felt seriously threatened by her screenplay, he would do anything to stop it from being made. Anything.

Dom picked up the telephone again and dialed Toni's number.

"Hello?"

"Toni, it's Dom."

There was a shocked silence.

"I guess I surprised you," said Dom. "I'm sorry. It's just that I need to find out something."

"That's okay."

"I'm curious about Justin's whereabouts this weekend. Do you know what he's doing?"

Toni said, "Just a minute," then she spoke in an undertone

to someone else in the room. Dom waited till she came back on the line. "Hi, Dom? Sorry . . . no, I don't have any idea. I quit working for him a couple of weeks ago."

"You're not working for Justin Groome anymore?"

"No. He fired me. At least, he threatened to fire me for walking out of a stupid discussion at eight o'clock on a Friday evening. So I told him to go to hell. Whitfield Communications is no longer representing him."

"Now I'm the one who's surprised."

"I'm sorry about your mother, Dom," said Toni.

"Thanks." Dom cleared his throat. "So you don't know where Justin is just now?"

"No. I left Whitfield Communications myself, actually. So I'm really out of touch with anything that's going on."

"You left? What are you doing?"

"I'm going to sail around the Caribbean."

"With . . . ?"

"A man. I'm really happy, Dom. So you don't have to feel guilty. This is really it for me."

"I can't tell you how happy this news makes me."

"Justin was driving me crazy with his obsession for finding Penny. I might as well tell you, all these newspaper reports really have me wondering about him."

"Did you find out something about Violet?"

"More and more things she did and said come back to me. I've been putting them together with the information Emmy Elson's uncovered and frankly it all seems horribly possible. Violet was moody and silly and she was difficult to understand," Toni's voice shook, "but I wish I'd made more of an effort. I was too impatient."

"Did you talk to Justin about it?"

"He's not interested in talking about anything except where Penny might be. He didn't even try to sue the *Monday Week*. That sure seemed strange to me."

"I have a feeling a lot of the allegations are true," said Dom.

Toni blew her nose. "If you do find Penny before that devil does, let her know that I'll do anything I can to help her in a court trial. All I have is circumstantial evidence, of course, but

it may help. Anyway, I'd like her to know that she can count
on me, if she's still alive."

"Thanks, Toni. That means alot. I'm glad you're not working for Justin, but I wish I knew where he was right now."

"Why?"

"I'm worried about . . . someone."

"Oh. Lark." Her voice was flat. "I heard something about a
screenplay. I would guess Justin isn't too happy about that."

"No."

"I don't know where he is."

"I'm glad I called anyway and heard your news. Give your
friend my best, will you? And have a great time. I like to
think of you on a boat."

"Good-bye, Dom. Good luck."

"Good luck to you."

Dom hung up, grabbed his jacket, and drove to the hospital. It was possible that Lark had been in touch with Carl
before she left.

Carl had another visitor.

"Dom, this is Bettina Smith," Carl introduced him. "She's
an old friend of mine from London. Her husband, Charles,
just went to the cafeteria for some coffee. Bettina, darling, this
is Dom Whitfield." As Dom absently shook Bettina's plump
hand, Carl asked, "Where is Lark? Bettina was hoping to see
her again."

Dom pulled up a chair. "She got a call from an investor
who's interested in financing her screenplay. He flew her to
France for the weekend so they could talk it over."

"Lark's written a screenplay?" said Bettina conversationally.
"I always thought that girl was talented. What's it about?"

"A documentary about a congressman called Justin
Groome."

Bettina's round eyes widened. "Well, my goodness! What a
coincidence. We know him. He's been in London recently.
Taken up with Isabella. Your Isabella, Carl, the one's that
been staying in your house."

Aghast, Carl struggled to sit up. "My God!"

"We all liked him very much," said Bettina, unaware of

Carl's distress. "Quite a charmer, isn't he? He even took Isabella to France recently."

"To France? Now?" snapped Dom.

"I believe so. Charles knows for sure. He spoke to Isabella just a few days ago. Ah, here he is."

Charles entered. Dom shook his hand automatically. The adrenaline was surging through his bloodstream. *What was Groome doing in France?*

"I was just reporting on Isabella," Bettina said. "Where did she go recently? France, wasn't it? Do you remember the name of the town?" She turned to Dom. "Charles is the gossip columnist for the *Sun*. He has a gift for remembering the smallest fact about practically everyone he meets."

"Nonsense," said Charles, deprecatingly. "But I do remember they were going to Soubriquet. It's near Cannes, I believe. Quite a fashionable little place on the sea."

Dom turned to Carl in bewilderment. "What does this mean?"

"I'm not sure."

They stared at each other, as though they were completely alone. Suddenly Dom said, "I've got to find her. Justin is ruthless."

"I know," said Carl.

"It can't be a coincidence that he's there at the same time."

"No." Then Carl added, "There is more reason for Lark to be afraid of Justin Groome than you know, my son."

Dom turned on his heels and strode out of the room.

CHAPTER SEVENTY-FOUR

CAUGHT in the apparent lie, Lark's pale face flooded with color.

"Emmy must have forgotten," she said. "We have met."

"Sure you have." Standing before her, Justin leaned forward, separating her legs with his body. "You're quite something, Lark. Dom is a very lucky man."

"Thanks."

"You're the sexiest girl in the whole town." He ran a finger along her bare stomach. "What made you dress up like this? Are you trying to drive us men crazy?"

"It was Isabella's idea."

His finger pressed her belly button. "I wonder why I get the feeling from your treatment that you're more interested in revenge than in justice."

She tried to move. "I don't know what you're talking about."

He held her thighs down on either side of his body so that she couldn't move. "Don't you? Then I'll try to explain. I think there's something about me that fascinates you. You're attracted to me, and you hate yourself for that. But you can't help it."

Lark glared coldly.

"You want revenge on me," Justin went on, "because mere justice wouldn't cut it for you."

"As I said before, I'm just interested in making an entertaining movie. Revenge or justice—they have nothing to do with it."

"There are lots of other entertaining people you could make a movie about. But you can't let me go, can you?" His face was close to hers. "You can't seem to let go."

"Let's go back inside," she insisted, pushing him away.

He stepped back at the same time, so that she fell off the wall. Laughing, he helped her to her feet.

"Sure. We have plenty of time to talk later."

They rejoined the group at the table. Oblivious to any tension, Frank asked Lark to dance. Away from Justin's immediate presence, she found she could think more clearly.

Frank gazed at her with moony eyes, and she remembered the sensuous outfit she was wearing. It might be of use after all, she thought. She glanced around the crowded room. A young man sat on a bar stool, watching her. She gave him a provocative smile. His face remained deadpan, but his black eyes flickered. When the music ended she told Frank, "I'll join you in a moment."

The man's eyes were still fixed on her. She went to the bar, and, standing beside him, she ordered a Coke. When she reached in her purse to get money, a hand closed over it. She jumped before realizing it was not Justin's; it belonged to the stranger.

"*S'il vous plaît*," he said, paying for the bill.

"*Merci.*"

There were no empty bar stools; the man got off his and offered it to her. She took it gracefully, smiling. He asked her something in French which she couldn't understand.

"English?" he asked.

She nodded.

"Mon Anglais eez verry bad . . ."

They both laughed.

"So what?" she said, half to herself.

"*Voulez-vous danser?*" he invited, a while later.

She nodded. The music slowed; he held her close in his arms. Justin sat talking with the others at the darkened corner table, but never once did he take his eyes off her.

Lark grew agitated.

The man kissed the side of her throat. His tongue licked the inside of her ear. Lark winced.

But the game had to be played if she was going to try to escape.

"Please," she gasped, "let's go outside." Anything for a change.

He looked pleased. He took her out the front door. The street was quiet. They stopped and kissed deeply and then they walked to a beat-up Citroen.

The man took out a set of keys and unlocked the front door, then urged her inside. Reluctantly, she got in. A moment later, the man was on top of her, breathing heavily, and tearing at her flimsy garments.

"Hey! Cut that out!"

The man did not stop at once, and she had to forcefully push him off before he comprehended the fact that she was not enjoying herself. He looked annoyed. His eyelids were heavy.

"*Qu'est ce que vous avez?*"

"Please can you take me to a hotel?"

"*Comment?*"

"*Pension?* Hotel?"

She glanced out the window and saw Justin and Miguel emerging from the discotheque. They were talking earnestly. Groome looked sharply up and down the street.

"Please," said Lark, desperately. "*Vite.* I need to go to a hotel."

Her urgency somehow conveyed itself to the man. Swearing and cursing, he climbed into the driver's seat and started the engine. A moment later they went screeching down the quiet village road. Looking behind, Lark saw Justin and Miguel watching them.

"*Vous pouvez rester chez moi.*"

"No . . . no! It must be a hotel." She couldn't stay at his house. If Miguel happened to know the man, they would track her down there.

Swearing again, he pulled up in front of a dingy building which said *Auberge* out front. She barely had time to say thank you and get out of the car, when the man pressed on the accelerator and screeched off down the road.

A sleepy porter was on duty. He eyed her suspiciously.

"I need a room for tonight," Lark said.

He shook his head. *"Complet."*

"Any room, just for tonight."

"Pas de chambres," he insisted, eyeing her outfit disapprovingly.

Lark tried to glare back, but she was at a loss. Now what should she do?

"Are there taxis?" she asked.

"Comment?"

"Taxi?"

As she asked, she glanced nervously outside. A jeep went racing past; she was certain she saw Justin in the front seat.

"Taxi," she urged the porter. "Taxi."

The porter said something in a rude tone of voice, picked up the telephone and spoke into it.

"Le taxi viendra ici," he said, hanging up.

A quarter of an hour passed. Lark sat on a wooden chair out of sight of the door, hoping she hadn't misunderstood the porter and a taxi was indeed going to show up. She prayed that Justin hadn't tracked down the man who'd brought her here and forced him to tell where she was. Her nerves were frayed.

The door swung open and she leapt to her feet. But it wasn't Justin; it was a tired looking Frenchman, chewing tobacco.

"Taxi?" he barked at her.

"Oui."

He motioned with his head. She followed him outside to the waiting cab.

"Ou voulez-vous aller?"

"Paris." She had decided on this while she'd been waiting for the cab. In Paris she could go straight to the airport and before she knew it she'd be in Los Angeles again. She knew Paris was a long way away, but she was prepared to pay generously for the trip.

"C'est impossible," the man refused. "Paris est quelques centaines de kilometres d'ici."

"Marseilles, then. I need to go to the airport. It's very important."

"C'est de beaucoup trop loin," the man refused again. "Je ne puis pas vouz apporter."

In the distance, Lark heard what she thought was the sound of a jeep returning. She jumped inside the taxi.

The jeep rumbled into sight.

"The train station," she gasped. "Train. Le train."

The driver got in also. With maddening slowness, he started the engine. Lark lay flat on the floor of the taxi. The jeep passed.

"Il n'y a pas de trains a Paris avant le matin. Vous devriez trouver un beau gite pour passer la nuit."

Lark sat up again and looked at her watch. It was almost three o'clock. She couldn't believe so little time had passed since she'd been talking to Justin on the balcony.

The man drove her to the neighboring town of Aix-le-Paix. He drew up at the closed-up train station. Gloomily, Lark gazed at the locked door.

"What time is the next train to Paris?" she asked the driver.

He made a "six" with his hand and a thumb.

"How much do I owe you? Combien?"

He asked for an exorbitant sum, but she was too distracted to argue with him, although he obviously expected her to. Mollified, he took the money and apologized for the station being closed.

Lark got out, wondering what she would do for two hours. The driver stared at her, as though he wondered also.

"Merci," she said in dismissal.

With another shrug and some parting remarks about these mad English, he drove off.

Lark realized that, after Justin had checked the various hotels in Soubriquet, he would most certainly check the train station. She could not simply sit on the curb, waiting for him.

She picked her way around the side of the station and climbed over a fence. The platform was below. On the far side of the tracks was another platform, and then an open field, edged with bushes and some trees. She would be better off hiding there.

Crossing the tracks, she climbed over a chicken wire fence and found herself in a field damp with dew. She made her way to the shrubbery where she could sit concealed from any curious eyes in the train station. It was only then she realized how exhausted she was.

The air was fresh and moist. Overhead the cloudy sky was growing milky in color. A bird chirped, then was silent. Then it chirped again.

Her eyes closed.

CHAPTER SEVENTY-FIVE

WHEN Lark awoke it was broad daylight. In the distance she heard the whistle of a train. She glanced at her watch; it was a quarter to six.

She jumped up and winced at the stiffness in her shoulder. Her calves cramped up and she shook them painfully. Peering over the top of the shrubbery, she saw no one on the platform but a light was on inside the station. She did not think Justin would have waited all this time on the off chance that she might appear.

Climbing over the fence, she hurried across the tracks to the station. Besides the man at the ticket counter, another man sat on a bench, reading a newspaper. He had gray, grizzled hair and he smoked a cigarette. He looked vaguely familiar.

"The train to Paris?" she inquired of the ticket seller.

"Il arrivera avant cinq minutes."

"One, please." She held up one finger.

She paid for the ticket. The grizzled man was talking on the telephone. From the back he looked even more familiar. Was she getting paranoid?

More people arrived. Lark felt conspicuous in the translucent skirt and revealing top. Her bare midriff was cold and her high heels were stained with mud.

Her fellow travelers glanced sidelong at her as though she were a whore.

The train pulled in. Lark was about to get on when she

noticed the grizzled old man watching her before climbing aboard the other end of the car.

That was when she recognized him. He had met them at the house when she had first arrived and he had carried her bags inside. She had seen him so briefly, she had hardly paid any attention to him.

She stepped back onto the platform, not sure what to do.

Trying to look casual, the man stepped back too. He buried his nose in his newspaper.

If he had been telephoning Justin, that meant Justin would be arriving at any moment. It was still safer to get on the train, wasn't it?

She climbed back on.

The whistle blew.

The man climbed on too.

She hopped back off onto the platform. The man delayed a moment, looking inside the coach for her, before he realized what she had done.

The train began to move.

He jumped back down also. He stumbled. It was Lark's chance. She leapt back on the moving train. When the man looked up again, there was no one else on the platform.

Lark found a seat in a crowded car. Self-consciously, she sat down, aware of the disapproving stares of the rest of the passengers. The window was open and she felt cold.

But at least she was on her way to Paris.

The train went slowly. She wondered how soon was their first stop.

An hour passed. The cold made her shiver. Apologizing, she got up to close the window. The passengers muttered and protested. As Lark looked out the window, she caught sight of a jeep on the road paralleling the tracks. She was certain it was Groome's jeep.

She sat down quickly.

Now what would she do? Was Groome planning to drag her off the train by force? He might make up a story that she was a whore, or even his runaway wife—any story that would sound plausible in a country where she could not be understood.

He could convince anyone of anything. . . .

She glanced out the window again. The jeep had picked up speed and was passing them. Probably he meant to wait for her when the train pulled in at the next stop. Some of the passengers gathered their belongings together, as though it weren't going to be long.

Lark gulped nervously. Now what should she do?

The train lurched to a stop. The passengers muttered in annoyance. Looking out the window, Lark saw there was no train station in sight yet. Nor was there any sign of Groome's jeep.

Immediately, she got up and went along the corridor to the door. It was easy to open. A moment later, she had leapt onto the tracks and was running into a grove of trees nearby. She crouched behind some thick rhododendron bushes. From here she saw what had happened to stop the train prematurely: A herd of sheep was blocking the tracks ahead.

Gleeful at her good luck, she looked around. She had no idea in which direction to go, but she knew she wanted to avoid the direction the train was headed. She headed east, toward the sun.

Her earlier rest had revitalized her. She took off her high heels, and walked barefoot across the meadow, skirting the few farmhouses and avoiding the road. She had walked for an hour when in the distance she saw a white church spire.

Please let that be a nice little town, thought Lark, *a little town that will offer me a hot cup of coffee, a croissant* (she was ravenously hungry by this time), *a change of clothes, and some means of getting to an airport.*

She could hear the church bells and they lifted her spirits. Walking had warmed her thoroughly. She felt everything was going to be all right.

As she neared the village she put her high heels back on and tried to smooth her tangled hair. Hopefully there would be a clothes store open where she could buy a pair of jeans.

The sound of church bells grew more cacophonous. A cafe she passed was closed up tight; so were most of the cottages and houses. It was still early.

She crossed the street. In front of the church stood several groups of women wearing flowery hats and men in dark suits. Children played, wearing their Sunday best.

Of course, Lark realized gloomily, as she grew conscious of the indignant stares in her direction, it would have to be Sunday! Self-consciously, she edged away from the churchgoing groups and headed for the main street of the village. She could feel the reproachful frowns of the churchgoers on her exposed back.

There was no point in skulking through the town. Holding her chin in the air, she marched along the street, looking for a place that might serve her a cup of coffee. A cafe at the far end of the street, with several tables and chairs set out in front, seemed to be open. She hurried toward it. Two tourists—they spoke in German—were seated at one of the tables. Lark went inside and chose a table that was out of sight of the windows. She felt conspicuous enough as it was.

A waitress approached. She appeared not to notice Lark's unusual Sunday garb.

"*Cafe au lait et un croissant,*" Lark requested in halting French.

"*Oui, madame.*"

The coffee was delicious. Lark ordered two more croissants; she realized she had hardly eaten anything the night before. When the waitress returned with her second cup of coffee, Lark asked, "Is there an airport nearby?"

"*Comment?*"

"Airport? With airplanes?" She gestured to the sky.

"*Oui, madame.* Marseilles."

She supposed she could hitchhike. "Which road do I take?"

"*A droite.* Turn right at the end of the street. There is a sign."

"*Merci.*"

Lark paid the bill and went outside. The sun was poking out from behind hazy clouds. The Germans were gone. All the stores were closed. She thought longingly of her blue jeans lying on Isabella's floor.

As she walked down the street, she passed a cafe that was closed. In front stood a scooter, with a denim jacket tossed carelessly on its seat. The key was in the ignition. Evidently the owner intended to return momentarily.

Lark hesitated.

But there was no time to lose. Hurriedly, she dug in her purse and took out a one thousand franc bill. She had no idea how much a scooter cost, but she thought that would cover it. She placed it on the nearest table, under a rock, where it could not be missed.

She climbed on the scooter and turned the ignition. Moments later she was hurtling down the road. No one yelled.

She was away.

The signs to Marseilles were clearly posted. Free at last, Lark began singing at the top of her lungs.

She stopped three times; once to put on the denim jacket, for the wind was chilly, and once to fill the scooter up with gas. As she neared Marseilles she stopped to ask directions to the airport. Once there, she parked the scooter in the parking lot and made her way to the terminal. As soon as she had her flight settled, she would call Dom in Los Angeles and tell him she was on her way home.

"I have a ticket for Los Angeles leaving tomorrow morning," she told the woman behind the ticket counter. "It's very important that I exchange it for a flight leaving as soon as possible."

The attendant examined her first-class ticket and then studied the computer in front of her.

"There is a flight leaving in a few minutes," she said. "I am not sure that you will make it."

"I have to make it," Lark said urgently. Justin would inevitably follow her to the airport. "Could you ask them to hold the plane while you adjust my ticket?"

The attendant spoke into the telephone, looked grave, and handed the ticket back to Lark. "It is gate twenty. Hurry."

Lark hurried.

Several minutes later she was seated and buckled into the last remaining first-class seat. The Jumbo cruised out to the runway to prepare for takeoff.

When the stewardess brought Lark her complimentary champagne, she felt she truly deserved it.

CHAPTER SEVENTY-SIX

DOM arrived in Soubriquet shortly before midnight on Saturday night. It took lengthy inquiries to discover where Justin Groome was staying. When he got there, a man told him they were all out "probably dancing."

Not knowing what else to do, Dom asked the taxi driver to take him to every discotheque in town. At Jackie O's he spotted Justin dancing with a tall redhead who wore hardly anything. He couldn't see Lark.

"Hello, Justin," he tapped him on the shoulder.

"Dom." Justin was disconcerted and surprised. "What brings you here? Oh, let me guess. Lark, isn't it?"

"Where is she?"

"She took off about an hour ago with a gigolo she met up with. Sorry, buddy."

Dom's jaw tightened. "Who exactly was this 'gigolo'?"

"A man about town. He probably took her to his house. It would be simplest."

"Know his address?"

"I'm sure Miguel does. Want it?"

"I certainly do."

"Come on, I'll introduce you."

Justin introduced Dom as "an old family friend" to the group seated at the table. Miguel did know the man's address. At Groome's suggestion, he offered to take Dom there himself.

"I hope you'll come back afterward and join us for a night-cap," Groome said.

Dom did not answer. He paid off the taxi; they took the jeep. Outside a particularly quiet looking house, Miguel honked loudly. Dom jumped.

"Do not worry—Auguste is still up. We spoke to him just a short while ago."

"You did? Here?"

"Naturally, Signor Groome wishes to find the young lady too. He is most worried."

Auguste grumpily refused to let them in. Apparently he had had a bad time of it with Lark. She had wanted to be taken to a hotel. Which hotel? He'd taken her to the *auberge* on Rue des Arbres. There he had left her. She had not particularly nice to him, Dom gathered.

"To the hotel?" asked Miguel with a grin.

Dom sighed. "You've already done this, right? Is she there?"

"Ah, no. There is no available room at the hotel. Unfortunately, the owner of the hotel took her for a—how you say?—a lady of the night. She is dressed for dancing, not for checking into hotels."

"Did he know where she went?"

"She ordered a taxi."

"And the taxi driver?"

"He took her to the train station. But there we lose her. You see, Mr. Groome wishes to find her as much as you do."

Dom looked around hopelessly. What should he do now? Carl's last words cut into him like a knife. Why did Lark have more reason to fear Justin than even he supposed? It could not just be because of the screenplay. The suspicion that had first taken hold when they were in Manaus, that Justin was the man who had raped her, resurfaced.

"Still, I'd like to check out the same places," he said.

Miguel nodded affably.

At the deserted train station, Dom finally gave up. *She wouldn't sit here and wait anyway,* he decided to himself. *Maybe she tried hitchhiking to Paris. Anyway, I'd better stick by Groome and make sure he really doesn't know where she is.*

"We may as well go back and join the others," he said reluctantly.

At the discotheque Dom refused a drink. He was bored and worried. It was five o'clock before the party broke up. "Maybe Lark got tired and went home earlier," Groome cheerfully suggested. "Maybe we'll find her there."

Dom doubted it, but he agreed to go with them. Inside the house, Groome showed him Lark's room. "You can sleep in here if you'd like," he offered. "As I say, she may turn up."

The telephone rang from somewhere in the house. Groome hurried off without waiting for his answer. A few moments later, Dom heard the sound of the jeep taking off down the road.

In a flash he bounded downstairs. But he was too late. Groome had been driving extraordinarily fast.

Dom returned inside, tense and worried.

Lark's clothes were unpacked. She hadn't brought much with her. Dom lay on the bed but was unable to sleep. He couldn't even close his eyes until he heard the jeep return about two hours later. By this time the sky was light and he was jittery from lack of sleep. He ran to the window and looked below; but only Justin emerged from the jeep. No Lark.

Groome looked up and waved.

"No luck," he called. "A wild-goose chase."

Dom returned inside the room.

He spent the morning scouring the town, asking people if they'd seen her. He couldn't bring himself to return to Los Angeles, but he didn't know what good he was doing staying in Soubriquet either.

At midday, he finally called his house, dispiritedly hoping Jonny might have a message for him.

"I'm calling from France," Dom said shortly. "You haven't heard from Lark, have you?"

"Yes, as a matter of fact, I have. She just called from an airplane phone. She's on her way home. Guess you must have missed each other."

"Thank God! I'm coming back right away. Did she tell you which flight she was on? Could you meet her at the airport?

It's very important that you don't let her out of your sight for a single moment after she arrives."

"I have an appointment tonight. It's important."

"Jonny," Dom said angrily, "this is more important than any damned appointment of yours. I wouldn't ask you to stick by her like a leech if it wasn't important. She's in danger."

"From whom?"

"Justin."

"Oh," said Jonny. "Him."

"Will you meet her?"

"Yessir," promised Jonny. "I won't let her out of my sight until you get back. Don't you worry about a thing."

CHAPTER SEVENTY-SEVEN

A S he'd promised, Jonny met Lark at the airport. He was unshaven but he didn't seem drunk. She was surprised to see him.

"I could have taken a cab," she said. "But it sure is nice to see a familiar face."

"Dom wanted me to look after you," said Jonny.

"Where is he?"

"France. I guess you guys missed each other."

"He went to France?"

"Yup. By this time he's probably heading back here, though."

Lark felt a wave of happiness that Dom had gone after her.

"I'm longing for a hot bath and a change of clothes."

"That dress is something," Jonny agreed. "The thing is . . ." he hesitated.

"What?"

"I need to go somewhere tonight. It's important. I'm meeting someone. But I promised Dom I wouldn't let you out of my sight. Would you mind very much going with me?"

Lark did mind, a lot. She longed more than anything to get back to her apartment, take off her torn sexy dress, soak in a hot bath, and crawl into bed and sleep for at least twelve hours.

"Just drop me off at my apartment," she told Jonny. "I'll be okay. Dom doesn't have to know."

"I can't do that," Jonny said unhappily. "I promised him. But I can't get out of this meeting. It won't take long."

"Dom's being ridiculous."

"I can't help that. Besides, maybe he's right."

Lark sighed. She felt so safe now she was back in Los Angeles that Dom's anxiety for her was an annoyance rather than a comfort.

"Can I change my clothes first?"

Jonny looked at his watch. "I'm late already. It won't take more than twenty minutes, I hope."

The club Jonny took Lark to was in the heart of downtown Los Angeles. Narrow stairs led to a large room jammed with tables. Lark's eyes watered from the thick cigarette smoke.

Great, brocade canopies hung from the ceiling overhead. On the walls were pinned shiny fabrics of gold, burgundy, and dark green. A band played eerie sounds on instruments she had never heard. She was the only woman there.

No, not the only one, she saw, once they were seated at a corner table. From the mesh of curtain near the kitchen stood another woman, veiled and waiting. She was scantily clad in crimson and gold. As Lark watched, fascinated, the music subtly changed. The lights dimmed. Slowly, seductively, the dancer came forward. Her arms and legs shimmered with gold bangles. A veil was draped provocatively over her, but as she began to move, and the music became more insistently rhythmic, she spun herself free of the translucent cloak. Smiling, she skipped among the tables, her large breasts heaving, her hips shimming in a vibration that took Lark's breath away.

Jonny ordered them both Arak—a Lebanese liqueur made of anise. He didn't seem interested in the dancer. His eyes roamed ceaselessly through the crowded tables.

The dancer approached—she was dancing from table to table, laughing, pouting, sparkling, seducing. It was wonderful to watch. Eventually, even Jonny couldn't help but be entranced. She took a red chiffon scarf that was tucked in her hip belt and wrapped it around Jonny's head, turban style. Then she reached for his hand. Lark saw that she pressed something into it. With a friendly wink at Lark, the dancer moved on, her zills ringing.

Jonny unfolded the piece of paper, hardly seeming to notice Lark. He looked tense and angry.

She put a hand on his.

"You okay?" she asked.

"No."

"What's the matter?"

"I'm in trouble."

"Maybe I can help."

Jonny laughed raggedly. "Not likely."

"Tell me what the problem is."

"Remember years ago, in London, you read my palm? You said I had a guilt line—"

"I was just teasing," said Lark. "I don't know how to read palms."

"I've been guilty of a hell of a lot of things in my life, but this last thing has got to be the worst. It makes me sick to think about it."

She put a hand on his arm. "I've done things that make me sick to think about too. Tell me, Jonny."

He stared at his glass. "It seems I have an illegitimate daughter. There's someone here who's using her to blackmail me."

"You don't have to be blackmailed. Everyone'll understand about your daughter. Even Emmy."

"Yes, she'll understand that part of it. But it's worse."

"How much worse?"

"The worst thing you can think of."

Involuntarily, Lark looked away. "I guess I don't want to hear."

"Of course you don't. But the girl needs to be found and looked after. I'm telling you because I'm scared out of my mind. If anything happens to me . . . Oh, what's the use?" He stood up. "I have to meet someone in the back room. I won't be long."

He dropped the piece of paper on the table and left. Lark picked it up. On it was scribbled a single word: "Fairusa."

Desperately tired, Lark ordered a cup of coffee to help her stay awake. Half an hour passed. There was no sign of Jonny. The dancer came back, but this time Lark felt less entranced.

The dancer ended her dance with a flourish and loud claps from the men near the stage.

To her amazement, Lark suddenly saw Dom standing in the front entrance, scanning the tables. What on earth was he doing there? He strode over to her table as soon as he saw her.

"Where's Jonny?" he demanded.

"He had to meet someone here. I thought you were still in France!"

"I took the Concorde as soon as I heard you were already back here. There was no answer at your apartment and no sign of you at my house. My maid said Jonny was out at this goddamn nightclub. I prayed he took you with him. You sure have led me on some chase."

"If you only knew just what sort of chase I've had." She felt so relieved to see him that she wasn't fully aware of his anger.

"Let's get out of here," said Dom.

Jonny was just returning. The brothers halted a few feet apart.

"How dare you leave her alone?" demanded Dom. "I asked you not to let her out of your sight for a minute. You *promised.*"

Jonny took a step back. "How'd you know we were here?"

"I went home and Benita told me."

"Oh, Christ."

"This is the last goddamn time you let me down," snarled Dom. "I mean that."

Grabbing Lark's wrist, Dom pulled her outside to his parked car and unlocked the door for her. When they were both inside he ground out, "What the hell was Jonny doing there anyway?"

"He had to meet someone," Lark repeated hesitantly. "It was important. Why are you so mad at him?"

"I've been worried sick about you all weekend. When I heard you were on your way back, I asked Jonny not to let you out of his sight. He didn't do it."

"I was perfectly safe."

Dom didn't answer. He stared straight ahead.

"Can you take me home?" she begged. "I've had the longest weekend of my life."

"Right. Your goddamn weekend." He started the engine and headed for the freeway.

"I didn't ask you to come after me."

"It was clear to me there was something fishy about the whole expedition."

"How?"

"Well, wasn't there? Why did you run away if you didn't think it was fishy?"

"Who said I ran away?"

"For God's sake, be straight with me! You left all your luggage behind! You didn't say good-bye to anyone! Look at what you're wearing! Of course you ran away."

"I guess I got kind of scared of Justin Groome."

He tensed. "I see."

"You don't see," she said. "Why are you being like this?"

"Being like what? All I know is that you decide to go off to France on some crazy whim, and I find out that the man you wrote a vicious movie treatment about is there too. I fly to France to try to find you, and learn you've already disappeared. I've had a hell of a weekend, thanks to you. And what in hell's name do you think you're wearing?"

"It's none of your business what I'm wearing!" shouted Lark. "I've had a hell of a weekend too! All I wanted to do when I came back was to climb into a bath and then into bed and sleep. Instead you made Jonny promise he wouldn't let me out of his sight so I had to come to some goddamn meeting he had!"

"That's all you're going to tell me?"

There was a silence. Dom drove a little faster.

"Dom," said Lark, almost quietly, "what's really the matter?"

"Why don't you tell me who you really are? Where you came from? What it is you're afraid of? You haven't trusted me as far as your delightful nose and yet you say you love me. You can't blame me for being mad as hell."

Waves of confusion poured through her.

"I can't think straight," she said. "I need sleep so badly it hurts."

Dom drew up in front of her apartment building. He reached over and opened the door, but he didn't get out.

"Good night," he said, harshly.

She got out. "Good night." She went quickly upstairs to her apartment.

She let herself in and felt for the light switch. Nothing happened. She didn't like that, but she went forward anyway.

Suddenly light flooded the room. She gasped, stepping back, reaching for the front door again. A hand closed on her wrist, dragging her away from the door, shoving her into the living room.

A gun pointed at her head.

She had never seen the man before. He was short, boxy-looking, with a broken nose, and dead-looking eyes. As soon as their eyes met, she knew that Justin Groome had dispatched him to kill her.

She screamed. She screamed and screamed. The man lifted his gun and swung it across her face, sending her flying. Then he pointed the gun at her again.

Lark closed her eyes. When the explosion came, she felt nothing. No pain, no shock—nothing. She opened her eyes. The man was sagging slowly to his knees, a look of astonishment on his face. He collapsed, facedown, on the carpet. His back was crimson with blood.

Lark lifted her eyes to the door. Dom stood there, a gun in his hand. She tried to get to her feet, but she was shaking too much. Dom didn't come over to help her.

Using every ounce of strength, she crept to the sofa and pulled herself up on it. Then she buried her face in her hands.

"That man was going to kill you." Dom was panting.

"Yes," she whispered.

He took a deep breath. "Now are you going to tell me?"

CHAPTER SEVENTY-EIGHT

DOM waited.

"I should have told you before," she began slowly, "but I was too frightened."

"Told me what?"

"My real name is Penelope Houten." A jolt went through her as she said her name.

Dom could only stare.

Someone pounded on the door. "Are you all right in there?"

Neither of them moved. The pounding grew louder. "Hey, in there!"

With an effort, Dom pulled himself together and went to the door. He opened it a fraction. "We're all right," he told two neighbors standing outside. "We're waiting for the police to come."

"Who screamed?"

Lark joined Dom at the door. "There was an accident. Sorry for the disturbance."

With difficulty, they got rid of them. Lark sat on the couch again.

Dom stood in front of her. He cleared his throat as if to speak, but didn't say anything.

"I saw Justin Groome murder Violet," Lark finally went on. "He knows I saw him. He threatened to kill me if I ever told anyone. So I never did. I ran away instead. But he must have found out who I really am."

"I can't believe you didn't tell me before now."

"I wanted to. I've felt so alone. I was afraid to trust anyone."

"Did you tell my mother?"

"She knew without my telling her."

"But how?"

Lark's eyes filled. "If it had happened to you," she broke out in anguish, "I would have recognized you anywhere."

He shook his head, unable to speak.

"It's true," she whispered.

He cleared his throat. "You're the one who contacted Emmy?"

"Yes."

"It was a good idea," he said slowly. "I'm not so sure about the screenplay."

"I'm not sure either." Lark was shivering. Now he knew she was Penny, would he fall out of love? Could that happen? For he had not loved Penny as he said he loved Lark. She lifted her head and glanced at the body on the living room floor. "What are we going to do?"

"Call the police. Unless one of your neighbors has already done so. But we'd better do it too."

She nodded. Dom went to the telephone.

He spoke into the receiver but Lark didn't hear a word. She still shivered from shock. If Groome was determined to murder her, he would succeed in the end. How could he fail?

Dom handed her a glass. "Drink this," he ordered.

It was scotch. The liquid burned her throat, but it stopped her shivering.

Dom had some too.

"I want to change my clothes." Lark realized she was still wearing Isabella's outlandish costume.

"I wish you would."

She went into the bedroom. Now that Dom knew she was Penny she started to *feel* like Penny: the unsophisticated teenager who had had such a crush on him.

She slipped into sweatpants and a T-shirt. When she returned to the living room, Dom was pacing restlessly. Aching with fatigue, Lark sat down again.

"Don't you think you should have done more about protecting yourself from Justin?" asked Dom.

"I thought my face was my protection." She added in a low voice, "If you didn't recognize me I couldn't imagine that anyone else would."

Dom had the grace to look abashed.

Peremptory knocks sounded on the door.

"Open up! Police here!"

Dom went to open it. Lark remained rigid on the couch, gathering her courage to face the ordeal with the police.

CHAPTER SEVENTY-NINE

A week after his return to New York, Groome made an appointment to see Miguel. They met in a small Italian restaurant on the Upper West Side where Groome could be assured of privacy. Miguel waited for him at the bar.

They were shown to their table. Not until the appetizers arrived (stuffed crab for the congressman; nothing for Miguel) did Justin Groome speak about what was on his mind.

"Your man failed us."

"I am aware of this."

"I thought you would try again."

Miguel gazed at the table, shaking his head slowly. "I am afraid we are trying to resolve our own business here now. We have not the manpower nor the will to do this thing for you."

Groome ate a bite of crab. It was delicious. He was not disconcerted. He knew from experience that everyone could be bought—for a price.

"How much do you want?"

Miguel spread out his hands apologetically. "We are not interested in the risk." He coughed gently. "It has recently come to our attention that you helped finance the Whitfield movie."

"Oh, that." Justin shrugged dismissively. "It's not important."

"But it is important."

"Nonsense. Do you want one hundred thousand dollars?"

Miguel raised both hands again in a gesture of apology. The

waiter brought their main course: chicken in white wine sauce for Miguel: *carpaccio* for Justin.

"The director of that movie is a friend of mine," said Justin. "I know him. The movie won't come to anything. It's over three hours long! No one will touch it."

"We do not share your confidence. We are trying to obtain the negative of the film, but so far we have been unsuccessful. We have tried to persuade Mr. Whitfield that it is in his best interest to give it to us. We do not want the film released." He coughed again. "We were sorry to learn of your involvement in the project."

"I'm a politician." Justin smiled coldly. "I do what I can to keep my constituents happy. The environment bullshit is hot right now."

"I understand this. We have no hard feelings, I assure you. But this movie will create a great deal of sympathy. We are having enough problems already trying to keep banks and businesses interested in our work."

"I shouldn't worry about that. As long as there's money to be made, banks and businesses won't let a sob story about Indians put them off."

"I am not so sure. We are in a new decade—and the United States is feeling a new sentiment."

"What do you want? I can get you practically anything."

The main course finished, Justin ordered Italian cheesecake.

"I am very fond of movies," said Miguel. "And I love California. I think I will go there for a few days."

Groome's eyes narrowed, waiting.

"I plan to be at the premiere of this film."

"I see." Groome picked a piece of cracker from between his teeth. His mind was working. No doubt Penny—Lark—would be at the premiere too. Maybe they could work something out.

"The premiere will be a benefit for the Indians living in our rain forest," went on Miguel. "One thousand dollars per ticket. It will be at the director's brother's house."

"Dom's house, eh? I didn't know that." Better and better.

"We are going to ask Jonny Whitfield for invitations for myself and my friends."

"But it's an industry thing," pointed out Groome. "Not for the general public."

"Still, I think in this particular case Mr. Whitfield will procure the invitations."

Groome gave an unpleasant smile. "I'm curious what sort of dope you have on Jonny that makes you so confident he'll get you the invites."

Miguel smiled back, not answering.

Groome spread some more cheese on a cracker. "The girl will be there too."

"Ah. So."

"You might find a hostage useful," suggested Justin.

"And she might accidently be killed while we negotiate for possession of the negative. We will not leave until every reel is in our possession."

"Hmm."

The men regarded each other, warily but with understanding.

"Will you be there too?" asked Miguel.

"Yes, I'm sure that I, as a major investor in the film, can get invited." He added, half to himself, "They'll be too scared *not* to invite me."

CHAPTER EIGHTY

A few days later Jonny left the edit lab after another discouraging battle with Roger Grigio, the film's editor, and went to Dom's office. He had an appointment with Miguel in less than an hour and he was a mass of nerves and determination. He looked at all the familiar faces at APG, at the secretary's smile, at Dom's hard eyes, as if for the first time, since he was sure it was to be the last.

"I have an appointment," he told Dom. "I don't know if I'll make it back."

Dom regarded him indifferently. Jonny had never told him any of his plans before, so why start now? But Jonny couldn't help it; he wanted to say good-bye. He lit a cigarette, knowing that Dom hated people smoking in his office, but unable to stop himself.

"Dom, that other night, I'm sorry I left Lark alone for a few minutes. It really wasn't for very long."

Dom didn't answer.

Jonny sucked on his cigarette. "I couldn't help it."

"Then get some goddamn control over your life. Who was it you had to meet—one of your gambling debts asking for payment?"

Jonny shook his head. "Remember someone broke into the vault? These Brazilians are determined to stop the release of *Flaming Forest.*"

"You had to meet in a seedy belly-dance club to discuss it?"

Jonny didn't answer. Besides, Dom didn't really want an

answer. He was goading him, hating him. Jonny had never realized before how little Dom liked him.

"Will you make sure the movie's released anyway?" he asked.

Dom's cold eyes flickered. "The movie's going to be released, you can be damned sure of that, after the trouble and money that went into it."

"That's all I wanted to make sure of." He drew on the cigarette again. "Also, if anything happens to me, I need you to do something for me. I have an illegitimate daughter who's in a lot of trouble. I want her taken care of."

"Jesus Christ."

"I don't know anything about her, except that her name's Fairusa and her uncle's name is Miguel Garcia y Reyes. She's from Brazil."

"You're crazy. Why on earth would I get involved in this?"

"Because she needs our help."

"'Our' help? I don't have anything to do with her."

"But if something happens to me—"

"Is something going to happen to you?"

"I'm not sure."

"What do you want me to do?" said Dom sarcastically. "Find her a husband?"

"Shut up!" Jonny interrupted sharply, jumping to his feet and pacing the room. "Don't do this! Can't you see?"

"I can't see a damned thing," Dom said. "You never confide in me; you never have. All I know about you are your tricks and confidences to get money. I find you jeopardizing your job, my job, the company itself, and then handing me flimsy excuses. So I'm going to tell you something. You're through with *Flaming Forest.* You've practically destroyed the film with your overspending, your tantrums with Jeannette, your drinking. Now it's your editing. You know a movie that's longer than three hours won't be shown anywhere. You're being impossible about it. I just spoke to Roger and he's all set to send the negative to the cutter tomorrow. When we get the answer print back we don't want you to even look at it. Roger and I will handle the final check. I don't want you involved in the making of the trailer. You'll have nothing to do with how the film is sold, packaged, or promoted. I've scheduled the premiere for June first, and I want to stick to that date. The film'll never be ready as long as you're still around. So you're fired."

"It doesn't matter," Jonny said hopelessly. He looked around for an ashtray, couldn't find one, and dropped the cigarette into Dom's wastepaper basket. Dom rifled through the papers to pick it out and extinguished the still lit cigarette on the side of the basket. Jonny watched in irritation. Then he said, "If anything happens to me—"

Dom's left eyebrow rose. "There you go again. 'If anything happens to me . . .' Is something going to happen to you?"

"I don't know."

"This hasn't got anything to do with Justin, does it?" Dom asked. "His offering to back the movie always did seem a bit strange to me. We can handle him together if that's the case."

"No, it's nothing to do with Justin."

"Money problems?"

"I always have those."

Dom heaved an impatient sigh.

Jonny said suddenly, "You've always been a coldhearted bastard, but in recent weeks you've turned into an icicle. I can't believe it's all to do with *Flaming Forest*. One movie like that isn't going to ruin your lousy company."

Dom stood up, his body rigid. All the anger he had been feeling toward Groome since he had discovered what he had done to Penny surfaced uncontrollably.

"You're right," he said, his voice low and furious. "I don't give a damn about your *Flaming Forest*. I'll tell you what I do care about. I care about the fact that you've known for years that Penelope Houten didn't kill Violet, and you didn't speak up and say one word in her defense. I know you're a coward, but I didn't know you were a crook too. Only crooks cover for murderers."

Jonny stepped back, startled by the outburst.

"You let that girl suffer in the hospital without standing by her," Dom's voice rose. "You let her run away. You let us all believe—*including Mom*—that Penny had committed murder. And all you had to do was say, 'She didn't do it. Justin did.' It makes me sick to think of it, Jonny. Literally, it makes me sick."

Jonny cleared his throat. "How do you know?"

"Haven't you been reading the papers?"

"Those are mere allegations. They could all be lies."

"Get out of here." Dom turned his back.

"Have you spoken to Penny?"

"Yes."

"Where is she?"

"You must be crazy if you think I'll tell you."

"I wouldn't tell Justin."

"I wouldn't trust you for the world," said Dom bitterly. "Why don't you tell Emmy that every word in those articles is true? That you saw the murder happen exactly that way? Why don't you make some little attempt to help Penny?"

Jonny was silent.

"I suppose the money he put up for *Flaming Forest* was the payoff," Dom said, his lips white.

"No. But how could you understand?"

Jonny turned and left. He was shaking.

On the street the sky hung low with muggy heaviness. He walked quickly toward the parking lot, feeling nothing but a strange numbness overtake him. This was it, he was thinking. This was the end of everything.

Miguel waited in his car, an innocuous-looking Ford Escort. He motioned to Jonny to get inside.

Jonny did so. They drove off.

"Where are we going?"

"Just for a drive," said Miguel pleasantly. "I want to talk to you. I want to give you one more chance."

Jonny looked straight ahead.

"The negative of the film was not where you said it was. We do not like being lied to."

"You can do whatever you want, but you're not getting my movie," said Jonny, despairingly. "It's going to be released as planned and to hell with you and everything you stand for." He grew impassioned. "So tell them about Fairusa. Go ahead —tell everybody! That's what you're going to do, isn't it? Go ahead—I'm waiting."

The sun was hitting them full in the face. Miguel lowered his sunshade. "Now . . . now," he said soothingly, "don't be anxious. We may have a different way of obtaining our end."

Jonny was unprepared for the coolness of Miguel's reaction.

"We have learned the negative is in your brother's house."

"How'd you find out?"

"We have our ways. We also know that the film is going to be released soon."

"I've been fired from the project again. I have nothing to do with it anymore." If the negative was going to the cutter's lab tomorrow, then it would no longer be at Dom's house. He did not have to worry about its being stolen.

"Still, you must know when the film will be premiered, no?" asked Miguel.

"June first."

"I see." Miguel regarded Jonny with his head tilted slightly, as though sizing him up. "Will you be there?"

Jonny shook his head. "I'm going to be as far away as possible. They're butchering my movie."

"But they will perhaps make it more effective," Miguel soothed him. "You will not be at the premiere?"

Jonny shook his head.

"A pity. There is nothing you can do about preventing its release?"

"No."

"Yet you surely do not want Hollywood to learn about Fairusa."

Jonny gazed straight ahead.

"If you were to procure four invitations to the premiere, then perhaps nothing need be said about Fairusa."

"What?"

"Surely this is possible."

"Why do you want to go to that? It's a benefit!"

"Perhaps the film is not as bad as we have heard. We wish to see it as soon as possible so that we know what we are up against in terms of our own public relations efforts."

"Okay," Jonny said slowly. "I guess I can arrange it."

Miguel pulled over to the curb and stopped. "I was sure we could work things out amicably. I am only sorry you will not be there." He smiled warmly at Jonny. "One more question: Your brother's girlfriend—what is her name?"

"Lark Chandler."

"She will be at this premiere?"

"Probably. She's practically living at Dom's house nowadays."

"I am sorry you will not be present, but I assure you your secret is safe with us, so long as you produce those invitations."

Jonny eyed the man warily.

"This is a bus stop," Miguel pointed out. "You have money for the bus?"

"Yes."

Miguel held out his hand. A bit dazed, Jonny shook it. Then he got out and closed the door.

"Good-bye," said Miguel.

Jonny stared after the car as it drove away. He was thinking how strange it was that procuring four invitations to the premiere for Miguel made him even more nervous than the possibility that his secret about Fairusa might be told.

CHAPTER EIGHTY-ONE

THERE had always been an indefinable link between Emmy and Jonny. Sometimes when Emmy had been highly strung for no accountable reason, she'd found out that he'd been at a tense meeting, pitching one of his stories. Or when he'd felt depressed, even if they'd been a country apart, she'd felt depressed too. Jonny had said it worked the other way as well.

Now Emmy had the unsettling feeling that Jonny was in danger.

She tried to ignore the feeling for a few days, reminding herself that even if Jonny were in some sort of trouble, it no longer had anything to do with her. But when she was a teenager she had heard Dr. Martin Luther King speak about the fact that everyone on earth was in some way interconnected and responsible for one another. Over the years, this belief, which had begun as a small, serious seed that made her embrace a career in journalism, grew consistently stronger.

She found she could not live with her anxiety about Jonny. First she called Dom at his office.

"I need to talk to Jonny," she told him. "You don't happen to know where he is, do you?"

"No. We had an argument about *Flaming Forest*. He says he's not even going to be at the premiere on June first."

"I can't believe Jonny wouldn't go to a premiere of one of his movies."

"He's bitter about the edit. We wouldn't let him take any

further part in that. He feels his movie is ruined. You know Jonny."

"Yes, I know Jonny. Still, I can't believe he wouldn't go to the premiere." She sounded absent. "He is the director, after all."

"Is everything okay?" asked Dom. "Maybe I can help."

She wondered if Dom would laugh at her fears.

"It's just a feeling I have that he's in some sort of trouble."

Dom hesitated. "Could you be more specific?"

"I wish I could. The only reason I might be having this feeling is because of an interview I did recently for a story I'm writing on a group of Brazilian terrorists who are committed to the continued razing of the rain forests. The man I talked to had heard of Jonny's film and was afraid it was too sympathetic to the Indians and ecologists. I don't know if there's any connection."

"I wonder if Jonny was being threatened." Dom sounded anxious. "He kept dropping hints before he left. You know how Jonny is. Evasive."

"Did you think he was in any danger?"

"No," admitted Dom. "I thought it was simply Jonny being melodramatic. But he certainly implied he was in danger."

Emmy bit her lip anxiously. "I know you're probably booked to overflowing for the premiere," she said. "But do you think there might be an extra chair for me? I feel as though I need to be there."

"Of course, Emmy," said Dom, surprised. "You're always more than welcome to come to anything like that. If I'd had any idea you were interested I'd have sent you an invitation."

"It's going to be a benefit for the rain forest, isn't it? How much are you charging?"

He laughed. "A lot. Don't even think about that, Em. You'll be our guest."

"Thanks, Dom."

"But, as I said, Jonny won't be here. I haven't been in touch with him since April."

Emmy smiled into the phone. "Jonny will be there. He wouldn't miss this premiere for the world."

Chapter Eighty-Two

A LONE. They say everyone is alone. But alienation is simply a symptom of the population explosion.

It used to be that ten miles separated you from your neighbor. Or a waterfall did, or a river, or a wolf. Then when you saw your neighbor on occasion, you'd have something to say, you'd do a square dance, have some fun together. But if every time you go to the bathroom you hear them, the excitement dulls.

You long for comraderie, lovers, understanding, but you keep bumping into wooden Indians, barber poles. Should you go about with an open heart on the off chance a person sympathetic to you will come along? Should you always be ready, like a virgin with an oil lamp, to be friends? Or should you close up, opening the impregnable gates to your heart only when the stranger has been tested?

Jonny didn't know. At night he locked his hotel door. In the morning he unlocked it and, unarmored, wandered vaguely out to do battle. Only there was no battle any longer, not down here on the golden Mexican beach, where he lay naked and brown-skinned and poor, and trying not to give a shit about what was happening in Hollywood with his movie.

But there are so many rings to aloneness. There is so much that is time-binding, even though sometimes the rings may be thorn hedges catching you and tearing you to bits. So many rings surround a person. Images of accomplishments, layers of the past, habits of the present.

He went swimming. The water was warm. It felt sticky. Great strings of unidentified things floated in it. He dove under. Green and clear. People spent hours drifting across the surface of waters, looking down. What did they see? Like players around a Ouija board, they seemed to be waiting for some otherworldly wizz-bang, some thunderbolt of enlightenment. He kept expecting one of them to stand up, to pull the snorkle from their mouth, and proclaim a profound thought, a moving experience. *I did it, I saw it, I felt it.*

Jonny put his head in the water again. Silently the fish swam deep under his feet. The water was clear. Hardly moving, like lazy thoughts. Like looking into the top of your own head, if there was a hole in it. Transparent thoughts gliding slowly here and there. Quick flashing thoughts, dazzling in the prism light. Opaque, unmoving thoughts, sitting there looking at you. What-for thoughts. And sea urchins. Black, prickly sea urchins. Like a porcupine inside your head, filling it up. Can't you get it out, get it out before it gets too big and takes up all the room inside your head. It prickles, it hurts, it grows larger and larger—

The sun beat down on his head and he turned over. His eyes hurt too much to open, his mouth was dry. His head ached as if someone were hammering it. Were they still drilling the street across from his hotel room or was it just a hangover?

Now it was nighttime. Jonny turned over in the wide bed and reached for her. But she wasn't there. No one was there. He opened his eyes.

His head ached. Where was he? He heard the murmur of the ocean outside his window. The blinds banged monotonously in the wind. *Bang. Bang.* Each time it felt like a bullet. He yearned for some cool water. He'd pour it over his head to stop it exploding: a long cool green glass of water. He wanted her to pour the cool water over the red inside his head, it would stop the noise, couldn't they stop drilling, banging, banging, banging . . .

He felt the last string of the balloon attaching his head to his body snap and float away.

Then there was blessed darkness. No noise, no blinds, no backfires, no drills. Just silence.

When he awoke it was still dark. He had no idea what had woken him, for the silence penetrated the room as deeply as the dark. But he had the distinct impression he was not alone anymore.

He sat up, trying not to make any noise. He felt no fear, only a sensational thirst.

Quietly, he reached for the bedside light and switched it on.

Its glare blinded him momentarily. When his eyes adjusted to the light, he found there was no one in the room after all. He felt confused.

He opened the curtains to let in some air. Dawn tarnished the dark silver sky. The sea was black. Naked, he lay back down on the bed. It was too hot even for a sheet.

For a while he tried to conjure up a vision of Emmy. The thought of her was usually able to arouse him. In spite of all the glamorous actresses and models he'd had, she was still his most exciting fantasy. They'd done such things together . . .

But tonight she wouldn't come.

Instead his mind kept filtering through the hazy events of the past few weeks. He felt as though he'd been missing something important. So wrapped up was he in *Flaming Forest,* he hadn't been paying attention.

That was what he thought now, anyway.

A breeze blew the curtains back and caressed his body.

Unexpectedly, he thought of Lark. His anxiety had something to do with Lark. Dom's urgent call to him from France had set something in motion that Jonny hadn't fully understood. He hadn't taken Dom's anxiety seriously.

Jonny propped himself up on the pile of pillows and clasped his hands behind his head. He had thought Dom was jealous of him, and that had amused him. Dom was usually so cold and unemotional. But he'd gone batshit over the little nobody from nowhere, Lark Chandler.

The little nobody from nowhere.

He liked that line. He thought about it for a long time.

He thought about Penny too. He felt bad about what had

happened to Penny. Dom's fury had been justified. He tried to imagine Penny's scared blue eyes gazing at him after Groome had punched him the night of the murder.

But instead he kept seeing Lark.

Who was she? Where did she come from?

Why had she written a screenplay that was certain to make an enemy of Justin Groome?

Jonny blinked and tried to conjure up Penelope again. But there was Lark again.

They had the same eyes.

Jonny sat up excitedly. They were the same height. Sometimes their voices seemed the same, except for Lark's English accent.

He remembered Justin Groome telling his mother, soon after Penny disappeared: "She's a liar, a thief, and a slut. Of course she'd run away."

And in London it had been one of the first things Lark had said to him. "A liar, a thief, a slut." And then she had pretended to read his palm and told him about his guilt line!

He stood up hastily. *Of course—of course. Plastic surgery can work miracles nowadays. No wonder she's crazy about Dom. She was always crazy about Dom.*

And now Groome knows. Somehow, he's found out. Does she know that he knows? He's going to kill her. That's why he hasn't bothered me lately. He's found out I'm the coward he thought I was, and I wouldn't do a thing to jeopardize my career. But Penny's no coward. She ran away because she knew she hadn't a prayer against him. But she was going to see justice done in the end. Of course she was.

The room was suddenly light; dawn was short down here. Jonny got dressed hurriedly. Did Dom know? He must. You couldn't love a girl and not know something like that, could you? But what if he didn't? What if Penny was alone, unprotected, vulnerable to whatever Groome planned?

What did Groome plan, anyway?

All this time Jonny had relentlessly pushed aside his suspicion with regard to Miguel's request for four invitations to the premiere of his movie. He was so relieved that his secret with Fairusa was safe, he didn't want to think about its price. But he had to face it. Miguel had asked him if Lark was going to be at the premiere. Could Groome and Miguel somehow be in league?

Of course they were.

Jonny hadn't intended to go back to Los Angeles ever again. He hated everything about it. It symbolized hope and despair, wealth and poverty, and the end of his career. No one would ever let him work in Hollywood again, not once they found out about Fairusa.

But he had to go back, for Penny's sake. His time of atonement had arrived.

His life was over. He had nothing to look forward to. No money, no career. No Emmy. He could stay in this third-rate hotel for another two weeks at most, and then he would have to move on. He had barely enough money for a flight back to Los Angeles.

But he would go back. He would go back, and he would warn Penny that she might be in danger. And he would tell her that if she wanted to, he would stand beside her in court and tell the world the truth about what had happened to Violet Sumner.

He had nothing to lose anymore by doing so.

Chapter Eighty-Three

EVERAL years before, Jonny had converted the basement of his house into a large screening room. Now Dom had had it festively decorated, with fifty chairs set up for the audience, and the projector waiting in readiness for the screening of *Flaming Forest*.

Upstairs the guests began to arrive. Distinguished as they mostly were, they were still thrilled to be invited to this particular premiere. So much secrecy and controversy had surrounded the film's creation that practically everyone in the film industry was eager to see the finished product.

Lark wore a midnight blue Jeran dress covered with sequins. Jonny's sapphire and diamond earrings swung from her ears.

She was nervous.

"Don't be," said Dom. "Justin can't do anything in so public a place. And I'm not going to leave your side for an instant all evening."

They were holding hands as they greeted the guests.

Justin Groome arrived with a blandly smiling model as his escort.

"What an exciting crush," he said. "Lark, dear, this is for you. A small hostess present—a token of my esteem. Just to show there are no hard feelings. If you want to make a documentary about me, go ahead. All I ask is that it be fair."

Lark took the prettily wrapped box. "Thank you."

"Excuse me," said Groome. "I see someone I know."

He took off with the silent model.

"Hey, Dom," someone called.

Dom moved toward the voice.

Lark placed the box on a side table to be opened later. The screening would not start for a couple of hours. First the guests were offered champagne and hors d'oeuvres in the living room. The buffet supper, some speeches, and a slide presentation would follow. Then the film would be shown and dessert and coffee served afterward.

A specially hired butler served drinks from behind a bar set up near the terrace. Two tuxedoed waiters passed around silver platters of stuffed mushrooms, shrimp remoulade, and chicken with snow peas.

Dom turned back to wait for Lark. As he did so he saw Emmy Elson at the door. She came over to him and he hugged her hard.

"It's good to see you," he said.

Emmy's eyes were scouring the room. "No sign of Jonny?"

"Not yet. Emmy, this is Lark Chandler."

Strangely, Emmy's strong premonition of danger increased as she gravely shook Lark's hand. "Pleased to meet you." She glanced around the room again. "I don't know why I got so worried about him. Maybe he's perfectly okay." Here in the gorgeous mansion where she had spent so many lonely years, it seemed incredible that she had even considered a terrorist attack might occur.

The living room was crowded. Lark was jostled. She gripped Dom's hand.

"There's Miguel," she said suddenly. "He was the man who was in Soubriquet with Justin that weekend."

"How'd he get in?" asked Dom angrily.

"Miguel Garcia y Reyes?" said Emmy, looking around.

"I don't remember his last name," said Lark. "There he is, standing by the bar."

"I see him. He gave me an interview recently for that story I'm writing about Amazonia."

"What's he doing here?" demanded Dom. "Who invited him?"

Before anyone could answer, Carl came up to them. He leaned heavily on crutches.

"You made it." Lark hugged him gently and took him to the couch. "I'm so glad."

"Can I get you something to drink?" offered Dom, following them.

"Just some water."

He went to the bar. Suddenly Lark jumped off the couch and followed him. "Something's wrong."

Dom turned to her. "What do you mean?"

"You know that present Justin gave me? I left it on a side table to open later. But he's moved it."

"Where is it?"

"I just saw him put it on the shelf in the dining room."

"If it were something dangerous—like a bomb—" Dom spoke both their fear, "Groome wouldn't stick around to see it go off."

Lark pointed with her eyes.

"I don't believe he is going to stick around."

"Wait here," ordered Dom.

He was gone in a flash. Masterfully but casually, he took Groome's arm and guided him back into the living room.

Groome looked decidedly uncomfortable.

What should she do? Certainly not "wait," as Dom had so peremptorily ordered. She thought rapidly. If the gift was some sort of timed explosive device, for when was it timed? Or perhaps it would not explode until she opened it? Or perhaps it had something more innocuous inside, like poisoned apples? She choked on a slightly hysterical laugh.

Carl looked in at the door. She hurried over to him.

"Are you all right?" he asked. "You look as though you are about to bawl someone out."

She gave him an anxious smile. "Not exactly." She told him her suspicions.

Carl became grave.

"Have you any idea what to do?"

"I want to get that box out of here. But I don't want Groome to see me do it."

"I can take care of it," Carl offered.

"What will you do?"

"Dom has an enormous garden. Perhaps the swimming pool would be the best place?"

Lark thought it might work. "But I'll take it. You're too tired."

"Nonsense," snapped Carl. "Tell me again where it is."

"On the shelf over there. It's wrapped in yellow paper."

Carl nodded and limped off.

A clap on Lark's shoulder made her jump. She turned and found Jonny looking wildly at her.

"Jonny!" she gasped in surprise. "What are you doing here?"

"I had to come." He was out of breath. "I don't give a damn about the film anymore, or my blasted reputation. Look, you're in danger. I realized it when I was alone down south. Groome's got this plan."

"A bomb? I think I know."

"I don't think he's going to use a bomb. I was just talking to Emmy and we think Miguel's a terrorist who's determined to get hold of the negative of my film. We think he's going to take you as a hostage while he demands it. He's in cahoots with Groome, I'm sure of it. As a hostage you could be accidently killed by the terrorists and then no one will be any the wiser about Groome."

Lark's face paled. "So you know too."

"It took me the longest time to figure it out, didn't it?"

She looked around for Dom, but she couldn't see him. The dozens of faces were blurred and noisy.

"If Miguel gets hold of the negative—" began Lark breathlessly.

"I don't care about that! We've got to get you out of here!"

"But you haven't heard. There was an explosion at the print lab. All the prints of *Flaming Forest* were destroyed before they went into distribution. We were able to get one made specially for this premiere, but without the negative we won't be able to make any more."

Jonny's face paled, but again he repeated, stoically, "We've got to get you out of here first of all."

"Where did Groome go? Dom was with him."

"Just come on—"

"Where?"

"Let's just get out of here. You're the one who's in danger."

They pushed their way through the milling crowd to the dining room where the tall side doors opened out into the garden. Dom was staring at the shelf, a puzzled expression on his face.

"It's gone," he said, looking up.

They ran over to him. "Carl said he'd get rid of it. But that's not what's worrying us. Groome's tricked us."

"For God's sake, let's get out of here!" yelled Jonny from the side doors.

Only then did Dom seem to realize that Jonny was there. "What's going on?"

They heard a loud commotion in the next room.

"Oh, God! I'm too late!" Jonny stared behind Dom. A man entered, a gun in his hand. "I wasn't even able to do this right." He sounded as though he might weep.

"All of you—come," the gunman snapped. He grabbed Lark and shepherded her into the living room. Fearful for her safety, the brothers followed.

In the enormous living room, all the guests were being forced at gunpoint to lie down on the floor, their hands behind their heads. Except for Lark, who was handed over to Miguel. His brown eyes gleamed as he caught her. He twisted her arm painfully behind her back and shouted a command at Dom.

"The negative of the film. Bring it to us or the girl won't live."

"Let her go," said Dom, desperately. "You can have the goddamn film. It's downstairs in the projector room."

"Get it. Bring every reel here."

Dom gazed helplessly at Lark, then turned to go down the stairs. Another gunman was on his heels.

Emmy Elson was the only one who had kept her head during the initial pandemonium. Quietly, she had slipped upstairs without being seen. There were too many guests for the terrorists to notice a sole maverick. Besides, she knew the house better than almost everyone there. In the maid's quarters, she picked up the telephone to dial the police.

But the phone was dead. The terrorists had thought of that. No doubt they had also disconnected the alarm that safeguarded the grounds.

She would have to get to a neighboring house in order to telephone the police. Drawing a deep breath, she crept down the back stairs to the garden. If only it were already dark this would be so much easier! But although the sun had set, the sky was still light. She hoped the gunmen were too busy with the hostages inside the living room to look out of the window.

On all fours, she crawled through the rosebushes until she reached the shelter of the bougainvillea.

Unexpectedly, she heard the sound of panting. She stopped short. To her surprise, she saw an old man on crutches hobbling up the path toward the house. She had noticed him earlier as one of Dom's guests.

"Hey!" she whispered.

Carl looked over questioningly.

"They're holding everyone hostage in there," she warned. "Better stay clear."

Carl limped over to her.

"I thought it was not a bomb," he said, confusingly. "I threw it into the pool nonetheless."

"I'm going to call the police, if I can get out of here without getting caught. Better try to hide if you can."

He shook his head. "Lark is in danger. I'll do what I can to help her."

Puzzled that he knew Lark was in danger, Emmy was going to ask him to elaborate, but then she realized she didn't have time.

"Good luck," she whispered. "I'd better take my chance now."

Carl turned back to the house.

Avoiding the main gate, Emmy skirted the wall surrounding the estate, looking for somewhere she could climb over.

A strategically placed orange tree helped. Within moments, she was on the other side of the wall, racing down the winding road toward the nearest house.

Chapter Eighty-Four

WHILE the hostages waited tensely for Dom's return, Jonny lifted his head and scanned the floor for Justin Groome. He was lying fairly comfortably, well out of harm's way, behind the couch.

Now was his moment, he decided. If the world was to know the truth, they had better know it now, while Lark was still alive.

"I have something to say." He rose slowly to his knees.

"Get down!" yelled one of the terrorists, pointing a gun at him.

Jonny raised a hand dramatically. "Not yet. There's no hurry, is there? You can kill me after I've had my say. That's only fair." He glanced at Lark's white face. "Let the girl go, won't you? Where can she run to? You're obviously hurting her."

For answer, Miguel smilingly twisted her arm even higher. Lark cried out.

Jonny stood up. The fifty or so bodies on the floor remained motionless, but he was acutely aware of their tension. Good. That meant they were all listening carefully.

"You're all witnessing something important. The man responsible for Lark being held up there is right now lying here with you, on this floor, pretending he's innocent. Get up, Justin. Get up and face us all."

"You bastard," Groome hissed. "Get down. They'll kill you."

"So what?" said Jonny, grandly. "That's not important any-more. What is important is that the truth comes out. Get up, Congressman Justin Groome. Stand up and face us. Stand up, I say!"

Glowering, Justin Groome got to his knees behind the couch. Some of the braver hostages craned their necks slightly so they could see him.

"I don't know what this is all about," he complained.

"All right, now listen carefully, everybody. Four years ago, this man, Congressman Justin Groome, murdered a woman. He framed a young girl for the murder, a girl who knew her only chance of safety from him was to escape and become a new person with a new identity. It was partly my fault that justice wasn't done years ago. Groome threatened to destroy my career—everything—if I revealed the truth about him. I was a coward. You see, besides the young girl, I was the only witness to this murder."

A collective gasp emerged from the people on the floor.

Lark broke in, her voice low but controlled. "I was the girl who was framed for Violet's murder. My name was Penelope Houten before I changed it, changed my face, changed my life, in order to be safe from Justin Groome. He had threat-ened to kill me if I ever spoke the truth about him. But now he's discovered who I am and he's already tried to kill me once before. I'm sure Jonny's right and he's in league with these terrorists."

As if to prove her words, Justin hissed furiously at Miguel: "Kill her, man. For God's sake, kill her."

"We're waiting for the film," Miguel replied implacably. "This is more important to us than any private feud of your own."

"Good God!" exploded Justin, standing up. Only then did he suddenly seem aware of all the people lying on the floor, listening. He subsided and added, more genially, "Anyway, this is all nonsense. I don't know what you're talking about. Evidently, there's been some sort of misunderstanding."

Carl appeared in the large open window directly behind Lark and Miguel.

"You're an ambitious man, Justin, and a powerful one," he said. Miguel swung his gun around, but when he saw the old, crippled man in the window, he turned his attention back to Lark. "But do you really think you can get away with murder again?"

"Who are you to talk to me about getting away with murder?" snapped Groome. "You murdered your lover's husband!"

"No. You know what happened better than anyone."

"To hell with you."

"You're a blackmailing crook," said Jonny to Groome.

"No . . . no. You've misunderstood." Groome tried to hold on to his temper. "As a politician, I have a job to do. I believe in what I do, and the men and women who vote for me believe in it too. It's important to all of us. Truth, justice, liberty: These aren't cliches my campaign manager wrote for me. These have meaning. They're important."

"What does truth have to do with blackmail?" shouted Jonny.

"Or being framed for murder?" cried Lark.

Dom appeared in the other door, the terrorist's gun at his throat. He had a black eye, but in his arms he carried several metal film cases.

"I've never blackmailed a soul in my life," Groome stated with appealing earnestness. "And as for murdering someone, I still don't know what you're talking about."

He looked pleadingly at them all, one at a time. Miguel snapped at the other hijackers in Spanish. Dom turned to him.

"Let Lark go."

"Bring the film over here," Miguel gestured.

Carl was the only one still watching Justin Groome. He saw him tense. Painfully, Carl climbed over the low windowsill and limped toward Lark.

"Let her go," repeated Dom.

"The film first."

"No. *Let her go.*"

Miguel released Lark and pushed her away. As he did so, he swung his gun toward her and fired. Lark screamed. In the same instant, Carl lunged between her and Miguel. The bullet lodged itself in his back. He collapsed on the floor.

Pandemonium broke out. The guests struggled to their feet and raced for the windows and doors. Dom dropped the metal boxes of film and grabbed Lark. She pulled away and rushed over to Carl's side.

"Are you all right?" gasped Carl.

She nodded, kneeling beside him.

They heard the wail of police sirens above the sound of the hysterical screams and shouts of the fleeing guests. Miguel and the other terrorists rushed for the exits.

Jonny carefully picked up the reels of film.

"Carl?" whispered Lark, taking his hand.

He tried to say something, but his eyes closed before he could speak again.

The police cars rolled up outside.

"Dad," she heard Dom whisper.

Dry-eyed, Lark gripped Carl's hand, gazing at his face. He looked asleep, not dead.

He had been killed because of her. Susan had died because of her too. How had it happened?

She wasn't a bad person. She didn't think she was, anyway. The bad things she'd done in her life seemed harmless initially. Much of it had been almost accidental, or even unconscious.

Evil is not a dragon. She didn't have a devil on her shoulder, urging her to steal the credit card or to seduce the boy. Nor did she have a good angel by her side, prompting her to be polite or to give up her seat on the bus.

The way she saw it, evil was amoral. It was a companion. It was always there, like a friendly, if overtalkative, guide. When Lark sat down to dinner, it sat down too. When she spoke, it spoke too. When she got upset, it did too. When she got excited, it did too.

"Lark . . . Lark . . ."

She blinked and shook herself. Dom was bending over her.

"Leave me alone," she whispered.

"It's not your fault."

"He saved my life."

Dom tried to pry her hand free from Carl's but couldn't. "Please, Lark." His voice was hoarse.

She still didn't move.

Jonny put up all the reels on the side table and stood protectively in front of them. "Where's Groome?" he demanded.

"I saw him running down the street," replied Dom, on one knee, beside Lark. "But he won't get far. Not now."

"Good."

Dom looked up at his brother. "Jonny?"

"I'll testify," Jonny answered his unspoken question. "I'll probably never be able to work in Hollywood again, but I'll testify. I should have done it years ago."

"We'll take care of Fairusa," said Dom. "We'll find her somehow."

"Thanks."

Dom added after a moment, "We couldn't have had a better promotional gag. The movie's a surefire box office hit now."

Jonny looked sick. "I don't care about that. I'd have given anything for this not to have happened. It was my fault those men were here."

"We'll talk about it later." He turned back to Lark.

Emmy came over to Jonny. "Are you okay?"

He nodded. "Good work," he said with a crooked smile. "I saw you out in the garden climbing that tree and knew you'd get help."

"I knew you'd come through eventually," she replied gravely.

Jonny looked away. He couldn't face anyone just then. After all, it was his fault that any of this had happened in the first place. He was the one who had not spoken the truth about Justin before now. And it was his movie.

He went through the French doors to the terrace, looking out at the garden. The fountain splashed in the darkness. He would have liked to have talked it all over with Emmy, but he couldn't. He felt too much of a jerk.

She gazed after him, her eyes hurt.

Dom put his arm around Lark.

"I'd better talk to the police and start getting things

straightened out here," he said. "Come with me, will you? I don't want you to be out of my sight just yet."

"I'm safe now." Her voice was low. "Justin's only hope now is to face me in a courtroom."

"I know. Still, I'd like you nearby."

"I'll come in a minute," said Lark, still looking at Carl. Dom waited.

"Come now," he said at last, prying her hand free of Carl's. "Please. I need you with me."

He put his arms around her when she stood up.

Emmy came over and put her arms around both of them.

"I can't believe how close we came to losing you again," she said to Lark.

"Me neither." Dom's voice was muffled.

"If it weren't for Carl," said Lark, "I wouldn't be here. He was a hero."

"Who was he?" asked Emmy. "I ran into him outside in the garden."

Hunched and despairing, Jonny came back in through the French doors. He heard Dom's reply: "My father."

"Carl!" exclaimed Jonny. "Of course!"

"It's a long story," said Lark, trying to pull herself together. "We'll tell it to you later, once everyone's left. You'll stay, won't you?"

Emmy nodded and held out her hand to Jonny. He took it.

"Carl wasn't the only hero," Lark addressed him. "You could have been killed just as easily."

"I guess we all have more than one side to us," said Jonny. "You sure kept one of yours dark for a long time, though. What idiots you must have thought us!"

"It was kind of fun," she said, sadly. "Like being at a masquerade ball. Especially when I first saw you in London."

Dom shuddered. *"Fun!"*

Lark leaned against Dom with a tender smile.

Evil is a carnival, a torrent, a wild hug, she thought. It is a force, an identity. Like an ancient god, it inhabits, it is not personified. When the pagan gods were reduced to statues of themselves they were dead, but did that leave the storm less awesome or the ocean less mysterious? When Pan became a goat-footed flute player, did nature become less frightening? Wouldn't you run from a lion? When evil became a bare-bottomed trickster with a mosquitolike sting, what was that fallout dust in your eyes?

COMING IN DECEMBER

YOU ARE SALLY JACKSON, DAUGHTER OF THE AMERICAN AMBASSADOR IN BERLIN. THE YEAR IS 1933. AND YOU'RE ABOUT TO LEARN THAT THINGS ARE NO LONGER WHAT THEY HAVE BEEN . . .

WAS out onto the pavement before the SA men realized it, and walking toward the corner. I heard them call me.

"Hey, girl. Miss Englishwoman."

I continued walking, wondering if they would follow. They did. I heard running feet behind me.

"Hey, stop. Hey, you." Their voices were very loud.

So I stopped and turned toward the men.

"Yes," I said in English. "What do you want? Why are you yelling at me?" I asked in an even tone.

The first man to reach me grabbed my arm and, outraged, I jerked it away.

"How dare you?" I yelled, even angrier than I had been when I entered the lace shop. "Don't you dare touch me or you'll have the government of the United States of America to deal with."

"America," he said. "You're an American?"

"What kind of a country is this that women are accosted on the street in broad daylight? You think you can just do anything? You're barbarians. All of you. You take one more step toward me and you'll be sorry!"

The young men looked at me in consternation. I suppose they were not used to being treated like that. I didn't care, I was furious at them. At that moment a taxi pulled up in the street next to me. Its brakes screeched, startling the SA bullies.

"Jesus Christ, Sally," said David, flinging open the door of the taxi. "Get in here—quick!"

"Go away, David," I said, "I'm all right. Oh, shut up," I yelled as an SA man started to speak. "You just shut up, all of you. I've had enough of this, being pushed around in this wretched country."

David appeared next to me and took hold of my arm, trying to steer me into the car. People were starting to gather. "Sally, come on, kid, this is getting out of hand."

"This used to be a wonderful place, but you and your damn Führer have spoiled it." I was yelling in English, but the crowd picked up on "Führer" and their mutterings began to grow louder. David grabbed both my arms, spun me around and pushed me into the taxi, jumping in and closing the door after us. He yelled something at the driver and the car sped off.

"Damn it," I said, beating my fists against my thighs. "Damn it, damn it, damn it! I hate this country!"

"Here, kid," he said, when I had calmed down, offering me a cigarette. My hands were shaking so badly, I could barely hold it in the flame of his lighter. "So, did you get your lace?" he asked. I held the package up. "I hope it was worth it." I nodded and placed the package carefully on my lap, smoothing out the paper.

"Whew," said David, "what a gal."

"I made a real spectacle of myself, didn't I?"

"Sure did. But it was magnificent."

"This is awful. How can you smoke these things?" And I thrust the cigarette at him. He took it and put it out.

When the taxi stopped, he put his arms around me and gently helped me out.

"Where are we?" I asked, looking around. It was a wide street, and treeless, which was strange for Berlin, the buildings all huge gray monoliths.

"I live up there," he said, and not giving me a chance to comment, led me into the courtyard of his building and up the five flights of stairs to his little flat. Three rooms, no kitchen, with two windows facing the courtyard. The small sitting room was empty of furniture except for a table and two chairs and a bicycle propped up on its kickstand, with a pair of aviator goggles hanging from the handles.

"I'll get you a drink," he said. "The bathroom's in there and I hope you appreciate the fact that I have one." He waved in its direction. When I came back he handed me a glass of very good brandy. We stood by the dirty windows. It was warm and stuffy in the room, and I unbuttoned the jacket of my suit.

"What's wrong, kid?" he asked. I shook my head. "You can tell me. We're pals, right?"

I looked at him, considering, but I knew I couldn't tell him what Christian had done to me, what I had let him do. I felt so guilty and angry about that afternoon, I could hardly think coherently about it, let alone explain it to someone, especially to David.

"Is it Heydrich?" he asked, handing me another glass.

"Oh, no, that's all over. My father didn't like it and we all agreed. Before I went to the States." I drank, then looked around the room. "How can you live here? It's so depressing."

Moving closer to me, David said, "It's dirt cheap. I don't get paid much. And I'm seldom here. Hold still, you've got . . ." and using his thumb, he gently wiped something away from under my eye. His hand was soft and cool on my flushed face.

"I look a mess," I said, raising my hand to my face. He caught my hand, palm to palm with his.

"Not at all," he said, spreading his fingers, letting my fingers coil around his. My thumb ran over his, our hands parted, the fingers stroking and parting, clasping and letting go.

I leaned against him as I watched our hands intertwine. Finally, he brought my hand to his mouth, lightly brushing my fingers with his lips. I felt a stirring inside me and raised my face to his. He kissed me, holding my face, holding me close. I'd never felt such physical closeness with another person, not even with Christian, and it made me breathless.

I backed away—just a step or two—from him. He searched my face for a long time, and when he was satisfied with what he saw, he leaned forward, bridging the space between us, and gently kissed me again, his lips barely touching mine, making me lean, in turn, toward him.

Still without a word, he led me into the tiny bedroom. We lay down together and he held me, until I lifted my face and he kissed me. It was dark in the room and I liked the darkness. I liked being able to feel nothing but his lips and tongue and that he needed a shave, and I could smell the sun his shirt had been dried in. I liked not thinking. I liked his kisses. I liked his lips on my breasts, soft and insistent, pulling and sucking, his hands gently cupping and molding me as though he were drinking me in. I unbuttoned his shirt and touched his bare skin and found I liked that too, especially the feel of his nakedness against my breasts. I liked everything he did to me there in the dark. And my mind finally was at peace.

Until I felt his hand between my legs. He'll know, I thought instantly. If I let him make love to me, he will know I am no longer a virgin. And I knew he would know who had had me. And he would hate me.

I sat up abruptly, wiggling out from under his hands and mouth. I pulled my skirt down and folded my arms over my bare breasts.

"What is it?" His voice was thick and husky, his hands were on my back.

"Where are my things?" I said. "I need my things. I should go home."

I expected him to be angry. Instead, he did a terrible thing. He tried to understand me in terms of that innocence he had talked about in the kitchen that night.

"Oh, God, kid, I'm sorry." He put his arm around me. "I shouldn't have let it go so far. You're so sweet, I just couldn't stop. I'm sorry. Shhh, that's okay. Sally, you're such a sweet kid. I'd never do anything to hurt you. I'm just nuts about you. Ever since we met. Remember how we necked in the taxi? You looked so fresh, like the girls on Fifth Avenue in the fall, all dolled up in their new autumn duds, ready to take on the world."

"Oh, shut up, David," I cried, jumping off the bed, grabbing my shoes, pulling my clothes together. "None of you knows anything at all about me. It's driving me crazy."

I hurried into the bathroom, and when I came out he was back by the window, fully dressed, smoking.

I stood by the door and tried to apologize. He waved his hand. "Forget it, kid. I'm the one who's sorry. But tell me this, what'd you mean, 'none of you'? You talking about the blond again? Did he make a pass at you too?"

I looked at him a long moment, tempted to tell him, just to shock him, to prove how wrong his notions about me were, but I didn't. "I didn't mean anything. I was talking about him, yes, and you, and my father. All of you." And with that lie, I left. I wouldn't let him take me home but he insisted on coming downstairs to get me a taxi.

When he leaned down through the open window to give me a kiss, I did something I have regretted ever since: I turned my head so that his lips just grazed my cheek. I know he knew that it wasn't an accident, but I couldn't look at him. I couldn't tell him why. I couldn't . . .

COMING IN DECEMBER FROM ST. MARTIN'S PAPERBACKS: *THE LAST INNOCENT HOUR* BY MARGOT ABBOTT, AN ELECTRIFYING NOVEL WITH ALL THE SWEEP OF *THE WINDS OF WAR*. WATCH FOR IT!